NEIGHBOURLY

A NOVEL BY NAT CUDDINGTON

This one's for me.
I hope that's okay.

CHAPTER 1

"So, that's a yes?" he asks, his eyes piercing into mine. They're soft, a quiet brown that reminds me of homemade chocolate, or melting icing on a warm cake. I shake my head, trying to stop making these stupid analogies that I always make when I'm around him.

"No," I reply with a smile. "It's still a no. A hundred times no." I can hear the playfulness in my voice as I say it, and he probably can too.

"Why not?" he whines. He steps in closer to me and I don't step back.

"I don't want a boyfriend," I say.

"That's exactly why you should say yes!" Oh, he's definitely excited now. "No one will even try to date you if they think you're dating me. It's perfect for both of us!"

I bite my bottom lip and look up at him, into his eyes, at his mischievous smirk that's familiar from interviews and blooper reels I've seen. The smirk that's even familiar from times since I've known him as my friend instead of just a celebrity. I let out a deep breath and his smile changes to something more hopeful, full of something deeper.

"Fine," I say.

He shakes his head. "No, it's okay, I need more than a fine. I mean, I want you to do this with me, but I need you to *actually* want to." He shrugs and starts to turn away.

"I don't know what I want," I reply quickly. "But what's the worst that can happen?"

His mischievous grin is back. "Surely nothing that bad. This is an excellent idea. I have excellent ideas."

He holds out his hand to shake, and I grab hold of it, not entirely sure how I just agreed to pretend to date one of the most well-known sitcom stars of the decade. Of course this isn't a good idea.

Okay. Sorry, I'm getting ahead of myself; we're too late into the story. Let's rewind.

"I can't do this anymore," Claire says. "Someone just asked me if the mushrooms on the pizza are cooked. Like, no, we just cook the pizza and then throw some raw mushrooms on top after it comes out of the oven!"

I smirk at her and shrug. "At least they didn't throw their salad at you because there wasn't enough dressing on it."

"When did that happen?" Claire's mouth drops open as she follows me to the back of the restaurant, away from all the customers.

"Last night. I can't handle this place anymore, either. Why am I still a server, Claire? I'm 27 years old."

"You're 29," she says, narrowing her eyes at me.

"Shit, I forgot you knew that. But see, this is my point! I'm lying about my age to feel better about myself because I'm still a server. I'm almost 30, Claire! *Thirty!* And I work in a pizza restaurant."

"To be fair, it's a fancy pizza restaurant. We have cloth napkins and fancy cocktails."

"And fancy pizza," I add, rolling my eyes.

"Yes! Fancy pizza! It's better than working in a fast food pizza restaurant."

"True. But still. This is not where I wanted to be when I was thirty."

"Twenty-nine."

I smile at her and head back out into the restaurant. "This is why I like you, Claire."

Okay, sorry, we're going to go back a little farther. I keep thinking I'm starting this story at the right place, but I feel like I keep leaving out important information.

My eyelids are actually swollen. I didn't know that was a thing. I've read books that mention swollen eyelids from people crying so much and I always thought it was an exaggeration, but I guess not. Because I'm staring at myself in the mirror and my eyelids… are definitely swollen. I look terrible. I'm not sure if I've ever actually cried this much before. I guess that's why I didn't know about the swollen eyelid thing.

I keep not going back far enough. I really don't want to relive it, to be honest. I mean, it's not like it was the worst thing in the world, but to me, it was kind of the worst thing in the world. I'm not some drama queen, I promise you, and I'm not one of those people who just absolutely needs a man in her life, but if we're continuing to be honest, I guess I'll just say that I thought I was going to have this particular man in my life. Like, for the rest of my life. Okay, okay, we're going back a bit further so I can tell you about it. This won't be fun for me, but I guess it's needed to set the story. Ugh, here we go.

Tyler comes home quiet. I try to ask him about his day but he just shrugs like he did the last three days and heads into the living room. What's his problem? Seriously, if anyone should be in a bad mood, it should be me, since he hasn't so much as kissed me in the last two weeks.

"Tyler, what's up?" I ask.

"Nothing."

"It can't be nothing," I say. "Did something happen at work?"

And this is when I feel it happening. I've felt it coming for a while. It's weird, knowing someone is about to break up with you, even before they say it. It's weird, knowing that someone has fallen out of love with you, but not wanting it to be true. Pretending it's not happening. Letting the question burn in the back of your head for months because you know if you say it out loud, they'll tell you that you're right. That the last eight years of your life are over as you know it, just like that. I know this is what's happening before he opens his mouth. Because the look he gives me, the sigh he makes, the way his shoulders slump, I can just feel it.

"I don't want us to be together anymore."

There it is. The one sentence that will continue to haunt me throughout most of this story. It keeps coming back to this one sentence. It keeps replaying in my head when I've got nothing better to do, which let's face it, is most of the time. All the damn time, actually. *I don't want us to be together anymore.* Done. Just like that.

I nod my head and sit down on the couch. The couch that we picked out together. Because we were going to be together forever. Now that it's out in the open I guess I can ask the question that I've been too afraid to ask. Too afraid to ask because I knew the answer anyway.

"Do you not love me anymore?" I manage to squeak out.

He runs his hand over his face and looks at me with the same pain I feel in my chest. There are tears in his eyes. "I think I'll always love you, Isla. But am I *in* love with you?" He shakes his head and lets out a long breath. "No. I don't think I have been for a while."

Okay. That's all you need to know. I was with Tyler for eight, almost nine years, and we were going to spend the rest of our lives together, and then he didn't love me anymore. Fast forward to me crying so much that I discover the swollen eyelid thing, and I guess we'll just skip over me moving out and finding a new apartment, and not keeping the couches we picked out, because they're so massive they surely won't fit in any apartment I can afford, and we'll skip a few months into the future where I appear to be okay on the outside, but on the inside, I still die a little. Because on the inside, I have thoughts. And my thoughts keep repeating to me that one sentence that started the end of my life. I don't want us to be together anymore.

Yes, let's keep going. Seven months into the future.

"I can't do this anymore," Claire says. "Someone just asked me if the mushrooms on the pizza are cooked. Like, no, we just cook the pizza and then throw some raw mushrooms on top after it comes out of the oven!"

Whoops, we covered this already. Okay, sorry, I'm not good at this.

I smile at her and head back out into the restaurant. "This is why I like you, Claire."

"Isla," Tom, my boss says, catching my attention. "How many tables are you covering right now?"

"Just one," I say. It is 2:30 in the afternoon, after all. Not many people come in for fancy pizza in the middle of the day.

"Okay great, I have a job for you. Claire can finish your table, right?"

I shrug and follow him to the back where the chefs are making pizzas, and wave at Claire to come with us so I can let her know what's happening.

"What's happening?" she asks.

"I don't know," I say, "But apparently you're covering my table."

"Oh. Alright, well I guess I'll go make sure everything's okay with them." She smiles and leaves.

"The people who are catering that big movie had to back out for the next two days," my boss says to me. "There was a family emergency or something, so the movie people asked us to cater! Isn't that exciting?"

"Yeah! Is the restaurant going to be in the credits?" I ask.

"I never even thought of that! I hope so! Anyway, can you bring everything over for me?"

"You want me to deliver pizza?"

"To a movie set, Isla."

"Yeah. Right. Okay. But like, isn't the main guy from that show going to be there?"

"I don't know what you're talking about."

"Uh, Logan Jackson," I say, trying to sound like I don't care who it is, or that maybe I'm not even sure that's what his name is. But I know. Oh, I know. When he doesn't respond with a look of recognition, I add, "From *Neighbourly*." He still looks at me like a deer caught in the headlights. "The TV show? It's on cable *and* Netflix, and it's super popular, there's no way you haven't heard of it."

"All I know is they chose our small town to film a big, fancy movie, and they're going to eat my pizza, and you are going to bring it to them. I also got the guys to prepare salads and baked brie with baguette."

"Wow, you're going all out," I say.

"Well I want them to enjoy it. Anyway, you can take everything over, I've got them in these warming dishes and all you have to do is light the dish burners under them to keep everything warm, and then bring all the dishes back. You can leave the leftovers they said."

"What do I do while they're eating?"

"I don't know. Hang out? I'm sure you can eat a little. You need a break too."

And before I know it, he's helping me load my hatchback with big black cases which hold the food that I'm going to bring to a movie set. I toss the warming cans on the passenger seat and start to drive over to the set. My fingers shake against the steering wheel as I follow the instructions Tom gave me, and I slowly drive through the alley behind the restaurant and other businesses that line the main street. I pull up to the back door of the community centre, where the movie people have set up their offices and resting rooms. Holding, they apparently call it. I hope I'm okay to just leave my car in front of the door while I unload everything because that's what I'm doing. I have to take three trips down the stairs and into the room they're using to eat, and once I've got everything unloaded and on the counter, I go move my car. I hope the director doesn't walk in while I'm gone and think I'm just going to leave everything like that. I drive around the parking lot a couple times trying to find a spot and finally back into a space and then run inside. There are already a few people flowing in when I get back, and I can feel my nerves shooting up my arms and down into my fingertips. There are going to be famous people in here soon.

"You must be from Carter's," a woman says from behind me.

I'm in the middle of pulling a catering tray out of the big container thing and I startle, almost dropping it. "Yes, I'm Isla. I'm just a server at Carter's. Tom Carter, he's the owner. But he's not here. It's just me."

The woman smiles at me and holds out her hand. She's tall, taller than me, and her dark hair is pulled back into a messy bun. "Awesome to meet you, Isla, I'm Zoey, the director."

I shake her hand and try not to choke on my words. "Cool. I'm just bringing the pizza."

She laughs a little. "I really appreciate you guys putting this together for us on such short notice. But the other place that was catering for us, Chives, had a family emergency and is closing for a few days. Their food is awesome, and they recommended you guys when they told us. I'll let you finish setting up, but feel free to stay and eat with us if you don't have to get back right away."

"Thanks," I say, feeling a little intimidated. She doesn't look that much older than me. And she's directing a movie? A movie starring Logan Jackson? I can't.

My hair is bothering me while trying to set everything up so I throw it up into a quick bun and then grab the lighter Tom gave me. I light the food warmer cans under the catering trays, and almost place one under the salads, but blow it out and set it aside after I realize that I'm an idiot. It looks good. And more people are coming in. Is Logan Jackson going to be in here? Eating? In the same room as me?

I grab a slice of Garlic Bacon pizza, my favourite, and dunk a few pieces of bread into the brie before placing them on my paper plate, and head over to a table in the middle of the room, away from any of the people already sitting and eating. The director, Zoey, smiles and nods at me from across the room, and I smile back and shove as much pizza into my mouth as I can because I don't know what else to do.

"Oh wow, this pizza looks fancy," I hear a familiar voice say. My heart starts to pound and I swallow my current bite of bread and melty cheese, afraid to turn around to see the person I know is standing almost directly behind me.

"It's awesome," someone from Zoey's table says. "Try the garlic and bacon one, it's amazing!"

"Oh I'm taking a slice of each one," Logan Jackson replies.

I still haven't turned around, but I know it's him. Logan Jackson is about to eat the pizza that I drove over in my car. Logan Jackson. *Logan. Jackson.* The star of *Neighbourly*, the show critics say is the best sitcom since *Friends*. I mean, the humour is a little different, and it's obviously more modern, but it's got a lot of hard core fans the way *Friends* did, or even *Seinfeld* did.

"Hey, you're the one who brought the pizza!" And I don't even have to turn my head to see him, because Logan Jackson sits right next to me at the table. It's like time stands still for a few seconds and I watch him in slow motion as he takes a bite of pizza and then puts it back on his plate. He's wearing a golden-yellow hoodie and a backwards baseball hat, the kind with the plastic snap, so some of his hair pokes through the hole above it. I wonder if it's part of his costume or if he changed to eat lunch. Surely he wouldn't wear a hat in between shooting scenes, it would mess his hair up. Right? Did I mention that Logan Jackson is sitting next to me?

"Um, how do you know?" I finally ask.

"Well you're wearing a fancy shirt that says Carter's, and those catering containers have a logo on them that say Carters, and I'm pretty smart, so I put the two together." He winks at me and I die a little inside.

"Then, yes, that's me." He smiles at me and I just stare at him, with my mouth gaping open, I'm sure. I want to add something else, something cool, so I say, "I brought food." Jesus Christ, what's wrong with me?

"Well this pizza's awesome."

I smile and give him a thumbs up, because I'm just *so* smooth, and then he gets up and moves to another table, bringing his pizza with him.

Okay, let's pause here. I'm sure you're wondering how I went from being a bumbling idiot to Logan Fucking Jackson asking me to be his pretend girlfriend. And I'll tell you. We'll get there. But it's going to take a little time. I had to tell you about my breakup first because I'm not gonna lie to you, it will come up again. It'll come up a lot, actually, and I want to say that I'm sorry about it, but you know I don't think I am. Also because from the sadness comes something good. Like Logan Fucking Jackson wanting me to be his pretend girlfriend. And we'll get there, I promise. We'll get there and keep going, my friend. I just started the story with that conversation because I wanted to get your attention.

CHAPTER 2

Yes, I'm that person. I'm that person who's going to do this to you. You might hate me for telling you the pivotal plot point before it shows up, but would you even want to hear my story if you didn't know it had me pretending to date Logan Jackson? I had to tell you ahead of time or you would just think I was a boring twenty-nine-year-old who worked at a fancy pizza restaurant and cried at home alone when she thought about her ex and the fact that no one will ever love her again. So yeah, I think I made a smart move telling you about the exciting thing first. Now you get to wait in suspense for it to get here.

"Thanks for bringing the fancy pizza," Logan Jackson says, knocking on my table a little as he passes me. I'm all done eating and just waiting to pack up the stuff, but I somehow still manage to make food fall out of my mouth when I answer.

"You're problem," I say, watching the piece of bread fall onto my shirt. "I mean no problem," I try again, wiping away the embarrassing piece of gross, soggy bread. But when I turn my head around to catch his gaze I notice that he's gone. I'm just correcting my stupid sentence to no one. Except the guy sitting at the next table. He definitely saw all that go down. I notice him smirking at me so I look away and get up. "Nothing," I say quickly, and too loudly to come across as in fact nothing. I cringe and also want to die.

"Okay," he laughs, grabbing his plate and bringing it to the compost bin.

I'm not sure if he's an actor in the movie or someone who works behind the scenes, but I'm still mortified. It doesn't matter who he is. He saw me spill food THAT I WASN'T EVEN CHEWING out of my mouth, mix up two possible responses, and then correct myself to no one. It doesn't matter if he's the co-star, the lighting guy, a camera guy, or a set designer, he saw it all happen and for personal reasons, I will now be passing away.

He looks back at me with a smirk before leaving the room and then I'm alone. I let out a deep breath and bang my forehead on the table in front of me. It's all I can do. I bang it lightly a few more times before finally getting up and putting the leftovers in the fridge.

"So?" Tom asks when he meets me outside to help unload my car. His eyebrows are raised and his eyes practically bulge out of his head.

I can tell he's eager to know what they thought of the food, but I bug him a little and say, "So, what?"

"Did everyone like it?"

"Yes, everyone loved it."

Tom beams at me and I just smile and roll my eyes. The restaurant is busy now so I grab my apron right away and ask Claire which tables she wants me to cover. The dinner rush goes by really quickly and luckily without any trouble, but at about 8pm Tom comes over to me and breaks the news that I have to bring pizza to the movie people again.

"Again?" I ask, surprised.

"Yeah, they get a meal when they're done shooting for the day as well, but you have to bring it to the hotel."

"Why do I have to do it?" I ask.

"Because you'll get to see Logan Johnson again!"

"Jackson."

"Sorry, Jackson Johnson. That's a weird name."

"No, Logan Jackson. His name is Logan Jackson. And I can't see him again; I'll make a fool of myself and die of embarrassment."

"Why? You're adorable. Plus isn't it about time for you to get back in the dating game?" He smirks and motions for me to follow him toward the back. I try to let his comment slide but it eats me up from the inside out.

"What does that have to do with anything?" I ask.

"I just thought it might be good practice, you know, for when you're ready."

"I don't need practice! That man is famous, Tom! And as gorgeous as-" I cut myself off and shake my head. "I don't have to date anyone if I don't want," I say firmly. "Ever."

"Of course you don't." Except he says it with a tone that clearly tells me I'm wrong. Or that I'm just lying to myself about not wanting to date. That I actually do want to; that this is just what I tell myself to make myself feel better.

"I'm not helping clean up when I get back," I say, eyeing the dishwashing room and all the guests out in the restaurant. "I've been here since 10:00 this morning. And I'm eating more pizza at the hotel. Or… what else did you pack? Are there ribs in there?"

"No ribs today. Meatballs."

"Meatballs are good. I'm eating all the meatballs."

Logan Jackson isn't here yet. I've set up the late dinner at the hotel lobby where the girl behind the desk told me to, and I've been sitting here eating my meatballs alone like a loser. How long is this going to take? I have to bring everything back to the restaurant when they're all done eating and I'm tired. I look at my watch and then startle when the main doors slide open.

"Hey! It's the fancy pizza girl!" Logan Jackson says with his arms up in the air.

I feel my face heat up and I look down at my plate of meatballs, afraid to even respond.

"Aw, it's also Jasmine," I hear Logan Jackson say. "Hey, Jasmine."

I look out the corner of my eye to see the girl behind the front desk blushing. That's nice of him to remember her name. But then to my horror, he sits right next to me before even getting food for himself.

"So do you like being a pizza girl?" he asks.

"Um, I'm not a pizza girl."

"What do you do then?"

"I'm a server…. At a pizza restaurant."

"So, you're a pizza girl."

"I prefer to just be called Isla." Where is this confidence coming from all of a sudden? Damn girl!

"My apologies. Isla." He smiles and I try not to look at him, but it's hard. Logan Jackson is smiling at me. And he's sitting right next to me. And he just said my name. "I'm Logan," he finally adds after I don't answer him. Oh and look, he's holding his hand out to me. Like, to shake. Logan Jackson wants to shake my hand.

"I know," I say quietly, and grab his hand. It's warm. And much bigger than mine. And strong. And sexy. Fuck. No. No, it's not sexy. I don't think people are sexy.

"I just thought it would be nice to introduce myself like an actual person, instead of like a celebrity." He lets go of my hand and I stare into his brown eyes, suddenly back to the Isla who can't function.

"I'm not a celebrity," I say.

He laughs and puts his head on the table in between his arms.

"Ha. *You're* a celebrity. I know. I'm not stupid."

"No, but you are cute," he says as he stands up. I will myself to disappear but it doesn't work. And get this. After he gets his food, he comes back to my table and sits next to me again. There are so many other free seats around for him to sit at, why is he sitting next to me? But that's when I realize that there aren't any free seats anywhere else, except for at my table. Everyone else from the movie is here and they're all eating. When did they get here? Did Logan Jackson really just put some sort of magical bubble around us where all I noticed was the two of us together like we were the only two in the entire universe?

"I have to bring all the stuff back to the restaurant when everyone's done eating," I tell him for some reason.

"That makes sense," he replies through a mouth full of pizza. "I have to have a shower and sleep when I'm done eating."

"That sounds nice."

"Yeah, showering and sleeping is nice after a long day."

"Yeah." And then we're quiet. Logan Jackson eats his pizza and I stare at my plate with three meatballs left on it, and I try not to puke up what I've already eaten. This is unreal. He looks at me and smiles every now and then as he eats, which makes me super self-conscious. The only makeup I'm wearing is mascara because I have a pretty big cluster of freckles over my nose and cheeks, which I like. If I wear foundation, they're less noticeable, and I've always thought they were pretty. I'm not good at makeup and stuff anyway, so in my mind, that's how I've always felt less plain. Not that I think I'm ugly or anything, just, next to Logan Jackson I'm basically a walking pile of, um, well, something bland.

Logan Jackson has a perfect nose with just a little bump that makes it look distinguished, and his hair is short, but long enough to have texture, and he's not wearing his hat anymore so it's flat in some spots and sticking up in others. But he still looks gorgeous! He has hat hair and he still somehow manages to look perfect. His whole being is so welcoming and attractive and confident, and here I am with my plain, dark brown hair that I just wear loose or in a messy bun. Plus I'm a wreck right now. I've been working all day, my hair is coming out of its tie and falling around my face, and I'm tired. I'll bet you I even have a bit of raccoon eyes going on from my end-of-the-night mascara.

My pretty freckles are not keeping me up to par on his attractiveness level.

"So do you like working at Carter's?" Logan Jackson asks after a few minutes.

I shrug. "It's okay. I like the people I work with."

"That's important."

"Yeah," I sigh.

"Well Isla, I hate to cut this short, but I'm beat, and I'm done my food, so I'm going to head up to my room."

"Okay," I say. "Have a good night."

He grabs his plate and stops to look at me, like he really looks at me, and he smiles. "You too."

How is this real life?

How is it possible to be this tired? I have never been this tired. I worked a total of 13 hours yesterday, and okay sure, that included an hour of sitting down and eating food, twice, but it also included lugging big heavy containers of food to my car and into a building and onto counters, and into my car and back into the restaurant… twice. But having to wait for everyone to finish their dinner so I could clean up made for a very late night. Why do they eat their meals at such weird times? And that was all on top of my regular job of being on my feet all day and carrying heavy trays and dealing with annoying people. So yeah, I'm back here at 10am again to get ready for opening and I'm exhausted as all hell.

"Oh my god, you have to tell me about the movie set!" Claire practically screams when she meets me at the back door. She's actually jumping up and down.

"It was really cool," I answer, unlocking the door. "But I'm way too tired today."

"You have to tell me more than that! Was Logan Jackson there? Did you talk to him? You know some people have seen him around town, eh!? Oh I wish I could meet him and also not be a total freak, because I have a feeling I would be. I can't believe he's filming a movie here, can you?"

"Well I can believe it because I've been to the... well, it wasn't the set. It was just the community centre. But yeah, I met the director... and Logan Jackson."

"NO WAY! Oh I'm so jealous! Imagine if you guys fell in love..." she trails off and looks up at the ceiling as if she's watching our wedding.

"Don't be ridiculous. I'm not falling in love with anyone, let alone Logan Jackson. He was just nice probably because he feels like he has to be."

"He was *nice?* Oh that's amazing! I'm so glad he was nice!"

"You wanted me to fall in love with him before you knew he was nice? Some friend you are."

I have been voluntold to bring the pizza, garlic bread, and salads over to the community centre again, but this time Logan Jackson doesn't sit with me. Because get this, Carly Bowman is sitting with him. Carly Bowman! She must be his co-star. I sit at the farthest table from them and eat my food slowly and carefully, just in case someone famous tries to talk to me again. I don't want another spilly situation like last time. But as everyone is slowly starting to clear away and leave the room empty, I notice Logan Jackson lingering. Even Carly Bowman has left. Everyone else has left, I now realize. I don't know what else to do, or what to say, so I stand up and immediately start cleaning everything and getting it all ready to bring back to the restaurant.

"Thanks for bringing us the food," Logan Jackson says.

"Oh. I mean it's my job. But no problem. Any time. It's nice to get a break from the restaurant."

He smiles and pushes his chair in. "I heard your restaurant was just filling in for a couple days."

"Yeah," I say. "After tonight it's back to Chives for you guys."

"Maybe I'll still see you around. After all, I know where you work." He smirks at me and my entire body blushes. I can feel the back of my neck heating up. This is ridiculous. But then his face sort of scrunches a little. "Actually, I don't know where you work. Like, I know where you work, but I don't know where it is."

"Oh. It's just down the road." I continue to pack everything up while I talk because otherwise I would just fidget and then probably do something weird.

"Cool."

"Logan, come on," someone says, poking their head in the room. "We're waiting for you."

"Sorry, I'm coming." He looks at me and smiles before following the guy into the hall.

Ohmygod.

"Jasmine's working again!" Logan Jackson says as he enters the hotel for dinner. He throws his hands up in the air as if he's excited to see the girl working behind the counter. Maybe he is excited to see her. Either way, she likes the attention, but I can see her trying to hide her reddening cheeks. "You don't have to work all night, do you?" he asks, stopping to rest his arm on the counter.

"Just till eleven," she replies quietly.

"Just till eleven," he repeats in a mocking tone. "That's basically all night, you know that, right?"

"Well I don't have to work past midnight, so that's good."

"I like your positivity." He knocks on the counter and smiles as he turns towards the dining area. But then he sees me and his smile grows. I can feel everything inside of me exploding with uncertainty as he makes his way towards me. Not even towards the food. He's coming right towards me. "Hey, Isla," he says as he sits next to me.

"Hi," I reply.

"How's it going?"

"Okay."

"Just okay?"

I shrug. "I'm tired."

"Are you having anything to eat?"

"Yeah, I guess." I turn to look at the spread I set up about twenty minutes ago but he puts a hand out to stop me and then rises from his chair.

"You stay put," he says. "You're tired."

I narrow my eyes at him but stay seated as he gets up and fills two plates with pizza and ribs. He brings them to our empty table and looks at me when he sits.

"Am I freaking you out or something?" he asks when I don't start eating.

"What? No. No, of course not. Why would you freak me out? You're only just bringing me food that I brought from a restaurant. We're just bringing each other food."

He chuckles and tears some meat off the rib bone with his fingers. "I'm sorry I'm freaking you out."

"I just said you weren't."

"Okay." He smiles and everything inside of me falls apart. How is he so beautiful? How is he doing this to me? He takes another bite of his ribs. "This barbeque sauce is amazing."

"Yeah," I sigh. "It always makes my mouth water when I bring it to tables."

"I can imagine." I stare at him as he picks up his pizza and takes a bite, and I stare at him as he chews. And the weird thing is, he's staring at me too. He's just looking at me as he eats, and I'm looking back at him, and I have no idea what I'm even thinking. I'm just staring at him and his somehow good looking hat hair. I'm staring at Logan Jackson eating pizza, while he stares at me. How is this even real life? What is happening?

He finally stops chewing and swallows. "Eat your fancy pizza, Isla." And then he smiles, stands up, grabs his plate, and takes it to another table. The crew members shuffle a bit to make room for him and he starts talking to them right away, making them laugh. He looks back at me once and raises his eyebrows at me, but I have no idea what message he's trying to convey with it. But I just raise my eyebrows back at him and eat my food.

That whole thing was weird, right?

CHAPTER 3

Okay, we're going to fast forward a little here, because otherwise you would be bored to tears. I stop bringing food to the movie because we were only filling in for two days, and literally nothing happens for the next two weeks. I work, go home and eat Kraft Dinner, cry a little, and work some more. Nothing interesting happens. I don't even know why I thought any of this would be good. Well, I know why it's good, it's because it's going to get good. Trust me.

I come out of the back room after dropping off some empty plates with the dishwasher and almost stop dead in my tracks when I see him. Logan Jackson is standing at the front of the restaurant with his hands in the kangaroo pocket of the same golden-yellow hoodie he was wearing the first day I brought pizza to the set. He's just standing there; his tall, muscularly lean frame is standing at the front of the restaurant that I work at, and now I have to hide.

"Oh my god," Claire says, grabbing my sleeve and pulling me back into the room I just came out of.

"What?" I ask.

"Logan Jackson is out there!"

"I know, I saw him too."

"Do you think he's here to talk to you?" she squeals.

"Absolutely not."

"I can't seat him. I can't talk to him. I'll mess up his whole order and spill drinks everywhere and make a fool of myself!"

"And you think I can do it?" I ask. "I embarrassed myself so much while I was catering for the movie! I'm a nervous wreck around him; he makes me forget how to… be a human being."

"I know, right? He's so gorgeous."

"Well someone has to greet him."

We both lean out of the back room just enough for our heads and shoulders to cross the doorway, and peek out at him standing there. The whole restaurant is pretty open, so we have a clear view past the cutlery station and the pizza oven. He's standing there with an innocent smile on his face and he's looking around the restaurant as if he's interested in the décor and not at all wondering where the employees are. Tom is behind the bar chatting up a regular and pouring him some beer, and the two chefs are laughing as they make pizzas almost directly across from us. And Logan Jackson is standing at the front of the restaurant, and nobody knows but me and Claire!

"Uh, guys," Charlie, one of the chefs says, "There's a guest waiting at the front, if you haven't noticed." He tips his head in Logan Jackson's general direction.

"Yes, we know, Charlie, thank you," Claire says.

"Well what are you doing?" He looks over at Logan Jackson and back at us, still hiding as best as we can from the rest of the people in the restaurant.

"Trying to figure out how we're going to talk to him without barfing," Clarie spits out rather aggressively. Charlie puts his hands up in surrender and turns around, back to the pizza.

"Well one of us has to go over to him before Tom notices that we're ignoring someone," I say.

"We're not ignoring him, Isla. We're staring at him."

"Well what are we supposed to do?"

"Do you want me to seat him?" Charlie asks.

"No!" Claire and I both yell at the same time.

Tom and his regular hear and turn towards us and I'm about to smile at them when I realize that Logan Jackson heard us too. Oh, and the two other tables currently in the restaurant.

Fantastic. Literally everybody in the restaurant is now looking at us, confused expressions all over their faces. I wave briefly at Tom and the bar guest, and pull Claire into the back room with me, the both of us almost crashing into Lance.

"Sorry," we both say. He shrugs and goes back to washing dishes.

"Okay," I say to Claire, "one of us has to go out and seat him."

"Not it," Claire practically shouts, putting her index finger on the tip of her nose.

"I don't understand why you don't want to talk to a famous man who is also incredibly attractive," I say with a huff.

"Probably the same reason you don't want to."

"Ugh." I spin around and march back into the restaurant, trying not to think about it. Thinking about it will make me nervous and I'll just become a blabbing mess of embarrassment. I make eye contact with him as I walk past the bar and he smiles, tilting his head up in a sort of hello.

"Hi, thanks for waiting," I say to him, trying to hide the shakiness in my voice.

"No worries."

"Are you dining alone?" I ask, grabbing a menu.

"Uh, yeah, just me."

"Okay. Would you prefer a table, or would you like to sit at the bar?"

He looks around and shrugs. "It doesn't matter. Whatever you recommend, I guess."

"Um." I try to think of something smart to say in response, but really I have nothing. I want to sit him at the bar so Tom can take care of him and I don't have to force myself not to barf everywhere, but I would honestly recommend the table in the corner window because you can sort of see the waterfront from it, and when the breeze comes in, it's really nice. "This way," I finally say, not sure if I was even loud enough for him to hear me. But he follows me to the newly wiped table in the corner and I give him a menu.

"I'll be right back," I say, stepping away as quickly as I can. I practically run to the back and collapse into Claire, who has clearly been watching from the doorway the whole time.

"Oh my god, Isla, you did amazing. I'm so jealous!"

"You have to come back with me. Please bring him his cutlery and stuff while I get his water. I can't. I can't do this, I'm shaking, look!" I hold my hands out to her so she can see my fingers tremble.

"Okay fine, I'll bring his cutlery for you, but I can't say anything. I'll probably just scream his name over and over if I try to say words to him."

"Thank you."

Claire follows me back to his table, where she sets it up for him, and I pour him a glass of water. "Anything to drink besides water today?" I ask.

"No, water's great, thanks." He smiles up at me and I put the pitcher on the table and follow Claire away.

"Isla, the water," she says to me.

"Yeah, he said he wanted water."

"No, you left the pitcher of water on his table."

"Shit." I let out a deep breath and close my eyes. I take a few more slow breaths and then head back to his table to see him eyeing the menu. I try to grab the water pitcher without him noticing, but obviously that's impossible. He looks up at me as soon as I pick it up. "Just… forgot this," I say, doing a weird curtsy thing. What's wrong with me?

"Okay. I think I'm ready to order too."

"Oh. Right. Okay. No problem. What would you like?" I put the water back on the table and grab my notepad. There's no way I'm going to remember what he says to me with the way my brain is working right now.

"I've been thinking about that garlic bacon pizza ever since you brought it to the movie set so I definitely need that again. And also some of those meatballs too."

"Awesome, I'll put that in for you." I put my pen behind my ear and make my way to the computer, leaving the water pitcher on his table. Again.

The rest of his meal goes fairly smoothly, but the water pitcher stays on his table the entire time. Another table actually asks me why they don't have a pitcher at their table and I just chuckle at them and tell them they're hilarious because again, brain, not working, and I'm surprised when they actually leave me a good tip. By the time Logan Jackson is ready to pay and I've brought him a takeout container for his two uneaten slices, the restaurant is really busy. It's helping me to focus a little better because I have less time to think about Logan Jackson and how I'm going to be normal around him. I bring him the machine to pay and he smiles up at me as I stand there waiting for him to put in his PIN. Why didn't he just tap his card? I'm getting all flustered again.

"Oh sorry, wrong PIN, I have to do it again," he says. Seriously?

"That's okay." I take the machine from him and put the total in again, hand it back to him.

"It was nice seeing you again," he says as he puts his PIN in again.

"Oh yeah, likewise."

"Dammit, I did it again." He hands the machine to me and I put the total in again.

"You should just tap it then," I say. "Or stop talking while you're pressing buttons."

"I had tap disabled on my card because it got stolen a while back. But you're right, I'm distracting myself."

"Actually," I say, "I'll leave that with you, I'm just going to take another table's order. Also I was trying to be funny when I said you shouldn't talk while you're pressing buttons. I wasn't trying to be rude. Just in case that didn't come through. Okay, give me a minute."

I notice him smirking as I back away and then notice my other table staring at him as I approach. Then they stare at me with giant smiles that are actually kind of creepy.

"Is that Logan Jackson?" one of them asks.

"Yes," I reply, getting my notepad out. "But I'm not sure if he wants people to know. I mean he didn't tell me not to tell people or anything, and I guess it's pretty obvious, I mean it's Logan Jackson, right here in the restaurant, eating pizza. Right there."

"Yeah. Anyway, we're not ready to order," someone else from the table says. "We've just been staring at him the whole time and haven't even looked at the menus."

I smile at them. "Take your time."

I reluctantly go back to Logan Jackson's table and pick up the machine. I rip his copy of the receipt and hand it to him, and notice on it that he gave me a $200 tip.

"Oh, I think you made a mistake here," I say, about to point to his receipt.

He smiles and holds a hand up. "Isla, shh, I didn't make a mistake." He remembers my name? But then I remember that I have a nametag on. Right. "I always do that. Is that okay?"

"Um, I mean, yes, yes that's great, I'm very grateful, it's just, it's like five times the cost of your meal and that's –"

"Isla," he says, cutting me off.

"Logan."

My saying his name sort of makes him pause and he smiles, his eyes widening in surprise for a split second. It surprises me too, first of all because I didn't say his last name, which I never thought I would be able to do, and because, well, I don't actually *know* him, and so saying his name seems weird. I don't know why I did it, or how I even did it, but it might somehow be the most normal thing that's come out of my mouth since meeting him. Except for my very professional server words at the beginning there, I'm quite proud of that to be honest. But saying his name, his *first* name without his last name, is that even something that's allowed? Will he be offended? Honestly I'm a little offended. He's Logan Jackson. I can't just call him Logan like we're fucking besties.

"If it makes you feel better, you can share the tip with your coworkers," he says quietly.

"Fuck that," I reply with a smile, which in turn makes him grin. "Um, I mean, thank you. I'm glad you enjoyed your meal."

I turn away and make my way to the cash register to take out two beautiful brown bills that I'm not stealing but that totally feels like I am. I fold them and stick them in my apron with my other tips, and try to go about my day as if I didn't just call Logan Jackson by his first name and he didn't give me two hundred dollars.

Logan Jackson says goodbye to me as he leaves and I call out my usual "See you next time," as if he's going to come back to our little restaurant. I can't help it though, it's a habit.

CHAPTER 4

Logan Jackson comes for an in-between-the-rush meal again the next day and Claire and I both almost faint again.

"I can't," Claire says, shaking her head. "You did so well yesterday."

"But he's so beautiful, Claire, I was a nervous wreck and he makes me feel like a slob!"

She gasps. "When did he say that?"

"He didn't, I said he makes me feel like that."

"Why? Did he give you a dirty look or something?"

"No. He's just… He's so gorgeous and I'm just… Me."

"Oh my goodness, Isla, shut up, you're so pretty. And you pull off that messy bun like you're hot shit; I'm so jealous."

"What? But I'm jealous of *your* messy bun," I say.

She pauses and then smiles. "Really?"

I just nod.

"Okay, you know what? We're both hot enough to pull off a sexy messy bun, but you don't even wear makeup and you're still beautiful. You know what I would look like without contouring?"

"Gorgeous," I say to her.

She shakes her head. "A girl with no makeup."

I tilt my head to the side. "A gorgeous girl with no makeup."

"Fine," she says with a huff. "I guess we're both pretty. What do you think of that, Isla Reid?"

"I think that's a fair observation, Claire Kishimoto."

She smiles. "Okay. But you're still serving Logan Jackson."

"Ugh. Fine."

I clench and unclench my fists as I make my way to the front to greet him and he smiles at me.

"Hey Isla," he says when I'm closer.

"Hi." I can't say his name again, it's just weird. I can't say 'Hi, Logan,' because it just slipped out the last time I did it, and like I said, we're not friends, and he's famous, and he's Logan Jackson to me, and so I can't just call him Logan to his face. I also can't call him Logan Jackson, because who actually refers to someone by their first and last name *to* that person? No one. Not me. That's why I just go with "hi" and nothing else. I bring him to the same table as the day before and this time he orders a beer to go with his water.

"Wow, that's some good head, Isla," he says as I set his glass on the table.

I notice myself cringing, but I'm not sure if he's trying to be funny or if he's serious. If he's trying to be funny, then he's not funny, and I hate him a little bit, but if he's serious, then I'm honoured, because yes, I gave that beer beautiful fucking head. I recover quickly enough I think, and give him a weak smile and leave him to look at the menu. And by leave, I of course mean run away.

"Um, Isla?" he asks after a few minutes. I look up at him from the podium at the front with the computer and register at it, and give him a smile. He beckons me closer with his fingers so I walk towards him. "I'm a little embarrassed."

"About what?" I ask.

"I realized after you left how that must have sounded when I complimented your beer pouring skills. I was honestly confused by your reaction, because you didn't seem thrilled, and I always thought it was hard to pour a good beer from the tap, especially creamy beer, and I thought it would be nice to let you know, and then I realized how it probably sounded in your head and I promise that's not what I was doing."

"Okay," I say, feeling the corner of my lips curl. "Well thank you. I take pride in my beer pouring skills. Especially the creamy beers."

"I'm not a creep, I promise," he adds.

"Okay. I believe you. Um, are you ready to order?"

"Yes."

When I take his food to him a bit later, I work up the courage to ask him a question. "How come you're eating here?"

"What? What do you mean?"

"Um, well, the movie people provide food for you for free."

"Yeah, but I really missed this pizza. It's seriously the best pizza I've ever had. I've asked some of the other people to join me but they're not bothered. I think they all sort of hate me."

"Hate you?" I ask, surprised. "Why would they hate you?"

"I dunno," he says with a shrug. "I think a lot of people think I'm annoying."

"Really?"

"It's probably just my anxiety talking, but yeah."

Logan Jackson has anxiety and thinks that people think he's annoying? But he's always so confident and funny. Also he's famous. Is his confidence just an act? I feel like I need to say something to him that doesn't make him feel any more self conscious than he apparently already feels. No one likes to hear that the person they're spilling their feelings to thinks that their feelings aren't valid.

"Well I don't think you're annoying," I try, giving him a smile.

He chuckles a little. "Good to know."

When he's done his meal, he tips me $200 again, and this time I feel bad and give half of it to Claire. She squeals and hugs me, trying hard not to jump up and down, but obviously, she fails. We all walk out together when we close up, but my car is parked way farther up the road than everyone else's and around a corner, so I venture into the dimly lit downtown on my own.

I'm just coming up to my car when I notice a man with his hood up, walking towards me. Then he starts to jog and I pull back, not sure what he's doing. Not sure what I'm going to do. The way he's jogging doesn't seem threatening, but I'm still nervous. I look around at the empty road and street lights illuminating the few unoccupied vehicles, and unlock my car. I start to run towards it, hoping I'll make it inside before he reaches me. But then he calls out my name. Do I know him?

"Who is that?" I ask, squinting.

"It's Logan!"

"Logan who? I don't know a Logan." I pull on my door handle but then he's close enough for me to recognize him. "Oh *Logan*," I say, a little embarrassed.

"Yeah. Logan." He stops in front of me and smiles. And I melt into a puddle and practically slide under the car.

"Um, what's up?" I manage to ask.

"I was just taking a walk. It's really pretty out here at night time."

"Well yeah, if you actually leave the confines of the buildings and go look at the water."

"No, I like the buildings too. They're so quaint."

I smirk a little, but don't really know what to say.

"And the streets are pretty, like you guys have all these twinkly lights like it's Christmas or something. Have you not even paid attention to where you live, Isla?"

Him saying my name so easily catches me off guard and I feel a weird lump in my throat. "Not recently, no. Maybe I should."

"You definitely should. It doesn't look like this anywhere I've been in the last eight years."

"Tell me about it."

He scrunches his eyebrows at me. "What do you mean?"

"Oh, nothing. Never mind. I was just thinking out loud. So have you walked to the water yet, or…?"

"Not yet. I mean I have a ton of times during the day, but not tonight. Or any night. I usually just go straight back to the hotel. We have two night shoots by the water next week, though, so that'll be fun."

"Yeah, for sure. Okay, well, have a good night." I start to get into my car but he puts his hand on the top of it and I stop.

"You don't want to keep me company, do you?"

"What, to walk to the water?" I ask.

"Yeah."

"Um. Sure. I guess. I mean, yeah, okay." I shut the door and lock my car twice, so I can hear it beep.

Our walk to the end of the street is silent and I want to ask him about Carly Bowman, why he isn't hanging out with her during his time off, but then I remember that he's hanging out with me and maybe if I say something it'll snap him out of this weird thing he's doing and realize that I'm not nearly cool enough for him to be seen with.

"So, have you lived here your whole life?" he finally asks.

"Since high school," I say with a bit of a nod. "My family moved here when I was in grade ten, so, yeah. I went away for school, just college, but then I came back after. Obviously."

"Nice."

"I don't know what kind of things to ask you, sorry," I say.

"You don't have to ask me anything. I was just trying to make conversation. I didn't want you to feel like I kidnapped you or something." His voice is very playful and it makes me smile.

We turn the corner onto the road that leads to the waterfront and Logan actually gasps. We're still a little ways away from it, so I'm sure he'll gasp again when we get closer and he can see the lights on the boats and the moon reflecting on the water.

"Sucker for small boating towns, are we?" I ask.

"I'm a sucker for all small towns. Small beach towns, small boating towns, small ... what other small towns are there?"

I look up at him and shrug. "I think you pretty much covered it."

"Small towns with one room school houses," he says.

"There's one of those close by. It also has the smallest jail in North America."

"That sounds exciting."

"It is, except the excitement doesn't last long. You can see the thing in like half a second."

"Right," he says with a smile.

We get closer to the water and already I can feel him relaxing next to me. He exhales so deeply and out of the corner of my eye I notice his shoulders fall. The wind makes the sail boats sort of sing, and the lights along the docks reflect across the water like fairies or fireflies.

"This is so magical," he says in almost a whisper.

It's not magical to me, because I used to come here with Tyler, and looking at the reflections on the water sort of makes me want to gag. A familiar ache in my chest works its way up to my throat and I close my eyes, willing the feeling to go away. This should be a magical moment. I'm staring at the water with Logan Fucking Jackson and all I can think about is my stupid ex-boyfriend who doesn't love me anymore. I can feel a sob coming so I fake a cough, hoping to make it go away, but it doesn't work. It's coming, I can feel it.

"I'm sorry," I blurt out, turning around, "I have to go."

"What?"

I cross the street even though the light is green in the other direction, but there are no cars coming, and I'm afraid that if I wait for the light to change, Logan Jackson will catch up with me and ask what's wrong. So I keep going, and once I turn onto the street that my car is parked on, I start to cry. I unlock my car and get inside. And then I sob. Big wailing sobs come out of me and I can't stop it. I need to just turn my car on and drive home, but I can't because of how hard I'm crying. What if he followed me and sees me or hears me? That will be the end of my life, for sure. A knock on my window both startles me and confirms my fears, and I scream a little, turning to see Logan Jackson on the other side of the glass.

"Are you okay?" he asks.

"No. Please go away." Another sob comes out and I take a deep breath.

"Well if you're not okay, I don't think I can do that."

"I mean I'm fine. Like, I'm not, but I will be. It's not a big deal, I'm just upset."

"Did I say something wrong? Or make you feel uncomfortable? Because that wasn't my intention, and if I did, I'm truly sorry, and you have to tell me if I'm-"

"It's nothing you did." I notice that my crying has calmed just a bit and I could totally drive home safely at this point. "And look, see? I'm not crying anymore." I sniffle and give him a fake smile.

"Well I don't know if I would call that not crying, but it's definitely better than it was."

"I just need to go home, okay?"

"To cry by yourself?" he asks gently.

"Yes."

"Crying by yourself is not something I would recommend. You can cry with me so you don't have to be alone."

"Um, I appreciate that, really, I do…" I pause and swallow, take another deep breath. "But… I don't know you. You're… You're Logan Fucking Jackson, and you're famous and you're… And I'm…"

He laughs a little and stands up. I guess he was crouched down so he could be at eye level with me through the window. "Okay. Fair enough. I'm sorry for overstepping."

"Okay." I fake another smile but it's easier this time, so I guess it's only half fake. I put the key in the ignition and look back through the window. He's still there, leaning down a little bit. "Um, thanks," I add.

"Any time." He smiles and steps away so I can start the car. I make sure I'm not going to run over his foot or anything when I pull onto the road, and as I drive away I can't help but look in the rear-view mirror. He stands in the middle of the road with an arm up in a wave, so I wave back, unsure if he'll even see. But any time I look into the mirror again, he's still there. He's there until I turn onto another street and then I don't know if he's still there or not. But he stayed until I was gone, and even though he's famous, and his niceness was probably fake or the beginning of a weird publicity stunt, it's nice to know that he stayed anyway. Most people wouldn't have stayed, but he did.

CHAPTER 5

The movie only has one week left of shooting and part of me is sad. I haven't seen Logan Jackson again since the night that I randomly started crying at the waterfront, but the excitement of it all is still fun. Seeing the cameras and the lights when I leave or come to work, and seeing roads blocked off so they can film is always something that lights something inside me. It's just so cool to know that our town is the setting of a big rom-com movie with two very well-known actors. Knowing that it'll be over soon and our town will just be a regular, small boating town again gets to me. It's weird to say or think about, but it's been sort of keeping me going. Keeping my mind on other things. Except for when I was at the waterfront with Logan Jackson, but you know what I mean. Besides that one time I've just been thinking about how fun and exciting it is to see movie stars and directors, and those fancy director's chairs on the sidewalk that I didn't even know were real things. It's sort of magical in a way.

I get to leave work tonight before we close, and I'm heading out at around 7pm, which is the most excellent feeling ever almost, and I notice that the movie is shooting down by the water. The sun's going to set soon and I have a feeling they're going to film a romantic sunset scene in a bit, so I decide to walk down and check it out. They have gates set up, I guess to keep the area they need clear, which is good because there are so many people trying to watch. I wonder if outdoor movie sets get crowds like this in LA and Toronto, or if this is just happening here because it's so exciting and new to us all.

I wander as close to the gates as I can, and I hear the director call action but we're too far away to hear what the actors are saying. They've got a camera set up on one end of the dock with a big boom mic on some sort of crane so that it can follow the two actors as they work their way along the dock. I watch as they stop walking and look at each other, get closer together as if they're about to kiss, and then the director calls "cut!" and I look around at all the other people to see if they're surprised to see how movie filming works too. They were filming for like two minutes and already they're stopping? They walk back to the other end of the dock where they started, and everything starts over again. They do it a few times and then a bunch of people start moving the camera and laying a track down on the dock. They're working so quickly that I'm worried one of them is going to fall into the water by accident. I notice a few more people joining the crowd, and before I know it there's basically a mob of people surrounding me at the gate. I wish we were allowed to get closer, but I'm sure they blocked off as much space as they did for a reason. Logan Jackson and Carly Bowman are walking up the grass a little bit closer to us, where their chairs are set up next to a table of snacks.

"We're shooting again as soon as the sun starts setting," the director calls.

Logan Jackson throws a hand in the air I'm assuming as an acknowledgement, and then looks behind him at the crowd and smiles. A bunch of girls "whoo" and then he gets off his chair. Carly Bowman grabs his sleeve and says something and he shakes her off and replies with a few words none of us can hear, and then starts walking towards us. Oh no. I look around for a way to leave but I'm surrounded by people and no one is moving out of the way. Why did I come right up to the fence? Why didn't I just stand behind some people?

"Excuse me," I say, trying to shove past people, but they're all getting closer to me somehow, sandwiching me and smushing me into the fence and other people. He can't know that I came to watch, he can't know. Maybe he won't recognize me. Everyone starts screaming and cheering and saying his name and holding out posters and magazines of him to sign and he immediately pulls a Sharpie out of his front jeans pocket to sign things for people.

"Hey, how's it going everyone?" he asks.

Everyone just cheers and screams his name. I try my hardest to back away but I can't. I just shove into the person behind me who shoves me back and I crash into the fence, making the most unattractive squealing noise anyone can ever make. Logan Jackson hears and sees the commotion; of course he does, and steps over to me with a huge grin on his face.

"Isla, are you okay?"

"I'm… I'm fine, I just got thrown into a fence. You know how it is."

He laughs and reaches over the gate to put his hands on my shoulders and sort of straighten me out. I realize standing this close to him that this is the first time I've seen him in person without a hood, a hat, or hat hair. He's got gel or wax in his hair or something, and it's just sort of messed up a little. It looks really good.

"Can you guys move back a bit?" he asks everyone. "I know it's exciting to see a movie get shot and everything, but this girl almost got hurt."

"It's fine, I'm fine, I didn't-"

"Come on, guys! Back up!" he shouts to the crowd.

Everyone sort of gapes at him but they do as he asks and they spread out a little from each other and from the fence at the front.

"Thanks guys! If you want to hang around until we're done shooting this scene, I'll come say hi again! Just be nice to everyone, okay?" he steps away from me and signs a poster for a teenager who's holding it out over the gate, and then he winks at me, at *me*, and heads back to the set. What is happening? It looks like they're ready for him to shoot again and he jogs over to the dock where it looks like someone touches up his makeup. Most of the crowd stays to watch, but some of the people who got autographs duck out. I can hear them freaking out about it as they walk away and it makes me smile. I'm not sure why I stay, to be honest. I don't really feel the need to get his autograph or a picture with him or anything, I mean I've eaten part of a meal with him, served him pizza twice, walked to the water with him and sobbed like a baby in front of him, what more do I need? I guess I want to stay for him to see that I'm a normal adult who can pull herself together and not be creepy or sad or depressing. Or maybe it's creepy that I'm here? No. No, of course it isn't. I'm super interested to see how the movie gets shot, and it's really cool to see the camera move backwards on the track as they walk along the dock.

A security guard ends up making his way to the crowd and I wonder why he wasn't here earlier, but am glad he's at least here now. It starts to get chilly once the sun goes down, and it looks like they're taking another break to set up another shot, this time farther away from the docks. The two actors go into a white tent and come out a few minutes later wearing different clothes, so it must be a completely different scene they're shooting now, just at the same location. Logan's got on the backwards hat and golden-yellow hoodie again, and I wonder if this movie takes place over a short period of time since I'm always seeing him wearing the same thing. More people start to leave, probably because they're cold, but I just wrap my arms around myself and pull my hoodie sleeves over my hands and keep watching. It would be more interesting if I could hear what they were saying, but it's still cool to watch. They even have a person stand in front of the camera with one of those clacky things before they start filming, which I also wasn't sure was actually a real thing until seeing it now.

Logan Jackson comes back to the now smaller crowd after they've done the same scene a bunch of times. This time the crowd says hi back and he smiles, leans over the barrier to take pictures with people, and signs things for people. It's sort of weird that Carly Bowman is staying back and not interacting with her fans. Some people are even shouting for her but she doesn't even turn around and acknowledge them.

"We're gonna be here for a while yet, guys. I don't want you guys to get cold watching," he says to everyone.

"We're okay!" some people shout.

He looks at me and I sort of shrug, but he stays on that side of the crowd for a few minutes talking to people. He hugs a few people over the top of the fence and then the fans run off squealing and jumping up and down. He eventually makes it to my area of the fence but he signs things for other people and takes selfies with them, and then finally steps up to me.

"Hey," he says.

My stomach shoots up to my throat and I have a hard time finding my voice. "Hi," I manage.

"You want to take a selfie?"

"Um. Yeah, okay." But the thing that surprises me is he takes out his own phone. He leans over the barrier and presses his face in close to mine, holds his phone up so we can see ourselves on the screen, and takes a picture. With *his* phone. I'm about to ask if we can take a picture with my phone too, but he starts talking before I can get any words out.

"That's a good picture," he says. "If you give me your number I'll text it to you."

My entire face turns red. And my neck. I can feel it. I don't dare look around at the people still left in the crowd. I don't want to see their expressions; I don't even want to hear what they're saying. They're saying things, they must be.

"Kay," I choke out, so quiet I can barely hear it myself.

He hands me his phone and I cringe at how noticeably I'm shaking when I take it from him. It's already open to a new contacts page in his phone so I type my name and put in my phone number with trembling fingers. This is ridiculous. I'm not putting my number in Logan Jackson's phone right now. But I'm totally putting my number in Logan Jackson's phone. I'm putting my number in Logan Fucking Jackson's phone. What the fuck. I can't.

"Logan, let's go!" someone calls from down by the water.

"Sorry!" he calls. He turns back to me and smiles, winks again, and runs back to set.

How is this real life?

"Did Logan Jackson seriously just ask for your phone number?" a girl squeals.

"No, absolutely not." I shove my way through the small crowd and speed walk towards my car. I didn't give Logan Jackson my phone number. That's just absurd. That didn't really happen.

"Logan Jackson asked for that girl's phone number!" someone else shouts from behind me.

"What girl!?" someone else calls.

"That girl there! Logan Jackson is going to date someone from our town!"

"No he didn't!" I call back. "He didn't ask for my phone number! That's ridiculous!"

"She's lying! I saw! I heard!"

"He didn't ask for my phone number!" I shout again, before picking up speed and running the rest of the way to my car. He didn't ask for my phone number. No. I don't want to give any guy my phone number, let alone someone *famous*. I'm not ready. I'm not ready to give guys my phone number. Not regular guys, not famous guys, no guys. It didn't happen. No. Absolutely not.

My phone chimes about twenty minutes after I get home and I open it to see a picture attached to a text from a number without a contact. The picture is of me and Logan Jackson, and the text says I'm glad you're not crying anymore. So yeah. I guess Logan Jackson has my phone number.

CHAPTER 6

I have no idea what to say, so instead I save the picture and post it to Instagram. I've been following Logan Jackson and the rest of the *Neighbourly* cast since halfway through the first season, but have never tagged them in a post. I think about putting a filter on the picture, but none of them look as good as the original. I write **You know how it is. Just hanging out with my bestie** for the caption with five laughing emojis. I tag him in the caption after the emojis and then erase it. Then I tag him before the emojis, and then I erase that too. Oh who cares if I tag him, he's probably not going to see it anyway. And he's probably not even the one who comments on pictures or makes posts anyway. I put in his handle before the emojis again and then post it. Was that a bad idea? No, I'm sure everyone who got a picture with him immediately posted it to Instagram. I'm just being a normal person posting it. Right? Yes. Right. I'm right.

I've fallen asleep on the couch watching *The Office* for the hundredth time, and am woken up by my phone. I look at the TV and Netflix is asking me if I'm still watching, so I turn the TV off and check my phone. I have a text and an Instagram notification. I look at the text first, which is from Logan Jackson, except I haven't added him to my phone yet so it's still just his number without a name.

So we're besties now, are we? it says.

Again I'm too nervous to answer so I check my Instagram. The first thing I see makes my heart jump into my throat, but the second thing just about makes me faint.

The first thing, the thing that would make any girl go wild with excitement, is a simple **TheRealLoganJackson liked your post.**

But the other thing, the other thing is

TheRealLoganJackson started following you.

No.

No way. Logan Fucking Jackson is not fucking following me on fucking Instagram. He also did not just text me. But my phone chimes and I'm afraid to look at it because what if it's him?

Oh no it's him. He says he likes my Instagram handle. Well I have to say something to him.

Thanks I type. I hit send and turn the screen off immediately as if that makes my text non-existent.

My phone makes a noise almost instantly and I actually squeal. But I turn my screen back on to see that it's just Claire. Not just Claire, sorry, it's Claire! Hurray!

OMG is all her text reads.

What? I text back.

You got a picture with LOGAN JACKSON and HE LIKED IT!?

Yeah, he actually took it with his phone I reply.

WHAT

I reply with a shrugging emoji.

HOW

Another shrugging emoji.

YOU MUST TELL ME THINGS AT WORK TOMORROW

I'm off tomorrow I reply.

WHAT

hahahaha I type. We'll talk on Friday.

YOU CAN'T DO THIS TO ME HOW AM I SUPPOSED TO LIVE

I love your capital letters and lack of punctuation I start. It really shows your excitement. But I'm really tired so I'm going to go to bed.

BUT LOGAN JACKSON

Maybe he'll get pizza tomorrow and you'll get to serve him this time.

He hasn't been in for a week.

Exactly. All the more reason for him to go in now. He probably misses us.

Misses you is more like it.

I reply with the wide-eyed blushing emoji and head to bed. She texts me again, but I'll read it in the morning.

I check my phone when I wake up close to noon and as it turns out, that last text from Claire wasn't from Claire, it was actually from Logan Jackson. He said, Pineapples hurt my tongue.

This is probably confusing to you. It's not actually confusing if you could see my phone when I posted the picture to Instagram, because then you'd see my Instagram handle, but you didn't see my phone and I didn't tell you what it was (because it didn't seem important, and honestly I didn't think you'd care, but I forgot about the part where Logan Jackson texted me about it so I left it out but I'm telling you now). So anyway my Instagram handle is pine.apple.tidbits and that's why he told me that pineapples hurt his tongue. I actually wanted it to just be pineapple.tidbits but someone else was also obviously amazingly cool already had it. So I had to put another period in there somewhere instead of thinking of something else entirely. Ugh, now I'm rambling about my Instagram handle. Anyway, I can't believe Logan Jackson texted me about his tongue.

Me too, unless they're suuuuper ripe, or cooked I type back.

He replies almost right away. Does this mean you like pineapple on pizza?

Of course I say. He doesn't reply after a few minutes so I think of something to add. I hope you do too or we can't be friends.

I turn off my phone screen as soon as I hit send, because again, it's like it never happened. But he doesn't reply. Hmm. I try not to think about it and check my Etsy page to see if I have any new sales, which of course I don't, so I grab my purse and go grocery shopping. I cook up a few meals when I get home so I don't have to cook after work for the next few days. I'm sitting down to watch more of *The Office* at five in the evening when my phone goes off.

It's Logan Jackson and it says, Surely it would take more than just an opinion about pizza for you to break it off with your BESTIE.

My eyes widen and my heart starts to hammer in my chest. What do I say? Like, really, what are you supposed to say to a celebrity that you're randomly texting? How is this happening?? My fingers are shaking. Of course my fingers are shaking.

You'd be surprised I type.

But then he doesn't reply again. I'm not really sure what I'm supposed to expect when texting a movie star, so I try not to read into it. Not that there's anything to read into anyway. Or anything that I want to be read into. I'm not making any sense. I'm going to have so much to tell Claire at work tomorrow.

Claire practically tackles me when she gets into work and pulls me into the back room.

"TELL ME EVERYTHING."

"Calm down," I say, laughing a bit. "So he followed me on Instagram…"

"WHAT!?"

"Claire, can you calm yourself?"

She closes her eyes and gives her whole body a shake before taking a deep breath. "Okay," she says, opening her eyes again. "I've calmed."

"Have you though?"

"Yes. Please continue."

"Okay," I say with a grin. "And then we texted… about pineapple."

"Because of your Instagram handle?"

"Of course."

"This is the greatest thing of my life; you have to tell me more!"

"That's it, we only texted back and forth a few times. And there were huge gaps of time in between his replies."

"Maybe he was texting you in between takes and stuff on set! Oh this is so romantic!"

"Oh, I never even thought of that. But no, it's not romantic. It's nothing. It's just a famous guy trying to have fun while he's in a small town." I pause, only just now realizing what that probably means. "And if that's the case, I mean, if he's trying to have *fun*, I'm not going to give it to him."

"Why not? I would!"

I shrug. "Because I don't know him. I don't want to have sex with someone I don't know."

"But he's Logan Jackson!"

"Yeah. He's nice to look at, I'll give you that. I do enjoy looking at his face. And hearing him talk. He's overall just very nice to be around when I'm not making a fool of myself, but that doesn't mean that I want to have sex with him. Or kiss him. Or have him touch me." I scrunch my neck into my shoulders as I get weird shivers just thinking about it. "Ew. No."

"You're weird," Claire says.

"Maybe *you're* weird."

The restaurant is busy all day, and even steady during the normally slow periods. People are probably in town for the weekend, hoping to catch some sightings of the movie and the stars. I'm glad to finally leave close to midnight, wondering why Tom had me in to open this morning because I'm dead tired. I'm strolling to my car when I hear someone call my name, followed by a bunch of high pitched screams. I turn around to see Logan Jackson being chased by about ten teenage girls, and the whole mob is coming towards me.

"Isla!" he shouts again.

"What's happening?" My first instinct to run away, but then they'll just be chasing me too, so what do I do? My car is just around the corner; maybe I can make it and lock the door behind me before they all catch up.

"Save me!" he shouts, which just makes the girls cry out and squeal.

"We won't hurt you, we promise!" one of the girls calls.

"Get in my car!" I shout to him without thinking.

I run as fast as I can and unlock my car with the fob when I'm super close. I pull open the driver side door and lock it as soon as I'm inside. Logan Jackson pulls on the passenger side door handle but nothing happens.

"Shit," I say. "I forgot about you."

"Geeze, thanks."

I undo the lock, but he's pulled on the handle again at the same time and it doesn't work. The girls are coming. They're drunk and in heels, so they're not as fast as we were, but if we can't get this door situation solved soon, they'll be on him like icing on a cake. Only more sexual and not delicious. I unlock it again but he's pulled the handle again.

"Stop pulling on the handle!" I yell.

"Sorry!"

I unlock it one more time and hear it release. "Okay now, hurry!"

He opens the door, throws himself inside and practically on top of me, and shuts the door behind him. I lock all the doors at once and breathe a sigh of relief at the sound of safety. But just as he sits up in his seat, all the girls swarm around my car and press up against the windows.

"Jesus," I whisper.

"Yeah," he says with a bit of a nervous laugh. "I thought it would be fun to check out one of the bars… it was not fun."

"Where did you go?" I ask.

"Roxy something or other?"

"Oh no, you don't want to go there. It's just filled with 17 year-olds with fake IDs. Always."

"So I've learned."

We stare at each other for a few seconds, and I get lost in his wonderful brown eyes that make me feel like I'm melting into my seat. But then a girl lifts her shirt and presses her lacy-bra-covered chest against my window.

"Oh that's inappropriate," I say casually, but with the tiniest bit of judgement in my tone. I put the key in the ignition and let out a deep breath.

"I'm too old for you!" he shouts through the glass.

"I've had sex before!" she shouts back.

"Congrats!" He gives her a thumbs up and looks back at me. "Can we just run them over?"

"Ha. I wish." I put the car into drive and honk the horn. "Move! I need to leave!"

The girls grumble but move out of the way.

"Oh, that was easier than I thought it would be," I say.

They all move onto the sidewalk but yell things like "I love you" and "I want to have your babies" as we drive away.

"So do you want me to take you back to the hotel?" I ask.

"No, they're probably all on their way over there now."

"True," I say. "I mean, we could go to my place if you want, but it's not like," I scratch my eyebrow, feeling embarrassed. "Uh, nice or anything." What am I doing? Why am I inviting Logan Jackson to my apartment? He's going to think I want to have sex with him!

"I'm sure your place is like, nice." He winks at me and I hope it's just an addition to his mocking of my unnecessary usage of the word like.

We pull into my parking spot at my apartment building and I look at him before I turn the car off.

"What?" he asks, narrowing his eyes at me.

I shrug. "I don't know. I just live in a shitty apartment and you probably have a mansion."

"So? Shitty apartments are the best. Plus my mansion is so big and filled with no one to share it with."

"That actually sounds sort of miserable," I say.

"It could be worse. Come on, show me your shitty apartment before those teenagers find us."

He walks beside me up the stairs of the two story building, and down the hall to my one bedroom apartment with the smallest kitchen known to man. He takes his shoes off as soon as we're inside and immediately heads for the couch in the living room.

"Do you want a tour?" I ask, feeling so awkward that I want to die.

"Do you want to give me a tour?"

"Um. Not really."

"Then I don't want a tour." He smiles and leans back into the couch, putting his hands behind his head.

"Look, I feel like I need to say something," I blurt out, standing across the room from him.

"Shoot."

"I don't want to have sex with you."

He starts to laugh, but stops himself when he sees that I'm not laughing. If my face is giving anything away, he can probably see that I'm downright terrified to have him in my apartment. In my living room. *On my couch.*

"Okay," he says slowly. "Well I wasn't expecting you to."

"You weren't?"

"No, I'm not a slime ball. At least I hope I'm not. That's so inappropriate."

"So you don't just have sex with your fans?"

"No. That doesn't sit right with me." He shakes his head and puts his hands on his knees. I realize that I've been pacing in front of the couch and his gaze follows me, a little grin on his face.

"Why are you looking at me like that?" I ask.

"I'm not looking at you like anything. I'm just… Hey, can you just… stand still for a second?" He's leaning forward on the couch with an arm out, like he wants to help me cross a stream or something. I finally stop and look at him with my arms crossed. "Do you want to sit down?" he asks.

"Um. No, I'm okay standing."

He smiles with half his mouth and tilts his head to the side for a second. It sends my stomach into my throat. "I understand the kind of … um, power? That I have over people? I don't want to sound full of myself or anything, but I'm really famous. I get that. And when people throw themselves at me, they're not thinking of what can come from that. Like, everybody thinks they want to sleep with Logan Jackson, but who they really want to sleep with is Cory Milligan."

I scrunch my face in confusion.

"From *Neighbourly*," he clarifies.

"Right. I knew that. I swear I knew that."

He smirks again but continues. "People want a character. Or if they say they don't, that they want me, what they really want is the idea of me. And they think they know what they're getting into, but I just… it's hard for me to explain. But having any kind of sexual relationship with a fan is hard core taking advantage of them. Like, if I were to try and sleep with a fan, she's not in the right mindset to make a proper choice about it. The famousness messes with it all. And also what if they don't want to have sex with me, but because I'm me, they feel like they can't say no? It's just not…" He pauses for a second. "I'm not about that."

"That's sweet."

"It shouldn't be. It should just be normal practice for anyone like me. I'm not… I'm not here to take advantage of you, Isla. And I'm sorry if I made you feel like that's what I was doing."

"You didn't. I swear you didn't. I just didn't know. Like, I just figured. Not that I thought I was worthy of um, sleeping with you or anything. I just thought… I don't want to say what I thought."

"Okay," he says quietly. "What do you mean by worthy?"

"What? Nothing. I don't know. Just. You're famous and I'm not. You know."

"No, I don't know," he says gently. "But please don't say that you're not worthy of something. Of anything."

"Okay," I say slowly.

"I'm serious."

"Okay," I say a bit more confidently.

"Good." He smiles. "So do you have to work tomorrow? When do you need to get to bed? I don't want to keep you up."

"Oh. Yeah, I do have to work tomorrow but not until dinner. Finally I don't have to work for twelve plus hours."

"So do you want to watch a movie or something? Give those girls some time to head home and forget about stalking me?"

"Yeah, sure. I can't guarantee I'll be able to stay up for the whole thing, though."

He stands up pretty quickly. "Ugh, I'm sorry, I'm imposing. Let me see if any of the security people from the movie are up; I'll get them to drive me back to the hotel."

"You're not imposing. But also, I can drive you."

"Are you sure?" he asks.

"Yes, I'm sure. I don't mind."

"Okay, that's awesome. Thanks." He stands up and I tilt my head at him. "What?" he asks.

"I don't have to drive you back right *now*."

"So what's with Carly Bowman?" I ask about twenty minutes into *Wonder Woman*.

"What do you mean?"

"Well the other day you came to meet all the people at the movie set and she stayed behind and didn't even look at anyone."

"Oh, yeah, that." He lets out a deep breath. "She's just private."

"That's it?"

"It's not my place to say."

"Okay, fair enough. Are you guys like…"

"Dating?" he finishes for me. "No. Not even close. But you don't have to go around telling everyone that I'm single. If people want to think we're dating, I won't deny it."

"Why not?" I ask.

He shrugs. "It's sort of exhausting being single and famous. It's all anyone cares about. They joke about me taking my shirt off for no reason, or ask when I'm going to settle down. Or if I've got my eye on anyone. Would I ever date a co-star? Would I date a fan? Am I dating the girl I was seen with in the tabloids last week? Sometimes it's just easier to say that I'm taken and I can't answer any of those questions."

"Oh. That's annoying."

"Yeah. It comes with the business though, so I can't really complain."

"Well I won't ask you to take your shirt off for no reason," I say.

The corner of his mouth curls into a half grin. "Good to know."

"They always make it seem like girls are way more sexualized than guys with that sort of stuff."

"Oh, they are, for sure. The questions some of my female co-stars have been asked at panels and in group interviews are ridiculous. But we get some of it too."

"Don't you think if you had a girlfriend though, they'd ask a lot of questions about the two of you? Or about her?"

"Oh for sure they would," he answers easily. "When I'm dating someone they always want to hear the cute stories about us, especially in the beginning. But it's better than talking about how I'm a 31-year-old single guy."

"It must be hard," I say quietly.

"What must be hard?"

"Meeting people. I already thought it was hard for *me* to meet people… Not that I want to meet people. But if I did want to, it would be hard. And everyone knows who you are, and if you were to meet a regular, non-famous person, they would just want to be with you because you're you, and not because of… you."

"Yup."

"Well what about, like, other people from movie sets? Like not necessarily other actors, but the set decorator, or the continuity person, or … what other jobs are there on movie sets?"

"I'm not looking to date anyone right now if that answers your question, or helps you out at all."

"Oh. Right. Sorry. I'm being an annoying talk show host, aren't I?"

"No, you're fine. This seems more genuine than a 60-year-old woman just trying to get cheers from the audience."

"Well what do you do during the weekends?" I ask.

"I usually just hang out in my hotel room and watch Netflix."

"All weekend?"

"Yeah. A lot of us live in Toronto so they go home on the weekend, but I live in LA now, so that doesn't work."

"Aren't you rich enough to have two homes?" I joke.

"Probably. And my parents live in Toronto, but I don't really want to spend the night with them more often than I have to."

"Oh you sound like such a good son."

"Hey, I love my parents, okay? But all weekend, every weekend for six weeks? No thanks. I'll visit them for a few days before I fly home. Hey, do you have any popcorn?"

"I do, actually."

He follows me to the kitchen and leans against the counter as I get out two bags of Redenbacher's and put one in the microwave. He crosses his arms and looks sideways at me as I take the lid off my butter dish and cut a chunk off.

"Extra butter?" I ask.

"Of course."

It's quiet for a bit and all we can hear is the popcorn popping. I want to keep talking to him because I'm finally starting to feel like a normal person around him, but I have no idea what to say at this point. I take the first bag of popcorn out and pour it into a big bowl and then start on the next bag. I can feel him staring at me but I try my best to ignore it and watch the bag get bigger as the kernels pop inside. He's silent as I take that bag out and pour it into the same bowl, and he's silent as I put the little glass of butter in the microwave next.

"Do you want to hang out tomorrow?" he asks.

His question catches me off guard and I drop the glass onto the counter. I manage to pick it up before more than a few drops of butter spill out, and inspect it to make sure it didn't break. It's fine, so I pour some of it on the popcorn and mix it all around in the bowl. I repeat the process until the butter is gone, and then I put the bowl back on the counter and stare at the buttery popcorn, pressing my hands into the sides of the bowl so I can't feel them shake.

"Isla?" he presses.

"Yes?" I ask, still looking at the popcorn.

"Did you hear me?"

I finally free my hands and turn towards him. "What?"

"Do you want to hang out tomorrow?"

"Oh right, that. Logan Jackson wants to hang out with me."

"You know you can just call me Logan."

"No I can't," I say with a bit of a choked laugh.

"Well I won't allow you to call me by my full name, that's just weird."

"Then I won't call you anything."

"So when you want to get my attention, you'll just say, what? You there?"

"That works," I say with a shrug. "Anyway, what would we do? Teenage girls will probably chase us everywhere."

"Not if you know of any places that teenage girls don't normally hang out."

CHAPTER 7

"Is the fake moustache really necessary?" Logan Jackson asks.

"There might be people, so if you don't want to get recognized, then yes, it's necessary." I'm standing just inside the door of his hotel room, trying to swallow the butterflies in my throat.

He sighs and sticks the moustache on his face, going into the washroom to look at himself in the mirror. "This is ridiculous," he says. I lean around the doorway a little but then he turns around and comes out. "I look like a 70's porn star. Why can't I just wear sunglasses and a hat?"

"You're also going to be wearing sunglasses and a hat," I say.

"You should have gotten me a full beard."

"They didn't have beards, only moustaches. But it's a pretty good moustache, don't you think?"

He takes out his phone and looks at himself in the camera. "It looks like a fake moustache."

"Fine, whatever, you don't have to wear it. But just remember that I sacrificed fifteen minutes of my morning to get this for you."

"Oh don't even; I know at least half of that was spent in the drive thru line at Tim Hortons." He smiles and shoves me in the shoulder so I shove him back.

"Well I also bought you that large drink and I make way less money than you. So remember that."

"Okay," he chuckles.

He puts on a Blue Jays hat so that the beak shadows his face, and presses the moustache onto his upper lip to make sure it's sticking well enough. I smile at him and we grab our drinks and head into the hall. Someone gives us a weird glance on the way to the elevator and we both nod at him while sipping from our cold, caffeinated drinks. It's quiet in the elevator except for the sound of me twirling the ice around in my cup. I guess I'm still nervous around him. I'll probably always be nervous around him.

I park the car in the lot across from the fancy condo down by the water and take the last few sips of my iced coffee. Logan Jackson's still got almost half of his ice cap so he grabs it from the cup holder and takes it with him.

"So are we looking at apartments today?" he asks as I lock the car and walk around it to his side.

"You're funny. Come on. This way."

He puts on his sunglasses and follows me out of the parking lot and across the road, through another parking lot and behind a senior's home.

"What are you trying to tell me, Isla?" he asks.

"Just come on."

The parking lot attaches to a paved trail that takes us under an archway of trees with purple flowers blooming in them. There are yellow flowers everywhere on the ground, but don't ask me what kind because I know nothing about flowers. They're yellow. Our footsteps are soft on the asphalt beneath us, and I can hear bumblebees close by as they work hard at pollinating.

"This is nice," he says quietly.

"Yeah. It gets nicer. Once we pass over the highway."

The inside of the overpass is covered in graffiti, but it's not ugly, spur of the moment or hateful graffiti. It's artwork. Thought out, colourful, obviously full of talent. I think it gets painted white every few months, but people just go over it again. I always like to look at them, and it's always interesting getting to see new ones after they've been given a new blank canvas. I wonder if that's how the graffiti artists view it, or if it makes them angry that their artwork and silent protests of love and equality have been covered. We watch the cars below us drive by for a few minutes before continuing along the overpass and into the wooded area on the other side. Logan Jackson tosses his empty Tim's cup into a trash can and we walk through the forest in silence. I hear a gasp next to me as we come into the opening leading to the bridge that crosses a small river.

"Yeah, this is really nice," he says.

I smile up at him and keep walking.

"The water's like glass," he half-whispers, stopping to look at the view. The sky is full and blue with perfectly white puffy clouds, and the water is so calm it looks like you could skate on it. He rests his elbows on the railing of the bridge and leans forward, looking into the distance. "So far I haven't seen any people, and I'm still wearing this ridiculous moustache."

I laugh out loud and throw my head back, and he laughs too, peeling the costume piece off his face.

"I forgot I was wearing it for a while," he says, still laughing.

"I forgot it wasn't real," I giggle.

He laughs harder and I start to wheeze like I do when I have a good laughing fit, and it makes him laugh more, which in turn makes me laugh more, and of course wheeze more, which makes him laugh more, and it continues until I can't breathe and my stomach hurts.

"It's not even that funny, but it's hilarious for some reason," he says through deep breaths of laughter.

I try to agree with him but all I can do is nod my head and curl in on myself as I continue to wheeze. I grab onto the railing for support but end up on my knees, my right arm above my head and clutching onto the wood. He sits down next to me, laughing harder every time I wheeze.

"Stop laughing," I manage to say.

"Stop wheezing!" he counters.

"I c- I… I can't!"

We both laugh for another few minutes but finally calm down and I have to wipe tears from my eyes and take a minute to catch my breath.

"I haven't laughed like that in a really long time," he says, smiling at me.

"Neither have I. I haven't… I don't think I've had a truly, genuinely happy moment like that since my boyfriend broke up with me."

"When did that happen?" he asks, slowly standing up.

"Um, eight months ago?"

"That's a long time to not be happy." He holds a hand out to me and I grab it, letting him help me to my feet.

"Yeah," I say slowly. "I mean, I haven't been unhappy the whole time. But I haven't… like I haven't been *that* happy, completely happy and unaware and… just not thinking about it in some way. If that makes sense."

"Yeah. Makes sense."

"I mean I guess it's been even longer than that, really. I wasn't happy for a while before we broke up."

"That makes sense too, I guess."

"Yeah." I kick a stone on the bridge in front of me and watch it fall into the water.

"Were you guys together for a long time?"

"Almost nine years."

"Ouch."

"Yeah. Sort of feels like I wasted my time. And like, it doesn't make *me* feel great, you know? Like I'm not good enough to love long term."

"That's not true."

"Okay," I say sarcastically. "You don't even know me."

"I know you a little bit. Enough to know that you deserve for someone to love you with their whole heart. You deserve to be loved, everyone does. Did he like," he pauses and says the next part really quietly. "Did he cheat on you?"

"No," I say, shaking my head. "He said he fell out of love with me. Which isn't his fault, I guess. But I don't really believe him."

"You don't believe that he fell out of love with you?"

"I don't believe that he was ever in love with me to begin with." I realize as I say it that I've never actually thought that to myself before. It was never something that I cried about or wished wasn't true. But it just slips out and whether or not I thought it was true before, I must think it is now.

"What makes you say that?"

I shrug and look away for a minute. "I don't know. I just don't understand how someone can just *stop* loving a person. I was in love with Tyler. I was so hopelessly in love with him, even when I thought he didn't love me, I still… I think I still love him, I just don't talk to him so there's nothing to really confirm my feelings, but every time I looked at him it made me happy. Hugging him after a bad day was like coming up for air. Sometimes I still thought about our first kiss and it always gave me butterflies. He didn't have to do anything to make me smile. Just being next to him, or lying next to him in bed, I always sort of felt safe, you know? And it always felt *so good,* like in a way I don't even think I can really describe. And I could never imagine not feeling that way about him. I think the only way you can stop yourself from being in love with someone is if you really try. I don't think feelings like that just go away on their own."

"Maybe for you they don't. Maybe he did love you. Maybe he was so in love with you and when he realized that all those things you mentioned weren't happening to him anymore, he tried. Maybe he tried so hard to make them come back. Maybe it ate him up inside that he wasn't in love with you anymore. Maybe it killed him a little bit. But what killed him more was dragging you along in a relationship that wasn't giving you what you deserve."

"Maybe." But what I don't say to him is that there's no way that's true. There's no way Tyler tried to fall back in love with me. Because I tried. I tried to get him to fall back in love with me when it felt like he wasn't anymore. I tried to get him to go on dates with me, I walked around the apartment naked, I bought him presents, I made him breakfast, and nothing I did made him want me. If I tried to bring up the fact that he was distant, or how long it had been since we'd had sex, he would get defensive, and we would fight. It didn't eat him up inside that he didn't feel the same way about me anymore. It didn't eat him up inside that it was clearly breaking me.

Logan puts his hand on mine and I look down at them, at his hand covering mine, both of them resting on the bridge that looks out over the water that's as calm as I wish my heart was. Logan Jackson is a really attractive guy, and while I certainly don't want to sleep with him, or even kiss him, I can't say that I don't enjoy him sort of holding my hand. It's warm and soft, and makes me feel safe for some reason. Like maybe he's my friend. I finally look away from our hands and up at him.

"Your face is red where the fake moustache was," I say quietly.

He smiles and chuckles a little. "Well we better not run into anyone now, because that might be even more embarrassing than wearing the damn thing."

"It looks like you just waxed," I laugh.

"Okay, that's enough out of you."

We continue walking, across the bridge and back into the forest on the other side, and we pass a couple walking their dog, who smile and nod at us. They either don't recognize Logan Jackson or don't want to bother him. I have a feeling they don't even know who Logan Jackson is, so even if he didn't have sunglasses and a hat on, or a fake moustache for that matter, they wouldn't have known who they were passing.

"Is it okay if I ask you a question about your ex?" he asks.

"Um, sure," I say slowly.

"You said that you think you're still in love with him, but you don't talk to him so you can't be sure…"

"Yeah…?"

"Do you want to test that theory?"

"What do you mean, like meet him somewhere?"

"Yeah. Or even just see him from a distance. Like does he work somewhere that's not creepy if we were to go there? Or something?"

"No, I don't think so. I mean he works at Sport Chek; he's a manager there, so it wouldn't be creepy if we went, but I don't think I want to do that."

"Have you been there since you guys broke up?"

"No."

"Are you in need of sports equipment? Is this depriving you of basic shopping rights?"

I laugh a little. "No, I'm okay, I promise."

"Okay."

I pull up in front of the hotel an hour before my shift at the restaurant starts, and Logan Jackson takes his sunglasses off. His eyes have so much emotion in them; somehow when I look into them, it's like I can feel what he's thinking. Except I have no idea what he's thinking. But it makes me feel like I do.

"Thanks for today," he says.

"Of course."

"I mean it. It was the most normal day I've had in a long time, and I didn't know that I needed it, but I did."

"I think I really needed it, too."

"Good. Well, have a good shift at work."

"Thanks."

He grins and winks at me before getting out of the car. He shuts the door and knocks on the roof before walking away. I watch him walk into the hotel and let out a deep breath before I can collect myself enough to drive home.

CHAPTER 8

"Your new boyfriend is here," Lance says, halfway through the dinner rush.

"What? I don't have a boyfriend."

"That Logan Jackson guy is here." He points behind him with his thumb and I feel my whole face heat up.

"Well I can't help him," I say in a panic.

"Why not? Weren't you squealing to Claire earlier about how you spent the whole day with him?"

"Okay, I wasn't *squealing*... Claire was. And I still- I'm still- I don't know!" I throw my hands up in the air and make my way to the front of the restaurant to greet him.

"Hey Isla," he says with a huge smile.

"Hey… Logan," I say with great difficulty.

He laughs. "Wow, you're going to need to work on that."

"It's still weird. I can't. Can we just make up a nickname for you?"

"No," he says, shaking his head. "I like my name, and it would bring me great pleasure to hear you say it. Without cringing. Or very noticeably trying."

"Okay. Hi Logan Jackson, how are you this evening? Will you be dining alone or with a guest?"

"I like my first name, not accompanied by my last name."

"Okay. Are you eating by yourself?"

He smiles and shakes his head a little. "Yeah. I've been having a craving for Hawaiian pizza for a few days now."

"Well you're in luck, because we have excellent Hawaiian pizza. But we only have seats at the bar left right now, is that okay? You came in at a busy time."

"Actually I think I'm going to take it to go if that's okay."

"Oh. Sure. Of course. I'll put your order in right away. Do you want anything else with it?"

"No, just the pizza is fine."

"How did you get here?" I ask as I type in his order.

"I had a security guard drive me. He wanted to come in with me but I told him that I'm a big boy and I've been here before by myself, so I can do it again."

"You're ridiculous."

He just shrugs and smiles, and waits at the front while I help my other tables. I bring him the pizza, he pays me, and tips me a regular amount this time, which wasn't even needed considering I didn't do anything, and he leaves.

It's 11am and someone is texting me. They won't stop. I groan and roll over in bed, grabbing for my phone on my night stand.

"I'm so tired," I say to myself as I unlock it and look at the screen.

Would you look at that, they're all from Logan Jackson.

I've discovered that the pizza restaurant you work at is closed on Sundays until the summer his first text says, which was sent at 10:46 AM.

I think you should take me on another adventure That one was sent right away, still at 10:46.

Are you sleeping? It's almost noon 10:53AM.

Okay, I guess you're sleeping, or possibly I've scared you away. If I've scared you away, I would love it if you could tell me what I did so I don't do this to potential future friends. If you're sleeping WAKE UP

Hi I reply.

Hey

I'm really tired and don't feel very adventurous I type to him.

You wanna hang out and watch movies?

And that, my friends, is how I proceeded to lie in a bed with Logan Jackson for almost ten hours.

I show up at his hotel room door with a reusable bag full of elementary school day snacks. The usual: Ah Caramels, Jos Louis, Passion Flakies, and vanilla Half Moons, which have seemed to replace the Twinkie all together, at least at the store I went to. I also have a 2 litre bottle of Nestea and a 12 pack of orange Bubly. I wanted to get actual orange pop like Fanta or Crush, but I figured it might be nice to have something in our day that wasn't overly sweet.

"Wow, that's a lot of sugar," he says as he lets me in. His hair is finally hat free and product free, and it looks great just laying on his head on its own. It looks soft.

"You were very vague," I reply.

"I said bring treats."

"Yes. But I don't know what that means! Was I supposed to get a pack of Timbits? Or maybe chips and dip? Chocolate bars? Doritos? Or all the classic prepackaged desserts that we loved so much and devoured at recess in grade five?"

"I'm sorry, you're right, you're absolutely right. Please, come in with your sugar and fizz and fake, sweetened tea, flavoured with lemon."

"Thank you," I say with a smile.

"No, thank *you*."

We dump everything out on the bed and start opening cardboard boxes so we can continue to dump everything out on the bed. I get some glasses from the little kitchenette and see that there's already ice in the freezer. Perfect.

"Do you want to watch movies or binge a show?" he asks me.

"Movies, definitely."

"What are you in the mood for?"

We end up scrolling through Netflix on his Fire TV Stick for a little bit but settle on *Mean Girls* to start with. It ends up being a high school comedy day, because we follow it up with *She's the Man*, at which point I go from sitting cross legged on the bed to lying back against propped up pillows. And then we watch *Easy A*.

"Man, these Half Moons are way better than Twinkies," I say, eating my third one. "I was a little sad when I couldn't find any Twinkies in the grocery store, because I remember loving them as a kid, but these have a way better cake to icing ratio. I can't believe I used to think Twinkies were better."

"Plus these have way softer cake. Also please don't judge me but I definitely called them Lune Moons growing up. I actually called them Lune Moons until this very second, when I heard you call them Half Moons, and I realized that Lune is just... moon... In French."

I laugh and almost spit my mouthful of icing and cake all over the comforter but I manage to contain myself. "To be fair, the packaging is pretty misleading."

"Right!?" he half squeals. "It says Lune before Moon! Since when is the French *first* on any packaging outside of Quebec?"

"It's okay, Logan, I totally get your side," I say with a giggle.

"Hey, you called me Logan."

"Would you look at that, I did. I didn't even have to try."

"Does this mean that we're real friends now and not just pretend, fangirly, Instagram besties?"

"I guess so," I say, hoping my face isn't as red as it feels.

"Okay, what next?" he asks, running his fingers through his hair, messing it up a little. "I feel like we need to keep it going with this theme. *The Duff? Pitch Perfect?*"

"Yes."

"Ha. Okay."

I've been cold for the last little bit and really want to get under the covers but even just thinking about it is making my heart pound. I know Logan said (oh look I called him Logan again and it came out totally normally), that he doesn't sleep with fans but since we're friends now, I'm afraid that I'm going to give him the wrong impression. I don't want him to think that I'm trying to get closer to him, or for him to think that I just want to get closer to him. Really I'm just cold and want to get under the blankets. But I can't do it. So I cross my arms and try to deal with it.

"Are you cold?" Logan asks halfway through *The Duff*.

"Yeah," I say quietly.

"Why don't you get under the covers, silly? That's what they're there for."

"Right. Yeah. I knew that."

"Isla, you don't have to be afraid of me. I'll stay on my side, I promise."

I smile at him. "Okay."

Both of us getting comfy under the covers proves to be innocent and we continue to laugh at teen movies as we finish *The Duff* and add *Pitch Perfect* to the marathon. Aaaand *Pitch Perfect 2*. Of course. Logan wants to keep going with *Pitch Perfect 3,* but I'm starting to feel fried.

"I can't, I think I need to head home. And eat some fruit or something. Maybe a vegetable."

He chuckles and gets out of bed. "That's probably a good plan. I need to be up early tomorrow anyway."

"I need to be up early-ish. But this was fun. You have excellent ideas."

"That's right I do," he says with a grin.

CHAPTER 9

I check my phone when I get up in the morning and see that I've got an Instagram notification. Someone whose handle is **EustaceScrubb** with a profile picture of a dragon has followed me. I click on their profile to see if I know them, but it's private. I shrug it off and get to work.

"Are you the girl that's dating that movie star?" someone from my first table of the day asks.

"Um, no? I'm not dating anyone," I reply.

"Oh my mistake."

But then someone at dinner points to me and starts whispering to the girl next to her. I scrunch my eyebrows at them and make my way over to their table.

"Are you ready to order?" I ask.

"My friend wants to ask you a question," the first girl says.

"No I don't, shut up!" her friend squeals.

"Um, okay. So are you ready to order?" I try again.

"Yeah," the first girl says with a sigh.

I check my phone after work and my Instagram has blown up. Logan added the picture of us to his Instagram and he tagged me in it. So I have thousands of new followers which is just absurd to me, and a bunch more notifications of people liking a bunch of my pictures. I go over to Logan's post to see what he said in the description of our picture.

Making friends.

That's all it says. That's innocent enough. Kind of sweet. Aww. Now my heart is doing this weird thing where it feels like it's crying and also like it's going to explode from cuteness overload. I don't know why I think it's so cute, but there's just something about an incredibly attractive famous man telling the world that he's made a new friend. I wonder if he waited to post it because he wasn't sure if we actually were friends or not, and he didn't want to seem too intense. I don't even know.

I'm so overwhelmed that I just stand there on the sidewalk looking through Instagram. I skim through some of the comments on his picture first, most of them are just heart-eye emojis, or people saying **aww** or **that's super cute** or **I wish we could be friends,** things like that. I go over to my notifications and scroll through some of the comments, which go back pretty far on some of my older pictures, but I don't really read them because there are so many.

"Isla!" I hear Logan call.

I look up at him, a little startled. "Hey, what's up?"

"We're just going back to the hotel for dinner, you wanna come?"

"You're inviting me to the movie set dinner catered by Chives at the little hotel up the road? Wow, that's really special, Logan, I don't know what to say."

"Okay I hate you a little bit right now."

"Hmm, not as much as I hate you."

His eyes widen in surprise. "What? Why?"

"You tagged me on Instagram! Now I have like ten thousand followers!"

"That's it? Only ten thousand?"

I hit him in the shoulder and pull out my phone. "That's a lot. And it won't stop notifying me! People are liking pictures that I posted like three years ago! These people are stalkers, Logan!"

"Oh relax, they're not stalkers. They're just interested in someone new."

"Well it's weird." And then it hits me. I gasp a little and Logan seems concerned.

"What?" he asks.

"People at work today! Everyone was asking if I was the girl who was dating you! I thought that maybe they were just at the set that day and heard you get my phone number, but it's making sense now."

"Well if they read the post, they would see that it clearly says 'making friends'. I didn't say 'making girlfriends'."

"I know but people jump to conclusions."

"Yeah. So, dinner?"

"What?"

"Do you want to eat with me?" he asks.

"Sure." I shrug, and we both walk over to my car.

"Hey Logan, you brought your girlfriend!" someone I don't recognize says.

"I'm not his girlfriend," I say quickly.

"Thanks," he says to me. I can't tell if he's being sarcastic or not.

He shrugs and makes his way to the spread of food and starts loading a plate up. I follow him and put some grilled chicken, pasta salad, and broccoli on my plate. We sit down at a table with Carly Bowman and the director, but I'm terrible and already forget her name. They both smile and nod at me, but don't say anything right away.

"You brought the pizza a few weeks ago, didn't you?" the director asks. Chloe?

"Yeah," I say just before putting a piece of incredibly tender and juicy chicken in my mouth.

"And now you're friends with Logan, that's super cute," Carly Bowman adds, with a weird, mocking tone.

"I'm so sorry I don't remember your name," the director says.

"Isla," I answer.

"Oh that's a great name," she says.

"Thanks, I got it for my birthday."

Logan and Maybe Chloe both laugh pretty loudly, and Carly Bowman looks at me like I'm an idiot. I feel myself blush and just sort of shrug. At least some people think I'm funny.

"Cute," Carly Bowman says in the same mocking tone as before.

"Carly, don't be a bitch," the director says.

Logan smirks and looks at me quickly, but I have no idea what to say so I just keep eating.

"The chicken's really good," I finally say after some awkward silence.

"Yeah, all the food from this place has been great," Logan says. "But Zoey misses the pizza." Zoey! I was close.

"I should really be smart like Logan and go get some for myself before we leave," she says.

"You should," I say with a smile.

It's quiet again and I feel super awkward. If it wasn't for Carly Bowman and her weird bitchiness, this meal probably would have been quite pleasant.

"Well I'm done," Logan finally says. "Isla, do you want to walk me to my room?"

"Sure," I say, grabbing my plate.

"Don't forget a condom," Carly Bowman says.

"Shut up, Carly," Logan shoots back.

My face gets hot and I follow Logan without saying anything.

"Sorry about her," he says in the elevator. "She's not very nice."

"No kidding."

My phone dings as we get to Logan's room and I pull it out of my back pocket to check it. I can see that I have a ton more Instagram notifications, but the one that just went off makes my heart jump into my throat and I think I even make a weird sigh.

"Something wrong?" Logan asks.

"It's a text from Tyler."

"Oh. Does he text you often?"

"No," I say, shaking my head. "I haven't talked to him since I moved out."

"Oh. Well are you going to read it?"

I take a deep breath and nod, but I still have my phone in my hand and I haven't unlocked the screen. I'm just staring at it like it's broken.

"Do you want *me* to read it?" he asks.

"No, I can do it, just give me a minute."

"Okay." He puts his hands up and then backs up towards the bed.

I let out another deep breath and close my eyes for a second. Then I unlock my phone and bring up his text.

I found that blanket your grandma knitted. Do you want me to bring it over? it says.

"What's it say?" Logan asks.

"He found a blanket of mine we thought we lost."

"Oh that's nice!"

"Yeah. He wants to bring it to my apartment. I don't know if I want him to come to my apartment. I don't… I feel… I feel like I can't."

"You feel like you can't," he repeats back, I think just trying to come up with a response. "Well that's understandable."

"I'm not having – I mean I'm having a hard time with this. I can't even think properly right now."

"It's okay, I get it. Do you want to meet him somewhere? I can come with you."

"Yeah, okay, that sounds alright. Not tonight, though. Oh my goodness, why am I freaking out about this so much? It's just Tyler… Like we were together forever, I don't know what's wrong with me."

"Well, you were together forever. It's hard."

"Yeah."

"Do you… Do you need a hug?" he asks.

I look up at him and feel my eyes start to burn. I open my eyes really wide to try and stop the tears from coming, but it doesn't work. Luckily I'm not crying-crying, like I'm not sobbing or sniffling or anything, but I'm still embarrassed. Why am I so embarrassing, and why is it always in front of the attractive celebrity? I cover my face with my hands so he doesn't see my tears start to fall, and I'm about to turn around and leave because Logan surely doesn't want to deal with this, but before I get a chance to even pick up my feet, Logan has his arms wrapped around me. My hands are still covering my face, so I'm just sort of tucked into his chest as he holds me, very tightly, I might add. But it's nice. He's warm and strong and smells *amazing* and his hug calms me quite a bit. I let go of my face and wrap my arms around his back, returning the hug.

"I'm sorry," I say into his shirt.

"What are you sorry for?"

"For being such a mess. You're just trying to be my friend and I keep crying like someone who can never hold it together."

He rubs my back a few times with both of his hands but doesn't let go. "You can hold it together most of the time. You've only cried twice in all the times that we've hung out. Also, letting yourself cry is a part of holding it together. You need to let it all out. If something is bothering you, let it bother you. You're allowed to cry."

I push away from him and look into his eyes. "But I'm crying about a boy. That's stupid."

"It's not stupid. He was your family for eight years. And then just like that, he wasn't. That's hard. And it's hard to talk to them knowing they're not your family anymore. That nothing's going to be the same with them. I get it. You don't have to be embarrassed. In fact, I encourage crying. I always feel better after I've had a good cry. Plus I wouldn't even call this a good cry. You're having more of a sample cry."

"A sample cry?" I ask, smiling a little.

"Or a mini cry. I don't know. You just got teary. It's not a big deal."

"Okay."

"So can we make Tyler jealous?" he asks, pretty excited. "Can I put my arm around you when we go get your blanket?"

"Oh, please don't. That's weird. I don't want to hurt him."

"Why? Didn't he hurt you?"

"Yeah, but because he didn't love me anymore…"

Logan nods his head slowly. "Right, okay. And you still love him."

"Well I don't--I don't know," I stammer. "I don't know if I'm still in love with him. But even if I'm not, I still don't want to hurt him."

"You're such a good ex-girlfriend."

"Well I like to think I'm just a good person."

"Right, of course." We're both quiet for a minute and I'm about to say something, but then he starts talking again. "Okay, well you think about the making-him-jealous thing and get back to me." His grin is so ridiculous it makes me smile.

"I'll think about it," I laugh.

His smile widens. "Great."

CHAPTER 10

"Who is that with him?" I wonder aloud as we pull into the Sport Chek parking lot.

"I don't know, I don't know anyone here," Logan replies.

"Is he dating someone? Is that his girlfriend?" I park in an empty area of the lot and stare at them through Logan's window. "Why did he bring a girl with him to give me my blanket?"

"Well in all fairness, you brought a guy with you to get your blanket, so…"

"Yeah, but … I'm the one hurting from this situation. He broke up with *me*, he shouldn't feel the need to bring a girl with him. Is he trying to make me jealous?"

"I don't know, I don't know either of them."

"Well what do I do?"

"I think we should get out of the car and go get your blanket."

Logan's about to open the door but I stick my arm across his chest to stop him. "Wait," I say quickly. "She's wearing a Sport Chek shirt!"

"Perfect, so they just work together. There's no crisis."

"But what if he's dating someone he works with?"

"Didn't you say he's a manager? He can't date an associate."

"What if she's a manager too? There's more than one, you know."

"I think they think we're super weird. We're just sitting here staring at them."

"Well we're also talking," I say. "Maybe--" but then I almost scream because *she touches his arm and he leans closer to her*. "Oh my god that bitch!" I screech.

"Okay, I think we need to go. We can get your blanket another day."

"No. No way. Let's go get the damn thing. I'm going to introduce you to them as my boyfriend." I hardly have enough time to see the enormous smile spread across Logan's face before I swing my door open, slam it shut and start marching around to the other side of the car.

"This is going to be fun," Logan says, catching up to me.

"Shut up, I don't want them to hear."

"Oh right, yes."

"Hold my hand," I whisper.

He takes my hand in his, but then he swings his arm up and over my head so that I'm tucked under his armpit, and my arm is across my chest, my hand up at my shoulder, still holding on to his hand. I feel strangely comfortable with it, and I smile up at him briefly.

"Hey," Tyler says as we approach.

"Hi," I say.

The four of us sort of stare at each other for longer than a few seconds, and then Tyler finally takes in a breath and says, "So your blanket is in my car."

"Okay," I say with a nod, keeping myself tucked into Logan.

"Are you Logan Jackson?" the girl asks.

"Yeah," he says humbly, as if someone has caught him doing something embarrassing.

"Oh my god, that's insane!"

"Yeah, it is, isn't it?" he replies. "But you're not allowed to kiss me or anything, or my girlfriend would get jealous."

"But she doesn't mind you putting your arm around Tyler's ex?"

"Okay, first of all, *Tyler's ex* has a name."

"Isla," I add, smiling.

"And my girlfriend doesn't mind because Isla is my girlfriend."

"Alright, well I'll just get your blanket," Tyler says quickly, practically running to his car.

"Can I take a selfie with you?" the girl asks.

"No, but you can take a picture *of* me, if you like."

"It's fine, I don't mind," I say, trying to step away.

"Okay, but Isla has to be in the picture with us. And you have to be beside Isla, so you can't crop her out."

"Logan," I say, "It's fine."

He presses his mouth to the side of my head and whispers into my hair. "Do you want to make Tyler jealous, or not?"

I sigh and nod.

"Great, okay, so you can get in beside Isla here, and take a picture with us," Logan says, still grinning from ear to ear.

She doesn't seem to mind at all, and skips over to us, tucks herself right up next to me, holds her phone out and snaps three pictures. "Thanks so much!" she squeals. And then she runs on over to Tyler, who's walking towards us with my grandma's blanket. I stare at them as she jumps up and down and grabs onto Tyler's arms. I watch as he smiles at her, and then jumps up and down with her, although she is much more enthusiastic than he is. She finally calms down and they meet up with us again.

"Here you go," he says, handing the blanket over.

Logan takes it from him. "Thanks, man."

"Of course." Tyler sort of fidgets a little bit and looks at me while also sort of looking at the ground. "Um, I'm glad to see you happy, Isla."

"Oh." I don't know what else to say. I guess I could say thanks? But that doesn't seem right. He just nods at me, and then turns around to head back to his car. His probably-girlfriend goes with him, but they don't touch on the way. Logan and I both watch as they get into the car, and we continue to watch as they drive away.

"Are you okay?" Logan asks, and it's only then that I realize I'm still cuddled into him. I don't really want to stop. I haven't been close like this with anyone since before Tyler and I broke up and it didn't occur to me until this very moment how much I've been craving physical touch. Like not sex or anything, just, closeness.

"I'm not sure," I say in almost a whisper. Because I really don't know how I feel and it bugs me a little bit that I know I feel *something* but can't really pinpoint what exactly that feeling is.

"You want to get ice cream and watch *Pitch Perfect 3*?"

"Yes."

We're in Logan's hotel room and halfway through the movie when I get a text from Claire.

UM. EXPLAIN, WOMAN it says, along with a link.

I click the link and it opens up Instagram, bringing me to the picture of me, Logan, and Tyler's maybe girlfriend. It's actually a good picture of the three of us, and Logan and I look oddly comfortable together. The caption is in all caps and says,

I MET LOGAN JACKSON AND HIS GIRLFRIEND TODAY! I GAVE THEM A BLANKET!

I half snort at that, and show Logan.

"Uh oh," he says. "Now people are really going to think we're dating."

My phone chimes again and Claire has sent me another link. It's to some celebrity news site, like a tabloid but on the internet, and there are pictures of me and Logan in the Sport Chek parking lot, arms wrapped around each other. It looks like the pictures were taken from across the street or something, and the headline reads "Logan Jackson Dating Local Girl?" I don't read the article, and head back to my conversation with Claire.

This is all so weird. We're not actually dating, I swear. We were just trying to make Tyler jealous I text to her.

Since I'm already on my phone, I decide to check some of my Instagram notifications that are getting out of control at this point.

I check the picture I posted of me and Logan first, and it has similar comments to the ones on Logan's picture. I go back into my notifications and scroll through the comments there, since they are on a lot of different pictures that I've posted. There are a few comments that make me smile.

you're gorgeous.

she's so naturally pretty i'm jealous

But then my heart hammers when I see one that just says **bitch.** It catches me off guard, but I keep scrolling anyway for some reason, and see a few more comments that make me feel a little like I might puke.

she's not even pretty. I know this person is just saying that to make me feel bad and that it isn't necessarily true, but it still stings. Just because I don't really wear makeup and a lot of other grown women do, especially ones who are popular on social media. And now I'm popular on social media. I know that comment isn't true, but right now I feel like it is.

Why would Logan want to date her?

Are they even dating? Maybe she's crazy and making it all up.

this girl is just looking for attention. she's just a crazy fan.

Wow. Crazy.

I feel sorry for Logan Jackson, having to deal with her.

I find it a little weird that these comments are talking to me in the third person, as if I won't be reading them. I swallow hard and try not to let them bother me. They're just trolls.

"Hey, do you want to come to set tomorrow?" Logan asks, catching me off guard yet again. "It's our last day of shooting."

"Oh. Yeah, that sounds fun."

"Cool. Can I tell everyone you're my girlfriend?"

My heart leaps into my throat and I almost choke on it. "Why would you do that?" I ask slowly, thinking about the comments I just read on my pictures.

"Because of what I said before," he replies quietly, as if he's embarrassed. He takes in a deep breath and puts his head down, but looks back up at me with just his eyes. "It's easier for me to have a girlfriend in this industry. It wouldn't be real." He swallows and tilts his face back up again. "We would just tell people it was."

"I don't understand," I say.

"What don't you understand? We just did it in the mall parking lot."

"Right, no, I mean, like…" Logan laughs, but I finally find the words I want to say and don't let him cut in. "I don't want to date anyone. The thought of dating someone new scares the fuck out of me. Like I can't even think about it. I was with Tyler for so long, I don't remember how to… Like, how to … be with someone."

"But it's just pretend," he assures me. "We won't actually be dating."

"Right," I whisper, my mind working, trying to decide if this could be a good idea.

"People already think we're dating. All we have to do is let them. I'm honestly so sick of being single in this industry, Isla. And I don't mind like, actually being single. But if everyone else thinks I'm taken, I'm more of a person and less of an object to them."

"That makes sense," I agree, also thinking that maybe if Logan confirms our "relationship" I will get less hate? People are hating on me now because they think I'm just trying to get attention, right? But if Logan tells everyone that we're dating, they won't be able to call me crazy anymore.

"So, that's a yes?" he asks, his eyes piercing into mine.

"No," I reply with a smile. "It's still a no. A hundred times no." I can hear the playfulness in my voice as I say it, and he probably can too.

"Why not?" he whines. He steps in closer to me and I don't step back.

"I don't want a boyfriend," I say. But all I can think about is everyone on Instagram calling me crazy.

"That's exactly why you should say yes!" Oh he's definitely excited now. "No one will even try to date you if they think you're dating me. It's perfect for both of us!"

I bite my bottom lip and look up at him, into his eyes, at his mischievous smirk that's familiar from interviews and blooper reels I've seen. The smirk that's even familiar from times since I've known him as Logan Jackson my friend, and not just Logan Jackson the celebrity. I let out a deep breath and his smile changes to something more hopeful, full of something deeper.

"Fine," I say.

He shakes his head. "No, it's okay, I need more than a fine. I mean, I want you to do this with me, but I need you to *actually* want to." He shrugs and starts to turn away.

"I don't know what I want," I reply quickly, making him face me again. "But what's the worst that can happen?"

His mischievous grin is back. "Surely nothing that bad. This is an excellent idea. I have excellent ideas."

He holds out his hand to shake, and I grab hold of it, not entirely sure how I just agreed to pretend to date one of the most well-known sitcom stars of the decade. Of course this isn't a good idea.

CHAPTER 11

I'm so nervous. What if Logan kisses me when I meet him on set? I'm supposed to be his pretend girlfriend, so he might. I should have asked him about this first. Why didn't we make up some ground rules? Everyone knows that when you pretend to date someone, you make up rules. I decide to text him, hoping he'll see it before he sees me.

You're not going to kiss me in front of everyone are you? I type. I read it over a few times before I hit send. I don't want it to sound like I'm not his girlfriend, in case someone else sees it for whatever reason. But I also don't want him to kiss me, you know? I think it sounds okay and I take a deep breath, hoping he reads it and understands.

He replies almost right away and my heart leaps into my throat for a second. Not if you don't want me to.

Oh thank goodness. A huge weight lifts off my chest and only then do I realize just how anxious I was before. But now I feel good. Excited, even. Okay. I can do this. I can pretend to be Logan Jackson's girlfriend. They're shooting at the docks again today, and I can already see the crowd huddled up against the barrier. Haven't people gotten over it by now? I can't believe how many people are still there trying to watch. My nerves start to come back as I get closer, knowing I'm going to have to pass through them, but tell myself that everything's fine. It will be fine.

"Isla!" Logan comes running up to the barrier with an arm in the air and I suddenly want to hide.

"It's his girlfriend!" someone shouts.

"It's the girl from the other day! Who gave him her phone number!"

"Her name is Isla!" another person yells, sounding incredibly excited.

The security guard steps into the crowd and tells everyone to move back. They all do, and they also part, leaving me a path to walk through. This is weird. Logan meets me at the gate and the security guard moves it so I can squeeze through. And then Logan puts his arm around me and presses his mouth into the side of my head, whispering into my hair.

"Thanks for coming," he says.

"Of course," I say, trying to fight back the nervous butterflies that have just been completely let loose inside my body. And I still don't want him to kiss me, but I don't particularly mind that he's whispering into my hair. It's a little weird for me, but since we've gotten pretty close over the last little while, it isn't uncomfortable like I would have expected. He walks me through the mostly empty marina parking lot, towards the water where all the cameras are set up. There are way more people involved in a movie than I thought. There are people operating cameras, lights, smoke machines, people with clipboards and headsets, and people taking pictures of literally everything with their phones. There's people just standing around watching, and people fixing costumes and makeup on the other actors.

"I don't want you to get jealous, but there is definitely a kissing scene being shot today," Logan says, I'm sure because people around can hear us talking.

"Oh. That's weird," I improvise. "But I mean, it's your job, so that's okay."

He smiles and pulls out his phone. "Can I take a picture of us?"

"Of course."

He presses his face into mine and we both smile as he snaps

a couple pictures. "I'll post it later," he says. He steps away from me a little once we get into the thick of all the movie stuff. They've got cameras and lights and white screen things set up on the docks. The director, Zoey, comes right up to me and smiles, holding out her hand for me to shake. I shake it and return a smile.

"Isla, it's great to see you again! Are you excited to be up close to all the action?"

"Yeah, this is all super cool."

"We have a chair set up for you over here, hon." She drags me away from Logan and I want to reach out my hand to him and make him come with us, but I know he's got a job to do. I can't help but look back at him though, and he smiles and waves as a makeup person walks up to him and starts powdering his face.

The chair that Zoey set aside for me is one of those fancy director's chairs, and it's lined up with all the other chairs, like I'm a part of the crew or something. Someone is sitting in the one next to mine, and I think I recognize her from a Netflix show that ended a few years ago.

"Hey," she says with a smile.

"Hi," I reply.

"I'm Taylor."

"Isla."

"Right, you're Logan's new girlfriend. I guess he invited you to watch. That's sweet."

"Yeah. It's kind of weird."

She giggles. "I hope you enjoy watching. I like watching the scenes I'm not in, get shot. A lot of the other actors just go hang out in holding when they're not in a scene, or to their trailers when we have them. But I love being a part of all of it."

"I feel like I would like to watch, too. Then it's like you're a part of the whole thing and not just the parts people see you in."

"Exactly."

Someone standing next to the director yells "background" and some people start walking in front of the camera, and then the director calls "action" and Logan sighs so big I can see it from where I'm sitting. He's on one of the docks, his feet dangling off the edge, and one of the cameras moves so close to him, I don't know how he can just pretend it's not there. He looks up and into the distance, when Carly Bowman's character starts walking along the dock towards him.

"I should have known I'd find you here," she says as she sits down next to him, her legs also hanging off the edge of the dock.

"I'm sorry I left," Logan replies. There's so much pain in his voice, and I don't even know what it's about, but it's tugging at my heart.

"Kyle, please don't apologize. I might not ever understand what you're going through, but I want to be here for you. I don't have to understand to care."

"I know."

"Please let me be here for you."

Logan rests his head on her shoulder and the camera moves around them and then I can't see their faces at all. But I'm so invested. I have no idea what's going on, but yes, Kyle, please, let her be there for you! The director calls cut and the camera moves away from them, and immediately they look like different people. Their little love thing is completely gone now that the cameras aren't on. They really don't like each other, eh? Someone walks up to the two of them and they all talk for a little bit, and then Carly Bowman gets up and walks in the direction she had come from at the start of the scene. Looks like they're resetting and doing the scene again.

They do the same scene three more times, and then the cameras change for a continuation of the same scene, it looks like. There's a guy holding a big mic over their heads, but the camera on them is on a different dock, getting a shot from farther away, I guess.

I'm super invested in their conversation until Logan looks at her in this… this *way*. His head is tilted down a little, but I can tell that he's still looking into her eyes, and then he moves his face closer to hers, just a little, and whispers "tell me to stop," before putting his hand on the back of her head and pressing his mouth to hers. It's a really fucking confident looking kiss, and I know they've probably done it a bunch of times, and he's kissed people in *Neighbourly*, but watching it in real life is different somehow. Both of their mouths open and I'm horrified. The kiss looks deep and passionate and like he really knows what he's doing, and even though he told me he wouldn't kiss me if I didn't want him to, I'm completely and utterly terrified. Especially when I realize that he never said he wouldn't kiss me if I didn't want him to, he said he wouldn't kiss me *in front of everyone* if I didn't want him to. What if he kisses me when we're alone? What if he grabs my head like that and whispers something meaningful to me and kisses me with his mouth and his tongue and his passion and his confidence, and I'm there just… being me? No. This can't happen. I cannot.

Oh this is ridiculous. As if Logan Jackson would actually want to kiss me. He's Logan Jackson! And I'm a server at a pizza restaurant.

But what if he does anyway? What if he thinks I want to kiss him? I get out of my chair as quietly as I can, and Taylor scrunches her eyebrows at me. I shrug at her and smile, but I desperately need to leave. Or at least just not watch this. I walk across the parking lot towards the path that takes you up and around the bay, but then I realize that there's a barrier there too. There's no one over at this one because you can't see them shooting from over here; there's a restaurant and trees in the way, but I don't want to have to move it. The restaurant is closed, probably so there aren't any cars coming and going since it shares a parking lot with the marina, or maybe they're using it as a filming location later and I'll be in their way. I make my way up to the wooden stairs anyway, and find a seat at a table. I can still see the movie making happen from up here, but I'm farther away and I can't see passion or fire from here. I just see people and cameras. I pull a chair out from a table by the edge of the patio and rest my arm on the railing next to me. I can see them getting up and moving, and I see cameras move, and I can hear voices but I can't make out any words. Yes. This is better.

I scroll through my phone a little and decide to look at Logan's Instagram profile. Is it really him posting, or a team doing it for him? The picture of the two of us that says **making friends** isn't his most recent picture, which surprises me. I mean, I guess since Logan blew up my page, I have been too afraid to really open Instagram at all. Especially since reading those weird hate comments, so I shouldn't be surprised that there's a new picture I didn't know about. It's a picture of the sunset over the water, and you can see the movie crew and camera as a silhouette in the foreground. It's actually a really good picture. The caption just reads **I love my job**. It has 470 thousand likes and 33 thousand comments. How does he even manage that? I guess he probably does have a team. But did he even take the picture? Did he decide on the caption? I'm not sure if I'm allowed, but I take a few pictures of the set from my spot, and then a selfie because why not, and then find something to listen to on Spotify.

Someone is shaking my shoulder and I wake up with a probably very unattractive gasp. Logan's face is about two inches from mine and I take in a sharp breath.

"Oh hey," I say, my voice scratchy with sleep.

"Hey." His voice is so calm and quiet that I want to go back to sleep inside it. "Why did you leave? Is everything okay?"

"Yeah," I lie.

He furrows his eyebrows. "Why do I not believe you?"

"I don't know." I stretch a little and make a bit of a squealy noise.

"Well that was adorable."

I look around to make sure no one can hear us. "Logan, we're not actually dating, right?"

"What? Of course not."

"Okay, so maybe don't say things like that to me."

"What, that your little stretch and noise that you made was adorable?"

"Yeah."

"Why not?"

"Because… that's something a boyfriend would say."

"Or a friend. I'm sorry, did I do something wrong? I'm really confused."

"I don't want to talk about it here," I say quietly.

"Okay, but we *can* talk about it?" he asks seriously.

"Yeah," I sigh.

"Okay, well we're just taking a break, and then we're shooting again when the lighting changes. Do you want to leave?"

"No." I shake my head. "But I think I would rather stay up here if that's okay."

"Of course it's okay." He stands up from his chair and looks around for a bit, then back at me. "I'll come get you when we're done."

"Okay." I smile at him and he smiles back, but I can tell he's unsure. He looks around again and then back at me before turning and leaving.

CHAPTER 12

Logan walks carefully up to my table when they're done shooting and slowly sits down next to me. I raise my head from my arms and smile sleepily at him.

"I'm sorry if you were bored. But I'm glad that you came."

"I wasn't bored," I say. "It was cool."

"Why did you move so far away then?"

I shrug and sit up straighter, but don't give him an answer. He raises his eyebrows at me, but I just shrug again and then stand up. "What now?" I ask.

"Do you… want to take me back to my hotel?"

Logan flops down onto his bed and I stand in the entryway feeling awkward. I want to talk to him about how I feel but I'm afraid to bring it up for some reason. Up until now he's been really easy to talk to. And it's not that he's suddenly not easy to talk to, it's that I'm suddenly afraid to open up. I haven't really talked about this with anyone before.

"Are you coming in?" Logan asks without raising his head to look at me.

"Um. Yeah."

That's when he sits up. "What's up? Is this whole thing freaking you out too much?"

My throat is so tight I feel like I can't breathe. I swallow and take a step closer to him, clenching my hands into fists so I can't feel them shake. "Sort of," I finally say.

"Oh my god, really? What part? We can stage a breakup if you want. I mean, I just posted that picture of us, calling you my girlfriend, but that's fine. We can stop if you want."

I smile and step even closer. "We don't have to stage a breakup. I just sort of freaked out I guess, because we didn't set any ground rules."

"Ground rules? I never thought of that. I mean, I don't know if I really have any. But if you do…"

"Well I feel weird talking about it."

He squints at me and pats the bed beside him. "Let's talk through it slowly then. What do you *not* feel weird talking about?"

"Well I guess I don't really feel weird talking about the fact that I feel weird talking about it?"

He laughs a little and nods once. "Okay, that's a start. But I feel like something happened today that made you upset."

I finally let myself sit next to him on the bed, but as soon as I do, I turn and shove backwards so that I'm closer to the headboard, both of my feet up on the bed with me. I bend my knees in front of me and wrap my arms around my legs. He stays where he is on the side of the bed with his legs dangling over, but turns his head to look at me.

"Okay, do you promise not to judge me?" I ask.

"I would never judge. People judge me all the time and it's not great. I would only judge if you, like, murdered someone or something."

"Okay." I let out a deep breath and lean back into the headboard. "I'm 29 years old."

"Um. Okay?"

"Okay," I try again, "I'm 29 years old but I feel like, sort of, like my feelings towards," I pause, trying to think of the right words and obviously failing, "everything, sort of makes me feel like… I'm a teenager."

"What do you mean?"

I almost blurt out that I've only ever had sex with one person, that I'm not just afraid to start a new (real) relationship with someone, but I'm afraid to even be fake-intimate with someone. I cut myself off before I even get a whole word out, and Logan narrows his eyes at me. Neither of us says anything, we just have a bit of a staring contest.

"I know that you know you need to explain this to me," he finally says. "But I can't quite figure out if you actually want to."

I let out a deep breath and tell him the one thing I know I need to tell him in order for this fake relationship to continue. "I don't want you to kiss me."

"Is that one of your rules?" he asks.

I nod my head.

"Okay," he says easily. "So I won't kiss you."

"Okay, but like, even when there are people taking pictures of us I don't want you to kiss me. Like, I think doing this with you could be fun, but I'll just ruin it. People won't believe that we're dating if they don't see us kissing."

"People will believe anything they want to believe. They don't have to get pictures of us kissing to think we're dating. And we can just say you're private. You don't want pictures of us kissing for everyone to see. It's not a big deal." He shrugs and moves on the bed so he's leaning against the headboard next to me. "Wanna watch a movie?"

"That's it?" I ask.

"What do you mean?"

"You don't want to know more?"

"Know more of what? There's more?" I feel my eyes widen and he squints at me. "The not kissing you thing isn't what you were having trouble telling me, was it?"

I shake my head.

"Then what is it?" he asks.

I want to tell him more, I want to tell him how I'm feeling but I also feel like if I do, I'm going to be giving away a big part of me. Like being vulnerable in front of a guy gives him the chance to steal part of your soul. I don't want to feel like he's stealing it, or even like I'm giving it to him. I want to know him well enough to *want* to share it with him.

"Nothing," I say.

"Okay. Do you have any other rules?" he asks.

"Um. No grabbing of my butt."

"Done. But you can't grab mine either."

I laugh a little. "Deal."

Logan turns on the TV and opens Netflix and I open my phone, ignore my Instagram notifications and upload the picture I took of the movie set. But before I hit post, I go back and find Logan's profile to see the picture that he told me he just posted. You can see the movie stuff and the water behind us, and the caption says **I love that my girlfriend is here to watch me work.** I decide not to read any of the comments, and go back to my profile to add the picture that I took. I might as well play along. I just put a heart emoji for the caption at first, but then add **Getting to watch @therealloganjackson film a movie is really cool**. Then I move the heart emoji to the end. People start liking it before it's even up for ten full seconds. I want to see if there are more supportive people in the comments this time, but I'm too nervous so I toss my phone to the side and pretend it doesn't exist. I look up at the TV to see that new episodes of *Neighbourly* have been added to Netflix.

"Oh my god, season five of *Neighbourly*!" I squeal. And then I realize that I'm sitting next to one of the stars and I feel my cheeks heat up almost instantly. "I mean, um, cool," I say in a forced casual tone, "new season of *Neighbourly*, that's whatever."

Logan laughs. "It's not new, this season just ended on TV."

"Yeah, I don't have cable. It's pretty expensive."

"Oh. Right. Well, do you want to watch it?"

"No, that's okay, I'm sure that's weird for you."

He shrugs and tosses me the remote. "I need to have a shower anyway. You can stay out here and watch it if you want."

I watch him walk around the bed and into the washroom, but I wait until I hear the shower start before I press play. He spends a while in the shower, which is good because I want to watch at least the first episode, and when I hear him shut the water off, I turn the volume down. I feel weird about him hearing me watch him on TV. The first episode is almost over when I hear the door open and I grab for the remote as quickly as I can and pause it. It's freeze-framed on Logan's character with his eyes half closed and his mouth open.

"Oh that's attractive," he says, looking at the TV.

I turn the TV off because I don't know what else to do. It looks like Logan didn't fully dry himself before he put his shirt on, because the shoulders and part of the chest are already soaking through.

"You don't want to finish the episode?" he asks.

"No, I can watch it at home."

"There was like three minutes left."

"It's not weird?" I ask.

"I promise it's not weird."

I take a deep breath and turn the TV back on, and it's still paused with Logan's open mouth and the timeline at the bottom of the screen saying how much is left of the episode. I press play and Logan's character finishes his sentence.

"Wait, I have a question," Logan says, grabbing the remote from me and pausing the show.

"Okay," I answer nervously.

"I think you have more rules that you're afraid to talk about."

"That's not a question."

"Well you got all weird earlier today when I called you adorable. Do you not want me to say stuff like that to you? Even if it's true?"

"Logan, you thinking I'm adorable makes me incredibly uncomfortable but also very excited and it's all very confusing and I don't like it."

"I'm sorry I make you uncomfortable."

"It's not…" I sigh and take the remote from Logan to turn the TV off because his character is frozen on the screen again, and again, it's not an attractive facial expression. "It's not that you make me uncomfortable. It's definitely a me issue. I don't want to talk about it."

"I think we need to talk about it, Isla."

"No, we don't."

For some reason all I can think about is Tyler telling me he doesn't love me anymore. *I think I'll always love you, Isla, but am I in love with you? I don't think I have been for a while.* All I can think about is me coming home from work every night for a month and Tyler not wanting anything to do with me. All I can think about is Tyler not opening his mouth when I try to kiss him, not putting his arms around me when I hug him. All I can think about is Tyler going straight to bed and turning his back to me after getting home from a dinner out, or a movie night. All I can think about is me trying so hard to get him to notice me, and him not even caring.

And then Logan Jackson goes and calls me adorable.

"Okay, I can see that you're upset, we don't have to talk about it," Logan says, startling me.

"Thank you."

"But as your pretend boyfriend, I would like you to know that I don't judge, and I'm always here to listen if you need. And right now, as your pretend boyfriend, but real friend, I will also sit quietly with you and watch the beloved sitcom *Neighbourly*, starring Logan Jackson and five other people who are less famous and less cool."

"Thanks," I say quietly, with a bit of a chuckle.

Logan smiles, gently pulls the remote from my grip, and turns the TV back on.

"What did I miss?" he asks.

"The whole episode."

"Yeah, but I don't remember what's happening here, catch me up."

CHAPTER 13

The hate comments have not gone away since Logan told everyone online that we're dating. They're getting worse. I hold my breath as I scroll through some of them, and can feel my eyes burning with tears. I know these people don't actually know me, and I know they're just trying to get a reaction out of me, but I can't help it. There are so many of them.

There are so many girls out there who are way prettier than her. Why would he date her?

Ugly

Logan, blink three times if you're in trouble

yeah she definitely brainwashed poor logan

Wow you want attention

But there are nice comments too, I think the mean ones just get pushed to the top because so many people reply to them, defending me. It just sucks though, because all I see are the mean comments, and not the angry replies. But I open one of the mean comments to see the thread of people defending me, and it makes me feel a little bit better.

Why would she be holding him hostage? One of the replies says.

Are we on the same instagram page here darlin? She's so blah looking and Logan is gorgeous. There's no way.

She's not blah! She's beautiful! Also those Freckles! Have you seen her freckles? You're just too insecure about your own looks and the fact that you need makeup to look half as pretty as she does with nothing caked on her face. I smile at that. But then I just go and block the original commenter, and then delete and block any other mean comments I see. I don't realize it, but I sit on my phone for the better part of an hour just deleting comments and liking nice ones.

But then a new comment comes into my feed that I can't ignore.

She's deleting and blocking everyone who says she's forced Logan Jackson into this, so you know it's true.

I block that person, and set my account to private. At least I won't get any new haters at this point. But I've been steadily gaining followers since all of this started, and I now have close to 50k. It's going to take me forever to weed out the bad ones. Or I could just stop looking at the comments. I can post pictures and then not pay attention to any of the reactions. Ugh, this is so exhausting.

Claire comes over on Saturday after work because we're both magically off at 8:00, and get a big spread from Harvey's and lay it out on my coffee table. We've got a burger and poutine for each of us, Nutella milkshakes, pop, and mini cinnamon donuts. Instead of picking a movie to watch, we just put on season one of *Neighbourly* so we can talk and not worry about missing stuff we haven't seen.

"So I need you to do me a favour," Claire says as she sticks her hand in the paper bag to get another donut.

"Anything."

"Can you please come with me to dinner on Tuesday with my parents?"

"Claire," I say slowly. "Have you still not told them?"

"I've been wanting to, I swear! But every time I open my mouth to tell them, I just… Ask them to pass the salt, or the potatoes or something. Maybe you can help me somehow. Like… tell them for me?"

"I'm not coming out to your parents for you," I say, shaking my head.

"What if you just did it sort of accidentally? Like you can ask me how my girlfriend is? Or if my mom or dad says something related to something and you can come back and say, 'oh yea, Claire's girlfriend likes that something!' and then it'll be easier for me to be like, 'oh yeah by the by, I'm bi.'"

"By the by, I'm bi," I laugh. "Just say that to them. I don't need to tell them that your girlfriend 'likes a something.' You can just say 'by the by I'm bi.'" I smile at her and grab a donut.

"Okay. Yeah. So anyway, dinner with my parents on Tuesday?"

Logan and I are talking on the phone the next day. He's back in LA and we're trying to figure out a plan for him to come visit me. Operation-make-people-think-we're-a-cute-couple-on-vacation. Or something of the sort.

"We could go to Toronto for the day. I don't know, like go to a Jays game, or the CN Tower or something," Logan suggests.

"Oh yeah, that sounds good. Lots of people would see us there."

"I would have to stay with you, though," he says with a bit of hesitation.

"Yeah," I reply, unsure why that's an issue.

"Well where am I supposed to sleep?" he asks.

"In my bed," I say.

"In your bed?"

"Yeah. My couch is really comfortable, I don't mind sleeping there."

"Right. Yeah. Yeah, that makes sense."

I smile. "Yeah."

"So I'm going to be on the season finale of Kate and Kat," Logan says, changing the subject.

"Oh that's exciting!"

Kate and Kat are a pair of super fun talk show hosts who have gained popularity over the last few years. They sit in fun chairs and drink flavoured fizzy water.

"Yeah. It airs the day after filming and my segment will probably be on their youtube channel."

"Cool, I'll have to watch it."

"Yeah. So I'll get to gush about you."

"You're not going to gush," I say, feeling my face heat up.

"Oh I'm going to gush. It's going to be great."

And boy, does he gush. But I can't tell you about it yet. I wish I could, especially because I really like transitions like that, but I have to tell you how dinner with Claire's parents went first. This one's good too though, so don't worry.

It's weird that we're having dinner with Claire's parents at Boston Pizza when we both work at a competing pizza restaurant. Well, I mean, they definitely draw different crowds. Boston Pizza is pretty casual, and Carter's is more classy. Well, as classy as pizza can get. Boston Pizza *feels* like you're eating at a chain restaurant, and when you're at Carter's, it definitely gives you the "I made this business myself from the ground up and it's my literal baby" feel when you're in there. The passion is really there. Anyway, I've gotten off track. My point is that we're eating at a pizza restaurant that isn't the one we work at.

None of us order pizza.

"Isla's dating a movie star," Claire says when our appetizer of spinach dip comes.

Her mom raises her eyebrows at me. "Is that so?"

"Yes. The guy who plays Cory in *Neighbourly*," Claire answers for me.

Then her eyes widen and she looks completely star struck. She must have a crush on him. "Seriously?" she asks me.

"I mean, well, it's not really…" I trail off and look at the table.

"She's too shy to talk about it, but it's true," Claire assures her.

"Yeah, Claire knows what that's all about," I say, nudging her in the elbow.

"I don't know what you're talking about." She says it so quickly I'm afraid that she's going to chicken out again.

Her parents both just look at me with tilted heads for a second but then continue dipping their fried pita pieces into the spinach dip.

"Well since we're on the topic of dating people, maybe Claire should share who she's dating!" I try.

"Oh you're dating someone?" her dad asks.

"Um." Claire shoves too much pita and dip in her mouth and takes a while to swallow it.

"Where did you meet?" her mom asks.

"What's his name?" her dad adds.

"Yeah Claire, what's his name?" I ask, a hint of playfulness in my voice.

"That's the thing," she says slowly.

"What?" Both of her parents seem very concerned.

"Isla. I feel like I'm going to barf."

"What's going on?" her dad asks. "Claire, you can tell us anything."

"I know." But her words come out strained.

"Claire," I whisper to her. "You've got this.".

She closes her eyes and lets out a deep breath, nods her head once. And then she slowly looks at her parents, who both stare at us with matching confused expressions on their faces.

"Her name is Emily," Claire says quickly. "I'm dating a girl named Emily."

Her dad narrows his eyes a little bit, and her mom puts another spinach dipped pita in her mouth.

"I'm bisexual," she adds.

"Emily's a nice name," her mom says after only a few seconds of silence.

"You never told me where you met," her dad says.

"Um." Claire sort of chokes, and then coughs, and then blinks a couple times at me. She turns back to her parents. "We met at the game store. She works there, actually. She helped me pick out a new board game. We talked for a while before we… before anything… I mean before -"

"Well this is exciting," Claire's mom says, clapping her hands together once. "Does she get a discount? Can we use it?"

"Mom!"

"What? I'm just asking the important questions." She shrugs and smiles.

"Well maybe we can have someone in the family who finally appreciates Monopoly," her dad says.

"Dad, nobody likes Monopoly."

Claire squeals and grabs onto my arm as we leave the restaurant and I smile and shove her.

"I can't believe I told them!" she says.

"I can," I tell her. "You're amazing."

Claire and I haven't been super close for long. She's only 23, and has been working at Carter's for about a year. Sometimes I forget how big of an age gap there is between us, but I guess it doesn't really matter. We've always had fun working together, but we didn't start hanging out outside of work until a few months ago. I guess all her friends from high school moved after college or university, and she moved back home when she graduated, so besides her new girlfriend, I'm all she has. Which I'm okay with, because I don't have a lot of friends either.

"Okay so I have to tell you something," I say before Claire gets out of my car at her apartment.

"Yes?"

"I'm not actually dating Logan Jackson. It's still pretend."

"But… But you went to the movie set and he had his arm around you and he was whispering sexy things into your ear. I saw pictures. I saw videos of pictures on youtube, with text on the screen about how you two are adorable together and you visit him on his movie set. People are calling you Lola."

I laugh a little. "Okay, he wasn't whispering anything sexy. And it's all for show."

"But why?"

I shrug. "Because he doesn't like being single. He's treated differently in interviews and stuff, and he said that people seem to take him more seriously when he's in a long term relationship."

"Well I guess that makes sense." But then she gasps. "But now you're never going to be able to get a boyfriend!"

"I don't want a boyfriend."

She grins at me. "A girlfriend?"

"No, Claire, I just, I don't want anything to do with… sex… and stuff."

"Sex and stuff. Nothing to do with it. With sex? Really? That doesn't make any sense to me."

"It doesn't have to make sense to you, but it does to me… And it's not just the sex thing anyway; I need more time with myself. Like, to be single. I was with Tyler for so long, and we started dating when I was like, 20, so I feel like I don't really know who I am without him, you know? Like my entire adult life had him in it, and everything that I did and thought and looked forward to had at least a little something to do with him, and I need to just be me for a while."

"Alright. That makes sense. I still don't get the not wanting to have sex thing, though. You've lost me there."

"Not everyone experiences sexual attraction the same way."

"Alright, alright," she says, putting her hands up. "But I should get in. I open tomorrow."

She grabs onto the door handle but I put a hand out to stop her.

"Wait, what did you mean a minute ago? That people are calling me Lola?"

"Not you, you and Logan. It's your couple name. Like Bennifer."

"People have given us a couple name? Already?"

"Everyone loves you."

How I wish that were true. Instead of saying anything more on the subject, I smile at her and wish her good luck with her opening shift. "I'm not in until 4:30," I tell her.

"Enjoy sleeping in!" She gets out of the car and I watch her walk around the house towards her basement apartment in the back. I would usually wait until I can see the person I'm dropping off get inside, but since I can't see her door from here, I wait until the flood of her porch light from around the corner turns off.

I'm thoroughly embarrassed to be me. Logan Jackson is acting like I'm the best thing that has ever happened to him and I'm just sitting at my computer in my PJs, literally dying. Okay, okay, maybe not literally dying, but you know what I mean. I'm sitting at my computer in my PJs, figuratively dying. Kate and Kat ask him about the latest season of *Neighbourly*, and they talk about how his character is Canadian, and what it's like portraying that as an actual Canadian, and then they ask him about filming his new movie, and then… And then Kat gets all squirrelly and smiles at him, and he blushes and smiles as if he knows what she's going to say (because he does know what she's going to say, believe it or not, they rehearse these shows!) and she says, "sooo, can we ask about a certain girl?"

"Yes, please do."

"We've all seen the pictures, and the videos, and you guys look adorable together, and already so comfortable with each other. A lot of people took videos of her giving you her phone number, which was *adorable*, but how did it all happen?"

He smiles and crosses one leg over his knee. "She actually worked on the set for a few days. She catered a few of the meals and ate with us. So we talked a little bit while she was there, and then we just kept running into each other."

"She ate her own catered meals?" Kate asks.

"Well, it was the restaurant she works at who catered, and she was the lucky person who got picked to bring it all over. If I had to bring a bunch of food over to a movie set and not get paid extra for it, I would stay and get some free food while I was at it, too."

Kate and Kat both laugh.

"But Isla's great. Everything is just easy with her. The first time we hung out on purpose-"

"Wait, what do you mean on purpose?" Kat interrupts.

"Well the first four or five times we hung out, it was just because we ran into each other, or she was saving me from screaming teenage girls." Kate smirks and raises her eyebrows, but they both let him continue. "But the first time we actually planned something, she bought me a fake moustache so no one would recognize me when we were out in public."

"And did it work?" Kat asks.

"We didn't even see anyone," he says with a little laugh. "She took me to this trail that was actually really beautiful."

"Is it weird dating someone who wasn't already well known like you?"

"No, it's refreshing, actually. It sort of keeps me grounded."

Kat and Kate both put their hands on their hearts and sigh and smile and the audience 'aww's. And I'm just sitting here thinking about everything he said and wondering if it's true or not. He said that everything is easy with me. That it's refreshing to be with me. I'm sure it's just him acting and playing the boyfriend part, but is it weird that hearing him say that sort of does something to me? Like it's making me smile. But like, in that way when you know you're not supposed to smile, you know the thing that makes you happy probably actually shouldn't make you happy, and you're trying so hard to keep a straight face, but your lips just can't help but curl a little bit, and you feel like you're doing something wrong by showing your happiness. It's that kind of smile. Because you know, everything is really easy with him for me too. I've never become friends with someone so easily before. It's like we were already friends and just hadn't seen each other for a while.

"When I fly up to see you, can you come get me from the airport?" Logan says over the phone that night. "Or do you want me to rent a car? No, you know what, I'll rent a car. If people see you picking me up at the airport they'll think it's weird if we don't kiss."

I pause and think about that for a second. "They'll also probably think it's weird that I'm making you drive yourself to my place from the airport. Everyone will think I'm a bitch."

"Hmm. Not if say, everyone thinks you can't get the night off work. I'll drive straight to the restaurant."

I smile. I try not to, but I can't help it. "Okay."

So I tell Tom the next day at work that I have to work until at least 8:00 on Friday.

"You want to work late the day before your vacation? That's weird."

"No, it's because Logan's coming and we need people to believe it's real in case there are people with cameras and stuff. He'll rent a car."

He scrunches his eyebrows at me. "That doesn't make any sense. Also I don't think you should be talking so casually about how you're not actually dating. Someone might hear you. You know, since you're trying to keep up appearances and stuff."

"Yeah," Claire agrees. "I didn't think it was a big deal that you told me it's not real, but you can't have everyone in town knowing. I can't believe Tom knows."

I roll my eyes at her. "Anyone who wants it to be real will brush it off as a rumour if they hear about it."

"I don't know," Tom says. "It could end up being messy."

"Well what am I supposed to do?" I ask.

"Pretend like he's your boyfriend." He starts walking out into the restaurant and I follow him. "Now I know you wanted to leave early to pick up Logan what's-his-face from the airport on Friday, but I don't have enough staff for that day. Two people already booked it off before you to go camping, so you're going to have to work at least until 8:00. I'm really sorry. But he's rich, right? He can rent a car or something, right?"

I smile at him and he raises his eyebrows. "This sucks," I say, immediately frowning and trying to sound genuine. "I was so excited to run and jump into his arms at arrivals!"

"I'm sorry I don't mean to be nosy," a guest at one of my tables says, "but is Logan Jackson coming back into town?"

I smile at her and walk closer to her table. "Yes. He's my boyfriend, so, you know, he's coming to visit me."

CHAPTER 14

Logan texts me a bit before 6:00 to tell me he's leaving the airport and I'm suddenly nervous. We talked about what would happen when he arrived, and how we would both act, what we would say, but I'm not an actor. I don't do improv. People are going to be able to tell that it's not genuine. I can feel my fingers shaking as I pick up peoples' plates, which is not good because he probably won't be here for another hour or hour and a half. Oh plus he's going the same way as the cottage traffic so it'll be longer than that. Shit. He might get here later than eight.

He walks through the restaurant door at 7:45 and my heart leaps into my throat. I take a deep breath and sort of run towards him. I'm excited to see him again, sure, but I have to play it up. I have to make it seem like I've been missing him the whole three weeks that he's been gone. I hug him and he hugs me back, squeezing tightly. When I let go, he leans in pretty seriously to kiss me, which catches me off guard, even though this is exactly what we planned, and I pull back.

"Sorry," I say, all flustered.

"What's wrong?" he asks, just like we planned.

"I'm at work," I answer. "I can't- It's not- I don't want-" This is all planned and basically scripted, but my inability to form proper words right now is completely genuine.

He laughs and cuts me off. "You're right. I didn't even think of that." And then he turns his attention to the side a bit, and notices a table of women staring at him. "Hi," he says to them. "How's it going?"

"I'll just go ask Tom if I can head out now," I say, backing away and going to find Tom.

When I come back all ready to go, Logan is taking pictures with basically everyone in the restaurant and I don't know what to do. I stand there awkwardly until he notices, and when he does he immediately smiles and ducks out of a woman's arm that had been around his shoulder.

"Isla!" he says excitedly. "Are you ready?"

"Yeah!" I reply. "So do you just want to follow me to my place then?"

"Yeah for sure." He turns back to the crowd around him. "I have to go now, but it was nice meeting you all! Enjoy the rest of your dinners!"

Everyone sort of sighs and watches us as we leave the restaurant. Logan grabs onto my hand before we're through the door and my breath catches for just a second. I look up at him and he smiles at me and gives my hand a squeeze.

But once we turn the corner outside, four people are there with cameras with big flashes on them. They don't even really say anything to us, they just start taking pictures and blinding us with their intense lights.

"Come on, guys, give us some space," Logan says calmly. He pulls me in closer to him and I tuck into his side as we push past them, but they just keep taking pictures of us! I'm probably horribly unattractive in all of them which is incredibly annoying, and I'm also seeing white spots everywhere already which is also very annoying.

Logan parked right behind me on the street, which is nice, but I'm afraid to go to my car alone. They're probably going to stay and keep taking pictures of him and not me, but still. And also why do they need so many pictures?

"Can you just kiss for the camera, guys? Come on, I need this," one of the guys says.

"Fuck off," Logan says to him. He puts his arm around me and I shove my face into his shoulder without even thinking. He hugs me and rubs my back and then whispers into my hair. "We can leave my rental here, okay? I'll drive."

Except now there's a fifth person taking pictures and it's suddenly hard to breathe.

"Back up guys, come on!" he yells, taking an arm off my back and waving it at them.

"Just one kiss and we'll leave!" the same guy yells. "I need a picture of it before someone else gets it!"

"You're not going to get one!" Logan says. "She's a human being who wants her privacy."

One of the other paparazzi guys shrugs. "She should have known what she was getting herself into when she started dating you."

"Come on," Logan says gently, walking me around my car. "Get in the car."

"Just one kiss, guys, come on! It's not a big deal!"

"It is a big deal, and you're an asshole!" He turns to me and whispers again. "Where are your keys? Never mind, come on," and he walks me to his car, unlocks it with the fob and opens the passenger door. I slide in the seat and he shuts the door, walks around to his side and gets in. He lets out a deep breath and looks at me. "Are you okay?"

"Yeah," I say quietly. "It's just… weird. And sort of scary."

"Yeah it is a little bit. But they're just people trying to get paid." He turns the car on and honks his horn when they don't get out of the road so he can get out of the space. They finally back up but keep taking pictures, and he drives us to my apartment.

"Wait," I say before he pulls into the parking lot. "What if they follow us? I don't want them to know where I live."

"I'll pull up in front of the building so you can go in and I'll park down the street."

I run into the building as quickly as I can and up to my apartment, realizing only then that I'm shaking. Which is a little ridiculous, right? They were just people taking pictures of us, it's not like they were going to hurt us. As I'm waiting for Logan to buzz my apartment so I can let him in, Tyler texts me.

The blanket okay? his text says.

I narrow my eyes at my phone and try to ignore the fact that my heart is beating way too fast. Why is he asking about the blanket? I mean obviously this is just an excuse to talk to me, but why? After eight months of being broken up, why now? And why three weeks after he gave it to me?

The blanket is fine I type back.

But then my intercom buzzes and I leap off the couch and run to the door.

"Identify yourself," I say into the mic.

"It's Logan and the paparazzi guys didn't follow me so please let me in in case they're wandering around looking for us."

I buzz him in and open my apartment door so I can see him coming up the hallway. He smiles and waves when he comes out from the stairwell and I wave back.

"I'm sorry that happened," he says when he gets closer.

"Why are you sorry?" I ask.

He shrugs and follows me into my apartment. "I sort of feel responsible."

"It's okay," I say.

We both sit on the couch and I pick up my phone again. Tyler replied while I was in the hallway.

How's your Etsy stuff going? it says.

Why is he so interested in me all of a sudden? It's nice that he's asking about me, but it sort of hurts that he's doing this now and not when we were dating.

"Who are you texting?" Logan asks.

"Tyler," I say shyly.

"Oh. Why?"

"I don't know," I groan. "I don't want him to be my boyfriend again. But I'm just… When we saw him to get my blanket, it made me…"

"Feel things?" Logan finishes for me.

"Yeah. But like, I don't know what kind of things. I don't know."

He half smiles at me and I lean deeper into the couch, wishing I could put into words what I'm feeling about Tyler. Of course I missed him for the first big chunk of our breakup, but after that I thought that maybe I didn't really miss *him*, I just missed the idea of him. Or the idea of having a boyfriend. And I only really missed him, or the idea of him, sometimes. Like when I had a reason to think about it. So I thought that I was doing a pretty good job of getting over him. But I guess I still miss Tyler, I just miss the Tyler from when our relationship was good. I don't miss the Tyler who didn't want to hang out with me, or the Tyler who snapped at me for no reason, or the Tyler who would agree to go on a date with me and then change his mind at the last minute and make me feel bad for being upset about it. I don't miss that Tyler. In a way I'm glad that Tyler broke up with me.

But I miss the Tyler who was supportive, and excited for me when I made a sale on my Etsy store. I miss the Tyler who woke me up at 3am when he couldn't sleep and asked me to eat pizza and watch Disney Channel movies with him. I miss the Tyler who looked at me like he was looking at the Earth from outer space, the Tyler who played with my hands and kissed my fingers while we watched movies. And when I saw him again in the mall parking lot, I wasn't reminded of the last year of our relationship, I was reminded of all the times that he was very clearly in love with me. Or when I *thought* he was very clearly in love with me. I don't know. I guess after not seeing him for so long, I thought I had stopped missing him, and maybe I had, but seeing him again brought everything back. I miss him. And I know that getting back together is a bad idea, and I don't want to do it, I just miss having the good Tyler in my life. And when he gave me my blanket, a small part of me wanted to let go of Logan and hug Tyler instead. And if I keep him out of my life like I've been doing for the past eight months, I'm sure these feelings won't come up again. Because I won't see him for it to happen. But when he texts me, it makes the feelings come flooding back in.

"Oh my god, is this a miniature *Neighbourly* set?" Logan screeches. I didn't realize he got off the couch, and I completely forgot about my Polymer Clay *Neighbourly* set on the window sill (Just FYI it's a fairly deep window sill. You could totally put cushions on it and use it as a seat).

I get up pretty quickly and grab his arm, trying to pull him back. "No, of course it isn't. Please stop looking at it."

He turns to me and smiles. "Wait, did you make this?"

"No, of course I didn't."

He narrows his eyes at me and then turns back to it. "This is amazing. This is Cory's apartment to the tee!" He picks up a miniature Cory from the miniature couch and inspects it. "This is incredible! How long did this take you?"

"I told you I didn't make it."

"Well where did you get it? How do I get one? I should Google this." He pulls his phone out of his pocket and I reach out to him again.

"Please don't," I say.

"Why not? You did make this, didn't you?"

I sigh and flop back down on the couch. He follows and sits next to me, but he still has the little Cory in his hand.

"Okay," I say, "please don't laugh."

"Why would I laugh?"

"Because it's embarrassing and nobody buys anything."

"What do you mean?"

"I make Polymer Clay things. Like of movie characters and stuff."

"What? That's amazing! Like what kind of movie characters?"

"Like Harry Potter, or Gollum, or Winnie the Pooh, or Iron Man. Lots of things. I do generic cute things too, like baby seals, or panda bears. Whatever."

"Can I see them?"

I sigh again and reluctantly head to my room. Logan follows me with a bit of a skip and it makes me smile, but one of those 'maybe this shouldn't make me smile the way it's making me smile' smiles, so I try to force it away. I pull a big Rubbermaid tote bin out of my closet and take the lid off, revealing, well, a bunch of tissue paper. I take one out and unwrap it, showing him a three-inch-tall Wonder Woman. He takes it and turns it around in his fingers, complete amazement on his face.

"This is so cool! And nobody buys these?"

"Well, some people do, but not enough for it to not be exciting when it happens."

"And you made that whole apartment and all the furniture and stuff?"

"Yeah," I say slowly.

"When? How long did it take you?"

"Um. I don't want to say."

"Why not?"

"Because it's embarrassing."

"Why is it embarrassing?"

"Because you're Logan Jackson! You play Cory Milligan on *Neighbourly*, and it's spelled with a U even though it's an American show and Americans don't spell it like that because it's about *your* Canadian character and you're in my apartment and I'm pretending to be your girlfriend and I feel like a crazy person."

"I don't want you to feel like a crazy person," Logan says, sounding a little hurt, like it's his fault.

"Neither do I, but I do!"

"Why? I like things too, you know. Like I'm a huge fan of *Lost*."

"Really?"

"Yes. I watched it in High School and during any down time when I was shooting movies, which I had a lot of, because I always just had small parts in things before *Neighbourly*, and any time I was feeling overwhelmed about something, or lost, I would watch *Lost*. Ha. If I was lost I would watch *Lost*. Anyway I've seen it so many times, and the season with the time travel I watched over and over. Sometimes I have to put it on to fall asleep."

"Really?"

"Yes. And if I could make things out of this clay stuff, I totally would have made *Lost* things."

"I have *Lost* things," I say excitedly. I start pulling things out of the bin and unwrapping them until I find a three-inch-tall Hurley.

"Oh my god, Hurley!" he takes him from me almost aggressively and holds him in both his hands. "Hurley is one of my favourites!"

"You can have him if you want," I say.

"Really?"

"Yeah, of course."

"Can I buy him from you?"

"No, I'm not going to make you buy him."

"But I want to. How much do you sell these for?" he asks.

"$25."

"That's it?"

"Well… Yeah."

"I'll give you 50 for him."

"Then let me find you another one."

"No, no, it's fine. I just want Hurley, and I want to pay you 50 dollars for him."

I stop and look at him for a second. "Okay."

"So can you tell me about making the *Neighbourly* set now?"

I groan and put the lid back on the tote. "I made it after Tyler and I broke up. And I made it while I rewatched the series, and it took me all four seasons. That's basically all I did when I wasn't working. It… helped."

He holds up his Hurley, and the much smaller Cory, and looks at them with so much pride. And then he looks at me with something else. Like he cares. I can feel it in his eyes.

"Well I'm really glad that I could help," he says. "Even if I didn't know you at the time."

I smile. "Me too."

CHAPTER 15

We're taking the GO Train to Toronto for a Blue Jays game, because neither of us wants to drive or park in Toronto and Logan thinks the train is fun. We immediately head upstairs when we get on the train, which is the quiet area, hoping people will give us space if they recognize Logan.

Someone does recognize him, a girl who looks to be about 18 or so, but she doesn't come over to us. She just takes pictures of us with her phone and looks away any time we look at her. It's cute.

"You should say hi to her," I whisper.

"Maybe. We've got an hour on this train, we can let her wonder if it's really me or not for a little longer," he whispers back.

"You're so mean."

"How is that mean? Hey, can I do something?"

I feel my eyes widen and my heart beat faster. "Something like what?"

"She's totally going to post these to Snapchat or Instagram or something, so can I like- can I just…" he puts his hand in my hair and moves his face in closer to mine.

"What are you doing?" I ask.

"Nothing, don't worry. Is it okay if I just get closer? I won't kiss you, I promise."

"I don't- I'm not," I stammer, "You're making me all nervous."

"Okay." He pulls back and puts his hands in his lap. "I just thought it would look good for the media. But I don't want to make you nervous."

"Can I tell you something?" I ask quietly.

"Of course." He makes circles on the back of my hand with his index finger.

"I don't particularly mind when you get close to me. Like, you can touch my hand like that if you want, and I don't mind when you whisper into my hair. And hugging you is nice. I like hugging you. But when your mouth is close to my mouth, or if you were to, say, touch my hip, or my thigh, or my lower back, it sort of..."

The corner of his mouth curls. "Turns you on?"

"No!" I almost shout. The girl who was taking pictures of us looks up from her phone, startled, and the other few people in our car look at us. "Sorry," I say, and then turn back to Logan. "No," I whisper, hitting him on the arm. "I don't want to hurt your feelings, because it's not a you thing. But it sort of gives me the heebie jeebies."

"The heebie jeebies? Like when you see a gross scene in a movie? Or when you're talking about ghosts and you get all freaked out and think there's one staring at you from the dark corner of the living room? Really? I give you the heebie jeebies?"

"No, that sounds bad. It's just- I'm not... Actually, can we talk about this at home?"

"Yes of course. But I'm not going to let it go until you explain yourself. Just so you're aware."

"Okay."

"I won't let you forget. As soon as we walk into your apartment, you're telling me exactly why I make you feel like a ghost is spying on you."

"It's not you," I try.

"It's fine. We'll talk about it at home. And I won't put my mouth close to yours." And then he turns in his seat so that girl can see him better, and he waves at her. Her mouth drops open and she goes beet red. She looks away and covers her face with her hand, clearly embarrassed. Logan turns back to me and shrugs. And throughout the rest of the train ride, she continues to stare at us, but looks away immediately if we catch her gaze. Finally as our train is rolling into Union Station, she gets up and walks over to us.

"Is it okay if I get a picture with you?" she asks quietly.

"Of course," Logan says with a smile. She crouches down in the aisle next to Logan's seat and holds her phone up in front of the two of them and I lean into the window.

"You can be in it too," she says to me.

"Oh. Cool." I lean into Logan and Logan leans into the girl, and she takes two pictures.

"Thanks," she says, standing up and immediately running down the stairs.

We wait until the train has stopped before we get up and then make our way into the station. It's pretty crowded and no one seems to notice us as we make our way outside. I'm not even paying attention to where we are; I just try to stay beside Logan as we navigate the crowds and streets, and after a few minutes he grabs onto my hand and pulls me closer to him.

"Is this okay?" he asks.

"Yes," I say.

"It doesn't give you the heebie jeebies?"

"No," I say with a bit of a laugh.

Any time the crowd is too tight and it's hard to walk beside him, I step behind him but he keeps a hold of my hand, pressing it against his back. We make it to the stadium and no one says anything to us as they scan our tickets and check our bags, and no one says anything as we walk through the crowds to our section. The ticket person letting us to our seats smiles as soon as he sees us, though.

"Hey, you're that Cory guy," he says.

"You caught me," Logan says.

"Cool. My girlfriend loves that show."

"Don't they all."

The ticket guy laughs and lets us through without double checking that we're going to the right spot. "Enjoy the game, guys."

We head down the concrete steps and find our row, and luckily no one is sitting in it yet so we don't have to basically crawl over everyone to get to our seats in the middle. We'll have to basically crawl over everyone to get out once the game starts though, if we want to go get food or use the washroom. I sat on the end with Tyler once though, and we were passing cans of beer down the row the whole game, and getting up constantly for those same people who had to pee 90 million times, so sitting in the middle is better. We'll probably only get up once or twice.

"So I don't know any of the players anymore," I say once we're seated. We're in the third row on the first base line, which is the closest I've ever sat at a Blue Jays game before. The field looks so big from this close; it's weird.

"I don't think I've ever known the players," Logan replies.

"Not even Bautista?" I ask.

He shrugs at me.

"Bat flip guy?" I try.

He shrugs again.

"What? Really?"

"I'm sorry, I don't usually watch baseball in my spare time. I think it's fun to see in real life, but I don't follow it or anything."

"Me neither. I mean I did. When I was with Tyler. Because Tyler liked it. It's fine. So we both don't know who any of the players are. That's good."

He smirks at me. "Okay."

"Oh no way, oh my god, no, turn around, I can't," I hear from beside us. I lean over Logan a little bit to see a man and woman maybe around our age standing in our row, but the woman is trying to make the guy back up. "We can't sit there," she says.

I scrunch my eyebrows at them, wondering what the problem is.

"It's fine sweetie, just sit down," the guy says.

"That's Cory Milligan," she says a bit quieter, except we can totally still hear her.

"Actually my name is Logan," he says.

"See?" the guy says with a smile. "It's Logan, not Cory Milligan. Who's Cory Milligan?"

"The character I play on a TV show," Logan answers.

"Oh no way! That's so cool! I'll sit next to him, then." He squeezes between her and the seat and sits next to Logan. "Hey man, how's it going?"

"Good. You?"

"Great! The sun is shining, the Jays are up in the series, and I'm sitting next to my fiancée's celebrity crush. All is good in the world."

The couple mostly keeps to themselves throughout the game, and the people on the other side of us either don't notice they're sitting two people away from a sitcom star, or they don't care. But just before the end of the third inning, something I didn't even think about happens. Something that never crossed my mind, but is now happening, and giving me so much anxiety I might actually throw up. The kiss cam. They are doing the kiss cam on the Jumbotron and I am so afraid that they are going to land on us. Especially if the people in charge of it recognize us, they're definitely going to pick us. I watch the screen in horror as it shows couple after couple being surprised and then kissing and being cute. They're going to put us on, I know it, and I'm going to have to kiss Logan Fucking Jackson. On the lips. Because who doesn't kiss their boyfriend on the lips when they're on the kiss cam?

Oh there it is. It's us. It's me and Logan Jackson on the big screen, and I try to look excited and shocked, but I'm sure everyone can tell that I look terrified. Logan shakes his head and tries to wave them off, but that's just silliness. No one is going to believe we're dating if I don't kiss him on a kiss cam at a Blue Jays game, where literally everyone kisses and is excited about it. It's not the same as being caught by the paparazzi and having a picture of a real, private intimate kiss. It's a kiss for show that everyone is excited about doing. This is ridiculous. Now I have to kiss Logan Jackson.

I lean in and he turns towards me when he notices what I'm doing, and I kiss him on the lips. He kisses me back, making it slightly more than a peck, but still basically just a peck, and then I pull away and try to ignore how hot my face is getting. I can hear the crowd cheer as if they're excited for us, wait, of course they're excited for us; they all know who we are. The cheering dies down fairly quickly, but it just makes it easier for me to hear the people left who are shouting things like "We love you, Lola!" and "Lola forever!"

I feel Logan let out a deep breath next to me and then he leans in, puts his mouth to my ear, and whispers into my hair.

"Are you okay?"

"Yeah," I mutter.

"I'm sorry I made it longer than half a second, I didn't mean to do that."

"It's okay," I say.

"I don't think it is."

"It's fine. I kissed you and you kissed me back a little bit."

"Come on." He grabs my hand and stands up, pulling me to my feet too. We squeeze past the couple from Logan's side - the guy and his fiancée - and shuffle past everyone else in the row until we get to the aisle. He keeps holding my hand as we walk up the stairs and make our way into the concession area. It's pretty empty since the game is still going on, but once the inning ends, it's going to be packed up here. He takes me to an area where we can still see the field, and presses us up against a concrete post.

"I feel like a jerk," he finally says.

"Why?"

"Because you've told me multiple times that you don't want me to kiss you."

"But I kissed you," I say, confused.

"Yeah, but I shouldn't have kissed you back like that."

"Logan, it's fine. It was almost nothing."

"Yeah, but almost nothing means it was almost something, too."

"It was a perfectly acceptable reaction. Plus it's not like you put your tongue in my mouth."

"Oh that sounds so attractive when you say it like that."

"Thanks for being concerned, Logan, but it's really okay. I kissed you, it lasted a second, we didn't make out, it was just a little kiss and it's over now and it's fine."

"Okay. As long as you're fine."

"I'm fine. I promise." But my voice cracks when I say the word promise, and Logan raises his eyebrows at me. "Okay, maybe I'm not 100 percent fine, but I'm basically fine."

Logan lets out a deep breath and tilts his head back for a second. His eyes find mine and he reaches his hand out to me. "I'm sorry," he whispers.

"It's not your fault, Logan."

"Yes it is," he says. He grabs my hand and rubs his thumb along my knuckles. "I'm the one who thought a Jays game would be a good idea because everyone would see us here. It didn't occur to me that they would put us on this kiss cam."

"It didn't occur to me, either." I shrug and look down at our hands. "Please don't feel bad. I'm feeling like this because of something *I* did, and *only* because of something I did. If you didn't kiss me back it would have been weird. You probably did a really good job of making it look real without, you know, turning it into anything."

"Okay," he says slowly, not sounding convinced.

"Please," I add, looking into his eyes. "Can we just forget about it and have fun for the rest of the day?"

"Sure," he says more confidently. "Do you want to go buy some Jays stuff?"

Logan buys me a jersey with one of the pitcher's names on the back, a hat, a water bottle, and a hoodie. I wear the hat and the jersey out of the store, and Logan wears his as well, and then we go get some food. It's crowded now, as the inning's ended, and we wait in line for food for what feels like forever. We take pictures with a few people while we wait, and only some of them freak out and scream. We finally head back to our seats with our bag of merch, giant cups of pop, and chicken fingers and poutine. We share the plum sauce for dipping our chicken fingers, and someone gets a home run, but I miss it because I'm taking a picture of my poutine for Instagram.

It's only 4:30 in the afternoon when we get out of the game, so we head next door to the CN Tower. There's a bit of a lineup inside, but we only end up waiting about twenty minutes, and then we pack ourselves into the elevator with ten other people.

"Hey you're the guy from that show!" someone says once the elevator doors close.

"What show?" Logan asks excitedly. "Where?"

"Oh, never mind."

Logan smirks and winks at me.

"I've never been to the CN when it's this empty before," I say as we walk along the windows, looking at Toronto below us.

Logan scrunches his eyebrows and looks around. "There are sort of a lot of people here."

"Have you never been up here before?" I ask.

"Yes. When there are less people than this."

"Well I've only been here when it's packed. Like. Packed. I find it weird that it isn't packed right now. It's a Saturday. In the summer."

"Maybe there's something else happening somewhere that's better than paying obscene amounts of money to look at Lake Ontario through a thick piece of glass."

I shove him in the shoulder and he laughs a little. "Let's go outside."

"Let's get dinner first," he says. "I feel like it's going to start to get busy for dinner, and I'm hungry."

We go to the regular restaurant, not the revolving one, because a, it's up another level and you need to pay more to get up there, and b, it's really expensive and fancy and we just want regular food. We get a good table next to the window though, and our drinks come with cute, plastic CN Tower stirrers. It does get busier as it gets closer to 6:00 and I'm glad Logan had the smart idea to eat before doing any more looking around.

"So, I have a question," I say, dipping my fry in some mayo.

"I might have an answer," Logan replies.

And this is a spot where we talk about Lost, *but I don't want to spoil anything in case you haven't seen it and are planning on it in the future. But just know that our CN Tower restaurant visit involves us bonding over* Lost *and excitedly agreeing with each other about a very controversial topic from the show. A lot of people are wrong about something, and we're both happy to find that we feel the same way about it as each other. Which is that we disagree. With the people who are wrong. They're very obviously wrong and we are correct and awesome.*

"Shall we go outside?" Logan asks when we've been done eating for a while.

"Yeah, let's go outside."

He grabs my hand and we walk together to the level with the balcony. As soon as we step outside, my stomach lurches and I feel like I'm going to fall over. I lean into him and put my opposite arm around him to grab onto his waist. We're basically hugging and I can't let go.

"Have you not been out here before? We're not even at the edge." He holds onto me too, but he's laughing as he does it.

"I have, and it never bothered me before. I don't know what's wrong." A gust of wind comes that makes it hard for me to breathe for a second or two, and my hat flies off. I squeal because it startles me and I want to grab it, but I feel like if I move, I'll fall over and somehow fall through the grate on the balcony and die. Logan pulls away from me and I squeal again, which is thoroughly embarrassing, but he comes back a few seconds later with my hat. He puts it on my head for me and I want to adjust it but I need to grab onto him again so I do that instead.

"I didn't know you were afraid of heights," he says.

"I didn't know I was either. I mean, they're not the best, but I didn't know this would happen to me. I want to walk around but I feel like I can't."

"What if we walked around like this?" he asks, meaning our practical hugging. "I promise I won't let you fall. But I mean, even if you did fall, you're not going to fall off the tower. You'll just fall to the floor of the balcony. Right here. That we're currently standing on."

"Shut up," I say, trying to joke. "I honestly have no idea what's going on. I don't think I can do it."

"When's the last time you came up the CN Tower?"

I shrug. "I don't know. In high school, maybe?"

"Well that was a long time ago. Your brain has changed since then. And it recognizes heights as something dangerous now."

"Sure, whatever you say. Let's go back in."

I keep holding on to him as we find our way back to the door and I feel better the second we walk through the threshold. I let out a deep breath and make my way to the glass floor. Maybe my brain will let me do that.

"Really?" he asks, as I stand in front of it.

"I can't come up the CN Tower and not stand on the glass floor. But you have to do it with me."

"But Isla, that'll be more weight in one spot. What if the glass breaks?"

"Oh don't even."

He chuckles and puts his arm around me and we stand at the end of the glass, looking down at the people below. I put my right foot in front of me and put it on the glass, and then take it back. I put my right foot on the glass again, and then quickly add my left foot. Logan follows.

"Okay we can't stay just on the edge here, though," he says.

"There are people in the way," I whisper, gesturing to the other guests in front of us, scattered throughout the glass floor.

"There aren't that many people," he says. He takes a step forward, forcing my shaky legs to follow. We just take a few steps so that we're not right on the edge, and then Logan takes out his phone. He holds it up above us so that you can see the glass below us and we both look up at the screen. He takes a few pictures and then we get off the glass and head for the exit.

I check my phone once we're on the train home and I'm surprised to see how many text messages I have. I have one from Claire and seven from my mom. That's weird. I open Claire's first since it's just one, and it says, There are already pictures of you and your guy online! This is so weird!

I shake my head with a smile and then reluctantly open the conversation with my mom.

Text one says Why didn't you tell me you were dating someone!? And why are there pictures of you on the internet!

Text two says Is this man a movie star?

Text thee: ISLA

Text four: YOU CANNOT DATE A MOVIE STAR YOU WILL NEVER HAVE ANY PRIVACY

PEOPLE WILL BE FOLLOWING YOU AROUND EVERYWHERE YOU GO AND NOW THERE ARE PICTURES OF YOU KISSING HIM AT A BASEBALL GAME

ISLA

Her lack of punctuation is really getting to me. She always texts with complete sentences. And there are never typos, probably because she proofreads them before she hits send. She must be really upset. All caps and no punctuation. This is new.

And text number seven: YOU NEED TO EXPLAIN YOUSELF AND TELL ME THAT YOU'RE OKAY

Oh boy. Explain youself. She wrote "youself".

"What's going on?" Logan whispers, leaning over my shoulder to see my phone. I lean away and turn my phone so he can't see the screen.

"My mom is freaking out."

"Does she not know about us?"

"Well she does now."

I type up a reply. I'm sorry I didn't tell you. I brought food from the restaurant to the movie set a few times and we kept running into each other. I swear I wasn't just trying to get with a famous guy or anything, and he's totally sweet. I promise. We're both okay, there are just pictures of us on the internet. It's not a big deal.

She replies almost immediately. We need to have a conversation about this.

Okay. Maybe we can have dinner this week. I'll bring Logan.

Fine.

"We're having dinner with my parents later this week," I say nonchalantly.

"Wow. We're at that step are we?"

"We're not at any steps, Logan, because we're not really dating," I say quietly.

"And do your parents know that?"

I take a second to answer. "No."

"Then they think we're at that step, and I have to impress them like we're actually at that step. So. We're at that step."

"Whatever you say, man."

Since I left my car downtown after work last night, Logan drives us from the train station to my car before going back to my apartment, and I smile at him before getting out of his rental.

"Meet you there," I say.

"Yeah, see you in a few."

It's just starting to get dark and the streets are fairly empty on the short drive to my apartment. It's calming, and I find myself smiling by the time I pull into my parking space. Logan is probably going to park down the road again so I wait in the vestibule of the building, looking out the window for him. I finally see him jogging around the corner and up the walkway so I open the door for him and he slips inside.

"I wanted to be fast," he says as we make our way up the stairs. "So no one would have time to spot me and then figure out where you live."

"Thanks."

He smiles at me and we head into my apartment. I don't even have time to take my shoes off before Logan starts talking.

"Okay, you have to elaborate on me giving you the heebie jeebies," he says. "It's been bothering me all day."

"Ugh I'm sorry," I say, slipping my shoes off and heading to the couch. "I didn't mean it in a bad way."

"Well it sounded bad." He joins me on the couch and puts his feet up on the coffee table. I sit sideways so I can face him without straining my neck.

"I just... I don't..." I close my eyes and take a deep breath. "This is weird to talk about. So. I don't know, I'm not, like, big on touching, and sex and stuff? Like, no, like, I like it, but with the right person. Like, the thought of having sex with someone I don't know, or even don't have strong feelings for already is not appealing to me. Like at all."

"So you're demi," he says easily.

"Um, I'm sorry, I'm what?"

"Demisexual."

"What's that?" I ask.

"What you just described. Someone who doesn't experience sexual attraction unless they have a strong emotional or romantic connection with the person."

"That's... a thing?"

"Of course it's a thing. You just described yourself as someone being that thing."

"But, like, so it's normal? I mean, I used to think that just nobody really experienced sex the same way, and that there wasn't a more popular way to be attracted to someone, but this year, just this year I found out how not common my feelings are towards sex, and how common it is for people to just … enjoy having sex with someone they've just met."

Logan smiles and takes his feet off the coffee table, curls them under himself and turns towards me so we're both sitting sideways on the couch, facing each other. "Of course it's normal. And it's also more common than you think, but you're right. Still not nearly as common as just being sexually attracted to someone because you think they're pretty."

"Are you demisexual?" I ask.

"No."

"Then why do you know so much about it?"

"I know a lot of people. I've learned a lot about the LGBTQ plus community since working on different movie sets and meeting different people."

"Well I'm not bi or gay or anything. I'm still straight. I still… like to have sex with men. And only men. Just not ones that I'm not in love with."

He shrugs. "I don't know, I think it counts the same way asexuals are a part of the community. Demisexual is on the asexsual spectrum, afterall."

"Well I don't know if I want to put a label on it or anything."

"It helps though, doesn't it?"

"I don't know," I say slowly. "It sort of makes me feel a little weird. Why can't it just be normal to tell someone that they're good looking but I'm not sexually attracted to them because I don't love them?"

"That is normal. Look, you don't have to call it anything. But if it helps you to understand, or helps other people to understand then maybe you can. But you don't have to. You can just tell the next guy who wants to date you that he's not allowed to kiss your neck until you're in love otherwise it will give you the heebie jeebies." I smile, and we're quiet for a minute before he continues. "I have a question, though."

"Okay."

"You said you didn't mind when I whispered into your hair."

"That's not a question," I say.

"Why doesn't that bug you, but it would bug you if I touched your thigh?"

"I don't know, the thigh thing seems more sexual and the whispering thing seems more friendly."

"But the whispering thing is really intimate, no?" he asks.

"Intimate but not sexual? I don't know. I don't know why I am the way I am, Logan."

He smirks. "Fair enough."

CHAPTER 16

I grab my laptop the next morning before going to the living room to see if Logan is awake (I tried to give him my bed, I swear, but he wouldn't let me sleep on the couch), and check my Etsy. And I almost scream. Why do I have so many orders? Almost all of my figurines have been sold. What is happening? I grab my phone and open Instagram to see that I have new notifications on my business page. Whoa. I have 74 thousand new followers. And there are comments and likes on basically all of my pictures! Especially on my *Neighbourly* set. How did people find me? Are the haters going to follow me over here too? I quickly look at some of the comments through squinted eyes, as if that'll make the mean ones less mean, but am surprised to only see good ones.

THIS IS GORGEOUS

CUUUUTE

I WANT

I JUST BOUGHT FIVE THINGS OMG

I smile, but then remember that I sold almost every figurine that I have, and start to panic again.

"Logan?" I call from my bed. "Logan!? What did you do?"

I hear his footsteps coming towards my room and then he opens my door with a ridiculous grin on his face.

"What did you do?" I ask again.

"Nothing! I just posted a picture of my new Hurley that I love so very, very much and tagged your page in it. I told people to go follow you and also that you had *Neighbourly* stuff." He shrugs like it's no big deal.

"But now I have to ship all these out and I have almost no stock left!"

"Isn't that what you wanted?" He scrunches his eyebrows in confusion. "You know that's the whole point of having a business where you sell things, right? The point is to sell them, and get rid of your stock. That's the best outcome really, is selling all your stock. Then you make more."

"I'm not going to have time, Logan! I've been making this for so long! It took me forever to build up this inventory!" I get out of bed and stomp to my closet so I can pull out one of my bins. "Now I have to go through all of these and find the ones people bought, package them, ship them out, and make more! When am I going to have time to make more like this again?"

"Well, first of all, I can help you with all the sorting and packaging and shipping, and maybe I can help you make a system for them for when you make more? So it's easy to find what you've sold? Also you could totally do custom orders, you know. You're popular enough now that you could do *only* custom orders, and you can charge a lot for custom orders."

"Well I'm so popular that I won't have time to keep up now."

"You would if you quit your job."

"I'm not-" I stop and look at him. He just smiles but I'm not sure what to feel. "I can't quit my job," I say quietly.

"Why not? How many figurines did you sell?"

I pause, for some reason caught off guard by the question, and then go back to my bed to check my Etsy on my laptop.

"Ummm... 234. But I only have like 250 of them!"

"I still don't know why you think this is a bad thing. So you sell them for 25 bucks right? That's almost 6000 dollars in one day, minus the supplies to make them, and minus the shipping."

"Shipping is extra," I add.

He smiles. "Well there you go. Plus if you sold them for fifty, like you should be, you'd have twice as much. You can totally quit your job and you obviously wouldn't need to sell that much every day. Even every month would be good. Can you make 234 figurines in a month?"

"No." I say. "But that's a lot of money for a month. I don't need to make that many sales in a month to make a living. I don't make nearly that much at the restaurant."

"So this is a good thing, no? Also hopefully your sales will slow down a little bit after the excitement of it is over, and it won't be so overwhelming to keep up with. But I don't mind helping you."

"Well you're only here for a week."

"I can come visit again, silly. And you can also visit me. You could come live with me!"

I feel my eyes bulge out and I almost take a step back, and Logan's expression immediately changes. The poor guy looks more horrified than I think I do.

"Wow, I didn't mean to say that," he says. "Of course you wouldn't come live with me. I seriously have no idea where that came from. I just meant like, since you don't have to work at the restaurant, and I don't mind helping you, and I live in LA, and since you don't technically have to live here if you don't have a job holding you here, you could live with me and I would always be there to help. But I don't- I'm just- Oh my god, please don't think I'm a freak. I don't know where that came from. You could also get your own place if you wanted to move to LA. But you also don't have to move to LA; you can obviously live here too. I don't know why I said that."

I can't help but smile. "You're ridiculous. Thanks for offering to help. I'm going to have a shower, and you should make us something to eat. And then we can sort all this figurine stuff out."

"Oh I should make us something to eat, should I?"

"Yes. That's what pretend boyfriends do. They make breakfast while their pretend girlfriend is in the shower."

I can't stop thinking about Logan while I'm in the shower. It's weird. Why would he say I could go live with him if he didn't want me to go live with him? I mean to be fair, he does get excited about little things often, and I guess it's also fair to say that it's normal for him to get carried away. It obviously didn't mean anything. He was just excited for me and my shop. I stop mid hair scrub when I realize I never told him what my Etsy store was, or what my business Instagram was. How did he find it? I turn the water off and am about to get out of the shower so I can put a towel on and go ask him, but then I remember I didn't finish washing my hair, or even do any other cleaning, so I turn the water back on, feeling stupid, and rinse out my shampoo. I quickly lather up everywhere else and make sure I'm clean and soap-free before I turn the water off again. I decide to actually put clothes on to confront Logan, and I throw my wet hair up into a messy bun.

"How did you –" I stop when I walk into the kitchen to see Logan setting the table with our breakfast. He made bacon and pancakes, and I think my celebrity crush on him just turned into a regular human crush. Except not really. I don't have a real crush on Logan. He turns around a little and smiles at me before taking a seat and putting his hand out and gestures for me to join him.

"Thanks," I say.

"No problem. Um, I made blueberry and chocolate chip." He points to one plate, with pancakes that have a blue tinge on the edges. "These ones are blueberry and the other pile is chocolate chip."

"You didn't have to go all out like this," I say.

He shrugs and smiles. "I'm just doing what any good pretend boyfriend would do."

Logan has a shower after we eat and I tidy up the kitchen a bit. I can't really wash the dishes while the shower's going, so I organize them so they don't look so messy in the sink and I wipe down the counter and table. And then I go over to Logan's Instagram to see the picture he posted. He said he tagged me, but I already had so many notifications by the time I woke up that I didn't even see it. He's holding the Hurley in his hand in front of his face, with a big goofy grin from ear to ear. I scroll to the right to see a better picture of it on its own, standing on my coffee table.

The caption says **Check out my Hugo Reyes I got from my amazing girlfriend! She made this out of clay! I love** *Lost* **so much, and I was so excited when I found out she had my favourite character. Now I have my favourite character made by my favourite person. Check her out! @claymatebyisla.**

Aww. I know he's not actually my boyfriend, and I'm not actually his favourite person, but it's still a nice post. It feels good to have someone brag about me. Logan gets out of the shower so I pocket my phone and start to fill up the sink but Logan comes into the kitchen before it's done.

"Etsy stuff?" he asks.

"I was just going to wash the dishes first," I reply.

"We can do that later. I'm excited to get this all organized." He actually hops on his toes a couple times.

"Okay."

The first thing that we have to do is get shipping supplies, because while I have some at home already, I most certainly don't have enough for 234 figurines. We go to the dollar store to get the bubble wrap and everything, and we try to be as inconspicuous as possible so no one recognizes Logan, which is mostly successful. Some people stare at us, and some people try to secretly take pictures of Logan on their phones, but otherwise we have no trouble. But as we're headed back to my apartment, Logan squeals and startles me.

"What?" I ask, half terrified.

"You guys have a laser tag place!?"

"Yeah," I say with a bit of a chuckle. "You wanna go this week?"

"Can we not go now?"

"I thought we were packing up my Etsy stuff now."

"But it's laser tag!"

I shake my head with a smile and turn left at the next intersection, making my way back up towards Laser Tag.

"I'm so excited! I haven't played laser tag in years!"

"I played a few months ago with work," I say.

"Nice."

I park the car and we walk into the building. It's got a small arcade as well, and there are a few people at the game stations who don't seem to care that new people have walked in. The girl working, Sadie, pales as soon as she sees us, though.

"Hi, Sadie," I say with a smile.

"Hi Isla." She looks from me to Logan, and back to me again. Back to Logan. It looks like she's trying so hard not to scream.

"Hi, I'm Logan," Logan says with a smile.

She just nods, clearly star struck and tongue tied.

"Is there anyone in the arena?" I ask.

"Hey, Sadie, do you want to get the birthday party started in the arena?" her Uncle Adam, the owner says, making his way behind the counter. "I tried but these kids like you better." He sees us and smiles, nods. "Oh hey, Isla."

"Hi," I say. I turn to Logan. "Sorry, they've got a birthday going on."

"Well I can go ask them if they want two more people to join," Adam suggests.

"I guarantee you they will be okay with Logan Jackson playing laser tag with them," Sadie says, hopping off her stool and basically sprinting around the corner towards the arena.

"Who's Logan Jackson?" Adam asks.

Logan just smiles and raises his hand.

Well. Laser tag ends up being fun.

That was sarcastic, in case you couldn't tell. First of all, the birthday party is for a thirteen-year-old girl, and is filled with screaming thirteen-year-old girls who can't stop screaming. It's just screaming on top of screaming as soon as we enter the room where everyone learns how the game works. Everyone in the party is wearing something white and they all have neon things in their hair and on their faces to make them extra glowey once the game starts. And none of them can stop screaming. Did I mention the screaming? Poor Sadie is trying to get everyone's attention, but can't, because of the screaming, until eventually Logan shouts over them and tells them they have to be quiet so they can learn the rules. And then the screaming stops, but the giggling starts. Now they can't stop giggling. I can tell that Sadie is nervous to be doing this speech in front of Logan, and the giggling girls don't help, I'm sure. But we finally get through that part, and find out that Logan and I have to be on different teams, otherwise we will make them uneven. So I don't even really get to play with him, which would normally be fine, but I don't know anyone else playing. And they're all star struck, screaming 13-year-olds!

"Can he be on my team!? I'm the birthday girl, he should be on my team!" the birthday girl screeches.

"Of course I can be on your team," Logan says, nudging her shoulder with a closed fist.

The birthday girl practically hangs off of Logan the entire time and only moves away from him to shoot me. And halfway through the game it seems no one even cares that we're playing teams. Everyone just wants to gang up on me and shoot me because I'm the reason Logan isn't single anymore. I'm the reason these teenage girls can't date the 31-year-old TV star. Makes sense.

Once the game is over, everyone takes pictures with Logan, and I take group photos of everyone with a few different people's phones.

Watching Logan interact with the girls is kind of endearing, because he's so sweet and patient with them, even though they're loud and screamy. He just talks to them like they're not damaging his eardrums, and treats them like friends. He asks them questions about school, and laughs with them, and hugs them, and it melts my heart. He's still excited about playing laser tag when we leave and head back to my apartment, so I try my best not to let on that I didn't have fun.

"You okay?" he asks once we get inside.

"Yeah," I say with a forced smile.

"Okay, you're just pretty quiet."

"It's nothing, it's stupid," I say. "I'm glad you had fun."

"You didn't have fun?"

"No, not really. We didn't even get to play on the same team and everyone was ganging up on me."

"Everyone wasn't ganging up on you," Logan says, frowning a little.

"Were you not there? They weren't even playing teams anymore. All the girls were screaming 'kill Logan Jackson's girlfriend!' and 'then I can be his girlfriend instead!' It was… not the best."

"I'm sorry. But you know they're just teenagers with a celebrity crush, right? They didn't *actually* want to kill you. I thought you were having fun."

"It's fine," I sigh. "I know they weren't being serious. It's just that a lot of people seem to hate me for taking you off the market or whatever, and it's sort of getting to me."

"Teenage girls who are too young for me anyway. I think they thought you were joking with them and having fun too."

I shrug. "Maybe. But it's starting to be a lot, especially after the Instagram thing."

Logan scrunches his eyebrows. "What Instagram thing?"

"Oh, nothing." Whoops, I didn't mean to say that.

"Doesn't sound like nothing, what Instagram thing?" He immediately pulls out his phone and I try to stop him but he turns around and lifts his phone up higher, out of reach.

"Logan, stop, I'm making a bigger deal out of this than it actually is."

"Nope, I don't think you are."

But then he finds it. Them. The comments on my pictures.

He looks up at me with one of the saddest expressions I've seen on him and he takes a step towards me. "Why didn't you tell me about this?" he asks quietly.

"I don't know," I say, shaking my head. "I didn't want you to feel like you were responsible, I guess. Or to feel bad, or think I can't handle it. Everyone gets hate online, I know that."

"It doesn't make it easy. You should block them."

"I was. I was blocking mean comments, but then I thought maybe I was being too sensitive."

"Isla…"

"It's fine. I know they're just saying that stuff to try to get me to feel bad or respond to them, but sometimes it still gets to me."

"Of course it does. People say mean things about me too."

"About you? People say mean things about you, Logan Jackson? I don't believe you."

"Okay fine." He touches a few things on his phone, scrolls a bit, and then clears his throat. **"You are dumb."**

"That's not that bad," I say.

"He's probably had surgery to look like that. Okay, sorry, that's a bad example. That one's obviously a compliment." He grins and looks at me over his phone for a second, but then goes back to his comments. **"You're show isn't funny.** This one doesn't count either because they spelled 'your' wrong. Okay here we go." He takes a deep breath before he reads the next comment. **"Kindly find a hole and die in it."**

My heart drops into my stomach. "People actually write that?" I ask.

He nods. "But these people are just looking for a reaction. They don't know me." He looks back down at his phone and smiles. "Oh, here's a good one. **Do people still like this guy? I thought we had all moved on. He's so overrated and he also looks like my grandma's butt."**

I can't help but laugh at that one. I cover my mouth with both my hands, but Logan is chuckling too.

"You know all the stupid shit people say about you isn't true, right?" he asks.

I take a deep breath and nod.

"It's not true," he repeats.

"I know," I say quietly.

"Do you, though?"

I don't reply, I just look at him for a second, and then down at the floor.

"Hey," he says gently.

I look back up at him.

"You know I heard the girls whispering to each other. They said they wished they were as cool as you."

"No they didn't," I say.

"Of course they did. I know it's hard to be your own biggest fan, I'm not always good at it either, but you have to try. Life is way more fun when you know how awesome you are. You're beautiful, okay? And I love that you're my pretend girlfriend."

I can't help but smile a little. "I like that you're my pretend boyfriend."

"Good. Now let's do this Etsy stuff."

Logan and I sit cross-legged on the living room floor with all my figurines piled between us. It's easier to find what we're looking for without them in their bins. I don't have a printer, so Logan writes down the customer information on different pieces of paper and when I find the figurines they ordered, we wrap the paper around them with an elastic. It only takes us a couple hours to get everything organized and another hour to get everything ready for shipping. I take a picture of all the packages, in a big, dramatic looking heap, (I organized it to look as big as possible) and post it to my business Instagram, with a caption that says, **I can't believe I'm getting ready to send out over 200 orders! I have to thank my amazing boyfriend @therealloganjackson for shouting out my shop with a picture of his Hugo Reyes, AKA Hurley, but I also have to thank all of you for supporting me and liking my stuff enough to want to buy it! Stay tuned for more exciting things from me!** And then I put a bunch of heart emojis. I'm a little nervous to post the picture, afraid that a bunch of the haters have followed me to this page, but I know I need to post something. So I just post it and try to think about the good comments I've already read. I take a deep breath and really look at the pile of packages. There are so many.

"Oh man, the people at the post office are going to hate me," I say with a groan. "I can't take this many packages at once."

"How about I take some to a different post office? We'll split it up into four batches, and ship them out on two separate days."

"Even that still sounds like a lot. But… Yeah. It's a good idea."

"Of course it is. I have excellent ideas." He grins and I reach over and shove him in the shoulder.

"You have ridiculous ideas," I correct.

"Oh, my mistake."

"How did you even find my Etsy page to begin with? And my Instagram?"

"Well your personal Instagram is following your business Instagram, and you're only following like 63 people, so it wasn't hard to find."

"Why were you looking at who I was following?" I ask.

"I was looking to see if you had an Instagram for your clay stuff, and most people follow their own accounts when they have multiples. I almost posted about it on my private Instagram by accident. Which I guess wouldn't have been a big deal, but I'm always afraid to tag people in it in case that makes it visible."

"You have a private Instagram account?" I ask.

"Yeah," he says with a bit of a sigh. "For my friends. And so I can post what I want, and you know, actually be able to read and respond to comments. It's nice when they're just from people I actually know, too."

"Can I follow you? What is it?"

"Um, it's EustaceScrubb," he says quietly.

"Wait, really? I remember when you followed me!" I grab my phone and open up Instagram. "It was right before you blew up my page so I got a notification for that on its own. That was you?"

"Yeah."

"Do you like *The Chronicles of Narnia*?" I ask, typing his name in the search bar.

"Yeah. I read them when I was a kid."

He comes up in the search and I request a follow. Logan takes his phone out and accepts it right away so I immediately start looking at his pictures.

"Just don't tag this account," he says.

"I won't. I understand why you have it."

"Okay."

"You post a lot on here," I say, scrolling past the thumbnails. "Way more than your famous one. Do you even post on it yourself?"

"Of course I do," he says, sort of defensively. "It's not always me replying to comments… But I have access to it too."

"So sometimes it's you replying to comments? And other times it's…?" I trail off, hoping he'll just answer by finishing my sentence.

"Sometimes it's my social media team. There are two other people who have access to it. They post on my Twitter too. But I'm always the one making the Instagram posts."

"Don't you feel weird about people pretending to be you?" I ask. "Like, people get so excited when you reply to them, or even like their comments, they would be so bummed if they found out it was some rando sitting in an office."

He shrugs. "I think most people know celebrity replies aren't actually from said celebrity."

I tighten my lips and deadpan at him and his shoulders slump a little.

"Okay, so *some* people know it's not the actual celebrity," he says, "but you can't expect me to be able to reply to comments myself. There are so many it's actually ridiculous."

"Well your social media team doesn't reply to that many anyway. How long can it take to just go to your Instagram and pick five random comments to reply to on each picture you post?"

"They reply to more than five, they just get buried with all the other comments so if you're not the person who got the reply, you can't see."

"Okay. Whatever. It sounds like I'm mad at you, but I'm not."

"Okay," he says with a bit of a chuckle.

"Hey, there's a picture of me here," I say, scrolling back to the top of his profile. I click on it to make it bigger. It's from the day I went to see him on set and the picture is taken from below the restaurant patio. You can see the wooden stairs leading up to the balcony and me with my chin in my hands, elbows resting on the table in front of me. The sky is a dark blue behind me, or really, beside me I guess, because it's my profile that you see in the picture, and I'm almost a silhouette. You can see a little bit of detail in my sweater and my face, but not much. There are white twinkle lights strung around the railing that are just blurry white blobs in the photo, but they're still really pretty and sort of serene looking. It's a very quiet picture. The whole atmosphere of it is pretty calming. "I didn't even know you took this." I go back to his main page and scroll through the thumbnails again, sort of feeling like he's letting me look through his desk drawers. There are pictures of him with friends, the cast of *Neighbourly*, at pubs, on the set, pictures of a beach, a boardwalk, a daisy, sunsets. It very much looks like the Instagram profile of a regular person just posting their life and not trying to stick to any kind of theme or structure. It's refreshing.

"Yeah," he says sheepishly. "Is that weird?"

"No." I smile at him and put my phone down. "Not weird."

CHAPTER 17

We're getting ready for dinner at my parents' and Logan is freaking out. I don't understand why he's so nervous. He acts in front of a live studio audience for a living, does interviews and red carpet appearances, and he's afraid to meet his fake girlfriend's parents?

"This is different," he says as we get into my car. "First of all, they don't know that you're my fake girlfriend. They think you're my real girlfriend, and that I'm your real boyfriend, and they're going to be worried about you. They're going to worry that I'm taking advantage of you -"

"How would you be taking advantage of me?" I ask, cutting him off.

"I thought we talked about this. It's the power thing."

"The power thing?" I ask.

"Yes, the power thing. From being famous. It's not appropriate for a famous person to date a non-famous person because there's a power dynamic. The non-famous person a lot of the time feels like they can't say no, even if they want to, because the famous person has a lot of power over them. They know a lot more people, everyone knows who they are… They also just sometimes will sleep with the famous person because they're star struck or whatever. I don't know, it's like someone dating their boss."

"Pretty sure lots of people are in relationships with their boss."

"Yes, of course, and there are a lot of famous people who are in relationships with people who aren't famous. But it's a tricky situation and you have to be careful."

"Are we not being careful? Plus we're not even dating!"

"I know but your parents think we are, and I don't want them to think that I'm only dating you because I know you'll sleep with me because of who I am!"

"Oooohh," I say slowly.

"Yeeesss," he replies. "Or that I'm making you feel like you have to sleep with me when you don't actually want to… because of who I am."

"I mean I understood it when you talked about it before, I swear I did, but I dunno, I just understand it more now." I glance at him quickly and then back at the road. "You just made it click easier just now."

"You're also not a nervous wreck around me anymore, so that probably helps your brain process what I'm telling you."

"Ha."

It's quiet for a minute before Logan starts talking. "Wait, you don't think it's inappropriate for someone to date their boss?"

"I never said that. I said that lots of people probably do."

"So you wouldn't say yes if your boss asked you out, right?"

"First of all, my boss is like 15 years older than me, and is in a happy, long term relationship, so no, I would not say yes. And second of all -"

"You know that it's okay to say no, right?"

"What?" I look over at him for a second. "What are you talking about? Of course I know that."

"I mean with me."

"Yes, Logan, I know that it's okay to say no to you."

"Okay, I'm just making sure."

"I mean, you did kind of pressure me to be your pretend girlfriend."

"What?" he says, sounding completely horrified. I glance at him quickly to see his face completely drop. "I did?"

"I said no to you like five times, Logan."

"I-" He cuts himself off and I can see him scrub his hand down his face out of the corner of my eye. "Jesus Christ, you're right," he whispers.

"So much for your famous-person-power speech," I say light heartedly.

"That wasn't even on my mind because we were friends! Like real friends, weren't we? We were just two regular people by that point, I didn't- I wasn't- oh my god. Oh my god, Isla, I didn't mean to pressure you. I mean, yes, okay, I did pester you, but I didn't mean to. I mean, I did, but I wasn't going to force you. I was," he lets out a deep breath. "I wasn't thinking. I wasn't asking you to sleep with me or kiss me or anything, I was literally asking you to play pretend, so it didn't occur to me that I was being inappropriate. And I know that's not an-"

"It's okay," I say, cutting him off with a smile. "You didn't actually."

"What? Why are you bringing this up, then!?"

"You're the one who brought it up! You said I was allowed to say no to you, so I thought I'd just let you know that you're a Peer Pressure Patty."

"A peer pressure what?"

"Patty. Someone who pressures their peers. I don't know, I just made it up. Like the Tommy Texters and Suzie Seat Kickers from the movie theatre pre-shows." I laugh a little. "I didn't say yes because I felt pressured to, I promise. Or because of your famous- person-power-dynamic thing. You're my friend, and yes, I also considered us real friends at that point, and I wanted to help you. I also, um, had my own reasons."

"Your own reasons?"

I shrug, but keep my eyes on the road. "I was getting a lot of hate when the rumours started about us and I thought it would go away if it became more official."

"Ouch. I guess that didn't work."

I chuckle a little. "It did not. But like I said, I also did it to help you, because you're my friend." I can tell he's about to say something but I keep going before he gets a chance. "I don't want you to feel bad, but you made me think of it so I thought I'd tell you. Just in case you find yourself in this situation again."

"Right, because as it turns out, it's actually common practice for me to befriend the caterer for my movies and then ask them to be my fake girlfriend." We both laugh, and Logan continues. "I'm sorry for being a Patty and I'll be more careful in the future. Peer pressure isn't cool," Logan says.

"Peer pressure *is* cool! That's what I learned in elementary school," I joke.

He laughs a little but quiets down pretty quickly. "Can I say something?" he asks.

"Of course."

"I'm glad you said yes."

I turn to him for a second and smile. "So am I."

My parents are both smiling at us like they're Stepford Wives. They've both met us in the doorway; they were here with the door open when I pulled into the driveway. It's weird walking up to the house with them staring at us, all giant fake smiles and wide eyes, just waiting for us to get closer. It's like they want to murder us and are doing a terrible job at trying to hide it.

"What's with the creepy smiles?" I ask.

"What?" my dad says. "We're not being creepy."

"You are, actually." I smile *normally* at them, and then grab Logan's t-shirt sleeve and tug him a little closer to me. "This is Logan."

"Hi," he says with a smile and a wave. Both of those non-creepy.

"Nice to meet you," my dad says, extending a hand towards him. They shake and I immediately push past everyone and into the house. Standing on the front step like this is weird.

"Would you like a tour?" my mom asks, still holding the Stepford Wife smile.

"Um, I don't need a tour. I mean, unless you were planning on giving one, and that would make you happy, then yes, I would love a tour." He turns to me and sort of cringes but I just shrug.

"We don't need a tour. Maybe I'll show him around after supper or something," I say.

"Okay. Well dinner's almost ready, but we can sit and have a drink first if you like," my mom suggests.

"Oh, also," I say to Logan, "You can call my parents by their first names. Patrick and Jenna. I know they didn't tell you their names when they met you, but that's probably just because they're nervous."

"Oh, we know all about that," Logan says. "This one was a mess when we first met. Just making no sense at all, and dropping food from her mouth."

My eyes widen and I feel my face getting hot. "You saw that?" I ask, horrified.

"That memory lives in my head rent-free, my friend." He smiles and winks at me.

"Um, excuse me," I say, stepping back and heading towards the washroom by the front door.

"Where are you going?" Logan asks.

"Oh I'll be passing away now. I just thought maybe you guys didn't want me to do it in front of you."

He grabs onto my arm and pulls me back towards him. "Hey come on, it was adorable."

"Remember what I said about using that word?" My face just keeps getting hotter and I can feel it creeping down my neck.

"Heeey," he whispers, stepping into me a little. "I'm sorry I mentioned it, I was just trying to keep the mood light. And make your parents not feel bad about being so nervous and creepy."

"Are you two okay over there?" My dad steps around the living room wall and into the hallway where we're still standing.

"Yes, sorry, I just need a minute," I tell him.

"Okay. As long as everything's fine."

"It is, I promise. We'll be right back." I head outside and Logan follows me to the front porch. I sit down on the first step and put my face in my hands. I feel Logan sit down beside me and I take a deep breath.

"What's going on?" he asks, lightly nudging my shoulder with his.

"I'm so fucking embarrassed, that's what's going on," I say with a little more anger that I intended.

"Why?"

"Because! Logan! Because!"

He snorts a little. "Okay, I understand now, thanks for clarifying the situation."

I get up and stomp down the stairs, down the driveway and onto the sidewalk. Logan chases me and grabs onto my wrist.

"Did I do something wrong?" he asks. "I don't understand what's happening."

I take a deep breath and shake my head. "I'm just so mortified."

"Because I saw food fall out of your mouth? Because way more embarrassing things have happened to people. And plus I'm so dreamy, I can see how it would be hard to keep your mouth closed around me, even while you're eating. It happens to the best of us."

"I am not… I'm not good at being… Like, I'm not good at boys. Men. Whatever. I'm not good at any of that."

"What?"

"I can't flirt, I don't even know when someone is flirting with me half the time, and I'm not cool, I'm not good at … pleasing anyone."

He scrunches his eyebrows at me. "What do you mean? Where is this coming from? Plus I'm sure you're great at all of those things, especially if you're with the right person."

"Thanks," I say quietly. "But I'm not. And I had a chance of a lifetime to deliver food to a movie set *and* eat with the cast and crew, which included my biggest celebrity crush, and I was just... A dork."

"You say that like it's a bad thing," he says with a smile.

"It's terrible. I made a fool of myself then, and when you came into the restaurant, like I'm just a bumbling mess around you and I hate it."

"You're not a bumbling mess around me anymore."

"Oh so you're not even going to try and make me feel better about it, okay, I see how it is."

"You want me to lie?" he asks. "Okay. You were the coolest girl I've ever seen. The way you talk so fast when you're nervous, I wish I could do that." I stare at him in horror but he keeps talking before I get a chance to say something. "Isla, you have to stop treating yourself this way. Who cares if you did something embarrassing while you were around someone super famous and super attractive?" The corner of his mouth curls while he says that last part. I've noticed he doesn't talk about himself being attractive unless he knows people assume he's using it as a joke. He always uses it in his humour, and I wonder if it's his way of dealing with his own insecurities.

"It's hard to be yourself when you're in a situation like that," he continues. "I never judged you, I still don't. Okay, so you weren't the smoothest person I've interacted with, but why should that matter? I'm a little worried when I talk to people who *are* smooth talkers around me, to be honest. They seem so... not human?"

I smile a little and he smiles back. "It's still embarrassing," I say.

"You're allowed to be embarrassed." He puts his hands in his jeans pockets and shrugs. "That's normal. But all of your interactions with me have been normal. I never once thought you were weird, or bad at... what did you call it? Bad at men?"

I snort at his last remark and he smiles and shrugs. "I just feel like I'm way more self-conscious than I've ever been," I say quietly. "Like, since breaking up with Tyler."

"Also normal."

"Okay. I'm sorry for just leaving like that."

"You have nothing to be sorry for. But I want to read you something before we go back in." Logan pulls his phone out of his jeans pocket and starts opening something on it.

"What are you doing?" I ask.

"Just listen." He smiles at me briefly and then looks back down at his phone. "She's so pretty. Hashtag jealous."

"Logan what are you-"

But he cuts me off and keeps reading whatever's on his phone. "I wish I had the courage to keep my freckles uncovered. You two are adorable. Hashtag couples goals. I love that Logan is with her. They both look so happy. Hi Isla! Can you two please be together forever? You two make me believe in love."

"What was that?" I finally ask.

"Comments on Instagram. There are a ton of really awesome comments about you, and about us. I know it's hard to focus on them when those assholes write what they do, but they're there."

"I don't know what that has to do with this."

"You're too hard on yourself, Isla. I just wanted you to know some of the nice things people are saying about you. I thought maybe if you knew how awesome you are, you wouldn't feel so embarrassed about the little things - *that don't matter,* by the way - or feel so self-conscious."

"Thanks," I half whisper.

"Of course. So you want to go back in now?"

I let out a deep breath. "No. But I guess we should."

"Should we hold hands or something?"

I smile at him and grab onto his hand, linking my fingers through his.

"Is everything okay?" my dad asks when we get back into the house.

"Yes," I say.

"We just needed to sort something out," Logan tries, and my mom smiles weakly at him. She thinks we had a fight and she already hates him. Great.

"We weren't fighting," I say.

"Okay." My mom smiles again and gestures towards the dining room. "Everything's on the table; let's eat."

"I swear," I say as we sit down around the table. It looks like my mom made meatloaf with roasted potatoes and asparagus. Which all looks and smells amazing. "I was having an issue of my own and Logan helped me around it. Because he's amazing."

My mom's smile seems more genuine this time. "Oh good."

"I'm sorry if we worried you," Logan steps in. "I just wanted to make sure she was okay."

"We appreciate that," my dad replies, putting some asparagus on his plate. When he's done he puts the dish back in the middle of the table and I grab it, putting some on my own plate.

"This all looks great," Logan says.

"My mom's meatloaf is amazing," I tell him. "Like, normally meatloaf is like, eh, whatever, but my mom's, it's the best. Like I swear I'm not being biased, it's so good."

Logan laughs and I notice my mom blushing.

"So can I ask an awkward question?" my dad says.

"No," I reply quickly.

He tilts his head at me and gives me a stern look so I put my hands up in surrender and let him ask his awkward question. "What are your intentions with my daughter?"

"Dad!"

"It's fine," Logan says, waving me off.

"No, it's not. We haven't even talked about this, we're not going to talk about it with you!" I half shout.

"I don't mean it like that," my dad tries. "I just worry that he's using his fame to his advantage."

"I assure you, sir, I'm not. I take this very seriously. I've also never dated someone who wasn't famous before, because I also have a fear that I would somehow be taking advantage. But it's different with Isla, first of all, because she wasn't just a fan, she had a job on set. That made her a part of the crew, and I always try my best to make all crew members feel important. Because they are. I find a lot of the more behind-the-scenes people feel overworked and underappreciated, especially by the actors. So I tried my best to make her feel comfortable, although I think I just freaked her out more than if I had left her alone." We all sort of chuckle at that, and I wonder if he's really good at improv or if this is actually what happened. "And by doing this," he continues, "I got to know her, sort of accidentally, I guess. She served me at Carter's a few times, and we kept running into each other outside. And if it makes you feel better, we were friends first."

"For how long?"

"I'm sorry?" Logan's face is pretty straight, but I can tell sitting beside him that he's nervous. We didn't make any sort of plan for this kind of conversation so we don't have a fake story lined up about how we actually started dating.

"How long were you two friends first before you started dating?"

"A few weeks," I say quickly. "We both went into our friendship thinking that was all it was going to be, thinking nothing of it, really, but it just grew. It was totally natural and no one was taking advantage. Can we please talk about something else now?"

My mom chuckles nervously and nods. "I hope you enjoy the meal."

It's quiet for a few minutes as we eat and I feel super awkward. I know it's normal for a few quiet moments during a dinner like this, especially when people just start eating, but it's making me feel so weird.

"I have a question, actually, that I can't believe I haven't asked yet," I blurt out.

"Yes?" Logan asks.

"Are you besties," I pause for a second and raise my eyebrows, "with Jennifer Lawrence?"

Logan laughs this weird, loud, short laugh and I can't tell if it's real or not. "We're not besties."

"Damn. Not even after she was in those three episodes of *Neighbourly*?"

"We're friends," he corrects. "I have her phone number. But we're definitely not besties."

"Oh my god," I say quickly. "Do you text her? Do you have her on Snapchat?"

"Okay, I don't even have *you* on Snapchat. You have Snapchat?"

"Everyone has Snapchat."

"What's Snapchat?" my mom asks.

"Something the kids do," my dad says.

"But they're not kids," my mom says, sounding worried.

"The younger generation. The techy generation."

"It's just a messaging app," Logan says. "You can send pictures and text and stuff."

The rest of dinner luckily goes smoothly and any time there's a stretch of silence, it doesn't feel weird. At least to me. We talk about where Logan went to high school, and how his parents live in Toronto and he visits as often as he can. We talk about how he likes working on a TV show and what it's like filming in front of a live studio audience, and then we talk about my Etsy store and how he made it sort of blow up. It feels pretty normal and by the time we leave at almost 10:00 I can say that I'm glad we came.

"Hey, you never gave me a tour," Logan says after we've been driving for a few minutes.

"Oh shoot," I say dryly.

"You didn't want to, did you?"

"Whatever do you mean? Why wouldn't I want Logan Jackson, star of *Neighbourly*, to see the house I grew up in? Nay, the *bedroom* in which I grew up? That's just absurd. Every self-respecting 29-year-old would be okay with their celebrity crush seeing their childhood bedroom."

"I was kind of excited to see it," he says with a shrug.

"Exactly why I didn't show you." I look at him for a second and smile.

CHAPTER 18

Logan and I are sitting on the couch after mailing out our first two batches of figurines, and I'm having a hard time believing I sold everything that I did. I mean, I know it was only because a famous person gave me a shout out, but he's not the one who made everyone make their purchases. He just let them know about me. No one would have bought anything if they didn't like them. People don't just buy things they don't want, right?

"Should I make my own website?" I ask.

"I thought you already had your own website." Logan raises an eyebrow at me.

"No, I have an Etsy store. But maybe I should make my own website instead, and people can order from there. It might work better. Plus it would seem more professional."

"I think that's an awesome idea. You have enough followers on your Instagram that you could announce your move on there, right?"

"Yes, definitely."

Logan and I spend the afternoon finding the right hosting company and emailing a web designer to set up my page so it doesn't look like a drag and drop site. I'm too antsy waiting for the proofs and can't sit still so we decide to go for a walk. I drive us to the same place we went before and I skip from the car to the paved trail, but this time I take us down around the condo so we can start our walk along the water. Logan laughs and runs after me.

"You're in a good mood," he says.

"Because I'm making a website!" I shout, still skipping and throwing my arms up in the air. "Oh my god!" I stop and turn around to face him because he's still behind me. A few boats rock in the water beside us, gently hitting the bumpers on their docks.

"What!"

"Should I still quit Carter's?"

"Do you want to quit Carter's?"

"Well I mean... Yeah. Working in a restaurant isn't my dream."

"Right."

"I should give them notice, though, right? I shouldn't just tell them I'm not coming back after vacation."

"I think we should go for a walk first," Logan says.

"Okay. Yeah, that's fair."

I check my Etsy when we get home and I have ten more sales. I also have a thousand more followers on Instagram. Which seems ridiculous to me.

"Time to write that resignation letter!" Logan says as he hops up and down on his toes.

"Yeah, really," I say. "Except."

His face scrunches a little. "Except?"

"What if people are just excited about this right now and it all blows over in a few weeks and I go back to getting one or two sales a month, or none for four months straight? And I've gone and quit my job? I should probably do both for a while. With the new website. Make sure it's still steady income."

"That's not a bad idea. But I think you're just scared."

"What? I mean, yeah, I'm scared that I won't have enough money to pay my rent. I'm not scared of something new, if that's what you're trying to say."

"Well, it was a little what I was trying to say."

"Obviously working evenings and weekends at a restaurant is not my ideal life choice. But I would also like to afford food, and somewhere to live. And like, I have student loans, and car payments, and I have to pay for hydro, and the internet, and Netflix, WHICH KEEPS GETTING MORE EXPENSIVE! I'm sorry I don't have the luxuries that you do."

He looks a little hurt and I almost apologize, but he starts talking before I get to. "That's not what I meant. I wasn't being super serious. I don't know, maybe sometimes I do forget what it's like to live paycheque to paycheque."

"Yeah," I say quietly. "Like, luckily my job allows me to have a little bit of extra money, like I can get a case of beer sometimes without worrying about my bank account too much, or I can get a birthday present for Claire or whatever, or go to Wonderland once or twice and get a funnel cake while I'm there, but if I want to save money I can have *no* fun. Ever. I can buy food, pay my bills, and sit on my ass. I'm not going to have anything saved for when I'm retired."

"Oh my god, we should go to Wonderland."

"Are you even listening to me?" I ask, getting annoyed.

"Yes. I'm sorry." He huffs and sits down on the couch. "I'm a douchebag, I'm sorry. I was just trying to …"

"To…?" I put my hands on my hips.

"I was trying to steer the topic onto happier things."

"You mean you don't want to have a conversation with me about how I'm poor compared to you?"

"I'm really sorry I said that; I just thought you were scared. You're completely right. If you don't feel comfortable quitting your job yet, then you shouldn't. I will support you with whatever decision you make."

"Thank you," I say quietly.

"But seriously, can we go to Wonderland tomorrow?"

"That depends. Will you go on Drop Zone with me?"

"Pretty sure it's called Drop Tower now."

"Yeah, I'm not calling it that."

Four separate groups of people have already stopped us to take pictures with Logan and we're still in the parking lot. How is this even possible? I don't even normally see that many people in the parking lot at once, and they all somehow found us like they've got some kind of radar on their phones. I take all the pictures for everyone with all their phones, but a couple people want selfies instead so I just step back and let them hang off my pretend boyfriend and get all close to him so they can both be in the shot. Of course. Selfies are great for that.

No one really seems to notice Logan once we're inside the park, probably because there are so many people and he doesn't seem to stand out or be as noticeable. He's also put on a hat and sunglasses, which I have no idea why he wasn't wearing them earlier, so that helps just a little bit. You have to be pretty close to know it's him, I guess. We take a selfie together in front of the fountain, trying really hard to get the mountain in the background.

"No, you have to hold the phone lower," I say.

"That's a terrible angle for us, though. I don't want a chin shot." He tries to just hold the phone higher without tilting it down but it's just our heads sticking out of the bottom of the picture.

"That's a ridiculous picture," I laugh.

"Okay fine, we don't have to see the top of the mountain in the picture, let's just take a good one of us." I lean my head into his chest as he wraps his arm around me, and I'm all tucked in all cute-like and we look adorable. We both smile at the camera as he takes approximately 37 pictures. "Now one on the bridge?" he asks.

"Let's go on Dragon Fire first," I say.

"You don't want to start with something small and work our way up? That one has loops."

"Are you afraid of the loops, Logan?"

"No." But I can tell he is.

"Yeah, we're going on one with loops."

"You're such a Peer Pressure Patty," he whines.

I wink at him, and he smiles and follows me into the medieval section. We stop in front of Riptide for a few minutes to watch people spinning around and getting soaked, and then we make our way to Dragon Fire. The lineup is super short and we weave through the gates and up the ramp until we get to the top and the lines for each separate train car.

"Front?" Logan asks me.

"No way, the back is so much better on this one," I reply as I go to the line for the last car.

"Really?"

"Yeah, because the hill drops right away, it doesn't feel like a real drop if you sit in the front."

"I'm not following."

"See how the first drop is right after the lift hill? It doesn't round a corner or anything first, so the back of the train is still going up as the front is starting to go down. You don't get the full effect of the drop if you're in the front."

"You're ridiculous."

"No, I'm smart."

"That too."

There are only two people in front of us for this car, so we basically don't have to wait at all. Once they get on their train and head off, our train pulls up and a worker ushers us forward. We step across the seats to put our bags in the cubbies and then get back on, Logan sitting on my left, possibly so people waiting in line can't see him, possibly because that's just how it worked out without him thinking about it. I pull my chest harness down and look at Logan who is still sitting with his up in the air.

"Are you okay?" I ask.

"I'm fine. I just haven't been on a rollercoaster in a very long time and I'm more nervous about this than I thought I would be."

"Do you want to get off? We can go on the Ghoster Coaster first if you want."

He shakes his head and pulls the harness down. "No, it's fine, I don't need to start with a kiddie coaster. I just have to do it."

"That's right you do!"

An employee comes by to make sure our harnesses are stuck down, which I always hate because it pulls it up a bit and I feel less safe. I push mine back down again and smile over at Logan.

"This'll be fun," I say.

"I hope so."

"It will. I promise."

The person in the booth practically chews on the microphone as she does her required announcement and all I can understand is "and enjoy the riiiiide" at the end as the train starts to move forward. I immediately get butterflies in my stomach and my fingertips and I let out a deep breath as we turn the corner and start to go up the hill.

"What was that deep breath for?" Logan asks. "I thought you weren't scared. I thought you were excited to sit in the back so the drop feels more like a drop?"

I watch the rest of the cars in front of us climb the hill and then I look out across the parking lot as we get higher and higher. "I am excited," I say. "But the being nervous part of it is half the fun, isn't it?"

"No. I don't like doing things that make me nervous."

"You're the one who wanted to come to Wonderland, Mister," I say.

"You're the one who wanted to go on the big ride first!"

"Have you been to Wonderland in the last 15 years? It's definitely one of the smallest roller coasters now besides the ones in the kiddie park."

He huffs beside me and I laugh a little. "I just thought it was interesting that you were trying to make fun of me for being scared of this ride and now-"

There's the drop.

I can almost hear his breath catch as we plummet to the bottom of the hill but as we start going back up and into the loop he goes back into his little speech.

"Now you're the one who's scared of the ride with the loops!" he yells. "You can't make fun of someone for-"

"I can't hear you over all the fun I'm having!" I shout back.

"Well guess what! I'm having fun too!"

"That's good!"

"Yeah! It is good!"

"I know!"

"Oh shut up!"

I know he's just kidding around, and I throw my arms up as we head into the corkscrew, letting out a long "wooooo" until we come out the other side.

"Whoa, that was dizzy," Logan says.

"But fun, right!?"

He doesn't answer and we go through the helix and then come to a fairly abrupt halt at the end.

"Fun," I say.

"Dizzy."

"Little bit."

Logan laughs and holds out a fist to me so I bump it with my fist. "Let's go on a smaller ride now," he says.

We go on The Fly next, which has a bit of a lineup and we take pictures and have to deal with screaming girls most of the time. It's not great, but I guess it comes with fake dating a famous person. The people sitting behind us in our little four-person fly cart are two teenage girls who can't stop giggling.

"I can't believe we're going to have a roller coaster picture with Logan Jackson," one of them says.

"I could reach forward and touch him," the other says.

"But you shouldn't," Logan monotones without turning his head around to look at them. They both gasp a little and then he turns back to smile at them. "It's not safe," he adds.

"Can I touch you now? We're just going up the hill."

"No, wait till after."

The girls both squeal and scream and then we're going down the hill and I scream too, and all four of us are screaming as the ride makes its twists and turns, and makes our stomachs drop as it swoops us and dips us. The girls giggle behind us and then scream again, and it makes me laugh too. By the time we get to the end, all four of us are out of breath and half crying from laughing so hard. As we wait to pull up, I see the girl behind Logan lean forward out of the corner of my eye and touch his shoulder. She just touches it, like she wants to see what a sweater feels like as she's passing it in a store. I turn around and see her sit back in her seat really quickly like she's embarrassed.

Logan just shrugs at me. "I did tell her she could touch me when the ride was over."

"It's true, you did say that, that's the only reason I did it," the girl says, her voice catching with obvious nerves every few words.

Once we can get out of our little fly cart, the girls run to get their bags and then scoot back over to us and smile and sort of hop from side to side but don't say anything.

"Do you ladies want a picture?" he asks them.

"Oh my god, that would be amazing!"

I take their phones and snap a few pictures of them as they squeeze in close to him, sandwiching him in between them. A few people are calling Logan's name from the line and the carts waiting to take off as we get pictures, but we ignore them, which seems rude, but I guess is also kind of normal to do?

"Can you take a video of us too with my phone?" the girl who touched him on the ride asks.

"Sure." I switch it to video and tell her it's recording and she smiles, waves, Logan waves too, and then she kisses him on the cheek and runs back over to me, snatches her phone from me and runs off with her friend, screaming and giggling.

"That was … fun," I say.

"It was," he replies. "Let's go look at our picture from the ride!"

The girls are at the picture booth when we get there, and they're screaming and jumping up and down with the guy from behind the counter.

"So we can like, get this picture put on a mug and all that?" one of them says.

"Oh yes, let's get a picture of you and I with two teenage girls put on a mug," Logan jokes, loud enough for them to hear.

"Oh my god!" they both scream, their elbows on the counter in front of them.

"Did you guys already buy photo passes for the day?" he asks them.

"No," they reply in unison.

"I'll buy them both a photo pass," he tells the guy behind the counter. "And I'll get one too, obviously with our pictures on them."

"Awesome." He scans three lanyards and the computer screen to put our pictures on them, and hands them to Logan and the two girls.

"Thank you! You're the best!" the girls say. They start to turn away but Logan calls after them.

"Wait!" he shouts.

They stop and turn back, smiles spread across their faces so big their cheeks must hurt.

"Can I get a hug before you leave? I might miss you guys."

Their eyes bulge with surprise and they run back over to him, both hugging him at the same time. He puts his arms around them both and then they run away.

"They were cute," he says to me. Then he turns back to the guy behind the counter. "Sorry, I'll pay with Visa."

A new group of people emerge from the ride before we get a chance to leave and Logan has to do a photo op with them before we can make our way to a new ride. It only takes about five minutes and then we're off on more Wonderland adventures.

We decide to go to White Water Canyon since it's getting hot out but it's still fairly early. This ride can have a two to three hour wait sometimes, so we head over to see how busy it is.

"I'm hoping since it's the middle of the week, there won't be many people," he says as we make our way through the park.

"Same. It hasn't been super busy so far, so hopefully there isn't much of a lineup."

We only have to wait in line for about twenty minutes, and when we get to the spinning platform I almost fall three times, which Logan finds hilarious. He grabs onto my arm gently and guides me to our raft and I try to laugh so I don't die of embarrassment. We get in and are followed by a group of three friends, two guys and a girl, and they all sort of look at us funny as they get in. Like they recognize Logan but are afraid to ask if it's him. We both say hi to them as they get strapped in and they mumble their 'hey's back to us and then lean in as close as they can to each other and start whispering.

"I hope we go under the waterfall," Logan says to me.

"I don't," I reply. "I didn't bring a change of clothes."

"Well that wasn't very smart of you, was it?"

"I suppose not. I brought a towel, though! And I'm wearing my bathing suit under my clothes."

"Oh yes, because wearing your bathing suit *under* your clothes when you go on a water ride will keep you dry and comfortable."

The group of friends in the raft with us keep smirking at us as we bicker but continue not to say anything about if they recognize Logan. The girl screams every time water splashes us and her two guy friends laugh at her, but then one of them gets half soaked by a geyser and he squeals unexpectedly. The rest of us all laugh and he shrugs, as if to say "I guess I deserved that". We're getting closer to the waterfall and I lean into Logan as if that will help me not get wet if we go under it, and he shoves me away, laughing.

"Oh no, you don't get to use me as an umbrella!" he says. "If we get wet, we're getting wet together!"

"That's why I was getting closer to you!" I try.

"Oh no," he says, shaking his head. "I know what you were doing! And that was not it!"

It looks like our raft companions are going to go under the waterfall and they all hunch their shoulders and brace for the cold stream to pound over them, but at the last second the raft spins and Logan and I get all of it. I squeal and scream a little and clench my fists, Logan laughs, and everyone else laughs and goes "ooooh!"

Logan helps me out of the raft at the end and keeps me steady. I have no idea how the corkscrew on Dragon Fire made him dizzy, but how he can just step off of a raft and onto a spinning platform without even stumbling, but whatever. The group of friends we shared a raft with grab their bags and then shout "Bye Cory Milligan!" to Logan as we head to the exit. He sticks his arm in the air and waves at the same time that he puts his other arm around me.

Once we get out of the exit walkway, there are a bunch of people with cameras waiting for us. People must have tweeted or something about where we were. Logan pulls me close to him and he nods at them but then continues to ignore them as we walk away and they follow us around. People see the camera crew and immediately run towards us, hoping it's because there's a famous person, and then of course there is, it's Logan, and we have to stop so he can take selfies with them all. It's getting kind of annoying, but Logan doesn't seem to mind, so I don't say anything. The camera crew end up keeping a distance, maybe to get better shots of us walking the park together, I don't know. Logan does such a good job of acting like they're not there; you'd think he does this for a living. Ha. (Insert nervous laughing emoji.)

"I have an idea," he whispers to me as he grabs my hand and pulls me into him.

"What?"

"It'll look super sweet for the cameras, but I think it'll still just feel friendly for you."

"Look at you looking out for my feelings," I say quietly.

"Of course. So, you said you brought a towel?"

"Yeah."

"Okay, here," he says as he pulls me to the side of the path so we're not in anyone's way. He starts to pull my backpack off, and I help him and then hand it to him. The straps and back of it are all wet from being against my soaking shirt. He puts it on the ground between us and bends over to unzip it, and pulls out my red towel with big black watermelon seeds all over it.

"Come closer." He holds the towel open in front of me and I step into him, dragging my bag with my feet so it stays between us. Logan wraps the towel around my shoulders and rubs it over my arms and shoulders a bunch of times. "Do you want to take your shirt off?"

"Not really…" I say slowly.

"Okay, that's fine. I just have a question."

"Yes?"

"What were you planning on doing when you decided to only wear your bathing suit under your clothes?"

"Well I was going to wear just my bathing suit if we went to the water park."

"Okay. I was just thinking, if I took your shirt off -"

"If *you* took it off?" I interrupt.

"Yeah. It would look so sexy. And you can walk around with the towel around you and I'll wear your shirt on my back so it dries."

"You think about this stuff too much, Logan. I'll keep my shirt on and wear the towel. You can carry my bag. How 'bout that?"

"Fair enough." He kisses my forehead and then picks up my backpack, keeping it on one shoulder and hanging on to the strap since he has his own bag on his back too.

"So, Drop Zone, then?" I ask.

"Drop Tower," he corrects. "You have to respect the name changes!"

"Ugh, you're right."

"Okay, let's go." He smiles and grabs onto my hand and together we step back into the middle of the path and make our way through the crowds, who right now, don't seem to recognize us.

"Logan Jackson! Logan! Logan!" Everyone from the line is calling out for Logan as we sit in our seats and wait to be brought to the top of the tower. And of course we're sitting in the seats that are facing the line, so we just get to stare at the groups of people screaming at us and taking pictures of us with their phones. He smiled and waved when we first sat down, but now he's got his head turned towards me and he's looking at me over his chest harness.

"Are you nervous?" he asks. "I do recall a certain someone being afraid of heights while we were in the CN Tower."

"That's different. I was walking free and could just fall. Here I'm sitting in a chair that I'm strapped into. It's not the same."

"Okay," he says with a skeptical head tilt.

And it seems everyone is strapped in safely because we start to rise. I swing my legs back and forth beneath me and look out at the park expanding in front of us as we go higher. We rise above The Bat (which looks like it got painted a different colour!?), and then I can see the mountain, and then we're above the mountain and still going up, and The Bat is a different colour?

"Why is The Bat a different colour?" I ask, trying to ignore the tingles in my toes as we climb even higher. Oh no, I can feel a weird sensation in my throat, and my balance feels weird even though I'm sitting down and I'm strapped into my chair.

"Oh yeah, it is a different colour!" Logan says back to me.

We finally stop at the top and I swing my legs back and forth a few times when I realize I don't even remember what colour it used to be.

"What colour did-" But then our chairs let go and my sentence is cut off by half a second of not being able to breathe as my stomach shoots up into my chest, followed by a short, high pitched scream. My legs push up and my knees straighten out just a bit as we fall, and just as soon as we started, our descent slows and we gently come back to the bottom.

"Woo!" Logan squeals. "Let's do it again!"

"We should come back on when it's dark and all the rides are lit up," I suggest.

"Oh yes, that's an excellent idea. We should make it the last thing we do before we leave."

"Okay, sounds like a plan."

We get out of our seats, grab our bags, and wave to all the people shouting at Logan as we make our way through the exit. Logan puts my towel around my neck and kisses my temple, and I lean into his lips a little as he does it. He lingers a bit, and then puts his arm around me and we make our way to the booth with our photos so we can get them scanned onto Logan's photo pass.

We get pizza and pop from Pizza Pizza, which is ridiculously expensive, but Logan's basically just swimming in money so he of course pays for it. A table of people talk to us without getting up to come closer as we eat, and Logan is super polite to them. They finally realize that I've just been eating my pizza in silence as they talk him up, and look embarrassed.

"We're so sorry," they say, "we'll let you enjoy your lunch."

"Thanks guys, we appreciate it," Logan says with a smile. "But it was nice chatting."

"Yeah." They nod and talk amongst themselves, and we stay long after they leave so we can try to have a bit of quiet.

We spend most of the afternoon in the water park, going on as many waterslides as we can, and spend as long as humanly possible in the Lazy River. It's really annoying putting my clothes back on when we're ready to go back to the rest of the park, because they're still damp, but at least they aren't soaked anymore. We share a funnel cake with strawberries, vanilla ice cream, and whipped cream, and then we peruse the gift shops along each side of the fountain. We pick up almost every stuffed Snoopy and ride themed mug, look through all the keychains, and sift through the hoodies and t-shirts. Logan buys me a Snoopy stuffy wearing a Canada's Wonderland sweater, and a Drop Tower keychain which I immediately put on the main zipper of my backpack. We go into the candy stores and come out with bags of gummies, chocolates, rock candies, and lollipops, and then we head back over the rides to get a few more thrills while the sun is still up. We go on Time Warp, which I'm only saying because Logan practically yelled at me when I called it Tomb Raider, and then we go on Back Lot Stunt Coaster, *not* The Italian Job. We decide to pass on Top Gun, or sorry, Flight Deck, because that ride has gotten far too rough over the years, and then try The Bat, which I'm surprised we didn't do after The Fly, since it's like, right there. We hit up Mine Buster, which I think is one of the best roller coasters, but Logan complains the whole time about how rickety it is and how much it hurts his back. We get some Tiny Tom donuts as twilight sets in and take the paper bags of deep fried deliciousness with us as we walk back to the front of the park to look at the lights on the mountain, in the fountain, and on the rides that we pass by. We sit thigh to thigh on one of the benches and finish off our donuts with cinnamon and icing sugar, lick our fingers (our own, not each other's), and then head back over to Drop Tower so we can look at the lit up park from above.

It's so gorgeous. As we rise, I can't help but hold my breath, looking out across the park as everything spins and flashes with different coloured lights. The sound of distant laughter and screams of joy fills my heart with happiness and I try to take in the moment as we come to a stop at the very top. I want to freeze this moment, live in it forever. I look around at the glowing world below us, this city of magic that can make real life seem so distant, even if just for a day. Even if just for three and a half seconds before we're dropped back down to reality. The air comes up beneath us as we race to the bottom and the wind in my hair makes me smile. I'm so glad we could do this. Even though we didn't really get the whole day to ourselves, we still got a lot of it, and most people respected our space.

I lean into Logan as we make our way out of the park, but then pull back and straighten up when I realize I wasn't doing it for show. I was doing it because it was comfortable.

"Are you okay?" he asks me as we walk through the parking lot.

"Yeah." I smile weakly at him. "I'm just tired."

"Me too. I can drive if you want."
My smile brightens at that. "Okay."
"I had a good day with you," he says.
"Me too. It was the best."

CHAPTER 19

HOW ARE YOU TWO SO CUTE WHEN YOU'RE NOT ACTUALLY DATING!? Claire texts me the next morning.

She sends me screenshots of articles on Facebook, Twitter, and Buzzfeed with pictures of me and Logan at Wonderland. There's a picture of us on Drop Tower and the headline says **LOGAN JACKSON CAUGHT CATCHING THRILLS WITH NEW GIRLFRIEND**. There's one with a picture of Logan putting my towel around me with the headline reading **LOGAN JACKSON THE GENTLEMAN.** There's one from Buzzfeed with a picture of me taking pictures for Logan and his fans, with a headline that reads **LOGAN JACKSON PAYS FOR FANS' SOUVENIERS** which I find weird because the people in the picture with us aren't even the girls from The Fly, but whatever.

I don't know I finally text back to her. We've gotten pretty close, and I guess also comfortable with each other.

Sure. Comfortable. She sends a winking emoji along with her text and I roll my eyes.

For real. I told you I'm not ready to get into a new relationship with anyone.

Yes, but that was before Logan Jackson started falling in love with you.

He's not falling in love with me I reply.

Whatever helps you sleep at night, miss. Did you even see his Instastories?

his Instastories? I ask.

Yeah, from Wonderland. He posted like 10 of them, all of you smiling and looking at him at all adorable-like. He tagged you in them.

I don't check my Instagram notifications anymore.

Fair. Anyway, when are you coming back to work?

Sunday.

Excellent I'm working Sunday too. Are you working lunch or dinner?

Dinner.

See you then.

I go to Logan's Instagram and play through his stories before getting out of bed, and I'm a little embarrassed to say that I watch them through a few times. He sounds so genuine in them, and watching me in the videos, not paying attention to him recording me, makes me feel sort of beautiful. There's a story of me holding his hand and dragging him along the path, of me saying something to him about a ride while we wait in line, and then realizing he's recording me when I turn to look at him.

"Why are you recording everything I do?" I ask him in the video.

"Because I never want to forget you when I'm old."

I smile and also roll my eyes at him.

I know the Instastories and the things he says in them are just for show, but it's nice to pretend for a few minutes that someone loves me like that.

I get an email notification on my phone from the site designer so I put my phone down and run to get my laptop.

"Aaahh I think I have a site layout!" I shout in excitement.

"Aaahh," Logan copies. He meets me on the couch and I open my laptop and go to my email so I can see what he sent me.

Oh my goodness, it's beautiful. It's clean and smooth looking, with a beautiful header in script font that's pretty but not hard to read, with boxy buttons across the middle of the screen to take the visitor to whichever part of the site they want to go to. The text inside each button is a very dark purple, in a sans-serif, all cap font, which I love. The buttons say: Shop, My Story, FAQ, and Shipping. When you click on the Shop button, it takes you to a new page with more buttons across the top of the screen, which say: Search, Super Heroes, TV Shows, Cartoons, Animals, and Custom Order.

"This is so nice looking," Logan says, leaning into me a bit so he can see the screen.

"Right? I'm in love with it."

"Did he make an interface for you, like for when people place orders?"

"I think so!"

I go back to the email and click on the next link he provided me, which shows me what my dashboard looks like. His email also says that we can have a Skype call to go over how it works, and for me to give him any other information he needs to add to the site. He recommends that I hire a photographer to take photos of all my figurines, and he can show me how to insert the photos when I make new ones.

"This is so cool," I say, looking over what the custom order form looks like.

"It's very cool. I'm really excited for you."

I hop on my Instagram and post to my business page, just posting a picture of a corner of one of the buttons on the site, with the caption saying **exciting things are coming soon!**

My comments section is almost immediately flooded with people saying they can't wait to get their orders and how they are already excited to order more. People are asking if I do certain characters, if I'll do custom orders, if I can make multiples of the same one, you name it. I might be able to quit the restaurant after all. But I'm still going to hold off on that and play it safe for a while.

"So when are you going to come visit me?" Logan asks.

"What do you mean?"

"You're going to fly out to LA right? What about when we start filming *Neighbourly* again? You can come watch."

"Oh. Yeah, that would be fun, actually."

"Of course it would."

"Can Claire come?"

"If she wants. Sure."

"Would that be weird? Or ruin our fake relationship?"

"No, I don't think so."

"Okay, I'll ask her about it at work on Sunday."

My phone goes off and I check it to see that Tyler texted me, which makes me a little flustered because it's only when I open his message that I realize I never replied to his last text, when Logan first came for his visit. I hate people who don't respond like that, and it's not like he was being rude or trying to get anything from me, it seemed like he was just being friendly, and I just stopped responding to him.

His text today says, Congrats on all your Etsy sales. It blew up pretty big this week and a lot of people are talking about it on the internet.

Thanks! I text back. I'm pretty excited about it, but it's also overwhelming. Also it's only because Logan shared it on his Instagram.

I'm sure it would have picked up on its own. Your stuff is amazing. A lot of people are saying that they like them better than Funko Pops.

That's ridiculous I reply. I could never compete with Funko Pops.

No. If you could, they wouldn't have the same quality anymore. They also wouldn't be handmade in order to keep up. But for some people to prefer them over a big brand like that is super cool. Plus you know you'll have repeat customers which is also awesome.

"Texting your other boyfriend?" Logan asks me, trying to peek at my phone.

"Well."

"Is that your ex?"

"Yeah," I say quietly, kind of digging my neck into my shoulders.

"Why do you seem ashamed?"

"I don't know… Because… You're my pretend boyfriend?"

"Even if I was your real boyfriend I would hope that you can talk to your ex without feeling like I'm going to be jealous or bite your head off because of it. He was your family for 8 years, was he not?"

"Yeah," I say slowly.

"And he wasn't a dick to you?"

I shrug. "Well. I mean."

"Wait, he was a dick to you?"

"Well he wasn't really a *dick*, but he was very… I didn't feel loved for the last several months of our relationship, let's put it that way."

"Really?" He actually sounds hurt, like he genuinely feels bad that I had to feel that way.

"Yeah. But it's okay. It's over now and I'm okay." I'm pretty sure you can hear the uncertainty in my voice.

"Well, that's good, I guess." I can definitely hear the uncertainty in his.

I shrug again and look back at my phone. Tyler texted me again. Do you have enough inventory for the festival in August?

My eyes widen and I almost choke. Oh my god. I completely forgot. How could I forget? I set up a table at the Tug Boat Festival every year, and Tom always jokingly gets mad at me for needing it off since the restaurant is always so busy that weekend, only I'm pretty sure he's actually mad at me for real, he's just too nice. With everything that's been going on I guess I just gapped on it.

"What's wrong?" Logan asks.

"I have a festival in August."

"You have a festival?"

"Well a festival that I go to. At the dock; there's a bunch of tug boats, and there's a contest, and there's vendors and a little carnival, and I always set up a table to sell my figurines and I completely forgot about it! How am I going to fulfill orders *and* make more inventory to sell at the show?"

"Do you usually sell a lot?"

"Yes, I usually use the money from it to get work done on my car or put a lump payment on my student loans or something."

"That's really smart."

"Yeah. Anyway it's always a great day, sales-wise, and fun too, but I have almost no pieces left! And a bunch more people want to buy more! What do I do!?"

"Why don't you close your shop for now? Say that you're making a brand new website, and you need to build your inventory back up. People will understand."

"What if they don't want to wait?" I ask, fighting back tears.

"Hey, don't cry, this is a good problem," he says gently. "You can do this."

"No I can't."

"Why do you think you can't do it?"

"Because I go back to work on Sunday and I'm not going to have time!"

"So quit."

"I can't just quit, Logan!"

"Okay. That's fine. You don't have to quit if that makes you nervous. But I don't want you to be worried or stressed about this if you don't have to be. When in August is the festival?"

"It's the August long weekend… So… the first week."

"Oh boy. Okay. Is there anything I can do to help? Do you only sell figurines at the tug boat thing?"

"I also make magnets. Canadian flags, Georgian Bay, Ontario with location pins, that sort of thing."

"Oh cool. If you need to make some of those, I can help by putting the magnets on them? I can get signage and business cards made for you. Do you need a tent? I can go get you a tent."

I let out a deep breath. "I have all that stuff. But." He raises an eyebrow, so I continue. "You might be right about closing my shop for a bit. Will you help me write a notice?"

ClayMate is temporarily closed in order to build my inventory back up! I'm so humbled by the response my little store has gotten recently, and all of your orders, messages, and kind words have warmed my heart. I am currently constructing a beautiful website for future orders instead of using Etsy, and believe me when I say I will be shouting from the rooftops when it's up and running! But if you are afraid of missing the launch, you can head over to the site now to sign up for my mailing list, and I'll notify

you when it's ready for browsing and ordering. Thank you all so much for your support and excitement, and I'll see you soon.

    <3 Isla

CHAPTER 20

Logan drove himself to the airport this morning and I'm currently getting ready for work, feeling weird about absolutely everything. I'm not sure why I feel weird, or what I feel weird about, but I feel weird. I feel like there's something stuck in my throat, like my stomach is empty, and like I'm too distracted to focus on anything.

I order more clay and supplies to be shipped to my apartment, and then I just pace around the living room, not sure what to do with myself. Is Tom going to ask about my store? He knows I don't want to work at the restaurant forever, but I don't think either of us really thought that my clay stuff would take off enough for me to leave. We always thought that if I left it would just be for a job that didn't require me to work most weekends, or touch food and pour beer. I'm a little afraid that he's going to ask about it and I'll mention that I don't have time to juggle both. I'm not sure why I'm worried about Tom, and me leaving his restaurant, but I've been working there since he opened the place eight years ago. I always thought it would be temporary, that I would get some kind of job doing art things, like maybe work at the gallery in town even, but thinking about leaving now makes me sort of sad. No, I wouldn't miss working evenings and weekends, or dealing with drunk customers, or being on my feet all day, but Tom is such a warm soul. He cares for his employees, and you can tell that everyone is happy to be there. He wants to take care of his staff, and he understands when people move on to bigger and better things. He just wants what's best for us. But I've been there since the beginning and thinking about leaving just…

I finally shake my thoughts away and get in the shower. I'll be late for work if I keep going at this rate. When I get out of the shower, I see the notification light blinking on my phone, so I wrap my towel around myself and grab my phone off the side of the sink. Ha. Would you look at that. Logan added me to Snapchat. His name is the same as his private Instagram: **EustaceScrubb**. I add him back and then head to my room to get dressed. I hear my phone go off while I'm putting on my jeans and once I'm fully clothed I open Snapchat to see that Logan sent me a picture out the window of his plane, the ground so far below and almost invisible through big patches of clouds. The caption is across the screen with the familiar grey text ribbon and reads ***I miss you already*** with two winky faces. I smile, close the app without replying, throw my hair up, and head to work.

The restaurant is already busy once I get there and my tables are staggered in a way that I'm running around almost all night with no time to talk to anyone. Claire smiles and widens her eyes at me a few times and any time I start to tell her a story or she starts to ask me a question, food is ready to be brought to a table, or another table is ready to order, or a table is leaving and I have to clear everything away. When it finally dies down near closing, Claire and I sneak into the back room.

"Do you want to come to LA with me at the end of the summer?" I ask her.

"What? Really?"

"Yeah! And we can go to the tapings of his show."

"Oh my god, that would be amazing!"

"Okay good. How was your week?"

"Isla, you have no idea." She grins at me and wiggles her eyebrows.

"Emily?" I ask.

"Oh yeah. Emily. Oh my god, Isla, Emily!"

I laugh and hold out my hands to her. "Okay okay, do you want to sleep over? We can catch up."

"Hell yeah I want to sleep over!"

"First of all," Claire says once we get in my apartment. "Congrats on your clay stuff! That's super exciting!"

"Thanks! But I'm really conflicted about it, actually."

I tell her about wanting to quit, and having to close my shop to catch up on inventory and being afraid that I won't have time to do that and still work at the restaurant.

"You should totally quit! I mean, I would miss you, but you deserve this."

"Thanks," I say.

We get into our pyjamas, make popcorn, and put on a movie.

"So, Emily?" I ask.

"Oh my god, Emily! I'm so in love with her, Isla."

"Aww," I say, putting popcorn in my mouth.

"I haven't told her yet, because we haven't been together for that long and I don't want to freak her out. She's also very… I don't know, like we'd kissed a lot before, and there was a bit of touching, but she mostly wanted to take it slow. I think she was afraid that I was going to sleep with her and ditch her or something."

"Understandable," I say with a nod.

"And like, the first time we kissed, it was amazing. Like, I've never had such an amazing kiss before, I'm telling you, and any time we made out after that, it was like…" she puts her hands on either side of her head and spreads her fingers out. "Like fireworks. Everywhere. Every time. And it was so hard for me to not be doing anything else, but she didn't want to, so we didn't, but theennnn…" she trails off, biting her bottom lip a little.

"But then?" I find myself leaning forward to get closer to her, as if that'll make her story even better or something.

"Then she just started… She just started undoing my belt, and then unzipping my jeans, and I asked her what she was doing, I thought she wanted to take it slow, and she just smiled up at me and said 'Yes, and we took it slow, and it was awesome, and now I want all of you.'"

"Jesus that's hot," I say.

"Right!? Anyway, it was amazing. I can't."

"When was that?" I ask.

"Thursday. And then she slept over every night since then. She's so amazing; I can't get her out of my head."

"I think you should tell her you love her," I say.

"Ha. No. There's no way I can do that."

"Why not?"

"Because! That's scary!"

"Claire, she's your girlfriend. You've had sex with her. I think it's pretty safe to tell her that you love her."

"No. No way."

"I'll bet you she loves you."

"What?" she scrunches her eyebrows at me.

"Maybe she was taking it slow with you at first because she needed to have more of an emotional attraction to you before she had that sexual attraction."

"You think she didn't want to have sex before because she wasn't in love with me?"

I shrug. "It's possible."

My phone makes the little bloopy Snapchat noise and I almost immediately pick it up, trying to ignore the fact that Claire is raising her eyebrows at me. I open the app to see that the message is from Logan, of course, and when I open his picture I almost scream.

"What?" Claire asks.

My mouth drops open and all I do in response is turn the screen towards her so that she can see the photo of Logan and JENNIFER FUCKING LAWRENCE sitting at a bar together! Both their mouths are open in an excited, playful smile and the picture is taken from above them, as if Logan had his arm way up above their heads so that you can see the bar and their drinks. The caption says **hanging with my bestie** and a winky face. He uses the winky face all the time.

"What are you going to say back!?" Claire squeals.

"I don't know! Oh wait, I do, I do." We recreate the picture, but in our pyjamas and at my kitchen table, and with glasses of chocolate milk. I put a caption that reads, **ME TOO!**

The next Snapchat comes almost immediately except it's a video, and I'm almost too nervous to open it. Claire isn't, though, she's practically jumping up and down in her seat yelling, "Open it! Open it!! Open it!!"

The video is of Jennifer Lawrence, but she's clearly holding Logan's phone, and she's mid-laugh when it starts. She looks at Logan off screen for a second and then back at the camera. "Hi Isla!" she says cheerfully. "I'm really happy that Logan found you. He's such a sweet guy and I know he's been bummed about being single for a while and--"

Logan cuts her off by saying "Okay, that's enough out of you," and takes it from her. He turns the camera from her and the video ends.

"That was amazing," Claire says.

"Should we send them a video back?" I ask.

"I don't know! What would we say!?"

"I don't know!"

I end up replying with another picture because I'm too nervous. I pose by smiling all innocently and looking off to the side, and the caption says, **I'm glad he found me too.**

The next picture is of Jennifer Lawrence smiling and the caption says, **awwwww**

Claire and I go back to our movie, and Logan texts me a little bit throughout the night, but not much. It's nearly three in the morning by the time Claire and I fall asleep, so it's lucky neither of us have to open tomorrow. Not that working the opening shift requires us to be up super early anyway, but it's still better this way.

One hundred people have already signed up for my mailing list! I can't believe a hundred people care about my stuff so much to be on an email list so they know right away when my site is up! Right now the site just has a similar message that we wrote up for my Instagram, and the button to sign up for the email list. And people are starting to get their figurines and are posting pictures on Instagram and tagging my account in them! I get all giddy when I see the notifications and am surprised at the quality of some of the pictures. It's like they collect stuff like this and stage them in photos for a living. But the thing that makes me the most excited is the way people are talking about their figurines, calling them Claymates as if that's the name of the actual items, and not just the name of my shop.

I got my David Rose claymate today and I LOVE IT SO MUCH now I need a Patrick to go with him! Everyone check out @claymatebyisla and get your own! Is the caption on one person's picture.

Pretty sure I'm going to be spending all my money on claymates from now on is another person's caption, who got a Spiderman figure.

And someone who bought three; Hopper, El, and Dustin from *Stranger Things* has a caption that says **I just got my claymates!**

I scroll through my mentions for a while during my day off on Wednesday but I know I should be working on building up my inventory. I put on *Neighbourly* while I make magnets and stop periodically to look up and watch what's happening. At one point I stop and watch an entire episode with a piece of clay in one hand and a shaping tool in the other hand, just sitting there like that, my elbows on my knees, glued to the TV. When I realize that I've just been watching the show and not doing anything, I shake my head and take a walk around my apartment. Maybe I should have a shower and try to wake myself up and get back in the zone. Before I do that, I take a picture of everything all over my coffee table and upload it to Instagram. Gotta let people know that I'm working on stuff!

My phone notifies me just as I hit post. Leave it to Claire to send me all the tabloids about my fake boyfriend.

Don't read the comments though her message says, along with a link.

I click on it to see a picture taken from a bar, behind Logan and Jennifer Lawrence, their heads close together, and a phone clearly between them. Even though the picture is from behind, you can tell it's them because their faces are turned towards each other a little but. But if the picture was closer, everyone could probably see that they were messaging ME! Ha. The headline says **IS JLAW BREAKING UP LOLA?**

I roll my eyes and text her without even reading the article.

It's funny because they were totally Snapchatting us when that picture was taken I type.

She just replies with a sly face emoji.

I put my phone down and go have my much needed shower, trying not to think about what the comments on the article must have said about me. Once I'm dressed, I scroll through Facebook for a bit, and a video of Logan being interviewed at an awards show shows up in my feed. I'm pretty sure it's from when he was dating Heidi Winters. The interviewer asks him insightful questions about filming a sitcom, and if he feels like he's type casted now, and he gives a good answer about how people don't usually do that on purpose, and it's not necessarily a bad thing to be typecast. "At least you know you're doing something right," he says in the interview. "People like what they see and they want to see you in more things like that. People get this comfort around who plays certain rolls, and it's an honour to be thought of for other roles like Cory, for sure. I do think it would be great to try something new, but if people think of me when they hear cute, silly

Canadian guy, or people think of me when they hear thoughtful boyfriend, then I'm okay with that."

I smile and click on another interview with him that's recommended. This one's definitely newer, like within the last year probably, and it's titled **LOGAN JACKSON PUTS REPORTER IN HIS PLACE**.

"Got any plans for after the show tonight?" the reporter asks. "I'm sure you could have all the ladies you want now that you're single."

"Well just because I'm single doesn't mean I'm going to mistreat anyone," Logan says shortly.

The reporter looks a little shocked, and he steps back a little, tongue tied for a second. "I never said you would do that," he says.

"But you're implying that I'm going to go home and pick from a group of women to sleep with, as if they're not actual people with feelings."

"I never said that. I just meant that you're famous and obviously the ladies think you're good looking."

"I'm sure there are men who think I'm good looking too," Logan says confidently. "But you know what I'm going to do after the show tonight? I'm probably going to have a drink with my friends, and then I'm going to go home and go to bed."

It's funny, the difference between questions from when Logan was with someone, to when he was single. Not that I doubted him before, but it's true. I get even more now why he wanted to do this, and I feel a little bad that he has to go through that. But I'm really proud of him for what he said. I watch a couple more videos that are recommended to me, and then get back to work.

My phone goes off in the afternoon and I check it to see that Logan has Snapchatted me again. I smile and open it, and then realize what I've just done. What I've been doing every time I see that he's messaged me. I've been smiling. Every damn time. His messages are making me *happy*. No. This just won't do. I close the app without replying to him, because I can't make myself think that I have a real-life crush on him. If I don't talk to him for a few days it will all go away.

It has not gone away. To be fair, I didn't actually stop talking to him. He Snapchatted me again at around supper time and I replied right away because I didn't want to be rude. And now it's Friday and he's Snapchatted me three times already today. I'm at work and I keep pulling my phone out of my back pocket to see if I've missed a message from him since it's on silent. What am I doing?

"What are you doing?" Claire asks.

I jump a little and put my phone back in my pocket. "What? Nothing."

"Are you checking your phone? Are you texting Logan?"

"No!"

"You are! While you're working! Isla!"

I shove her in the shoulder and laugh. "Shh."

I don't have a crush on Logan, I've concluded. I only think I have a crush on him because I miss having someone to love. I miss having that person to text when I'm excited, or having someone that I think of when certain things happen. Logan is kind, and sweet, and funny, and sends me silly messages that make me smile and it's making me think that I have a crush on him. But really I just have a crush on the idea of someone liking me. Which I don't even really want someone to like me, because if someone liked me then he would want to do something about it and even just addressing that sounds terrifying and also horrible. Plus I still don't want to kiss Logan or anything, so no, it's definitely not a crush. It's a crush on the idea of having a crush. That's a thing, and that's what it is.

I'm still thinking about the fact that I absolutely do not have a crush on Logan as I'm walking up the stairs to my apartment, and then I remember that I forgot to turn the sound back on on my phone, so I grab it out of my pocket, and oh, would you look at that, Logan Snapchatted me. I turn the sound up and then I open his message and it's a picture of him sitting on his couch, looking at the camera with big brown puppy dog eyes, with a caption that simply says, *hi.*

I call him when I get into my apartment and he picks up pretty quickly.

"Hey, what's up?" he asks.

"Nothing, I just got home from work. You seem lonely."

"What makes you say that?"

"You've been Snapchatting me a lot, and your latest one is dripping in loneliness."

"Really? I was just saying hi."

"Okay. Sorry, just, my friends and I usually only Snapchat each other if we have something to say."

"I did have something to say. Hi."

I chuckle and flop down on the couch. "Okay. Um. Hi."

"I gotta go," he says quickly.

"Oh. Um, okay. Talk to you later then."

"Bye." And the call ends just like that.

That was weird.

CHAPTER 21

The rest of July goes by in a flash. I go to the beach with Claire and Emily a couple of times, and the rest of my spare time is spent on building my inventory. I stay up way too late and get up way too early, but I need to make sure I have enough stuff for the Tug Boat Festival and have a head start on stuff for my shop. I talk to Logan mostly every day, but his texts and snaps are less frequent since the time I told him he seemed lonely. I think I might have offended him, but I don't know what to say about it. I mean, I know I could just apologize, but I don't want to make it into a bigger thing and make it seem like I'm worried about what he thinks, or worried about how I make him feel. I don't want him to think I want him to be my real boyfriend.

There is far less hate on my ClayMate page, so I check that often, and try to respond to as many people as I can. Especially the people who bought things and tagged me in their pictures. I still don't check the comments on my personal page, but continue to post pictures on it like I would have before it blew up.

"Isla, go home," Tom says to me two hours before the end of my shift the Thursday before the festival.

"What? Why?"

"You're exhausted. I don't want you working so much that it's hard on you. I know you've been making more clay figurines every second that you're not working and I want you to go home and rest. Don't work on your art, just go home and sleep, or put on a facemask and watch a movie."

"Are you serious?" I ask.

"Yes."

I count out my tips and thank him about nine times as I'm getting ready to leave and he practically pushes me out the door. The Shoppers Drug Mart is still open so I take Tom's advice and head over there to get a Korean facemask. I pick up a personal size bag of Lays ketchup chips as well, and a peanut butter Oh Henry. It's hard to not work on my stuff when I get home, but I'm off all day tomorrow for last minute prep, so I try my hardest to relax. I snap a picture to Logan with my sheet mask on, with a caption that says **tom made me go home and rest.**

He replies in text form and says that was nice of him.

Yeah! I text back.

Are you watching a movie?

Yeah I'm watching *To All The Boys I've Loved Before.*

Why?

What do you mean why? Because it's adorable and wholesome and warms my heart.

But it's about teenagers he texts.

Says the guy who spent an entire day watching teen movies with me

Those were all classics!

So?

Okay. Enjoy your wholesome, probably not funny, non-classic teen movie

Oh I will

The Tugboat Festival is going well so far. I've only been set up for an hour and I've already sold four figurines and six magnets. Two of the people who bought from me have bought my stuff from previous years here, and one other person came because of my Instagram post! She was also hoping that Logan would be here with me, and I told her that I would tell him hi for her. She didn't seem too bummed though, and she bought an Ironman figurine with his helmet open. Most people who come by know what I'm selling and call them claymates, which is really cool, and by noon, all I have left are magnets. I had way more of those to start anyway, since they're all way faster to make, but I've never sold this much by noon before. It would be really cool to have to pack up because I sold everything, but it would also suck to have to pack up so early. The festival is two days, too, what am I going to do tomorrow?

"Hey, do you have any *Neighbourly* stuff?" I hear a familiar voice say.

I look up and take half a second to register that it's Logan. He's got a beard! It's not super thick, but it's full enough that I almost don't recognize him. He's also got a hat and sunglasses on, so really I can see basically none of his face, which was probably the whole point, but still!

"Oh my god hi!" I squeal, running around the table and hugging him.

"Hi! Surprise!"

"It's so cool that you came! When did you get here?"

"Just now!" He steps back and looks around at the other vendors lining the path that runs along the water. "There are so many people here."

"Yeah," I say, "People come from out of town for this. For some reason." I smile a little and he starts to look at my stuff, so I slowly go back behind my table. "I would have brought an extra chair if I knew you were coming," I say.

"Oh I'm fine, I can stand. You didn't make any claymates for today?"

I try to play it cool that he just casually called them claymates like it's a brand, but I'm too excited, and my response comes out way more enthusiastic than is probably necessary. "Yeah I did, I sold them all!"

"No way!" Logans seems just as excited as me, so maybe I'm not being over the top about it.

"Yeah!"

"That's awesome, congrats! Are you selling them for fifty?"

I bite my bottom lip and sort of look away.

"Isla," he says slowly. "Thirty at least?"

"No, I'm still selling them for twenty five. I always sell them for twenty five; people who have bought from me before would be mad! People come looking for me at this thing, you know."

"You should still charge more. You've got to be paying yourself less than minimum wage to make these, right? These are so detailed, they can't be easy to make. If people really like your stuff and want to support you, they'll understand."

"Maybe."

Someone comes up to the table and I say hi, but she just smiles, looks at some magnets and starts to leave. "Thank you," she says as she walks away.

"Have a good day!" I call to her. Then I turn back to Logan. "So you have a beard."

"I do," he beams. "I thought it would be good to come in disguise."

"It's a good disguise. Is that why you haven't been sending me pictures of your face for the last week and a half?"

"Maybe." He shrugs and smiles a little, picking up a magnet and then putting it back on the table. "Can I buy a Georgian Bay Magnet?"

"Yep. Ten bucks."

"What? That's it?"

"It's a magnet, Logan."

"Yeah, but it's an awesome magnet."

"An awesome magnet that costs ten dollars." I picture him rolling his eyes, but he's still got his sunglasses on, so I can't be sure that he actually does. He hands me a ten and I put it in my pouch. "Take your favourite one," I say. "They're all a little different."

He inspects them and takes one with the most noticeable imperfections. "I like this one," he says with a smile, picking it off the table and putting it in his pocket.

"I almost didn't bring that one."

"I'm glad you did. Because it's my favourite."

"Why?" I ask.

"Because it looks the most homemade. And I know you made it, so it looks the most Isla made."

Logan has decided to wander and check out the other vendors and look at the boats, and not long after he leaves, Tyler comes up to my table.

"Hey," he says casually.

"Hi," I reply a little shortly.

"Can I buy a magnet?"

"Of course you can."

He picks up a few different ones and puts them back on the table, taps them with his fingertips a few times, but doesn't actually pick one.

"Are you okay?" I ask.

"Yeah," he says with a shrug.

I smirk a little and tilt my head. "Are you sure about that?"

He laughs and looks away, then back to me. "I miss you," he finally says.

"You miss me? Really? After we've been broken up for almost a year, you want to tell me that you miss me?"

"It's not like that. I don't know."

"I miss you too, Tyler."

"Really?"

I sigh. "Yeah. But not like that. I mean I missed you when we were still dating for crying out loud."

"What do you mean?"

"We were still together but you didn't pay attention to me. I tried so hard, Tyler. I tried so hard to get you to notice me, to get you to want me again, but you didn't. I miss the Tyler that loved me. There's a difference."

"But you cried when we broke up."

I narrow my eyes at him. "Okay? So?"

"I don't know what I'm trying to say."

"Neither do I."

"I'm sorry," he huffs. "I'm not… I'm not trying to get back together, I just…"

"You just what?"

"Are you really dating that Logan guy?"

"Yeah. Are you jealous?"

"Yes."

"Well. Good. Aren't you dating that girl from Sport Chek?"

"No. Not really."

"So you're sort of dating a girl and you're coming to tell me that you miss me?"

"Okay, I didn't come here to tell you that. I came here to support you. It just slipped out."

"Okay," I say slowly.

"I guess I'm just lonely."

"No," I say shortly. "You don't get to do that to me."

"Do what?"

"Are you being serious right now, Tyler? You broke up with me, and you sort of have a girlfriend, and now you're telling me that you're lonely? Why don't you tell your sort of girlfriend that you're lonely?"

He shrugs. "She doesn't know me like you do."

"Give it time," I say quietly. He nods and it's quiet for a minute. "You don't miss me," I add. "You miss having someone. I just happened to be that someone for so long you think it's me that you miss. But it's not."

"Yeah," he sighs.

"It's hard always having someone there for so long and then just… not."

"Yeah. It's not the same having a girlfriend I don't live with."

"I thought she was only sort of your girlfriend," I joke.

He smiles a bit. "Whatever. I still come home to no one most days. When we were living together, even when we were doing our own thing, you were still there. I could just talk to you whenever I wanted."

"I know," I say. "I'm in the same boat as you. Have been since you broke up with me."

"Right," he says quietly. "So have you quit your job yet?" he asks.

"No," I say easily. "I'm going to wait and see what kind of orders I get when my new site is up."

"That's smart. I'm sure Tom would hire you back in a heartbeat if you needed him to, though."

"Yeah, probably."

"So this Logan guy, he's cool?"

"Yes," I say with a bit of a smile. "He's very cool."

"And you're happy?"

"I'm okay," I say honestly.

"Just okay? Logan doesn't make everything better?"

"Logan can make things better sometimes, yeah. But my happiness is not determined by me having or not having a boyfriend." And as I'm looking at Tyler, I can say with full confidence that I'm not in love with him anymore. There is nothing there that is making me ache for him to hold me, there is nothing that is making me want to kiss him, or run my hands through his hair... There is nothing that is making my chest hurt because I know I can't have him. Talking to him doesn't feel the same as it did when we were in love, and it doesn't feel the same as it did when I could tell he didn't love me anymore, and it doesn't feel the same as it did when we first broke up or when we met him to get my blanket. It feels like I'm talking to an old friend. But then that starts to make me sad in a way I didn't expect.

"Right," Tyler says.

"You're okay though?" I ask.

He shrugs. "I'm okay."

"Well, okay is better than bad."

"True enough." He finally picks up a Canada magnet. "I'll take this one."

"Ten bucks," I say.

I feel like I'm pretty quiet for the rest of the afternoon, and not very talkative once Logan comes back. He's excited about all the stuff he bought, like butter tarts, a wallet, and a Tug Boat Festival t-shirt, and I'm excited for him but it's hard for me to show it. I feel so weird ever since talking to Tyler. And because I feel weird about it, I feel sort of stupid. Like, it's stupid to be sad about not loving your ex anymore, right? That's stupid.

"Are you okay?" Logan asks as he helps me pack up my table and take my tent down.

"Yeah," I say quietly.

"You want to go get wings?"

"Sure."

He stands up straight and puts his hands on his hips. "Okay, something is wrong."

"Nothing is wrong."

"What kind of wings do you want? I'll meet you at your place with them if you want."

"It depends where you're getting them from," I say. "Winghouse or Wild Wing?"

"Oh boy. I can go to both places."

"Then I want Hangover from Winghouse and I am Canadian from Wild Wing."

"Sounds good." He helps me pack my stuff into my car and then he heads on his way to get our food. Dammit. He's going to bring the wings home and he's going to want to talk about why I seem so bummed and then he's going to think I'm a loser. Ugh.

I leave my stuff in my car and just bring in my leftover product, which all fits in my purse, and wait anxiously for Logan to buzz my apartment.

It doesn't take long for him to show up, so I buzz him in and unlock my apartment door, and before I know it, he's walking in with two bags and putting them on the coffee table. I'm about to get up from the couch but he tells me to stay sitting while he grabs a plate for each of us. We eat in silence for a bit, and Logan softly chuckles at how messy my Hangover wings are; the sauce is getting everywhere, but I just try to wipe my face as often as I can so I don't look gross. I leave my hands alone until I'm done though. They're just going to get all saucy again. Logan eventually turns on the TV and puts on The Office, picking up from where I left off the last time I watched it. And we keep eating our wings while Michael Scott makes a fool of himself and Jim flirts with Pam.

"So what's going on?" Logan finally asks.

"Um. I feel weird talking about it."

"Okay. Well if you ever don't feel weird talking about it, I'm here. You can tell me anything."

"Thanks," I say. And we watch *The Office* for the rest of the night, not saying anything. Which is actually really nice.

"Okay," I finally say. Logan stops putting a sheet on the couch and turns back to look at me standing in the corner.

"Okay what?" he asks.

I let out a deep breath and close my eyes for a second. "Tyler came to my booth today."

"Ah. Okay."

"I feel sort of stupid about the way I'm feeling about it."

"Why?"

"Well it's weird, like, when we were talking, I was looking at him, and I was talking to him and listening to him, and the whole time I was thinking, 'yup, I'm definitely over him. I'm definitely not in love with him anymore.' But then that made me really sad." My voice cracks a little and I try to clear my throat. "The fact that I'm not in love with him anymore made me sad. That's so stupid. Like. I don't want him to be my boyfriend. But I don't want to not love him. No, that's stupid, I want to not love him, but I don't..."

"Realizing you don't love someone anymore is hard."

"Shouldn't it be a good thing? Shouldn't I be happy?"

He shrugs. "Not necessarily. It's hard leaving a part of your life behind. And when you realize that you don't love someone anymore, even if that's the outcome you're hoping for, it's sort of like..."

"Like it was the last piece of the relationship left to hold on to and it's gone," I finish for him.

"Yeah."

"But shouldn't that mean that I'm still in love with him? If I have this new sadness about it being over? How can I be over him, but be sad about it at the same time?"

"Letting go of someone is complicated, especially when you were with them for so long." I nod, but don't say anything. He continues after a minute or so. "Can I ask you a question?"

"Yeah."

"Was Tyler your only relationship?"

"Well I mean, no?"

"No? Why did you answer that like it was a question?"

"Because I don't want you to think I'm a loser."

"Why would I think you're a loser?"

"I don't know."

"Okay, so this is your first breakup. And it's a huge breakup on top of that. I would say your feelings are even more normal now that I know that. You're not just trying to fall out of love with someone; you're trying to live your life without the thing that made up a huge part of it, for a long time. He was in your life for basically your entire adult life so far."

"Yeah."

"I'm sorry this is so hard for you," he says gently.

"Thanks."

CHAPTER 22

I can't believe Claire and I are at the airport on our way to visit Logan! To watch an episode from season six of *Neighbourly* get filmed! Ahh!

"Where do we go?" she asks, looking around once we get through the doors of Terminal One.

"We have to find our airline."

"How do you know what to do?"

"I've flown before. Have you not been on a plane before?" She shakes her head and I smile. "Oh this'll be fun."

We check in at the self-serve kiosks, make our way through security pretty quickly, and then stop dead when we get to customs. The lineup is huge. It snakes back and forth so many times and everyone looks so empty and bored to tears.

"Why is it so busy?" Claire asks.

"Maybe a bunch of people are on lunch," I say with a shrug. "Because the line really doesn't look like it's moving. I guess this is why they tell us to get to the airport three hours early."

Everyone must have come back from lunch at the same time because after about twenty minutes of hardly moving at all, the line suddenly starts to go so quickly we hardly have time to put our bags down each time. We tell the customs officers that we're on our way to visit my boyfriend and they smile at us, or at least, my customs officer smiles at me, I'm not sure about the one Claire gets, and we're off to our gate!

"Ooh this is so exciting!" Claire says, skipping along with her carry-on rolling beside her.

We stop at a restaurant since we're still pretty early, and take a seat with our bags under the table by our feet. We laugh about funny customer stories and talk about how Tom is going to react when I give my notice at some point. Probably soon. She says our regular customers will miss me, and I guess in a way I'll miss them too. But I have over 500 people signed up for my mailing list at this point, so I'm not super worried about being able to make money. Especially if I raise my prices like Logan keeps saying I should.

We finally head over to our gate and wait for our flight to board, and we get to go on in one of the first groups since we're sitting in business class, which is very exciting for me. I've only ever sat in economy before, and while some planes are definitely more spacious than others, most economy seating is pretty cramped.

"Wow," I say out loud as we enter and I see how wide the seats at the front are. There are only two per row instead of three, and there's *so much leg room*!

"What?" Claire asks.

"Oh Claire," I say with a bit of sympathy. "Sitting in these seats is going to ruin planes for you."

"What do you mean?"

We find our seats and I put my carry-on in the overhead compartment and then put Claire's up for her. I take my backpack off and take a step forward so Claire can get in first. "You take the window seat," I say to her.

"Thanks!" She puts her bag on her lap as she sits down and then I take my seat, getting the stuff out of my backpack that I'll want during the flight. "But what do you mean this is going to ruin planes for me?" she asks.

"These seats are so spacious. You'll never want to fly economy after this."

"Maybe I'll just make sure any time I fly somewhere, your pretend boyfriend will want to buy my tickets for me. Maybe next time he'll get us tickets for those absurd first class seats that turn into beds and stuff!"

"Excuse me, he's my real boyfriend," I say, widening my eyes at her, because there are people on this plane with ears, ears that hear, and they could totally hear us!

"Right, of course, your real boyfriend. I hope you guys never break up, because I really want a bed seat the next time I fly somewhere."

"You're ridiculous."

She smiles at me and then looks out the window. "I know."

Claire lets me lean over her after we take off so we can both look out the window at the ground getting farther and farther away, and at the clouds and sky in the distance. I love looking out windows of airplanes; I could do it all day. Who needs in-flight movies when you have a view from thirty thousand feet? We eventually pull away and lean back in our seats after flying through clouds for so long that we get bored.

"It's weird that when we're going through the clouds, it just looks like fog," Claire says.

"Yeah, that's what fog is. Or what clouds are. Whatever. It's the same thing."

"Oh, I guess that makes sense. I thought going through them would somehow be more magical."

We decide to watch movies on our personal screens that are in the backs of the seats in front of us, and hit play at the same time, but mine takes a second longer to load for some reason, so when I watch both of our screens at once it's like watching a movie and its shadow. We look at each other and laugh any time something funny happens, and look at each other and grab our chests with welled eyes if something sad or heartwarming happens. We take our earbuds out to eat when they serve us supper, and look out the window a few more times before starting a new movie to watch together.

"I'm excited to fly back already," Claire says as we walk the bridge into the airport. "That was fun!"

"Well I hope LA ends up being more fun, otherwise that's a little disappointing."

"Nah. If LA is half as fun as the plane ride was, I'll call it a successful trip!"

"Okay," I say with a chuckle.

There's a man in a suit with a sign that says Isla Reid and Friend as soon as we come into the arrivals gate, surrounded by families and friends running to hug their loved ones.

"Oh look, it's our driver," I say to Claire. "Come, friend."

"Why am I just 'friend'? Why isn't my name on the sign?"

"Obviously you're not important enough," I joke. We make our way over to him and he smiles and shakes both our hands.

"How was your flight?" he asks as we follow him through the busy airport and into the parking garage.

"Awesome!" Claire half screeches.

"Excellent!"

We get into a fancy black car with slippery seats, and cup holders between us in the back, and look out the window as we drive towards my pretend boyfriend's mansion.

He legit lives on a street that has gates and giant mansions way back from the road. Like, does he live next door to other movie stars? This is wild. The driver puts a code into a keypad and then the gate swings open and he drives up a winding, grey brick driveway and stops in front of a white, well, mansion. That's the only word I can use to describe it. It's massive. And there's a fountain. A fountain! Logan comes out of the front door and I half run up to him and hug hum. He kisses the top of my head and then smiles at Claire.

"Hi," he says to her.

Claire nods and smiles but doesn't say anything.

"Claire's shy," I tell him.

"That's okay. She won't be shy by the end of the week. How did you both manage to get a week off, by the way? Who's working at the restaurant?"

"People who aren't as good as us," I say.

"Of course."

We follow him inside and I'm blown away by just the foyer. The floor is this slate-like tile, in big, dark pieces, with light grey walls and teal accent colours. There's teal abstract art on the walls and teal benches.

"This is really nice," I say. Even though the floor is tile it feels super cozy.

"It's because the tile is dark and there are bright accent colours. I didn't do it. But I like it."

"Well that's good."

He takes us into the kitchen which is *beautiful* and enormous and has shiny counters that go on for days. The fridge is the size of like, four of my fridges. And the island has twelve stools around it. *Twelve!* And they all fit comfortably too, like if you needed to add a few extra there would totally be room. The kitchen has French doors that lead into the backyard which has a pool with a waterfall and a hot tub and a waterslide and I just can't.

"Can we go swimming later?" I ask.

"We can go swimming right now if you want."

"No, let's go later," Claire whispers to me.

"Come on, I'll show you your room. You guys want to share a room, right?"

"Yeah, that'll be fun," I say.

The stairs are super wide and very twisty, it's like the staircase in Jumanji, which I'm okay with, and the runner that goes up the middle is plushy and squishy under my toes. The room we're staying in has two queen size sleigh beds in dark cherry wood and I can't help it, I leap onto one and let myself flop into the floofy comforter.

"This is nice," I say. "I could get used to this."

"I would be okay with that," Logan says from the door.

I look up at him from the bed and give him a bit of a smile because I don't know what else to say. Is he saying that for show, or because he really thinks it would be fun for us to live together? He must know that Claire knows this isn't real, or he wouldn't suggest that Claire and I sleep in the same room, right?

"I'll let you two get settled. You can unpack your stuff into the dressers if you want. Just come down whenever you're ready. I'll be in the kitchen."

"Okay," I say quietly.

He nods once and leaves the room, gently shutting the door behind him.

"Oh my god," Claire says, flopping onto the bed next to me.

"I know, right?"

"Why can't you actually date him? Please date him for real."

"I don't know," I groan. "I don't really want to date anyone right now."

"But if you had to, like if someone put a gun to your head and said you had to pick someone to date, you would pick him, right?"

"No," I say slowly.

"Then who would you pick?"

"No one?"

"So you would rather die than date someone?"

"No."

"Then? You would choose Logan."

"Or Tyler."

"Really?" she asks.

"I don't know, maybe. I don't want to get back together with him, but if I was forced to, I dunno," I shrug, "like, I already know him. There would be no scary firsts with him."

"Why does it have to be scary? Why can't it be exciting? And fun?"

"Because it just sounds terrifying to me. I can't even think about kissing Logan, let alone having sex with him. With anyone, not just Logan. I don't know, I've only ever been with Tyler, and I was comfortable with him, and up until the end I was never insecure about myself or my body. He always made me feel beautiful, and loved."

"And you don't think someone else can make you feel like that?"

I just shake my head as an answer.

"Why not?" she asks. "If someone loved you, and you loved them, they would definitely make you feel loved, and beautiful, and safe, even."

"Yeah." Even I can hear the uncertainty in my voice. "It's just…"

"It's just what?"

"I feel like I'm not good at any of that. I have no idea what I'm doing, Claire. Even if I loved someone new, and I felt comfortable with them, and they made me feel beautiful or whatever, I would be so self-conscious of how I'm doing things. I don't know what people like."

"So you ask him."

"What?"

"You're allowed to ask guys what they like. It's encouraged, even."

"Yeah, I know. I guess I feel like at this point I should just know. When I was with Tyler, I felt different about asking about things because I was younger. But I'm almost thirty so I feel like someone will judge me if I ask questions or do something weird, or I'm not… good."

"Listen, if you're with someone who judges you for stuff like that, then you don't want to be with him. The right guy will gladly guide you through anything you're unsure about, and he'll do it like a sexy mother-fucker, too. Trust me."

"You're probably right. But it still scares me."

"And that's allowed. You're allowed to be scared. Just don't let it stop you from living your life, or from being with someone who will compliment it so well."

"When did you get so wise?" I ask.

"Probably when Emily became my girlfriend. She's super smart and mature."

CHAPTER 23

We finally make our way back downstairs and find Logan cooking up beef in the kitchen. He's got a spread of taco stuff on the island, and it looks awesome.

"You don't have a cook?" I ask.

"I do," he says with a shrug. "But sometimes I like to make things myself. And I thought it would be fun if I made something for you guys."

"That's nice of you," I say, pulling myself up onto one of the stools. "Can we do anything to help?"

He shakes his head. "No, it's almost done. Thanks though."

We mostly eat in silence, but I wish Claire could bring herself to say something in front of Logan.

"How was the flight?" Logan finally asks.

"It was good!" I reply. "Claire loved it, right?"

She nods and takes a big bite of her taco.

"It's okay, we'll get her to talk at some point," Logan smiles.

We're in the pool and Claire still hasn't said anything in front of Logan! Also can I just say that this pool is *amazing*? The water is the most comfortable temperature while still being a little refreshing, and there's this waterfall that comes down from this river thing on the second floor patio and I don't know how it works but Logan says it's on a continuous running loop like a fountain, and all I can think to respond with is, "Like the fountain in your fucking front yard?"

He laughs a little. "Yeah."

"Oh my god, we should swim in the fountain," I say.

"It's not really deep enough to swim in," he says.

"I don't care. I've always wanted to play in a fountain and I can do it in this one without getting in trouble!"

"How do you know you won't get in trouble?" he asks, so I splash him. "Hey!" he laughs. "I splash back!"

"Do you now?" I splash him again and he pushes both his palms through the water in front of him to hit me with a practical wave.

"Can I see the river thing that makes the waterfall?" Claire finally asks, her voice barely a squeak.

"YES!" Logan shouts. "Let's go see the river thing!"

We pull ourselves out of the pool and walk across the cement, towards the wooden stairs that lead to the deck on the second story. We get to the top and before I even get a chance to, Claire steps right into the little river along the edge. I guess it's more like a stream than a river, and it only goes up to her ankles. It's sort of like a little trench or ditch at the edge of the deck where the water can run. I get in behind her and walk along the water, letting it splash as we drag our feet through. We turn the corner it makes as the deck branches out over the pool and stop at the edge where the water drops below us. There's a railing here and we keep our feet in the water, our elbows on the ledge as we lean forward to watch it splash into the pool.

"Is it better or worse than you expected?" Logan asks, squeezing in next to me.

"I think it exactly met my expectations," Claire says.

"Oh, well that's good."

I smile up at Logan and he shoves his arm into mine.

"Are you two excited about seeing the taping tomorrow?" he asks.

"I am!" I say.

Claire shrugs.

"She doesn't think anything will be as fun as the plane ride was," I tell him.

"That's absurd. Okay, something else cool is happening this week, and I was going to let it be a surprise but now I can't hold it in."

"What?" I ask.

"I'm taking you to a super cool and exclusive celebrity party on Friday."

"What?" Claire and I both say at the same time. Except I sound excited and Claire sounds like she wants to barf.

"Does that not sound fun?" Logan asks.

"No," Claire says, shaking her head. "I'll just stay here." She walks through the deck stream and heads back to the stairs.

"Claire," I call, going after her. "Claire, do you really not want to go?"

She sits down on the top step and rests her elbows on her knees so I sit next to her.

"A really big part of me wants to," she starts, "but I know I'm going to make a fool of myself. I'll drink too much to try and calm my nerves and I'll stumble all over the place and probably puke on some fancy food platter."

"Well we don't have to drink," I say. "We can just have soda water all night. Or Coke or something."

"Then I'll be nervous and make a fool of myself in other ways. I'll say stupid things. Or do what you did and leave water jugs where they're not supposed to be left."

I smirk at her. "I think we'll both be fine. It's just the initial idea of talking to famous people, but once you do it a little bit you realize they're just regular people like us. They're just regular people, Claire."

"Yeah," she sighs.

"Come on," I say, "Let's go back in the pool."

We play and swim in the pool until it's dark and by then Claire and I are both wiped. Our bodies are still three hours ahead so even though it's only 9:00 it feels like midnight for us. We both yawn as we wrap ourselves in Logan's fluffy towels and head inside.

"You can't go to bed at 9:00," Logan says to us as we start to head upstairs. "You'll be up at 4am."

"Yeah, I feel like we have to try and stay up at least until 10:00," I agree. "Or we won't get used to the time change."

"I can't," Claire says with a shake of her head. "I'm so tired that I'm dizzy. Travelling today just exhausted me so much."

"Okay," I say. "I'll come up with you to get changed, but is it okay if I try to stay up later?"

"Yeah of course. I'll probably sleep at least until seven to be honest," she says. "I love to sleep."

Claire and I both get changed into our PJs in our room, facing away from each other, and then she gets under the covers of one of the beds.

"Oh man, this is so comfortable. I'll be asleep in less than five minutes." Claire smiles and closes her eyes.

"Okay. I'll try to be quiet when I come in later."

"Oh I don't think you have to. I'll be like the dead for the next 10 hours."

"Okay," I say with a bit of a laugh. I turn the light out for her and go to find Logan.

"You can go to bed if you want, too," he says when I find him back in the kitchen.

"No, I need to try to stay up or I will definitely be awake too early in the morning."

"Okay. You wanna watch a movie?"

Logan has a theatre in his house. A theatre. In his house. With stadium seating. I mean there are only four rows of seats, but still, they're on steps like in an actual movie theatre. And the seats in the front row are two person couches. He immediately sits on one of the couches so of course I sit next to him or that would be weird. There are cup holders on each arm rest, and they recline. I pull the foot rest up but don't really recline it, and Logan does the same. The screen takes up almost the entire wall and he takes a remote out of a compartment in his armrest and turns on the projector above our heads.

"You pick something to watch and I'll go make us popcorn. What do you want to drink?"

"Um, just Coke, please, with ice."

"Great."

I pick *The Hunger Games* because Jennifer Lawrence, and also Peeta is just the sweetest thing, and I haven't seen it in a long time so I thought why not. We share a bowl of popcorn and I stay up for more than half the movie, but end up falling asleep at some point. Logan wakes me up when the credits are rolling and I shuffle my feet upstairs to mine and Claire's bedroom and sleep for what feels like forever.

Claire wakes me up at 8:30 and we lie in the same bed, under the covers together for about twenty minutes, whispering about Logan.

"Did he try to kiss you?" she asks.

"Why would he try to kiss me?"

"Because he's in love with you."

"He is not. Why do you think he's in love with me?"

"Have you seen the way he looks at you?"

"He's not in love with me; that's ridiculous."

My phone goes off and I check to see that Logan texted me.

"Breakfast is ready," I tell her.

"Yum."

We make our way downstairs to the giant and beautiful kitchen. And there are pancakes on the island. Piles and piles of pancakes and piles of crispy bacon.

"Who do you think is going to eat all this?" I ask.

Logan shrugs and sits down. "The cook made it. We'll have snacks for later. Do you like leftover pancakes?"

"I do, actually. I like them cold," I say.

"Me too," he says with a big smile.

Claire just smirks at me and I widen my eyes at her. She keeps smiling and then she winks. I tilt my head at her, widening my eyes a bit more, trying to tell her she's wrong, that what just happened is not because he likes me, but she's not having it. She slowly shakes her head, still smiling, and grabs a pancake from the pile in front of her.

We're sitting in the front row for Logan's show taping, right in the middle of the audience, which is pretty cool. They announce all the actors and they each run onto the set when their names are called, and I woo and shout when Logan comes on. They show us the first scene that was filmed somewhere else first, on a screen, I think to get the audience laughter and stuff for it, and probably also so we're not lost while watching the rest of the taping. It's really cool watching them film, and it's the best when they mess up lines and laugh about it. They all look like they're having so much fun together, and I have to say I'm a little jealous of Logan and everyone else on the show. I never thought about acting, and I'm definitely not a good actor, and I could never memorize lines or anything, so I'm not saying that I'm jealous of them for being actors. I'm just jealous of them for having a job that genuinely looks like a lot of fun and doesn't necessarily feel like work. I'm sure there are parts of it that feel like work, or are tiring or annoying like any other job, but I've never had fun at work the way it looks like they're having fun. They all talk and joke and laugh in between takes like they're all best friends.

I thought it was going to feel like a long time, especially when I first heard that it takes about four hours, but it went by so fast. I can't believe we were sitting and watching people act for four hours and now it's over. Everyone gathers around the edge of the seating to meet the actors, which is something they apparently only just started for this show last season. We don't need to meet them because, hello, I'm fake dating one of them, so we hang around in our seats until the crowd clears out, which takes another hour or so.

"Heeeey," Logan says, running over to us. "Come meet everyone."

He grabs my hand, and Claire and I walk with him to the set where three of the other cast members are sitting around the TV show kitchen table.

"Guys, this is Isla," he says to the rest of the cast that are still here.

"Hey Isla, nice to meet you," Jack Roy, the guy who plays Chas says.

"Who's your friend?" Sarah Thorne asks. She plays Jen.

"This is Claire," I say, grabbing her arm and forcing her to come closer. "She's afraid to talk in front of famous people because she thinks she'll say something embarrassing."

"Yeah," she manages to say.

"No judgement," I add. "I was a huge mess around Logan before I got to know him."

Everyone laughs a little.

"I would love to stay and chat, but I'm beat," Jack says, getting up. "I'm glad I got to meet you, though. Are you two going to the party on Friday?"

"Maybe," I say.

"Aw you should, it'll be lots of fun," Sarah chimes in.

Seth Watson, who plays Brett, hasn't said anything yet but he nods along with Sarah about the party being fun. I wonder where the other two girls from the show went. They must have gone home while we were waiting for the crowd to get smaller.

"Okay well maybe see you at the party, then," Jack says. He waves and heads off set.

The three of us watch a movie in Logan's theatre, and we all sit in the seats at the back to make it feel more theatre-y. Claire announces that she's tired when the credits start to roll and she makes her way upstairs but I stick around with Logan. I have a feeling Claire has done this on purpose in hopes that we will kiss and fall in love. Well guess what, friend? It's not going to happen.

"You up for another movie?" Logan asks.

"Sure. Something fun."

We put on *Bill and Ted's Excellent Adventure* because, hello, hilarious, and we both laugh together at all the silly parts. I notice about halfway through the movie though, that he's sitting with his legs sort of wide, so the side of his knee is touching the side of mine. I'm not sure if he's doing it on purpose or if he doesn't even realize our knees are touching, but it's all I can think about. There's this weird warmth that's radiating across my skin where his jeans are touching mine, which is ridiculous because it's literally the side of our knees. He's probably just relaxed and that's how his leg is sitting on its own. But what if he wants to get closer to me but he's afraid of me rejecting him, and this is all he has the guts to do and he's hoping I'll read it into it and then move myself closer to him? What if this trip was all a part of his elaborate plan to turn me into his real girlfriend? I finally cross my legs away from him so that there's nothing to think about. Our legs aren't touching anymore and he doesn't seem to have reacted to it, so of course this was all in my head. And now I've missed a funny part of the movie because I was thinking too much about Logan instead of how Bill and Ted are going to get their history presentation ready on time.

"Claire's having fun, right?" Logan asks me when the movie's over.

"Yeah. She's way more outgoing in real life, I promise. This is just weird for her."

Logan scrunches his eyebrows at me.

"What?" I ask.

"In real life? She's way more outgoing in real life? You think visiting your fake celebrity boyfriend isn't real life?"

"Oh," I laugh. "I didn't mean that. I mean like, when she isn't around intimidating famous people. I'm a little surprised, actually. I mean, I know she was afraid to serve you at the restaurant and stuff, but I didn't know it would extend this far."

"Okay. As long as she's enjoying herself. I would feel bad if she came all this way with you and stayed for a whole week to just feel out of her element the whole time."

"Yeah," I say slowly. "That wouldn't be fun. But anyway, I'm going to head to bed."

"Okay. Goodnight."

"Night."

Claire is totally awake when I get into our room and it scares me a little. I wasn't expecting her to be sitting up in bed. She must have heard me coming; I'm sure she wasn't sitting up and staring at the doorway the whole time.

"So?" she asks.

"So… what?" I gently shut the door behind me and grab my PJs out of my dresser.

"Did anything happen?"

"No, of course not. This isn't real."

"Ugh." She flops back into her pillow. "I really thought I was doing you guys a favour by coming up here! I've been so bored!"

"Okay, well next time just hang out with us, because nothing will happen between us, whether or not other people are there."

"But you realize if we go to this exclusive celebrity party, something has to happen, right?"

"What do you mean?"

"Well you guys are supposed to be boyfriend and girlfriend. And according to when you apparently first started dating, you've been together for what? Three months? There's going to have to be some closeness."

"I'm okay with closeness."

"Are you, though?"

"Yeah, we've been close before. Like he'll put his arm around me and I'll snuggle into his side or under his arm or whatever."

"No, you're going to have to amp up the cuteness."

I'm in my PJs now but instead of crawling into my bed I get under the covers with Claire. "Like how?" I ask.

"Like you're going to have to sit on his lap and steal his snacks, and drink from his drink, and at least let it look like you want to kiss him all night. If you guys act the way you've been acting around me the past two days, no one is going to believe that you're together."

"Shit," I whisper.

"Yeah. Aren't you glad you have me?"

I get out of bed and march towards the door.

"Where are you going?"

"I have to talk to Logan about this!" I say back in an intense whisper.

"You're going to talk to him about this right now? At almost one in the morning? In your sexy pyjamas?"

I look down at my cartoon owl PJ pants and oversized Schrute Farms t-shirt. "I'm sorry, sexy?"

"I was being sarcastic."

"Well I don't want to be wearing something sexy while I have this conversation with him!" my hand is on the doorknob and I can feel it shaking. My hand, not the doorknob.

"Okay, then away you go, my friend. Let your feelings soar. Let his feelings be reciprocated."

"There are no feelings," I say quickly.

"Whatever you say. Have fun in his room. Don't forget to put your PJs back on before you come back in here."

"Oh shut up." I stick my tongue out at her and she just sticks hers out back at me. I take a deep breath and head into the hall. And realize Logan never gave us a full tour of his house and I have no idea where his bedroom is.

"Logan?" I half whisper. I pad down the dark wooden floors and peek into each room, but mostly they are just empty bedrooms or bathrooms. Oh. I've found an arcade. I turn the light on and almost gasp at how big it is and how many games are in here. There's a Star Wars Pod Racer game! Where you actually sit in a pod and use the controls like you're young Anakin! I sit in it and press the coin slot, hoping it's been rigged to work without needing to insert anything, and I'm right! I get to choose my track! I just go for the obvious and pick the race on Tatooine, but before it gets started, Logan comes in and announces himself.

"Hey," he says, leaning against the doorframe.

"Hey," I reply, starting to get up.

"Your game's about to start." He nods towards the game and I turn back to the big screen in front of me. The countdown is already at one and I hardly have time to prepare myself. I don't even know how the controls work. There are two levers on either side of the pod in front of me, like an airplane I think, and after crashing a few times I start to get the hang of it, pulling down on one to turn in that direction, or pushing up on both of them to go faster. I come in last, but playing was fun and I definitely want to try again. But instead I look over at him. He came a bit closer while I was playing and I reluctantly pull myself up and swing my legs over the side of the pod and hop out.

"Why are you exploring the place without Claire?" he asks.

"Oh I was actually looking for you. Claire's sleeping. I think."

"Oh you were looking for me, were you? Whatever for?"

"Well, Claire actually made a really good point."

"And that was?"

"That we can't just keep acting like friends if we go to that party tomorrow. People will know we're not dating if we act like we've been acting this whole time so far."

"Why? We acted like friends at the Jays game, and at Wonderland and stuff, and everyone ate it up. They think we're adorable."

"Yeah," I agree. "But a party isn't public in the same way, right? When a couple is at a party together they usually get … closer to each other than they would in a crowd at the CN Tower, or in a lineup for a rollercoaster."

"Fair."

"Um, I'm sort of nervous about it, but I think Claire is right."

"So do we need to set new ground rules? Am I allowed to grab your butt now?"

"No, you still can't touch my butt."

"Okay." He steps in a little closer to me. "What about this?" He puts his hand on my lower back and gently pulls me into him. His fingers are grazing the top of where my back meets my butt, but technically he's not touching it. He puts his other arm around me and places that hand in the same spot, and presses his body into mine. I don't know what to do with my hands but before I have a chance to even do anything, his fingers find my wrists and he puts my arms around his neck. "Is this okay?" he whispers into my hair as he puts his hands back on my lower back.

"Um, yeah, I guess."

"You guess," he chuckles. And then he steps away from me really abruptly. "'I guess' isn't okay. Come on, let's go somewhere and talk about this. I don't want you to be uncomfortable tomorrow, but I also don't want to make people question us."

"Okay." I follow him out of the arcade and back into the hall, and down two doors into what must be his bedroom. It's really simple, but cozy. The king size bed is under the window and there's a TV mounted on the wall with a couch and a round chair, a fireplace on the wall adjacent to the bed, and a door leading to either a walk-in closet or bathroom.

He sits on the bed and crosses his legs so I do the same, sitting facing him.

"Okay," I say.

"Okay."

"What do we do?" I ask.

"Well I guess we have to figure out the kinds of the things we should do that you're comfortable with."

"I don't know what I'm comfortable with," I say quickly.

"That doesn't help me at all, Reid."

"That's a new one," I say with a smirk.

"No?"

I shrug. "It's cute. But probably something like babe or sweetie would be better at the party."

"I've never really been a fan of babe," Logan says.

"Me neither, actually."

"What about sweetie? Or sweet pea?"

"Sweet pea is kind of cute, I guess," I say, trying it out in my head. "But actually maybe I like the last name best."

"Yeah, but calling someone by their last name is more of a friend thing."

"Jim calls Pam 'Beesly' in *The Office* and it's adorable. Even after they're married."

"Okay. So I'll last name you. And maybe I'll throw a sweetie in there every once in a while."

"Okay, sounds good."

"So what kind of things should we do at the party? Should I have my arm around you the whole time? We could just pretend that we're on the balcony of the CN Tower and you'll be hanging on to me for dear life and no one will question it."

I laugh and hit him in the arm.

"It's true," he says.

"Should I take sips of your drinks?" I ask.

"Definitely."

We stare at each other in silence for a good twenty seconds, because we're both probably thinking the same thing. Should we kiss at all? I don't want to, but I feel like we should. But obviously we shouldn't if I don't want to.

"Maybe-" I start, but Logan says "Can I-" at the same time and then we both stop.

"Sorry, you go," we both say at the same time. And then we both say "Jinx, you owe me a Coke."

"Oh my god," Logan says with a sigh, putting his face in his hands. "We're ridiculous."

I smile and look away for a second, and then back at Logan, who's staring at me with this… look. I wish this look had a name so I could say it and you would be like "oh yes, that look, I know it well," but there aren't many names for the types of looks people can give. But his eyes have so much emotion in them. He's not smiling, but his cheeks and mouth are set in a way that shows he's not mad, or sad, or bored. He's not smiling, but he's smiling, but he's not necessarily happy. He's just looking at me, and I'm looking at him, and I have no idea what he's thinking, but this look he's giving me is somehow comforting. Like he's not sure what I'm thinking either, but that we both know we enjoy each other's company, and we both know it's going to end at some point, but we both know we're here now, and that we're friends, and that… I don't know. I'm getting a lot from him from this look, but all that I'm getting is just what I'm reading into it myself. It looks like he's feeling things and he's looking at me with his feelings but I don't know what his feelings are. Yes. That's the best way to describe it. He's looking at me with his feelings.

"What if I…" he whispers and leans into me, slowly, putting his hand on the mattress beside me to brace himself. He puts his face next to mine, and turns his mouth into mine but doesn't press our lips together. All I can focus on is my breathing, and the fact that I don't want him to kiss me but how I also wonder what it would be like if he kissed me. "I won't kiss you," he says quietly. "But what if I…" and his other hand is up by my face, his fingertip trailing along my jaw. He moves his face around mine, slowly, like he's thinking about where on my face he wants to kiss me, and in what order, but he just hovers, over my cheek, over my jaw, over my ear. My heart is hammering and my stomach is twisting into knots, but not necessarily in a bad way. Or maybe in a bad way. I don't know. But I feel weird just sitting there letting him do this so I raise my hand and put it on his neck, trailing part of his jaw with my thumb.

"Yeah, something like that's probably good," I manage to say.

"Okay, but we're not going to be sitting across from each other on a bed at a party."

"Should we stand up?" I ask.

He nods and we both get off his bed and stand facing each other. He grabs onto my wrists and then runs his fingers along my arms, up to my shoulders, around my neck, and then gently into my hair. I step in closer to him and put my hands on his back and he leans down and whispers into my ear.

"I can just whisper random things to you all night. I'll get all close to you, like this, and whisper Dwight Schrute quotes into your ear."

"Okay," I chuckle.

"You should run your fingers up and down my back."

"Why?"

"Why are we doing this at all, Reid?"

I run my fingertips up his back, slowly, and then back down, stopping when I can feel the waistline of his track pants. I do it again and he cups the side of my face under my ear, bringing his mouth close to mine. "Is this okay?" He moves his face back a little and says, "Is that closeness okay?" I can't find my voice, so I just nod, and he slowly moves closer to me again, not close enough to kiss, but close enough that I can taste his minty breath and I'm suddenly worried about my own. But the knots in my stomach are loosening and it's just my heart that's still racing.

"We only have to do something like this once at the party and no one will question anything," he whispers.

"Okay, so I guess we're good, then," I whisper back.

"Okay."

I slowly step away from him and he stands up straighter as if he's been startled.

"Okay," I say in my normal volume, but still feeling like I should be whispering. "Okay I'm fine with that. Uh, you can do that if you want."

The corner of Logan's mouth curls up just a bit. "Okay."

"Well I guess I'll go to bed, then."

"Okay," he says.

I step towards his door and he just watches, smiling at me.

"Goodnight, Logan."

"Goodnight, Isla."

CHAPTER 24

The celebrity party is at a bar, but you have to be on a list to get in, and only celebrities and their friends and/or pretend girlfriends are on the list. There are people outside screaming at all the famous people as they go in, as well as people with cameras, the flashes blinding us as we cross the sidewalk from the car to the building.

Logan puts his arm around my waist and I grab onto Claire's hand and the three of us go in together. The music is loud and there are less people than I was expecting, I think just because when I found out this party was happening at a bar I was picturing it being packed like karaoke night at a regular bar. But there are still a fair amount of people here, and any time I recognize a celebrity, my heart jumps into my throat.

"Would you ladies like a drink?" Logan asks.

"Oh no, nothing for me," Claire says. "I need to be as smooth as possible tonight."

"What about water?"

"Oh yeah, sure. With lemon?"

"For me, too," I add.

"Okay, two waters with lemon, coming right up."

Logan leaves us to go to the bar and Claire and I just grab onto each other's hands and try not to scream.

"There's another Logan nearby," Claire says.

"What?"

"Logan Lerman. He's behind you."

"Oh my god." But then I notice Paul Rudd behind Claire. "Paul Rudd. Paul Rudd is behind you."

Claire's eyes go wide and she squeezes my hands. "We cannot make fools of ourselves in front of Paul Rudd."

"Even if we did, he'd probably be a sweetheart about it," I say.

"Right? It's Paul Rudd."

"Paul Rudd's the best."

I realize as we're talking that we're actually yelling, so we can hear each other, and that Paul Rudd is much closer to us than I thought, and I think he can hear us. He smiles when I say that he's the best and then he just comes right up to us.

"I hear he's only okay," he says.

"Oh my god," Claire squeals. Her nails are now digging into my skin.

"We're obviously not basing this on real life experiences," I say. "So I guess you'd be the one to know."

He smiles and nods. "Definitely. He's just okay."

And then Logan comes back with our drinks, holding our two glasses and his bottle of beer with both his hands and Claire and I both try to help him let go of our drinks without him dropping anything. He nods to Paul Rudd, who nods back, and Claire and I take our waters. My hands feel better now that Claire isn't tearing them to shreds.

"You guys want to go up on the roof?"

"The roof?" I ask.

"Oh the roof is great," Paul Rudd says. "Way better than that okay guy you were talking about earlier."

We both giggle and then follow Logan, and Paul, it seems, to the other side of the bar where a door leads us to a set of stairs. We slowly make our way up, and once we get to the top, I lose my breath for half a second. First of all, there are less people up here, and the music is soft, but there are twinkle lights *everywhere.* Along the railing, around the bar that's apparently also up here, around skinny trees near most of the tables, around lattice that goes up the back wall where we just came out of. It's sparkly and calming, and makes me want to melt. The night sky isn't quite as dark as I was expecting, probably from all the city lights, but looking down at the city below is also calming. Brake lights and headlights on the road, warm yellow glows coming out of windows in buildings from across the street. I can still hear the traffic and everything, but somehow it feels quiet up here.

"This is nice," I say.

"I love it up here," Logan says. "Plus there usually aren't many people up here, which I tend to like."

"Which is weird," I say, "Because it's so pretty up here."

"I think people just don't like that the music isn't as loud, and you can hear the traffic and stuff."

I shrug. "I like it."

"I thought you might." Logan runs his hand down my arm and then links his fingers through mine. "Come on."

I narrow my eyes at him and then turn to Claire. "You'll be okay?" I ask her.

"Of course, she's hanging out with her new best friend," Paul Rudd says with a smile and Claire looks like she's going to faint.

"Yeah, I'll just hang out with this… okay guy," she jokes.

"Sounds good," Logan replies, and then he drags me to the edge of the roof.

He stands behind me and puts his arms around my shoulders and top of my chest, so I lightly grab onto his forearms.

"We didn't talk about this," he whispers, pressing his face in next to mine. "Is this okay?"

"This is okay," I squeak out.

I have knots in my stomach for about three seconds and then I feel them loosen and I relax into Logan's chest. It feels nice letting him be close to me like this. I'm not really sure why, but I like it, and I don't want it to end. I want to be closer to him, so I lean my head back a bit so that it's going into the crook of his neck.

"This is cozy," he says quietly.

"Yeah, it is."

"Do you think any paparazzi are getting some pictures of us from the street? They've got some pretty good zoom lenses."

"Probably."

"Can we make them think we're going to kiss?"

I slowly turn around and wrap my arms around his neck, letting him drop his face closer to mine. His breath is on my lips and he slowly moves from side to side, his mouth hovering over mine.

"You still don't want me to kiss you, right?" he asks.

"No," I manage. "No, not really, but thanks for asking."

He chuckles and tilts his head away from mine a little. "Okay."

We finally break apart a bit and go to find Claire, who's been sitting at a table and laughing with Paul Rudd.

"This guy's amazing!" she says to us as we sit down.

"No, actually, she's amazing!" Paul Rudd says. "I'm just okay."

"Pretty sure you're up there with Keanu Reeves," I add.

"Hey, what about me?" Logan asks, faking being hurt.

"You're in a different category," I say, tapping his cheek with the palm of my hand.

"I don't know what that means, but okay."

We mostly hang out with Paul Rudd all night, but a few people come to say hi to us, well, to the two celebrities at our table, and Claire and I just sit quietly while they catch up. Logan always introduces us, and we shake their hands, and I can't even remember who they all were now, but they're all pretty quick interactions.

"You guys, there are more people up here all of a sudden," Claire says, leaning over the table to get closer to us. "You should uh… You know."

Logan immediately grabs my hand and I scoot in a little closer to him. "We should what?" he asks, playing along.

"Bring them over here so we can meet more famous people, obviously."

"They'll come over on their own," he says with a shrug.

"Hey, new friend Paul Rudd," Claire says, getting Paul Rudd's attention.

"Yes new friend, Claire Something," he replies.

"Kishimoto," she says.

"I'm sorry?"

"Her name is Claire Kishimoto," I jump in.

"Oh yes, that makes sense. Yes, new friend, Claire Kishimoto?"

"Would you like to accompany me to the bar?"

"That would be lovely." They both get up and make their way to the bar in the corner and Logan slides his chair closer to me so that our thighs are touching.

"She did this on purpose," he whispers into my hair.

"I know."

"She's doing it so we can get close again. Since there are no people sitting with us to make them feel awkward with our PDA, we have no excuse to behave."

"Ha. Okay."

He cups my face and does his almost-kiss thing, this time making me lose my breath for half a second. I must have sucked in some air or something, because he smirks at me and says, "You alright there?"

"Fine," I half whisper.

He laughs quietly on my lips and then ever so lightly, kisses my jaw.

"This okay?" he asks.

I nod slowly, so he does it again, and then kisses the corner under my earlobe, and then *he puts my earlobe in his mouth* and I can feel him stopping almost as quickly as he starts, but I pull away almost immediately anyway.

"Okay, that's enough of that," I say with a nervous laugh.

"Sorry," he says. "I thought-"

"Thought what?" I ask. "Definitely not that it might make me uncomfortable."

"Did it?"

I pause, about to tell him that it did, but I can't. I can't, because I sort of wanted him to suck on my earlobe, pull on it gently with his teeth, and then I wanted him to kiss me. But I also didn't want him to kiss me. I wanted him to kiss me but I didn't want him to kiss me. You know? This doesn't make any sense. Also I never said he could do that!

"You liked it, didn't you?" he asks, probably trying to read my expression.

"No," I lie, covering my face with my hands.

"You liked it but you don't want me to do it again," he says quietly.

"I didn't like it."

"Okay. I'm sorry. I thought for a second that it would be okay because you just said it was okay that I was kissing your jaw, so I put your earlobe in my mouth, and then I took it out right away because then I thought maybe it was too far."

"Okay," I sigh.

"I'm sorry." He leans in closer again and whispers, "This fake dating thing is complicated sometimes."

"Yeah, it is."

"Hey you two can stop kissing now that we're back," Claire says, sitting down across from us.

"We weren't kissing," I say automatically, and regret it right away.

"Ah, you were doing *something*," Paul Rudd says. "Claire Kishimoto made me watch."

"Okay, I didn't make you watch, I just told you to look at how cute they were."

Paul Rudd half smiles and shrugs.

I feel weird about liking the fact that Logan was about to suck on my earlobe, and I try to brush it off. I look over at him and he gives me a weak smile, shrugs, and then nudges my shoulder with his. I nudge him back and grab his drink from him.

"Hey!" he shouts playfully, trying to get the beer bottle from my grasp.

"I just want a sip!" But then I take a big guzzle.

"That's more than a sip!" He takes it back and drinks the last of it. "I'll get you your own beer if you want one."

"No, I just wanted some of yours."

"Did you, now?"

I can't help but notice Claire smiling at us from the corner of my eye. This playfulness is sort of coming naturally now that we're doing it, and I feel a little less weird already.

"Let's go get another drink together," I suggest, "and these two new-found friends can hang out here for a bit."

"Okay, but you're going to get your own drink, right?"

"No, we can share!"

"Okay, I'm getting you your own drink."

We walk up to the bar together and there are a few people in line, but the bartender also isn't going super quickly. He's chatting up all the celebrities as they order their drinks and they seem to be having a good time talking to him. I grab onto Logan's hand and lean into his arm, resting my head on his shoulder. I swear I can feel him sigh, feel his tension slip away as I press into him.

"This is fun," I say to him.

"Yeah, it is. I'm glad Claire is finally breaking out of her shell."

"Me too. Who knew Paul Rudd would be the one to help her do it?"

It's our turn at the bar and Logan asks the bartender how his night is going.

"Oh it's great, and you?" he answers.

"We're having a lot of fun."

"That's awesome. What can I get you?"

Logan orders two beers and we take them back to our table, where Claire and Paul Rudd are laughing. Logan hands me one of the beer bottles and I shake my head at him.

"No," I say, "I told you I only wanted to drink from your drinks; I don't want my own."

He huffs and takes a drink from it and then hands it back to me. "There, I drank from it so it's sort of mine."

I shrug and take a sip from it myself. "You know, I don't really like beer."

"What?" he shrieks.

"Haha, I'm kidding." I take another drink and clink my bottle against the neck of his. "Cheers."

"Cheers." He stares at me as he takes a sip from his beer and I narrow my eyes at him.

"You two are adorable," Claire says.

"Thanks," we both say at the same time.

"Okay!" Paul Rudd announces to our table. "Cutest couple award! We deserve some pie."

"You mean we deserve some pie," Logan corrects.

"That's what I said."

"No, you said 'we' as in all of us, but I mean 'we' as in just me and Isla."

"Hey, is Spiderman here?" I blurt out.

"You mean the guy who did that hot lip sync battle?" Claire asks.

"I thought we were getting pie," Logan says.

"I can't believe I hung out with Paul Rudd all night!" Claire screams when we get back to Logan's.

"So you're glad you went then?" I ask.

"Yes! I'm so cool now! I can be so smooth around any and all celebrities! Just throw one at me! I'll be cool!"

"I don't think it's a good idea to throw people," Logan chuckles.

"I'm so wired! Can we swim in the pool!?"

"It's 2:30 in the morning," I say.

"We can swim in the pool if you want," Logan counters. "Time of day shouldn't make a difference."

"But we should probably go to bed, no?" I ask.

Logan shrugs. "What for?"

"I don't know?"

So that's that, then. We put on our bathing suits, turn on the lights outside and jump in the pool. We swim and go down the waterslide and play under the waterfall until almost four in the morning. And it's amazing.

Okay, here is where we're going to try and go deep inside my head so I can try to explain the 'I wanted him to kiss me but I didn't want him to kiss me' thing. I swear it all makes sense to my brain, and even though it does confuse me a little bit, it mostly doesn't. It can be very complicated for people to develop or not develop feelings for others, and we're going to attempt to break down what it's like for me.

So yes. I wanted Logan to kiss me at the party. But only a part of me wanted him to kiss me. I wanted him to kiss me, but I didn't want him to kiss me. Oh wait, we covered this part already. Ha. I'm sorry.

Okay.

There was a part of me, yes, that thought it might be nice to kiss Logan. I'm not sure when this part of me started to become a thing, it's like it just sort of snuck up on me, I guess. But here's the thing. Although I thought Logan kissing me at the party might be nice, I also thought that it would be scary. I'd kissed other guys before kissing Tyler, but only two. I had huge crushes on them, so kissing them was nice, and not scary. But I was younger, then. Now I'm old, and have only kissed the same person for almost nine years. I got used to what it was like to kiss Tyler. Kissing Tyler was comforting. It made me feel at home. It gave me little flutters in my stomach, but not in an anxiety kind of way. In a magical kind of way. And when I kissed Tyler, I didn't think about how I was doing it, or if I was any good at it. But kissing Logan would be scary because I don't know how Logan kisses. I don't even know if I'm good at kissing anymore. The time at the party, I hadn't kissed anyone in almost a year and I basically completely forgot how to even do it. Also when you kiss someone, you usually do other things not long after that, and that scares me even more. Being naked in front of someone new, after having only one person see me naked, is not something that sounds like fun to me. I'm absolutely not ready for that kind of intimacy.

On top of that, there's the scary idea of falling for someone new. Trusting someone new. Being vulnerable with them and basically giving yourself over to the idea that they just might shatter your heart into thousands of tiny pieces. Like Tyler did. If Logan were to kiss me, and I were to let him, and I liked it, that would mean for sure that I like him. That would mean that I want there to be something more, and if that something more never happens, or does happen but gets broken, it would suck. A lot. And I'm not sure if that's something I want to subject myself to.

CHAPTER 25

Claire and I don't wake up until almost one in the afternoon. It seems like Logan's still sleeping so we take turns in the shower and then head into the arcade, and play Dance Dance Revolution until we're sweating. We probably should have waited on the showers. Logan comes in after about an hour and joins us. We take turns playing the winner and we just end up having a great afternoon filled with ridiculous video game dancing, and lots of laughter. We go in the pool after supper, and then head to the theatre room to watch some movies. We continue this routine for the rest of our visit, not even leaving Logan's property. And you know, it was exactly what I needed.

I realize on our last full day here that I still haven't played in the fountain, so without telling anyone what I'm doing, I make my way to the front of the house and step outside, planning on going in with all my clothes on. Everyone knows that when you play in a fountain, it has to happen fully clothed. It's just not as fun or as authentic if you're in a bathing suit. I step up onto the stone and look down into the clear water. There are a few pennies at the bottom, which I think is cute, and it looks like the water will go up to the middle of my shins or just below my knees. I jump off the ledge and let the water splash around me as I land, and then I put my arms up, stepping under the stream that's coming down from the addition above me. I spin around and close my eyes, my head tilted back as the water pours over my face. I straighten up and shake my head because I remember that I like breathing (ha), and then I just start skipping around in the water, kicking it up as much as I can and letting it splash me. I wish there was music playing so I can pretend I'm in a music video.

Logan and Claire jump in without me even realizing they had been there and I startle a little but we immediately start laughing and running around the fountain together. Logan sort of tackles me and we both fall in, my knees scraping along the bottom.

"Oh ow," I say through a laugh.

"Oh my god, are you hurt?" he asks.

"I'm okay." I roll onto my back and bend my knees so that they poke out of the water and Logan looks at them.

"You did get hurt," he says, lightly touching them with his fingertips.

"It's just a scrape."

"Just kiss them better, already," Claire calls.

"Gross," I say.

"Come on," Logan says, standing up and holding out a hand to me. "Let's get dry and cozy in some PJs."

"Can Logan please just be your real boyfriend?" Claire asks me as we're getting ready to leave. We're in our room with the door closed, packing up our suitcases.

"No."

"But you didn't even think about it," she whines. "He's so great and you two are so cute together. Like so cute it almost makes me sick. But it doesn't. It makes me go 'awwwww'."

I laugh at her. "I told you I'm not ready for a relationship."

"That was a while ago, though."

"It wasn't that long ago."

"It kind of was. Look, if you guys visit each other again and you're still single by the end of it I might lose my shit."

"There's nothing wrong with being friends with someone, Claire."

"There is if you clearly have feelings for each other and you're already making everyone else think you're dating, and you clearly have feelings for each other."

"We don't have feelings for each other," I say, ignoring the fact that she said that part twice.

"Keep telling yourself that," she says with a smile.

"It's true."

"I saw you guys at that party."

"We were pretending."

"It didn't look like pretending."

"We were pretending!" I repeat. "We practiced it the night before, in his room."

"I'm sorry, what?"

"We practiced what we would do to make people think we're dating."

"Nope. This has gone too far." Claire throws her hands up in the air. "What exactly were you doing?"

"Just… I don't know. Like, almost kissing."

Her eyes go wide and she grabs at her hair. "You're killing me, Isla!"

"Why?"

"Nobody does that! Nobody practices their pretend almost- kisses! He likes you!"

"No, he's just being cautious because he knows I'm not comfortable with a lot of stuff. He wanted to make sure I was okay."

"Because he's in love with you."

"He's not in love with me. And even if he was, I'm not in love with him, so it doesn't matter."

The plane ride back into Toronto is a little awkward because Claire seems to be mad at me for not wanting to date

Logan for real. She keeps telling me everything's fine, but she's not herself. Any time I try to be funny with her or get excited about something, like our movie options or the amazing view, she's only at about 50 percent. Maybe 65 sometimes.

"I don't want you to be mad at me," I finally say when there's only about an hour left in our flight.

"I'm not mad at you."

"But you are."

"Ugh." She turns towards me. "I'm not mad. I'm just… I don't know. Mad?"

I laugh a little. "But why? Because I want to be single?"

"Nobody wants to be single, Isla."

"I'm sure there are lots of people who want to be single. Not everyone has to feel the same way as you. And yeah, okay, I don't want to be single for the rest of my life. I would love to have someone to share my life with. To have someone to come home to and tell them about my day. To make supper with, or cuddle on the couch with while we watch TV. Yeah, all of that sounds great. But I don't *need* it. And I want to be okay being by myself before I try to spend my life with someone new. I need to be okay in my own skin before I let someone else in."

She rolls her eyes a little. "I guess that's okay."

"Of course it's okay."

"But the second you feel amazing being you, you better go jump Logan."

"You're ridiculous."

I have built up more stock for my website, but I still don't feel like it's enough to open it up. I'm so overwhelmed by the amount of people who have signed up for my mailing list. I feel like once I make the site public and open up the online store, I'm just going to sell out of everything right away. And I'm still not sure what to price my figurines at. I'm putting my magnets on the site and keeping them at ten dollars, but I guess the figurines should be more than twenty five, especially considering how much work I put into them. Maybe thirty five would be okay? I also took the site designer's advice and found a digital photographer to take photos of all my stuff, but they said it would probably be easier for me if I did the photos myself since I'm constantly updating my inventory. I felt bad for them so I paid them to give me a little lesson on framing and stuff and now I'm waiting for a lightbox with seamless white background thing to come in.

How's it going, pretend girlfriend? Logan texts me one night.

I'm okay, I'm just making a t-rex I reply.

A t-rex? From what?

From the cretaceous period? I type to him.

Oh so it's not from a movie?

I guess it could be from any movie that stars a t-rex

Har har. Logan types. You should make him wear a hat.

Too late, I'm making her a purse.

For real?

Yes for real. It's going to look adorable hanging off of her tiny little t-rex arm. What are you up to?

I'm just watching *The Office*.

So am I! I'm on season 8.

We chat back and forth a little bit and then I tell him I have to go or I'll never get my work done.

Sounds like someone needs to quit their restaurant job he says.

I need to see how everything goes when the site is live.

I know, I'm just bugging.

I know. Okay. Talk to you later. I add a smiley face emoji.

Later, Reid. Winky face.

People keep messaging me and commenting on my Instagram pictures asking when I'm opening my store. I reply to as many people as I can, telling them that I work a full time job and it's hard to build my inventory back up in my spare time but I'm doing the best that I can. It takes a long time to make these, I say. Most people don't reply to me but some people say nice, supportive things like, "Take your time, hun, don't wear yourself out!" or "Okay! I'm sorry, I thought this was your job!" which is nice. But it still stresses me out. I want to take more time off but I only have a week of vacation left this year which I'm using to visit Logan on my birthday. And I'm really hoping to have my shop up and running before then anyway. I'll just be tired for a few more weeks. It's fine. I'll be fine.

A text from Tyler pops up on my screen as I'm replying to Instagram messages and I try to ignore it for a little while so it doesn't look like I'm waiting by my phone waiting for him to text me or something. I reply to two more messages and then look at his text.

Can I do anything to help you with your shop? the text says. I can see a lot of people in your comment sections are getting impatient.

Not really, but thanks I reply. But then I realize I still need photos of everything. I've had the supplies for it for a week or so now, and haven't had the energy to set it up or go through them all yet. Actually… I text to him before he answers.

Yes?

You want to be my photographer?

Tyler is at my apartment in less than an hour and I realize he's never been in here before. He offered to help me move, which was nice of him, but I thought it would be weird. He helped load my stuff into the truck, but didn't come with us to the new place.

"It's really nice in here," he says looking around.

"Thanks."

"Small, though."

"Yeah, well, I am just one person. I don't have someone to split the rent with."

"My place is small, too."

"You didn't keep the apartment?" I ask.

He shakes his head. "I couldn't afford it on my own. And it's shitty too because I'm actually paying more now for my place than I was for half of ours."

"Same," I say. "It's tight sometimes but it's doable. I just can't do as much fun stuff anymore."

"Well you can now, now that you have a super-rich boyfriend."

I smile a little. "Yeah, I guess."

"So how long until you move into his mansion with him? I saw your Instagram pictures."

"Oh probably never. It's not like that."

He narrows his eyes at me. "What does that mean?"

"Nothing. I just don't think this is a forever thing, you know?"

"Ah."

"It's not like that, either."

"You don't need to explain yourself to me, Isla."

"Right," I say with a nod.

"Anyway, pictures?"

"Yes."

He helps me set up the lightbox, and we take a few photos to make sure we have the exposure and angles right, and then he starts taking the pictures for me while I make more figurines. Every once in a while I look over at him and wonder what it would feel like to kiss him again. But it makes me feel weird every time, so I guess that's a good thing. But then he turns and looks at me and gives me this weak smile, and for some reason "I don't want us to be together anymore" starts playing in my head. I'm just immediately taken back to the moment I knew for sure that he didn't love me anymore, and I feel like breaking down. I almost sob right there in front of him, but I take a deep breath and hold it in. But I suddenly don't want to be in the same room as him anymore. All I can think about is the fact that he stopped loving me and couldn't be bothered to try and make his feelings come back. That he didn't seem to care about me at all. That any time I tried to talk to him about it, instead of listening to me he would get angry and make me feel like it was my fault that I felt lonely, or that it was my fault I didn't feel beautiful anymore. And for some reason I feel like our breakup is happening all over again. I'm not in love with Tyler anymore, I'm sure I'm not, but it still hurts. Remembering how he hurt me still hurts. I get up from the couch and make my way to the washroom. I shut the door and sit down on the closed toilet, putting my face in my hands and taking deep breaths to try to stop myself from crying. But no matter what I do, I can't hold it in anymore. I take a gasping breath when I feel a sob in my chest and I get up from the toilet and immediately turn the shower on so Tyler can't hear me. I take off my clothes and get in, and the second I'm under the hot water I start to cry. Like, full on shaking sobs. I can't help it.

Why is my life such a mess? What if I could have made it work between Tyler and I? What if I didn't try hard enough to make it work? What if I shut down too easily when he got defensive? What if I didn't try hard enough to talk to him about it? What if I could have taken a different approach?

And now I'm in a fake relationship with someone and I'm afraid to admit that I might have a crush on him. No, I don't have a crush on him. Even if I did have a crush on him, I don't want to be in a relationship right now. Even if I did want to be in a relationship I'm too much of a chicken to do anything about it. There's nothing to do anyway, because I don't have a crush on him. But what if Claire is right and he does like me? But I keep pushing him away by telling him I don't want him to kiss me? Ugh, what am I, thirteen? This is ridiculous.

Plus I want to quit the restaurant so bad, but I also feel bad about doing that! I don't want to leave Tom after being there with him since the beginning. I don't want to get my hopes up and have my store fail after three months. What if it fails after three months? *What if it fails right away?* What if it *doesn't* fail and I can't keep up with the orders?

I thought I would have my life together by now. I thought I would have everything figured out. I didn't think I would be crying over boys and my stupid job.

I hear the bathroom door creak open and I'm still sobbing. Big, loud, whaling sobs.

"What's happening?" I hear Tyler ask.

I just keep crying. I can't stop.

"Isla," he says, a painful crack in his voice.

And then the shower curtain is being pulled back and I pull my hands away from my eyes to see Tyler standing at the opening, looking at my face.

"What's going on?" He doesn't sound annoyed. He sounds very much like he's worried about me.

"I hate my life," I cry.

"Everybody hates their life." And then he gets in the shower with me. With his clothes on!

"What are you doing?"

"I don't know! I don't know what to do!" he half shouts.

"Why didn't you care this much while we were together?"

"What?"

"You didn't care about not loving me anymore." My sobs have quieted down now, but I'm still really sniffly and still have to take weird shaky breaths.

He reaches around me and shuts the water off. "I'm sorry," he says. "I know that must have felt really shitty. But I was…" He lets out a deep breath and wipes the water off his face. "I did care. I guess I just didn't realize how much *you* cared."

"That doesn't even make any sense!"

"I didn't want to break up with you. I mean, I did, but I didn't want to hurt you. It hurt me that I didn't love you anymore."

"Why didn't you try?"

He looks at me without answering for longer than I would like, and eventually I think we both know that he doesn't need to. He probably did try, for a long time, and it didn't work. He had just stopped trying by the time I could feel it.

Tyler finally lets out a deep breath and opens the shower curtain, leaning out to grab a towel from the bar on the wall. He pats himself down and squeezes his clothes inside it, so that he doesn't drip all over the place.

"Where are your extra towels?" he asks.

"In the closet in the hall," I say quietly. "Just outside the door."

He leaves and comes back in with a towel, handing it to me and then immediately leaving the room. I realize just then that I was naked that whole time. I mean it's not like he hasn't seen me naked before, but it's kind of weird now that I'm thinking about it. Only now that I'm thinking about it, though. At the time it didn't faze me. Is that weird?

I go into my room to change, and when I come out, Tyler is gone.

CHAPTER 26

I'm in a weird funk for the rest of the evening and I try to make more clay things but I keep stopping and staring at the wall. Not even at the TV. Just the wall beside it. I end up going to bed early and crying into my pillow until I fall asleep.

My head is in a weird place at work the next day and everyone seems to notice. It feels like I just got broken up with all over again, which is ridiculous, and I feel weird about how upset I am. I feel like I shouldn't be upset when I think about my ex falling out of love with me. I don't need him to complete me. I don't need a man for my life to have meaning. My life has meaning all on its own and I can do whatever the fuck I want on my own too. I can do whatever makes me happy by myself; I don't need someone to do it with me. I'm telling myself all these things, and I know they're true, I know I don't need anyone to be in love with me. But I want someone to be in love with me. Nobody needs a PS4, or a trip to Europe, but most good things in life aren't really *needed* are they? Most good things in life are luxuries. But those luxuries help us in other aspects of our lives. Like when I said I really needed mine and Claire's trip where we basically hung out in Logan's mansion the whole time; I didn't actually physically need it the way I need water, or food, or a shower. But I needed it in order to not feel so exhausted, and frazzled, and overwhelmed. It was a break from my life. I didn't need it to continue living, but I still needed it, you know? And I don't need a man in my life as my partner to not be sad about myself, or to make me feel good about myself, but I need one because I need a companion. Someone to share my life with.

Anyway I'm still bummed about everything at work and finally Claire asks me what's up. I just shrug and continue trying to smile for my customers.

"Why are you still working here?" someone asks me near the end of my shift. She's a little drunk and I just scrunch my eyebrows at her.

"What do you mean?" I ask.

"Aren't you the girl who makes those polymer clay mini statue things?"

"Yes."

"Girl, you need to quit this place!"

"I need to make sure my shop will be successful first," I say.

"But you're not giving it a chance to! You're spending all your energy on this place and you should be putting it into what you love! People are waiting for you to open back up and you would be by now if you weren't still here, bringing us pizza. I mean, don't get me wrong, it's fucking delicious pizza. But girl!"

I give her a half smile and walk away. She's right. I know she's right. I've known this the entire time. But if a stranger is telling me to do it, I can't ignore it anymore. I find Tom behind the bar and suddenly my hands are shaking. My arms are weak with nerves and my mouth is dry.

"Tom, can I talk to you for a second?" I ask him.

He looks over at me with a tight expression and I can tell that he knows what I'm about to say. He nods, and follows me to the back room.

I let out a deep breath and he puts his hands on his hips.

"Tom, I'm really sorry, but I have to focus on my business or it's never going to take off the way I want."

"I know," he says softly.

"I'll work the next two weeks."

"The schedule's only out till next week."

"It'll take you longer than a week to hire someone new and have them trained."

"Claire and Mark can handle it until then. Plus the part-timers might want to pick up a few extra hours."

"Are you sure? I don't mind."

"I'm sure, Isla. You should have done this a while ago."

I smile at him, hug him, he hugs me back, and then I go cut a piece of peanut butter chocolate cheesecake and bring it to the girl who told me to quit.

"This is for you," I say, putting it on the table in front of her. Her friend smiles but kind of scoffs, like, she doesn't understand why I didn't also bring her a free piece of cheesecake. "Share it if you like, but it's on me."

"Why?"

"Because I just quit."

"What!? Yaaasss!" She puts her hands in the air, her fork clenched in her right fist.

I'm actually happy when I get home. I have a real, genuine smile that I can't seem to get rid of.

I call Logan immediately, but it goes to voicemail and I realize he's probably working. He's three hours behind me and they usually shoot until at least 8PM.

"Hey, it's Logan, leave a message," is all he says on the answering service.

"Logan! Oh my god! Call me as soon as you're done shooting or whatever! Ah oh my god I quit my job! Like, not on the spot, I didn't just up and quit, but I gave notice! My last shift is next week! Aaahh oh my god, call me!"

I want to shout from the rooftops, I want to dance around outside in the rain, except it's not raining. Claire wanted to celebrate with me and she was going to blow off her plans with Emily and I told her not to be ridiculous. I can be happy on my own. It's fine.

I keep checking my phone every ten minutes, hoping I just missed Logan's call or text, but there's nothing. No notifications from anyone. My excitement starts to die away and I feel weird. Now I'm sad about the fact that I have no one to celebrate with and the first person I called lives in a different country and couldn't even come over to be excited with me if he wanted to. I need more friends. Instead of thinking too much about it and letting the sadness take over, I put on *Neighbourly* and start it from the beginning. And then I get out my clay and start making stuff.

Logan doesn't end up calling me by the time I go to bed and I hate to admit that I'm a little sad about it, but I guess it's okay to be sad about not being able to share your excitement with one of your best friends, right?

He does call me though, at three in the morning, and my ringer scares the shit out of me. I gasp and squeal a little as I wake up and then I grab my phone from the nightstand and see that it's Logan.

"Hey," I yawn into my phone.

"I'm sorry I just realized how late it is for you. Like just as you answered, I realized. I'm so sorry. You can go back to sleep."

"It's okay, I want to talk to you."

"So you quit, eh? That's pretty cool. I knew you had it in you!"

"Yeah," I chuckle. "So hopefully I can have my site up and running soon."

"We need to throw a party for your launch."

"Oh I never thought of that. I don't know many people though, so it wouldn't be much of a party. You could come visit, though."

"I wish I could but I'm so busy. I have so many events scheduled it's absurd. The movie's coming out soon and there's so much press for it it's making my head hurt a little bit."

"Oh. I thought it wasn't coming out until December?"

"Yeah, that's soon."

"Oh. Am I still going to be able to come for my birthday?"

"Yes, definitely. There might be a few days that you have to hang out by yourself, though. I just have interviews and stuff. But not the whole time, and not on your actual birthday. I checked already."

"Okay."

"But you're coming for a whole week, right?"

"That was the plan."

"Yeah, it'll be fine. I'm doing one talk show, and you could sit in the audience for that," he says.

"That might be fun."

"There ya go."

I smile and curl up deeper into my blankets. "I might have to go back to sleep," I say.

"Okay, wait, before you do. I love your freckles."

"Um. Thanks?"

Logan chuckles quietly. "I'm reading nice comments on your latest Instagram picture."

"Oh."

"May I continue?"

"You may," I say through a smile that I'm sure he can hear.

"**Your smile makes me happy.**

I love this picture of you.

Oh my goodness gracious me, what an adorable human.

I feel like we could be friends in real life

Why do I want to be friends with her? Can I be friends with her?

She always looks so confident. I'm really glad I met you. That last one wasn't a comment, that's from me."

"I'm glad I met you too." I hide my face in my pillow as if he can see me blushing.

"Okay, you need to get some sleep. Goodnight, Reid."

"Goodnight, Jackson."

ClayMate is here! Thank you to everyone for waiting patiently, and thank you for all your words of encouragement! I'm so excited to share my website with you, and I'm excited to be a part of your fandom experience! Please explore the site at your leisure and definitely check out the section where you can get custom made pieces especially for you!

<3 Isla

I already have three orders. The site has been live for twenty minutes and I have three orders. Were people just waiting by their phones and computers for me to email them about it being ready? I've sold a Charlie Pace (*Lost*), a Canada magnet, and a No-Face (*Spirited Away*). I'm so excited that I immediately move their orders into the processing phase, print out their paperwork and package them up. I go back to my computer to move them to the shipping phase and I've also sold a Black Widow and a Wonderwoman to the same person. This is so exciting!

I notice over the day that people are putting things in their cart but not buying them. Which might be good. I don't want to get hundreds of orders all at once and be overwhelmed by it, like last time. I get a few more orders before the end of the day and I have them all mailed out before the post office closes.

Logan calls me to congratulate me and I talk to him for about an hour and explain how the custom order form works on my site. The price mostly goes by size, with an extra fee tacked on for the fact that it's custom. But I'll do up to eight inch pieces for it. Eight inch ones obviously use more clay, but they're a little bit easier to get the details right, at least in my opinion. I haven't done many big pieces in the past so I'm a little excited to do some if anyone places an order for them.

Claire comes over when she's done her shift and she helps me package the next four orders that I get in, and we talk about her day and laugh at silly customers. She leaves fairly early because I need to get up in the morning to make more pieces so

I don't get behind. Plus ship out any others that people may order.

I've been making and shipping out Claymates during most of my days, but I've decided to give myself weekends off to keep myself from burning out. Which is cool because I've never had regular weekends off since I started working in high school. Look at that, I'm less than a month away from turning thirty and I finally have a job with a schedule that I like.

I get my first custom piece on my website, which is an eight inch Sabrina from the new Netflix reboot, and I'm so excited to get started on it. I look at reference photos online to make sure her outfit and hair is right, and that her hair band is in the right spot. I know I just said that it's easier to do details on bigger pieces, but I guess it's also harder, because when it's bigger it's easier to tell if it closely resembles the thing or not. It takes me a long time to do her face and my fingers are crampy by the time I'm happy with it. That definitely took much longer than it takes me to do the faces of the small characters. Maybe my custom fee should be even more. No, I think it's still a decent price, even if it takes me a bit longer. I'm just not used to doing bigger pieces, so I'll get better and faster, I'm sure.

We're going to skip ahead a little bit because I don't really know how to transition, but I guess I'll just say that things go well after this, but also nothing very interesting or exciting happens. I get a few more large custom pieces and I get faster pretty quickly, so I'm not worried about the price point like I was when I made the Sabrina. Logan and I talk on the phone every night and text a little bit through the day, and I catch myself every time I notice that his messages make me smile. I tell myself it's just because he's Logan and I'm lonely, and most of the time I believe it. But that's it. Nothing else happens. So let's end the chapter here and start the next one with my birthday trip to see Logan. Because that is definitely interesting.

CHAPTER 27

There are so many people in Logan's house. Most of them are celebrities, but some of them are crew people from *Neighbourly*, and I'm very overwhelmed with how many people know I'm turning thirty and how many of them think I'm Logan's girlfriend, and how many of them know this party is for me. The music is loud and I'm drunk but not too drunk, just happy drunk, and I don't know where Logan is.

"Have you seen Logan?" I ask a group of incredibly good looking people in the kitchen. They all shrug at me and then continue their conversation.

I make my way up the stairs and into Logan's room to find him looking through something on his bed.

"There you are," I say, relieved.

"Oh sorry, I didn't think I would be gone this long. I have a birthday present for you."

"You do?"

"Yeah. It's just something small." He shrugs and looks down at his feet.

I feel myself smirking a little bit. "Small things are great."

He grabs a little gift bag off his bed and extends it out to me. I step in closer to him and take it from him. He's going all red. I take out the tissue paper and pull a long, slim box from the bag. I'm afraid that it's going to be some ridiculously expensive necklace that I would be too afraid to wear, but when

I pop the box open I'm pleasantly surprised. It's a rose gold chain with two little rosegold disks, each with different numbers on them.

"Logan this is adorable," I say.

"I thought it suited you."

"It does. I love it."

"I'm sorry I didn't get you something more expensive."

"It's okay," I laugh. "It would have felt weird if you got me something super expensive. Plus you paid for my flight." I look at the numbers on the little rose gold discs and rub my finger and thumb along the edges. "What are the numbers?"

"Um, where we met, and the date." He's so quiet I almost can't hear him.

"Really? Like the address?"

"Um." He sounds very unsure of himself. "No, the coordinates."

"Are you for real?"

"Yes…"

"Logan, that's so weird and cute. Are you sure that was the date we met?"

"I'm sure."

"Well now it's even cuter."

"I'm glad you like it."

"I love it. Thank you."

"You're welcome."

"Can we go swim in the pool now?" I ask.

"Can I put your necklace on you first?"

I hand it to him and turn around, about to pull my hair out of the way for him, but Logan does it first. His fingers gently sweep across the back of my neck as he gathers my hair in his hands, and I get goosebumps down my arms. I try to be subtle when I take in a deep breath, and he lays my hair over my shoulder. I bunch it in my own hands when he starts to put the necklace around my neck, and I pull it over the chain, letting it rest over my shoulder again. I feel him clasp it behind my neck, and then I don't feel his hands on me at all anymore, and I want them to be.

The two charms hang just below my throat and I touch them gingerly with my fingertips before turning back around to face him. I smile up at him and he smiles back at me and we just stare at each other for a good ten seconds. I swallow and rock back and forth on the balls of my feet, telling myself that he got me this cute necklace because he's my friend, not because he has feelings for me. But why would a guy get someone a necklace with the *coordinates of where they met* on it, if they were only friends? Oh right, because everyone needs to think we're dating and if anyone saw it and asked about it, everyone in existence would be talking about it and how freaking adorable it is. They would probably all call it the *Lola Necklace* and want replicas for themselves. Of course. Why do I even let myself jump to these absurd possibilities? Of course it's for show.

Except what if he has feelings for me? It's easy enough to know where we met and find out the coordinates of the location, but how does he remember the date? I don't even remember, and it was more significant for me! I was meeting a famous person! I sort of just want to kiss him and see what he does. I sort of just want to go on my toes and press myself into him and taste his breath on my tongue.

"Pool?" he finally says.

"Yes. Pool. I have to get changed first."

I go into the washroom attached to his bedroom to change (all my stuff is in here because some celebrities will be staying over so we have to act the part) and I come out with my hair in a ponytail, and wearing my purple bikini and the necklace. Logan had changed too while I was in the washroom, and when I come out, his jaw almost drops.

"What?" I ask.

He blinks a couple of times. "Nothing. Just. Nothing."

"You're acting like you haven't seen me in a bathing suit before," I say.

"I feel like I haven't."

"What does that mean?"

"I don't know. I'm a little drunk."

I smile and move closer to him. "Me too."

"Okay so do you want to practice our pretend dating thing again before we go downstairs?"

"Like… How?" I lick my lips and swallow.

He steps in closer to me and lightly grabs the charms from my necklace. My breath hitches and I step a little closer to him.

"I forget what we did last time," he whispers.

"Um," I say quietly. "We just sort of…"

I put my hands on the back of his arms, and I never thought about how in shape he was until this second. I'm touching his bare arms while his chest is also bare, and he's not overly muscular or anything, he's kind of slim, but he's definitely in shape. And I'm touching his tight triceps and I can feel my face getting hot, and then he steps closer so that our chests are touching and he lets go of my necklace so that his hand can cup my chin and tilt my face up to his. He leans in and brings his mouth to my ear.

"We just sort of did this, right?" he murmurs.

"Yeah."

He kisses my jaw right under my ear and my knees almost give out. "Okay, I remember," he says softly. "Let's go back to the party."

I nod and let him step away from me.

We go downstairs together, holding hands so people think we're in love. But I still feel weak everywhere from being close to him in his room. I would like to do more of that.

There are only a couple other people in the pool and I have no idea who they are, but it's okay, I just want to be silly in the water with Logan. We take pictures under the surface with his underwater camera and laugh hysterically every time we come back up to look at how bad we are at posing underwater. I keep thinking I've framed the photo right, and that I have a great expression on my face, but every picture comes out with only half my face in the picture and I look like I'm having a painful poo or something.

After who knows how long of laughing at ourselves and having mostly sobered up, I swim over to the waterfall and stand under it with my elbows on the edge of the pool behind me. The water falls gently on my head and Logan comes up to join me. He catches me off guard when his hands go right to my hips under the water and he presses his chest right up against mine. But it only catches me off guard because I'm not expecting it. He did it so quickly without thinking, it seems, as opposed to slowly and carefully like up in his room earlier. I like it, but I sort of hate that I like it.

"Is this okay?" he asks, bringing his face close to mine.

"Yes," I breathe on his lips.

"Really?" he presses himself even tighter against me and his mouth is mere millimetres from mine. My stomach flutters and I press myself into him.

"Really," I whisper. I have butterflies in my fingertips.

"What if I…" and he kisses me. His warm lips are on mine and I wrap my arms around him and he presses me into the wall of the pool behind me and I feel like I can't get close enough to him. He grabs the back of my thighs under the water and pulls me up a little so I can wrap my legs around his waist. The waterfall streams down over us as I breathe him in and he holds me up against him. His tongue is so delicious and his hands on my butt are fantastic. He finally pulls back but I'm not ready to stop and I lean my face in closer to him. He smiles and kisses me again.

I don't really know how it happened, but we're on the stairs now. I guess he pushed us off the wall and we sort of drifted through the water, but I'll be honest, I really have no idea. I'm sitting on a lower step so that the water comes up pretty high on my chest and Logan is kneeling on the step below me, but he keeps pushing me back into the concrete so I crawl out of the pool backwards and he follows, hardly taking his mouth off mine the whole time. He grabs both my hands and pulls me to my feet.

"Hi," he says, which is adorable.

"Hi."

He kisses me again and I press up against him, not feeling close enough to him. He scoops me up in his arms and I have no idea where we're going because we're still kissing, but he's walking somewhere and I just hope that he's got his eyes open or something, but then he stops walking almost right away, probably because he can't see. I move my mouth away from his and I kiss his jaw, his neck, his collarbone, and he continues walking until we get to the hot tub. He carries me into it, and the water feels extra warm since I'm a little cold after getting out of the pool, and I'm glad there's no one else out here anymore because I just want to kiss Logan until the end of time. We slip into the hot, silky water and continue making out.

"Hey!" someone shouts from the patio. "Stop playing tonsil hockey and come in here and have birthday cake!"

"You want to go have cake?" Logan asks, his lips still brushing mine.

"Not really," I breathe. My stomach erupts with butterflies again and I get tingles everywhere. But these aren't nervous butterflies. They're the kind that sort of feel like magic, the kind that make me sigh because I can't handle how much I love the fluttering inside me. They're the kind of butterflies that I feel like I can relax into.

He kisses me long and slow, pulling my hair tie out and running his fingers through my wet hair. He pulls me into his lap so that I'm straddling him and I almost gasp when he starts to play with the string in the back of my bikini. It doesn't feel like he's trying to untie it, but it isn't double knotted, and there's a whole house full of people who could just look out the window and see. Even if I wanted him to untie it, I would want it to be more private. So just in case, I reach behind me and grab onto his hand, shaking my head.

"I wasn't," he says between kisses that are continuing to take my breath away. "I wasn't going to untie it, I was just playing with it." He kisses me again but takes his hands away.

I open my eyes to see that he's holding his hands up beside him.

"What are you doing?" I ask, grabbing them. "Put your hands back. Just don't take my top off."

He grins into my mouth and I kiss him again, sighing when he runs his hands up my back, and back down to my hips.

"Like this?" he asks.

"Yes, that's good," I say, kissing him again.

"Guys!" the same person calls, and I realize that it's Jack Roy, the guy who plays Chas on *Neighbourly*. "Cake!"

"Okay," Logan calls. "Come on," he says quietly to me. "I think everyone gets the idea now anyway."

He gently slides me off him and gets out of the hot tub and walks towards the house as if none of this even happened. And I suddenly feel like I can't breathe. And not in the good way like a few minutes ago. I feel my face getting hot and my eyes welling with tears but I swallow it down as best as I can. I'm such an idiot. I can't believe I didn't realize he was only doing all that for show. All his famous friends are right in the kitchen and could see us easily this whole time if they wanted to. I can't believe I kissed him back like that, like I *meant it*, because I did mean it, while he was just acting. Now he's going to think that I was acting too, and that I'm okay with it. But how could he think that I was just doing this for show? I was into it. But of course he would think I was just doing it for show; that's what this whole thing has been, hasn't it? A show?

Logan stops on the deck and looks back at me with raised eyebrows. "Are you coming, Reid?"

I huff and get out of the hot tub and storm past him into the house.

"Whoa," he says, coming through the door after me.

Everyone starts singing happy birthday as soon as I walk in, and I hate that I still feel like I'm about to cry. I'm on the verge of tears and I'm doing absolutely everything I can to hold it together while a bunch of famous people sing me the happy birthday song. This is ridiculous. They finally stop singing and I grab a towel from the pile by the door to wipe myself down. I make sure I won't drip all over the place, wrap the towel around my head and walk over to the cake that's on the island. I take a deep breath and blow all the candles out, letting everyone cheer and clap around me.

"I'll be right back," I say with a smile that feels so fake I'm afraid everyone can see through it.

I run upstairs to Logan's room and grab my clothes to change back into. Logan opens the door without knocking while I'm in my underwear and bra, and I almost tell him to get out, but it's basically the same as a bikini, so I just keep putting my clothes on with him in the room.

"Are you okay?" he asks.

"I'm fine. Why?"

"You seem mad."

I take the towel off my head and pull a t-shirt on. "Why on Earth would I be mad?" I try to say it sincerely but it comes out dripping in sarcasm; I can't help it.

"I don't know."

I throw my hair up in a quick bun and go into the washroom to make sure I don't have messed up mascara from the pool. It looks fine so I go back into his room and keep walking into the hall.

"Maybe you should think about it, then," I say as I pass him.

"What's that supposed to mean?"

I shrug and head downstairs, back to the kitchen where most people are still gathered. Some people are sitting around the island and some people are at the table, but there are also a few groups of people standing. They're all eating cake so I go cut myself a piece and eat it while I stand alone. It doesn't seem like anyone has even noticed me come back.

"What's going on?" Logan asks, coming up behind me.

"Nothing. I'm eating cake."

"Can I have some?"

I shrug and point to the cake on the counter with my fork. "Be my guest."

"No, I mean some of yours."

"Fuck no, this is my cake."

"But we could…" he leans in closer to me and whispers, "we could share. Like a cute couple."

"Except that we're not. A cute couple."

I wish I could just tell him why I'm upset. I'm sure it was an honest mistake on his part and he doesn't realize that I didn't want to kiss him for show, that I kissed him because I just wanted to kiss him, but I can't tell him that. He'll be freaked out and not want to be my friend anymore. If I tell him that I caught feelings, he's going to second guess everything he says to me and everything he does around me. He's going to be worried that I think everything he does is because he likes me and then we're going to fake break up and we won't even be friends anymore.

But we are adults. We can handle things like this. If I still want to be his friend, and me liking him doesn't freak him out, then we can still be friends, right? Why is this so hard? I thought that telling someone about my feelings for them would be easy once I was older. But it's not. Nothing is easier. Everything is just as hard as when I was a teenager, except now I have other stupid adult things to worry about on top of the stupid stuff.

"Right, but we're… pretending that we are." He's being really quiet and has to get really close to my ear so I can hear him.

"Right. Pretending."

He tilts his head to the side and scrunches his face at me a little. "I'm so confused." He backs up and then goes to cut himself a piece of cake. I suddenly feel incredibly awkward in my own skin so I go up to bed. I'm really tired anyway.

I wake up pretty early in the morning and it seems like Logan didn't come to bed. Which is fine, but concerning for our image. I hop in the shower and get dressed, and decide to dry and straighten my hair. I put on a bit of eye makeup and go to find Logan but instead find hungover celebrities. I walk the entire house and not only do I not find Logan, but I also do not see Jennifer Lawrence anywhere. She wasn't at the party last night, so I don't know why I hope to find her now, but still. Rude. I finally go out onto the back deck and find Logan in the pool with Chris Hemsworth and I sort of want to throw up a bit. They both see me right away and Chris Hemsworth pulls himself out of the pool and walks around to the deck. He nods at me as he passes, but thankfully doesn't say anything or I definitely would have puked everywhere. I'm shaking a little bit. Logan gets out of the pool too then, and walks over to me.

"That was Chris Hemsworth," I squeak.

He laughs. "Very observant."

"I don't remember seeing him last night."

"There were a lot of people here. Plus you went to bed pretty early. What was that about? I feel like I did something to ruin your birthday. You want to come in the pool? Or the hot tub? We can pick up where we left off."

"Um yeah, no."

"Oh. Okay. Well did you at least sleep okay?"

"Yes," I say shortly. "What about you? You didn't come to bed."

"I haven't been to bed yet. There's no other way I would be up this early after partying."

"It's not that early," I say, looking at my watch. Eh. It's 8am; I guess it's pretty early for the morning after a party. I shrug and look back at him. "So are you going to bed now then?" I ask.

"No no, I want to hang out with you."

"Oh." I don't know what else to say. I don't want to be a bitch but I still feel weird about last night. "You didn't even come to see if I was okay."

"What?"

"When I left the party early, you didn't come to make sure I was okay."

"I did, actually, but you were asleep."

"I didn't fall asleep that fast," I argue.

"You did. I followed you up like fifteen minutes later. I thought you were going to come back and join us, but when you didn't, I went to see if you were okay, and you were out. I didn't want to wake you."

"Oh."

"Yeah. I'm sorry you're so wiped. But what do you want to do today? You want to go to Venice Beach?"

"Sure," I say with a shrug.

"Hey. Are you sure you're okay?"

"I said I'm fine."

There aren't a lot of people at the beach, probably because it's the end of October and it's "chilly". It's also before 10am on a weekend, and everyone is probably sleeping or getting coffee somewhere instead. Most people are wearing hoodies but I'm fine in my jeans and t-shirt. I guess it is a bit cooler by the water, but I mean, it's still warm out.

"Aren't you cold?" Logan asks me after we've walked quietly for about ten minutes.

"No," I say. "It's like 18 degrees."

"Yeah but the breeze off the water is cold."

"It's nice," I say.

"Alright. So are you going to tell me what's bothering you?"

We pass the outdoor gym thing, and there are a few people using the rings. I sort of want to try them, but I don't want anyone to judge me or anything so I just keep walking past. I think about how to word what to say to Logan, but when he sees me taking a while to answer, he suggests something else.

"Do you want to check out any of the vendors?" he asks. "Or… do more of what we did last night?"

"Wow you really want to kiss me again, don't you?" I say, feeling my cheeks blush.

"Yeah, of course I do."

And I almost stand up straighter, I almost go up onto my toes and kiss him myself, but I can't. If I kiss him again I'm going to fall deeper into this and I can't let that happen. Kissing for him isn't the same as it is for me. He can kiss someone he's not necessarily attracted to just because he thinks it's fun, but I can't. And having to say it out loud again makes me feel like a prude. Plus it's bad that I already let myself get a crush on him, so it can't go any further. If he liked me back that would be a different story, but the fact is, he's just doing this so people will continue to believe that he has a girlfriend. I step away from him and he grabs my hand to pull me back.

"But you don't want me to, do you?" he asks.

"Ding, ding, ding, what does he win!?"

"Why are you being like this?" he asks, letting go of my hand. "You said it was okay to kiss you."

"No I didn't."

"What? Yes you did! I asked if it was okay and you said it was!"

"You asked if it was okay that we were really close. You never stopped to ask me if it was okay to kiss me."

"Oh. Well, I'm sorry. I thought you wanted to, what with all the kissing me back you were doing! You had your legs wrapped around me for Christ's sake." He says the last sentence a bit quieter, and leans in so I can hear.

"You practically put them there!" I shoot back, not caring about keeping our voices down.

"I did not! You did that all by yourself! And what, you're going to tell me you didn't want to kiss me, even though when I pulled away from you, you *pulled me back!?* And you were all, telling me not to stop touching you, and kissing my neck and stuff!"

"Yeah because I wanted to!" It just comes out of me. I feel my eyes widen a little with the shock of admitting it, and now it's going to dawn on him that I like him.

"What!? That doesn't make any sense! That's what *I'm* saying!"

"I kissed you, Logan, because I wanted to kiss you. Okay? I wanted you to kiss me all night, and then I found out that you were just doing it because people were there to see!"

"What!?"

"This fake dating thing is going too far and someone's going to get hurt. Like me."

"Why would you even call it that?" And now he's acting because there are people around.

"You mean why would I call our fake relationship what it actually is?" I ask.

"Isla, shh, stop, you're upset, okay, I get it, but can we-"

"No! We can't! You know that physical stuff is a big deal to me! You know that! Why would I suddenly be okay with making out with you just to uphold our image?"

"I wasn't-"

"I was never going to make out with you just to uphold our image, Logan!"

I turn around and he reaches out for me and grabs onto my shirt. "Isla, wait, please, can we talk about this?"

"You want to talk about this now? In front of all these people? In front of all their cameras?"

He looks around at everyone watching, everyone filming with their phones, and he sighs.

"I didn't think so," I say.

I keep walking away although I have no idea where I'm going, and Logan jogs to catch up to me.

"Isla," he calls. "I'm trying, okay?"

I don't answer him but let him walk beside me. Some people follow us but we both ignore them.

"Are you guys breaking up?" one person says, probably a reporter or something.

"Were you two faking it this whole time?" another person asks.

"Can we be left alone, please?" Logan spits at them, turning around rather aggressively. "Why is it your business what we do behind closed doors?"

"It wasn't behind closed doors," the first person says. "It was right here at the pier."

"It doesn't matter. Just write whatever you want about us in your stupid tabloids."

Logan's driver picks us up and we're silent the whole way back to his place. We're silent as we make our way into the house, and we both silently sit at the island in his kitchen.

"Can we talk about this?" he asks.

"No," I say shortly. Now I have the not-good kind of butterflies. The kind I get when I'm nervous.

"No? You don't want to talk about the fact that you're mad I kissed you, even though you said you wanted to kiss me?"

"No. Maybe I should go home early." I get off my stool and pick up my purse.

"Excuse me? How is that going to solve anything?"

"There's nothing to solve, Logan. You're not my boyfriend."

"But we're friends!" He gets up too and huffs. "Aren't we?"

"Yeah, we are. But we're not dating, and I don't think that we should keep pretending that we are." I'm so mad at myself because my eyes are welling with tears as I talk and I don't want him to know that this is hurting me. He clearly hasn't clued in that I have feelings for him at this point, and I don't have the courage to spell it out for him. Nothing can come of this anyway, so I have to leave and hope I just get over it. I'll find some other guy eventually who I'm comfortable with. Or I can be single forever; it's fine.

"Why are you crying? Just tell me how to fix this!" Logan's phone starts ringing and he looks at it quickly. "Fuck, it's my publicist," he says.

"You should probably get it, then."

"Please don't go anywhere." He holds his hand up a little and then answers the phone. I can hear her on the other end even though he hasn't put it on speaker.

"Why are there videos of you on the internet fighting with your girlfriend? And why are people saying that you've been faking it this whole time? Why wasn't I aware of this?"

"Look, I'm not- I didn't- It was just something we decided to do ourselves!"

"You both decided to pull a publicity stunt without running it by your *publicist?*"

He turns around and lets out a deep breath and I take this opportunity to run upstairs and pack my stuff. I almost stop and go back downstairs three times to tell Logan that I'm mad because I thought he stopped pretending, and I thought he knew that I did too, but I'm too embarrassed. I have these images in my head of him saying he's been waiting for me to tell him that I like him, that he's been waiting for me to make the first move so that I don't feel uncomfortable, and now that it's out there he's so happy. I just picture Logan literally sweeping me off my feet and kissing me as he carries me through his mansion and into the pool, not caring that both of us are still fully clothed.

But then I snap out of it and realize that that scenario is absurd because no one is here to watch and that's the only way he would do that again. Because there's no way that Logan Fucking Jackson caught feelings for me during this whole thing. I'm *so* embarrassed about even considering the possibility. I feel so stupid. Like can you imagine Logan Jackson *actually* dating me? Like actually being attracted to some nobody like me? He's Logan Fucking Jackson! He dated Heidi Winters for crying out loud! He's not going to go from dating someone like Heidi Winters to someone like me. That's why so many of his fans love it so much. Because it's so unexpected and *unrealistic.* Logan Jackson falling in love with someone who isn't famous is a literal fantasy.

And I know I said before that I'm not a drama queen, and right now you're probably calling me a damn liar, but you have to understand how scary this is for me. Logan and I have become such good friends, and telling him that I fell for him will not only embarrass me more than I already am, but it will also surely ruin our friendship. When has someone ever fallen for a friend who didn't feel the same way, and not somehow ended up becoming mortal enemies? Never. Unrequited romantic feelings in a friendship will always be disastrous. But if I don't tell him, he can at least still be in my life. We can still be friends. And the only way that I can deal with not telling him right now, is to leave. I know it's childish and ridiculous; I know it as I get an Uber, and I know it as I sneak outside to wait for it. It makes me feel stupid all over again, but I can't stop. I just feel stupid for everything. I'm stupid for falling for Logan, I'm stupid for letting myself think he fell for me too, and I'm stupid for running away.

I can hear Logan on the phone still as I tiptoe through the foyer and out the front door. The Uber pulls up in front of the gate as I'm walking down the brick driveway and I breathe a sigh of relief knowing I don't have to wait for it. But as I get closer to the gate I realize I have no idea how to open it. I get to the control box hoping to find an *open* button, but there are only numbers. You actually need a code to open the gate from the inside? That's ridiculous! Now I'm locked in! Logan Jackson has kidnapped me!

"Are you coming?" the driver says, leaning out his open window.

"Um," I say, "I'm trying."

"You don't know how to open the gate?" he asks.

I shake my head but keep my head down, looking at the keypad.

"Is the guy who lives here holding you prisoner? It's the guy from that show, isn't it? That Canadian guy. I knew he seemed sketchy."

"It's not him," I say quickly. "And he's not holding me hostage."

"Open the gate, then."

"I'm trying!"

He holds his hands up in surrender and leans back in his seat. I guess I'm going to have to climb over the gate. I pick up my carry-on and try to shove it through the iron detailing, but it's not small enough to smush it through even the widest part of the design in the gate. Dammit.

"I don't think it's going to fit," the driver says to me.

"No shit."

"Toss it over the top, I'll catch it."

"I don't know if I can get it over the top."

He gets out of the car and shrugs. "Try."

I pick up the bag and look up at the top of the gate. It's pretty high. I don't think I can chuck a suitcase over the top. I don't know why I even thought I would be able to squeeze it through; it's obviously designed to keep people out, and people are often smaller than suitcases.

"You know what? The bag isn't important." I put it back down and make sure my backpack is tight on my shoulders. And then I grab onto a swirl of metal in the gate, step onto the bar across the bottom, and start to climb. I get to the top and swing my first leg over, but I have to stop when the whole gate rattles. I tighten my grip on the metal and look down at the Uber driver on the other side of the gate.

"Come on, you can do it! Swing your other leg over!"

"I'm trying!" I yell.

"You say that a lot!"

I let out a frustrated grunt and try to swing my other leg over, but the gate moves any time that I move, and I'm afraid I'm going to fall. I try to move slowly but then I'm not even sure I know how to do it anymore. I can't even picture in my head how I'm supposed to bring my other leg over without it making me fall. I fall and die in every scenario in my head. I'm about to try one more time to get my other leg over when I hear Logan calling my name.

"What are you doing?" He runs down the driveway, but what surprises me is he doesn't stop when he gets to the gate. He doesn't even think about it; he immediately starts climbing it too.

"Logan stop!" I scream as he comes closer, making everything shake and making me feel like I'm going to fall off.

"I knew it!" the driver says. "I knew it was him!"

"Logan!" I yell, but he's up at the top already, swinging one leg over so that he's straddling the top with me.

"What are you doing?" he asks gently.

"Trying to leave."

"Why? Running away is not the way to figure out what's going on."

"I know what's going on," I say, "and I can't be a part of it anymore."

"Okay, that's fair, but you don't have to leave so abruptly. We don't have to keep doing the fake-" he stops himself when he notices the Uber driver on the other side of the gate. "We don't have to keep doing this if you don't want," he continues, "but you don't have to leave."

We stare at each other for a second or two. He's doing that thing again where I can see that he's feeling feelings, and he's looking at me with his feelings, but I don't know what he's feeling.

"Why didn't you just open the gate?" he asks, when I don't answer him.

"I don't know how!"

"You press the green button."

"What!"

He laughs a little. "Isn't it obvious?"

"No! I thought that was the enter button! For like, after you type in your code!"

"You're silly."

I don't reply, instead I glare at him, and he furrows his eyebrows.

"Are we really not going to talk about this?" he asks.

I hold on tighter to the gate below me and slowly look down at the driver, who is staring up at us. He smiles and gives me a thumbs up.

"There's literally nothing to talk about."

"Okay, that doesn't seem true. I'm sorry that I …" He pauses and looks down at the driver as well. "Do you mind giving us some privacy?" The Uber driver sighs and gets in his car. "With the window rolled up?"

"It doesn't matter," I say to Logan. "I'm too embarrassed and I just want to go home."

"Why are you embarrassed?"

"Can we not?" I say shortly. "I'm really not good at this and I'M STRADDLING A VERY TALL GATE AND I AM IN DANGER OF FALLING TO MY DEATH!"

"Okay," Logan says calmly. "Can I talk, then?"

"Not up here!"

"Right. Okay. Let's get down, then."

"I don't know how," I say slowly.

"What do you mean you don't know how?"

"I don't know how to swing my other leg over without falling."

"The same way you swung your first leg over."

I shake my head. "No, nope, can't do it."

"Well you're going to have to."

"I don't like that answer." Logan chuckles and I glare at him. "Don't laugh," I say.

"Here." Logan's voice is coated in confidence. "Let's do it together."

"Okay," I breathe.

"Grab hold of the gate."

"Yeah, like I'm not doing that already."

He half smirks and tilts his head to the side. "Okay, lean forward a little, and lift your back leg up, behind you."

"Behind me!?" I screech.

"Yes, it's easier to do it that way if you're afraid of falling. Come on, you can do it. Like this." He leans forward and swings his leg out behind him, and then turns his body towards the gate and he's magically standing on the metal, looking at me and waiting for me to follow.

"I can't do that," I say, shaking my head.

"What did you think you were going to have to do when you started climbing?"

"I wasn't thinking that far ahead!"

"You can do it, Isla, just swing your leg out behind you and turn towards the gate at the same time."

I sit at the top of the gate, shaking my head.

"Here, how 'bout I get down and stand under you? I'll catch you if you fall."

"I'll break your head if I fall," I say.

"You will not." He climbs down and stands below me, his arms up in the air. "Come on, you can do it."

I let out a shaky breath and do what he told me, my arms trembling beneath me. I feel like I'm going to slip any time I move, but I manage to get back over and climb down.

"See I knew you could do it!"

"Thanks," I say. "Can you open the gate now?"

"You're still leaving?" He sounds hurt.

"Yes."

"But I haven't gotten to say-"

"Logan, I can't," I interrupt. "I just need to go home."

He sighs and presses the green button. We step back as the doors swing open towards us and once there's room for me to get through, I grab my suitcase, nod at Logan, and slip between them. I throw my stuff into the back seat and then look over the car door at him. He's just standing there staring at me like he's just lost something he doesn't know how to get back.

"See ya later, Logan," I say. And then I get into the car and shut the door.

CHAPTER 28

Logan texts me the whole time that I'm in the airport, but I can't bring myself to reply. If we're going to end up talking about this I don't want it to be over text anyway. There's a flurry of texts from him once I land and have access to data again, but they stop by the time I get through customs.

I start to feel uneasy on the shuttle to the Park n' Fly lot. I wasn't originally supposed to leave so late in the day, and I'm kind of scared to be sitting on this shuttle alone when it's pushing midnight. And then I'm going to have to find my car in the dark. I look around the bus at the rest of the people on it and they all seem harmless. There's a guy looking at something on his phone with earbuds in and an older couple who look like they're so incredibly in love. I'm sure it'll be fine. When the bus stops at my lot I take a deep breath and collect myself, and make sure my phone is handy and I have my keys in my hand just in case. I thank the driver and speed walk to where I thought I parked my car but it's not there. Shit. I have the right lot, right? I press the lock button on my key fob to make my car do its little honk thing, and I see the lights flash in the distance. I let out a sigh of relief as I race towards it, glad that I don't see anyone else around. I throw my suitcase and backpack in the trunk and get in the car, locking the doors behind me. And before I even have a chance to turn the car on, I get a call from Claire. I squeal in surprise and answer it once I've collected myself.

"What happened?" she asks before I even get to say hello. "There are articles everywhere about you guys being fake!"

"Yeah. I don't really want to talk about it," I say.

"Okay. Do you want to have a sleepover?"

"That sounds great."

I drive right to Claire's apartment; I don't even go home first. And even though I told her that I didn't want to talk about it, I start talking about it basically right away. I cry through my whole story about kissing in the pool and how hot it was and how amazing it made me feel until he mentioned that he was only doing it for show.

"He didn't actually say that, though," she observes.

"He said 'they get the idea', Claire. It was for show."

"Maybe he was just saying that because he thought maybe you were doing it for show, and he was embarrassed. And he was just trying to play along."

"Absolutely not. As if he would have actual feelings for me."

"Why is it so hard for you to believe that he would have feelings for you!?"

"Because he's Logan-"

"Jackson, yeah, I get it. But he's just a person. You said that to me once. He's a person with feelings, real human being feelings like you and me. Everybody just knows who he is. That's the only difference."

"I can't let myself believe that, it'll hurt too much."

"Are you in love with him?"

"I don't know! I'm... I'm something."

"Oh my god, he tweeted about it," Claire says, looking at her phone.

"Well, I'm sure *he* didn't. His publicist did."

"I'm reading it anyway: **I'm really sorry that Isla Reid and I broke everyone's trust. We never meant to hurt anyone by doing what we did, but please know that we have always been real friends.**"

"Well that sounds like a bunch of horseshit," I snort. Then I add, "Are there any replies?"

She nods and reads some. **"It's not that you broke our trust really, it just doesn't make any sense. It's kind of weird.** Someone else said, **How can we believe anything you tell us now? Why would you make up a girlfriend?** and someone else said, **I knew he was gay. This Isla girl was helping him hide it.** Oh this girl with a Tinkerbell profile pic said, **Lola made me believe in love and now I don't even believe in fairies."**

"Harsh. Should I say something?" I ask.

"To the Tinkerbell girl? No, she's just being dramatic."

"No, to Logan."

"Do you want to?"

"I don't know what I would say. Plus it's probably not a good idea to say something before running it by Logan first."

"But you're not talking to Logan," she says in a mock whiney voice.

"I'm just so mortified, Claire. I can't- I don't... Ugh, I don't do stuff like that! I'm not... It's not the same for me. Physical stuff isn't the same for me, and the idea of being passionate like that with him, just so that people might see, makes me feel so uncomfortable."

"You need to tell him that."

"I can't! He'll just ask why I did it, then!"

"Yeah! And then you can say you did it because you're in love with him!"

"I can't tell him that! And I'm not in love with him."

"Remember when you said you didn't have a crush on him?" She narrows her eyes at me.

I narrow mine right back at her. "Vaguely."

Claire's phone chimes and she picks it up and smiles. "Is it okay if Emily joins us? She might be able to help."

"Sure," I say. "The more the merrier."

Emily has brought beer. We fill her in on what's going on while we drink, and she gives us a lot of head nods, and shushes me anytime I try to correct Claire when she uses the word love. I find myself crying again by the time we get to the end and I feel stupid. They both tell me that it's not stupid.

"I feel like a teenager," I whine.

"Doesn't everybody?" Emily asks.

I shrug.

"I feel like that's the secret nobody tells anyone. Everyone thinks that when they get older, they're going to *feel* older. I'm 25 and I feel the same as I did when I was in grade 12. I mean, I've had more life experience since then, so I know more and I feel like I know how to handle certain situations better, but I still *feel* the same. I have more of an open mind I guess, but I still like to be silly, and have fun, and I also still get nervous about small things, and overthink literally everything. And I know that before I met Claire, even when I had met Claire, that was scary for me! I don't ever want to be single again because I would also be too afraid to let anyone know how I felt. I would be too afraid to put myself out there with anyone. I feel like this whole dating thing actually gets harder as you get older. Especially because as you get older, you have more to lose when it comes to telling people how you feel. In high school if someone doesn't like you back, or you lose a friend over it, who cares? You're sixteen and you still have your entire life ahead of you, and you probably weren't going to stay friends with them long after high school anyway. Am I right? But when you're older you can form deeper connections with people. Friends stick around longer. There are tougher things going on in your life that they can be there for, and if you make them feel uncomfortable because you have feelings that they don't, losing that can be hard. Plus you're even older than I am so it's probably even more intense for you."

I take in a deep breath and stare at her. "People also expect adults to have sex."

"Are you ace?" Emily asks.

I shake my head. "But being physical with someone isn't something I just… do. I honestly don't understand how people can just have sex with strangers. I need to have a strong emotional connection with them first and I feel like, because I'm thirty, guys will just expect me to sleep with them basically right away, and I'm afraid that when I don't, they won't want to be with me anymore, or they won't want to wait until I'm comfortable with it. They'll just think I'm a prude. So that makes it even harder for me on top of all the other stuff you said."

"Isla, if you tell a guy that you aren't comfortable being physical with him right away and it makes him not want you, you don't want to be with him anyway. I don't care how old anyone is."

I smile a little. "Thanks. Claire said something like that too."

Emily grins and looks over at her, but she's on her phone and isn't paying attention to us. "Of course she did." Emily turns back to me. "From what I've heard, Isla, it doesn't seem like Logan would be the kind of guy to turn you away just because you want to take things slow."

"But he's the kind of guy who will kiss me in front of his celebrity friends just so they will believe we're dating."

"I know it's hard, but I really think you should talk to him about this. I think you'll be surprised by the outcome."

"But if he doesn't like me back then-"

"Then he'll either be good about it, and you'll stay friends, or he'll be an ass, and you don't want to be friends with an ass anyway."

"Oh my god!" Claire screeches. "Logan is live on his Instagram!" She goes to his live stream on her phone and turns the volume up.

"-So that's my day in a nutshell," he's saying. We huddle into Claire, each of us on one side of her, lying on our stomachs on the floor, propping ourselves up with our elbows. I wonder if he told everyone what happened today. "Heeey, I think I just saw Claire come on." Claire squeals and covers her mouth with her hand. "Hey Claire, if that was you! The comments are going so fast, I can't even find it now."

"Isla, go on with your phone," Claire says to me.

"No way, you're being absurd!"

"Of course I'm not! Get your phone!"

My fingers tremble as I get my phone from my purse and go to Instagram. I go to my notification of him going live and click on it. Logan's talking about *Neighbourly* and the comments section is blowing up with questions about me and if our relationship is really fake.

"He didn't see you come on, you have to say something," Emily says.

"What am I supposed to say?"

"How about 'hi'?"

"Ugh." I type hi and press send, but so many other people are commenting at the same time and mine is gone in less than a second.

"Isn't that his maybe fake girlfriend?" someone comments. And then everyone is commenting telling him I'm here.

"It looks like everyone is convinced Isla's on the stream," Logan says, clearly looking at the comments and scrolling through them. "That can't be true though, because she hasn't so much as answered a text from me since this morning. It's also, like, 3am for her right now, there's no way she's on here." He looks at the constant stream of comments for about twenty seconds and then steps back with his hands up in mock surrender. "Okay! Wow you guys are intense." Most of the comments are in all caps, repeating "she's here!" over and over. "Oh okay, yeah, there she is. Isla, I'm inviting you to join me."

"Oh no, absolutely not," I say out loud.

"He can't hear you," Claire says.

But the invite is there on my screen and I don't know what to do. I almost hit decline, but I shake my head and accept. And just as I do I have a mini panic attack inside my head because I don't even know what I look like and I've done a lot of crying over the last couple hours and oh no I'm on the screen and thousands of people can see me and my red, puffy face.

"It's Isla!" he says.

"I don't know why I accepted this, Logan. What are we supposed to talk about?"

There are comments flying up the screen saying I should talk about why I pretended to be his girlfriend, ones saying that I should tell everyone we aren't faking.

"You saw his tweet today, though, didn't you?" I say, hoping the people who wanted me to admit we are actually dating know that I'm talking to them. "Your comments were gone so fast, I don't know your usernames," I add. "But to the people telling me to convince everyone we weren't pretending… I mean, you saw Logan's tweet today, didn't you?"

"I didn't actually confirm anything in my tweet," Logan says.

"You didn't deny anything either," I say, narrowing my eyes at him.

"Can we… Can I call you?"

The comments are going wild with heart eye emojis and sly face emojis, and all caps comments and I don't know what to say.

"I mean, it's better than talking in front of thousands of people," I finally say, "so, yeah."

"Okay. Give me a sec." And he ends the live stream without even saying goodbye to his fans.

Logan video calls me and I answer it right away, and Claire and Emily squeeze in behind me so they can see.

"Hi," he says.

"Hi," I reply.

"Oh I see we still have an audience."

Claire and Emily both wave and he nods and smiles a little.

"Are you okay?" he asks. "I have no idea what happened; I'm still so confused. Like I don't understand why you wouldn't answer me. Did you even read all the messages I sent you?"

"I stopped reading them before I got on the plane. You just kept saying the same stuff and I didn't know what to say to you."

"You could have at least told me if you were okay. I was worried about you. So what's going on?"

"I would really like to talk to you about this," I say. "But I'm having difficulty finding the right words."

"Okay," he replies slowly. "How can I help?"

"Why don't you ask her more questions other than 'what happened'?" Emily says.

"I don't really know what other questions I can ask," he says.

"I'm just going to take this in your room if that's okay, Claire."

Claire nods and I get up off her living room floor and walk into her room, shutting the door behind me. I lay down on my side on her bed and hug her pillow to my chest, holding the phone out in front of me.

"Hey," he says.

"Hey."

"So what's going on, Reid?"

I sigh and bury my face in the pillow. "I told myself I wasn't going to tell you this."

"Yes, I know. You flew five hours away from me just so you could keep that promise to yourself."

"Yeah. I'm sorry about that."

"Sure you are. So what is it? What were you not going to tell me?"

I let out a deep breath. "I'm not good at this."

"Good at what? And take that pillow away from your mouth; I can hardly hear you."

I sit up and cross my legs, but keep the pillow in my lap. "Okay." Another deep breath. "I really am sorry that I left like that. And I'm sorry that I didn't answer you after I left. That was shitty of me. The leaving too, that wasn't cool. It was stupid. But I left because I thought you were kissing me because you wanted to kiss me. Like because you like me, and it had nothing to do with keeping up appearances or whatever. I thought you just wanted to kiss me. And I thought you knew that I would never kiss you, especially like that, unless I had feelings for you. But you just did it because of the pretend dating thing and I got so embarrassed. I'm so embarrassed, Logan, that I would even let myself think that, and I feel like a complete idiot and I don't know why I let my brain go there, or my heart, or whatever. I just. I'm sorry. I like you, Logan, and I kissed you because I wanted to kiss you and for some reason I thought we were on the same page. But I know that we're not, and that's why I had to leave."

"Because you were embarrassed?" he asks.

"Yes! And because I don't know."

"And because you don't know."

"Don't make fun of me. I feel so ridiculous. Like a little girl with a crush."

"Okay."

"Okay? That's all you're going to say? Is our friendship ruined now? What should we tell all your fans? That I was just yelling about our relationship being fake because we had a fight and I'm unreasonable when I'm angry and make stuff up, and then we broke up? Or do we tell them we're staying together? What are we supposed to do?"

"I have an idea, actually. But I have to go."

"What!?"

"I'll talk to you soon, okay?"

"Are you being serious right now? I just told you that I have a crush on you and you said *okay* and now you're hanging up on me!?"

"I'm not… Just… I can't. Please don't worry. I'll talk to you in a little bit."

"No, what's happening?"

He chuckles. "Bye, Isla."

"No!"

But then he hangs up. What the fuck.

CHAPTER 29

The three of us sleep until noon and then go out for breakfast together. We all get French Toast and bacon and laugh with our mouths full. They try to keep my mind off the fact that Logan basically ran away from me, and it mostly works. Emily tells us about a really cool board game they just got in at the store she works at, and how she and some of the other employees played it after the store closed. It sounds fun, and I suggest we get together to play it one night.

"Yeah, that would be great." Emily smiles and looks at Claire with so much love in her eyes it almost makes me sigh. I pay for all our meals to thank them for hanging out with me while I cried about a guy until four in the morning.

I have a shower as soon as I get home and straighten my hair so I can feel cute. I don't know what else to do so I log onto my shop and start to put orders together. My phone rings about an hour later and I answer it without even looking at who it is.

"Hello?"

"Isla you have to come get me." Claire is frantic on the other end.

"Claire? What's wrong?"

"I don't know, Emily and I were on the trail and she said she doesn't love me and I don't know what to do!"

"Oh my god, but everything was fine this morning!"

"I know! Can you come get me?"

"Are you on the trail by yourself?"

"Yes!"

"Okay, I'm coming, how far are you? Can you start walking towards the water and meet me?"

"Yeah. But we went pretty far."

"It's okay, I'm coming. I'll be right there."

I throw my phone in my purse and practically run out the door. My hands shake against the steering wheel and I try my best to stay calm on my drive towards the trail entrance that's closest to my apartment. I park in the free lot across from the condo that overlooks the bay and run across the street. The trail runs between the condo and the water, but if I run up the road and go behind the retirement centre to get onto the trail, it saves me a bit of time. I run the winding trail through the trees and across the highway overpass, looking out for Claire the whole time in case she's off the path. I'm out of breath and sweating despite the cool fall temperatures and have to take my hoodie off. I slow down a bit as I come to the bridge that crosses the river, and as I get closer I notice a guy standing in the middle. I probably look like a mess so I slow to a walk so I can catch my breath and prepare myself for our passing. He'll probably just say hi, and I'll probably just smile and nod, and then I can be on my way. I get closer, and what? It's fucking Logan!

"Logan?" I call.

He moves to the middle of the bridge and stands facing me with his hands in his jeans pockets.

"What are you doing here? Have you seen Claire?"

"Claire's not here," he says.

I stop walking and squint at him. "That doesn't sound sketchy at all."

He laughs a little. "Claire was helping me get you here."

"So Emily didn't break up with her out of the blue on a romantic walk?"

"No."

"Well what's going on? Why did you conspire with her to get me to meet you here?"

"I didn't want to have this conversation over the phone."

"What conversation?"

"Can you come closer?"

I roll my eyes and take a few steps forward, but I'm still on the paved trail under the cover of trees and he's standing well towards the middle of the bridge.

"Come on, Reid, closer than that."

"Ugh." I meet him on the bridge and stand a couple feet away from him. I'm not sweaty anymore and the cool air is making me shiver so I pull my hoodie over my head and then comb through my hair with my fingers. "Okay," I say to him. "What did you want to tell me that was so important you had to fly five hours and make me think my friend was having a crisis?"

"I'm in love with you."

I stop and almost choke on my own breath. I blink at him. I swallow. A smile starts to crack my lips apart but I stop it.

"What?" I ask.

He takes a step closer to me. "I kissed you in the pool because I wanted to kiss you. I wanted to kiss you in my room before the party, too, and when you were visiting with Claire, but you said you didn't want me to. I've wanted to kiss you so many times, Isla. For so long. For longer than you've wanted to kiss me, I'm sure. I only said that thing about people getting the idea, because…" he runs his hand through his hair and looks to the side, at the river stretching out below us. "Because I was afraid that you were only doing it to help me, that you were still just pretending. And I didn't want you to think that I wasn't anymore. I didn't want you to think that it had been real for me for so long."

"But you know that I don't like being physical unless-"

"Remember when I said I have anxiety, Isla? I know the logical explanation for you kissing me is that you like me, but my brain kept telling me that you were just doing it for show. That you were comfortable enough with me to take the pretending up a notch, and that you still only saw me as a friend."

"How long?"

"What?"

"How long have you been in love with me?"

"I don't know." He takes another step closer to me. "A while."

"Before you asked me to be your fake girlfriend?"

He shakes his head and takes another step closer. "No, it was after that. Wonderland maybe, is when it started. And I tried to deny it at first, tried to just keep being your friend, but I..." He trails off and looks out at the water. He finally looks back to me and continues. "I know that this is scary for you, and that Tyler was your only boyfriend, so that makes it even scarier, and I know what it's like to be afraid of getting hurt, and I know that you're demi, and it's okay if you want to take things slow, but I love you. I love you so much that it hurts, Isla. Like I actually get this pain in my chest when I think about you, or when I want to kiss you but don't, and when you-" he cuts himself off for a second and shakes his head, starts over. "When you kissed me back it was like, I don't know, I don't have words for it. It was amazing. A kiss has never felt like that to me before. No one has ever made me feel the way that you do."

I stare at him, wanting to say something but afraid of saying the wrong thing. I'm not sure if I'm in love with him, and I don't want to tell him that. There's nothing worse than telling someone you love them and having them tell you they don't. I obviously have feelings, I just don't know if I want to call them love. Not yet, anyway. I gasp when he finally steps into me and closes the gap between us. He puts his hand on the back of my head, his fingers tangled in my hair, and his mouth hovers over mine, his breath warm on my lips.

"Can I kiss you?" he whispers.

"Yes please."

CHAPTER 30

We take a bunch of selfies on the bridge, making sure that you can see the pretty sunset behind us. We're going to make an Instagram post about us later, but when we figure out what we want to say and how we want to say it. Logan takes one of us kissing and it's actually really cute. We continue to walk along the path, holding hands and laughing, taking more pictures of us being adorable, and of course stopping every now and then to kiss. I feel like I can't get close enough to him. I never thought that I would even want to kiss someone new again, let alone kiss them and enjoy it. It's not even weird that it isn't Tyler.

"I can't get enough of you," Logan breathes into my mouth.

"Same."

"Can we go back to your place?"

"Yes please."

We hardly make it into my apartment before we're kissing again and I can't even shut the door properly because Logan is walking me backwards down the hall. I kick it and hear it latch, but only just. He picks me up before we get into my room, and I wrap my legs around his waist like in the pool, and he sighs into my mouth.

"That's so hot," he says.

"Shut up," I laugh.

He lays me down on my bed and crawls on top of me. If someone told me six months ago that I would be making out with Logan Jackson on my bed, I would have laughed in your face. But here I am, making out with Logan Jackson on my bed. His hand slides up my ribcage under my shirt, and then he stops at my bra.

"Is this okay?" he asks.

"Yes," I say.

He grins, and before I know it, I'm not even wearing my bra anymore, or a shirt at all, and neither is Logan.

We fall asleep curled up under my blankets together, still wearing our jeans but no tops. And let me tell you. It's incredible.

I wake up in the middle of the night and nuzzle closer to him. He sort of wakes up and pulls me into him with his arm, and breathes in my hair, which gives me shivers down my arms and butterflies in my stomach. The good kind. I sigh and relax into them, closing my eyes again. I want to lie in bed with him forever. It's easy to fall back asleep, even though I'm trying not to. I want to be aware of all of this. I want to cuddle with him forever and I want to be awake for it all.

I wake up in the morning to Logan gently kissing my temple, and when he sees that I'm up, he kisses me on the lips, slowly opening his mouth against mine. I melt into him and pull on his belt loops to bring him closer to me. He grabs my hips and pulls me on top of him, and I lean down to keep kissing him.

"Your lips are like magic," I say.

"Are they really? How so?"

I shrug and kiss his neck, just below his ear. "They make me all tingly."

He smiles and I pull back a bit so I can look at him. "And I haven't even kissed you in all the places that I want to kiss you yet," he says.

"Well you definitely know how to make me blush," I say, getting off him and crawling out of bed.

"Where are you going? I wanted to do some of that kissing right now."

"I'm sure you did." I smile at him and put on a t-shirt. "You want breakfast?"

"Yeah," he sighs. "That would be nice."

We make pancakes together and then we watch *The Office*. I finished my latest rewatch already, but Logan hasn't and I've seen the show so many times already so it doesn't matter. Plus we don't really watch it anyway. We just make out most of the time.

"So what are we going to say on your Instagram post?" I ask later in the evening.

"I don't know. We don't have to post it now. We can have our little bubble for a bit. Just us two. Like, with nobody else knowing about us. Just for a while."

"I'm okay with that."

"Okay."

"Can I … Can I tell you something?" I ask, feeling my nerves taking over.

"Yes, of course, you can tell me anything."

"So I'm sure you've deducted on your own that I… That I've…"

He kisses me quickly and says, "That you've what?"

"That Tyler's the only person I've slept with."

"Yeah I figured as much. Why is that important?"

"Well because I don't know."

"Well because you don't know. You say that a lot."

I chuckle and shove him in the shoulder. "And you mock me a lot for it. I'm trying to be serious."

"Okay, sorry." He lets out a deep breath. "Serious time."

"You're making this even harder!" I whine, but with a laugh coming through.

"I'm sorry!"

"No you're not."

"You're right, I'm not."

We stare at each other for a few seconds and I want to tell him how much I like him, that I'm falling in love with him, but how scared I am to move any further with him, physically and emotionally. I want to. But there's something in my throat that's stopping me, and it's fucking annoying. He finally kisses me, but it's slow and gentle, and his hands on me are careful and soft. I run my hands up his chest under his shirt, and he reaches behind him to take it off. I help him pull it over his head and then he's kissing me again and laying me back on the couch. Every time he touches me it gives me goosebumps and I can't help but sigh into his mouth.

"Are you okay?" he whispers.

"Oh I'm better than okay."

Logan kisses me slowly and lingers on my lips before he pulls back. "So what are you trying to tell me?" he asks.

I shrug and he kisses me on the forehead and gets up from the couch. I smile after him and tell him I need to have a shower first. He smirks at me and I shake my head, heading to the washroom by myself. I think about how I want to word my serious stuff that I want to tell Logan while I stand under the stream of hot water, but know no matter how I go over it in my head, it'll come out terrible once I start to actually say it. I put on my PJs when I get out of the shower and Logan asks if he can have a turn. While he's in the shower, I put some orders together from my site and let *Neighbourly* play in the background.

"Oh this was a good episode," Logan says from the edge of the living room, startling me.

I immediately turn the TV off. "Oh that's weird," I say.

"Why?"

I cringe. "I don't know. It's weird that I watch you on repeat when you're not here."

"You watch me on repeat when I'm not here?"

"Shit, I didn't mean to say that."

He laughs pretty loudly and sits next to me on the couch. He smells like my shampoo and it's very sexy. "What did you mean to say then?"

"Nothing. I meant to say nothing."

"You're adorable. You're allowed to watch my show on repeat. But wait, like, do you watch all five seasons and then just start it over right away?"

"Pretty much," I admit.

"Really? Why?"

"I don't know," I say with a shrug. "It's comforting. I miss you when you're not here."

"Really?"

"Yes. How is that even a question? I mean… Obviously."

"Okay, you have a point."

"So what I was saying before… It's actually, um, it seems silly, I guess, but I still want to talk to you about it."

"Of course."

"I'm just really nervous about sleeping with someone new. I feel like I have no idea what I'm doing."

"You're right, that is silliness. Not knowing what you're doing is actually not a thing. You just think you don't know what you're doing because you're overthinking it and we're not actually doing it."

"Well I still feel that way. And I feel silly because I'm an adult. An adult who's done this before… And I still feel …" I let out a deep breath and let myself trail off.

"You talk about this stuff as if adults aren't allowed to be self-conscious, or be afraid of things. I'm an adult too, remember? And I was afraid that you didn't like me back so I pretended that I was still pretending. It happens to me too. And I know that you can't help but feel the way you do, but you don't have to feel that way with me. I'm not here to judge you. I'm here to be there for you. Being with someone new can be scary for a lot of people. But it should also be fun. And comforting. And if you're not having fun, or you don't feel comfortable with me, then we shouldn't be doing it."

"Right," I say.

"Is that all you wanted to tell me?"

"Yeah," I sigh.

"Really? You just wanted to tell me that you're embarrassed to be an adult who's afraid to have sex with someone new?"

"Why do you have to put it like that?" I ask.

"How about this," he says, "We're not going to have sex until you don't feel that way anymore."

"How do you know I won't always feel that way?"

"Because that's how it works, Reid."

Logan has to leave already because he wasn't even planning on coming to see me. I was supposed to be traveling home tomorrow morning from my visit with him that I cut short, and he has to work tomorrow afternoon so he's already on his way to the airport and I'm in my apartment by myself. Just a regular day, I guess. I look through the pictures that we took with Logan's phone on our trail walk. He sent them to me and told me to pick my four favourite ones to post to Instagram when we tell everyone what's going on. Definitely the one of us on the bridge with the sunset behind us. And another one of us on the bridge but we're kissing. My nose doesn't look the best, but Logan's nose is of course perfect, and we're still cute. I've never really been a fan of kissing selfies, but we do it well, it seems. Plus no one has seen us kiss beyond the Blue Jays game incident and I'm sure they all want to. I look for too long at a picture he took with me in the background. I'm holding a fallen leaf between my thumb and index finger, looking down at it like I'm inspecting it. But what I love so much about it is that Logan is clearly looking at me in the screen as he takes the picture. And his smile is so full of life. I don't want to sound full of myself, but he's very clearly admiring me. It makes me all warm inside. The fourth picture that I choose is one of him giving me a piggy back ride and we're both laughing and looking at each other, and it's a little blurry because I'm sure it's hard to take a selfie while you're laughing and someone is on your back, but I love it. My arms are around his neck and my face is turned towards his a little bit, and you can tell that we're having fun. I text the four pictures to him and tell him those are my picks.

Excellent he replies. A few minutes later he adds, We'll come up with something for the description the next time we visit. I have a lot of talk show appearances soon and then the premier for the movie. You're going to be my date, right?

Fuck ya I text back.

Excellent

You use that word too much I say.

Impossible And then a heart emoji.

CHAPTER 31

It's been a month and we still haven't posted about our relationship yet. We haven't had a chance to visit each other again since he confessed his love for me, but we talk every single day, and snapchat each other pictures as often as we can. He reads nice comments to me from my latest Instagram pictures before I get ready for bed, and I usually fall asleep on video chat with him every night. He's told me that he always keeps the call going for a little while after I've fallen asleep because he finds it comforting. Which is cute.

Luckily for us, no one has asked about us at his interviews so far; they've been pretty focused on the movie. He told me that one interviewer made a comment about it, but he just brushed it off and didn't say anything about it. He said that interviewer is always an ass anyway. I ask him about Carly Bowman and he scoffs.

"Are you jealous, Reid?" I love that he basically always last names me now. It makes me all gushy inside every time he does it.

"Maybe. I mean, I'm not going to act on it, but I mean, yeah, a little bit."

"First of all, Carly's a bitch," Logan says.

"Logan!"

"It's true! Just don't tell anyone I said that. But you've met her."

"Yeah," I agree.

"Anyway, when's your car coming to pick you up?"

"It should be here any minute. Maybe I'll go wait outside for it."

"Good plan."

"I'll call you when I land, okay?"

"Oh I'll probably be working. I'll be home to meet you when you get there, though."

"Okay."

Logan and I talked about how I used Park n' Fly with Claire, and then again when I visited alone, and how uneasy it made me finding my car in the dark by myself, so he paid for a car to pick me up, and also to drive me home when I come back. I also like that I can take the stress of driving myself there out of the day, and just relax. Plus sleeping. I'm excited to be able to sleep. Which I do for most of the ride. I wake up every now and then when a song I like comes on through my earbuds, and I look out the window at the snow on the side of the highway and then go back to sleep.

I watch movies on the plane and send Logan some snapchats of the view, and of the movie I'm watching, and of my food, and of me… And I realize I should probably stop spamming him with pictures. So I spam Claire with pictures instead, and I send her ones of the clouds out my window, and of the movie I'm watching, and of my drink, and of me…

Having fun are we? she replies in the text feature.

Trying to I say.

But the most fun is when I get to the car for Logan's driver. He smiles over at me before opening the back door for me, and when I start to slide inside, I scream. Logan is in the backseat!

"Oh my god!" I screech, tackling him and pressing him into the door behind him. "I can't believe you did this!"

"All I did was show up in the parking garage," he says. "It's not like I met you at baggage claim."

"You would have been recognized at baggage claim. This is better."

I kiss him, long and slow, and I swear it gives me life. I melt into him and tuck my head under his chin, enjoying the quiet butterflies in my stomach as he holds me.

"I missed you," I say quietly.

"I missed you more."

I sit in the middle seat so that I can lean into him on the ride to his place, and I fall asleep pretty quickly. He brushes my hair over my forehead and tucks it behind my ear to wake me up and I nuzzle into him more, not wanting to move.

"We're here," he whispers.

"Can we just stay like this forever?" I ask.

He giggles. "No, but we can do this in my house. Like on the couch, or in my bed, which is much more comfortable."

"Yeah, okay," I whine.

He carries my stuff in for me and I immediately head to his room without even saying anything.

"Oh we're doing that now, are we?" he says as I take my jeans off and crawl into his bed.

"It sounded so nice when you suggested it. We can cuddle and watch something."

He grins at me and takes his jeans off too, getting under the covers with me. We watch *Captain Marvel*, but I fall asleep before it's over. I'm not sure what it is with me and all my sleeping today, but I can't help it. Plus sleeping all tucked into Logan isn't the worst thing in the world, so I don't fight it.

"Are you excited for the red carpet tomorrow?" he asks me when I wake up during the credits. "Well, I don't know if it's going to be red. But there's definitely going to be an area where the stars walk, and you'll be walking it with me."

"I'm sort of excited, but I'm also nervous. I'll probably trip or something."

"I'll be holding on to you the whole time, you won't trip."

"What if they ask me questions?"

He grimaces a little bit. "They probably won't. Sorry, Reid."

"Why not?"

"They might tell you that you look pretty, or ask you if you're excited to be there with me, or if you're excited to see the movie, but they don't usually talk much to the dates."

"Yeah, okay, that's fair. People want to hear from the people who were actually involved in the movie."

"I can ask you questions if you want," he says, kissing my neck.

"Like what kind of questions?"

"What do you want for Christmas?"

"Nothing."

"You can't want nothing," he says. "Really? Nothing?"

I shrug. "I want to hang out with you. Oh, you can get me cozy PJs and new slippers. And we can hang out all day in our cozies and just like, play video games and kiss."

He kisses me on the mouth. "That sounds fun. But don't you think we should spend it with our families?"

"You are my family."

He pauses, a shocked but happy look on his face. "But I'm not your only family…"

"True," I say. "So what if you came to my place? And we spent Christmas Eve in my apartment, got pizza and watched *Die Hard*, and then spent the morning together, just us two, until like, two in the afternoon? And then we can go to my parents'."

"What about my parents?" he asks.

"We can visit them on Boxing Day?"

"Oh that sounds good, actually. Yes, let's do that."

I smile at him and pull him closer to me so I can kiss him.

"You do realize that this will be your first time meeting my parents," he says.

"Yes. Why, is Boxing Day not a good time to meet your parents for the first time?"

"Well I don't know, they'll feel like they have to get you a gift and it might be weird."

"Tell them not to get me a gift, silly."

"But what if they want to?"

"Then they can if they want, but why are we still talking about this?"

"Why, what else would we talk about?"

"About the fact that I'm trying to do things to you and you keep talking about your parents!"

"You're trying to do things to me?" he asks. "Like what? It doesn't seem like you're trying very hard."

I laugh and shove him a little bit, but then pull him back so I can kiss him. The mood changes very quickly and the things I wanted to do to him are happening and I never thought that I would be comfortable with something like this again. I guess I just needed time with the right person. Logan and I are doing very dirty things to each other and I'm not nervous about it at all or uncomfortable in any way. It's fun, and hot, and Logan definitely makes me feel safe, and that he cares about me.

"Wait, do you have a condom?" I ask.

"Of course I have a condom. I have many. Oh, I have so many to choose from! What kind do you want?" He opens the drawer in his nightstand and pulls out a few boxes, making me laugh. "These ones are ribbed. They're supposed to feel good for the lady, I don't know."

"I don't care, Logan," I chuckle.

"You should care," he says, mock concerned.

"Logan, you're killing the mood."

He laughs and kisses me, putting his hand between my legs. "Is that better?" he whispers a little hoarsely.

"Fuck," I breathe, and he laughs softly.

"So you want me to keep doing this, or do you want me to put a condom on?"

"I mean…" I sigh into his mouth and let him kiss me, but then he pulls back again.

"Mmm, that wasn't an answer," he says, the fun tone still in his voice.

"I'm trying," I say. "You're too good at this, I can't…"

He laughs again and I actually sort of love that we're giggling through this. And not like we're teenagers who are both shy, it's more like… We're two adults who are comfortable with each other and just feel relaxed enough in the other person's presence to laugh while also having sex. Who would have thought?

"Okay," I try again, "you can put the condom on."

"Okay, which one do you want?"

"The ribbed one, I guess."

"You guess," he chuckles, opening the packet with his teeth. I watch him put it on and then he comes in closer to me again, pressing himself against me, but then he stops. "Wait, does this mean you love me?"

"I'm sorry?"

"This, what's happening right now. You want to do all this because you're in love with me, aren't you?"

"Logan, just–" and my words catch in my throat, my breath hitches, and I gasp into Logan's mouth.

"Yes?" he murmurs into my ear, his silly tone of voice gone. How does he go from funny to sexy so fast like that?

We move slowly together at first, and I don't answer him, because I can't, I can hardly breathe. I can hardly even kiss him. It's okay though, because he's mostly kissing my neck, except that's also a part of why I can't breathe, because he's just *so good at everything*. I finally find the air in my lungs and bring his mouth to mine, pulling him closer, not wanting to let go. I roll us over so that I'm on top, and his hands run all over my body, making me shiver.

"Yes," I say, before leaning forward and kissing him.

"Yes what?"

"I'm in love with you."

"Say it again."

I kiss him, brush my tongue against his, and linger on his lips before pulling away. "I'm in love with you."

CHAPTER 32

Everyone is screaming. I didn't expect there to be this much screaming. Or people. I really didn't think there would be fans here, behind a fence, screaming everyone's names as they walk the carpet. I squeeze Logan's hand and he squeezes back, leans into me and whispers into my hair.

"Are you nervous?" he asks.

"Yeah," I say.

"You'll be amazing. Plus you look incredible. Not that you don't normally look incredible. But you're-"

"Thanks," I say, cutting him off. "You look pretty good too."

"Thanks." He's wearing a dark grey, fitted suit with a yellow tie and I've got on a yellow dress with some slightly poofy ruching in the skirt, which goes almost to my knees. It's strapless and also gives me a bit of tasteful cleavage which I'm not mad about.

"Logan!" Oh would you look at that, it's Ryan Seacrest. Logan walks towards him, taking me with him. Ryan Seacrest is on the other side of the fence, his microphone pointed over to our side.

"Hey," Logan says into the microphone.

"It's so good to see you, are you excited for the movie?"

"Yes, I'm really excited to see how it all came together. Filming it was such a joy, so it'll be fun to watch."

"And what about you, are you excited?" He moves the mic towards me and I'm taken aback a little.

"Oh. Um, yeah, definitely. I brought food to the set, so it'll be exciting to see them, um, not eating."

The three of us all laugh a little, but I'm immediately embarrassed because what I said was absolutely not funny. "So it's true how you met, then?" Ryan Seacrest asks. "You weren't just a fan?"

Logan scrunches his eyebrows at me a little, but I'm not sure why.

"Um," I start, unsure of myself. "Yeah, it's true."

"You don't have to answer anything you're not comfortable with," Logan says quietly.

"I'm sorry, I wasn't trying to make anyone feel uncomfortable," Ryan Seacrest says.

"I know," Logan replies with a genuine smile. "I'm just trying to take care of her."

"I understand. Well I hope you two enjoy the movie."

"Thanks, I'm sure we will."

Logan puts his arm around me and we start to walk away, towards another eager reporter.

"I loved American Idol in high school," I call back to him, and he waves and laughs.

"Logan, hi darling," a woman reporter I don't recognize calls.

Logan raises his eyebrows and walks us closer to her.

"Hello darling yourself," he says.

"How are you two doing tonight?" She sounds really genuine and excited to be interviewing us, and I like her right away.

"We're great, but the real question is how are you doing?" he asks.

"Oh I'm doing alright!"

"Just alright? Come on, you've got to be doing better than alright!"

She laughs and blushes. "I'm great."

"That's good."

"So tell me, was playing this character different from playing Cory on *Neighbourly*?"

"Yeah, actually. This movie is fun and romantic and everything, but it definitely has a deeper side to it that *Neighbourly* doesn't really have. There were a few scenes in this that were hard for me to do."

"Because they were more serious?" she asks.

"Yes, definitely. This movie gets pretty deep with the characters and their stories. I'm really excited for people to see it."

"That's really cool." And then she turns to me. "What about you? Are you nervous to be here?"

"A little," I say.

"Is it intimidating being around all the famous people?" The way she asks really makes me feel like we're friends. Like she's not asking in the voice of a reporter, she's asking in the voice of a person who just wants to know things.

"No, I've luckily gotten some practice with that over the last little while. It's actually the crowds of screaming fans behind you that make me a little uneasy."

She laughs and actually throws her head back a little. "Well I hope you two have fun tonight."

"Thanks, you too," Logan says, taking me along with him to meet another interviewer. We go closer to the backdrop thing they've got set up to take a few pictures, and it's weird because some photographers ask me to move out of the way, and some ask me to get closer to him. Every time they ask me to get out of the shot I feel offended, even though I know I shouldn't, and super awkward. I don't know what to do, and I mean he's only taking a few photos and then his arm is immediately out to me, but I still feel weird.

"Hi," he whispers into my hair, giving me butterflies and making my knees weak.

"Hi," I whisper back.

"You're doing amazing," he says.

"Thanks."

"Are you having fun?"

"Sort of."

"Just sort of?"

"Yeah. I'm not having a bad time, though. I definitely like that I'm here with you."

He smiles. "I like that you're here with me too."

"Logan, hi," someone else says. We walk over to him and Logan says hi back. "So was your experience filming this movie comparable to your experience with filming *Neighbourly*?"

"Not at all, actually, we filmed the movie on location and *Neighbourly* is all filmed in a studio."

The interviewer laughs. "Sorry, I meant acting-wise. Are your characters similar?"

"Nope, they're completely different, and I thought it was great being able to break away from Cory for a little bit. Don't get me wrong, I love Cory, and playing him is pretty comforting, but it's nice being able to challenge myself and try new things."

"So is this movie pretty serious then?"

"It's got its moments."

"Well I'm excited to see it."

"As you should." Logan smiles at him and is about to keep walking, but the reporter keeps talking, so he turns his attention back to him.

"I saw your Instagram post this afternoon and I think everyone really loved what you two said."

"Oh, thanks," Logan says. "We wrote it ourselves."

"Are you excited to be here, Isla?" he asks me, pointing the mic at me.

"Yeah, super excited," I say.

"You look great, by the way."

"Thanks, but so does Logan."

"You're right, he does."

"And so do you," I add.

He smiles and blushes a little. "Thank you."

"Of course."

Logan moves us on and we stop to talk to six or seven more people, who all ask Logan the same questions about the movie being different from the show, and I can tell he's trying to answer the questions differently every time, but the last three answers he gives are exactly the same. I guess it gets pretty tiring having to answer the same questions over and over. They ask me all the same questions too, but I can usually answer mine with a simple 'yes'. He ends up signing a few posters and t-shirts and stuff for people over the barrier, and he even leans over and takes selfies with some of them. Some of the fans just want to take pictures of the two of us together, which is sweet, and then we finally go inside.

The movie's amazing. And I'm not just saying that because I'm the star's girlfriend, I swear. It's well shot, the dialogue is great, and it makes me laugh out loud. And he was right, the characters are deep, and the few serious parts in the movie are heart wrenching. And that scene that I saw them film, when they kissed and I freaked out, is so much better on the screen, with all the close-ups and the music and good lighting and everything. I blush when they kiss though, and feel really weird.

"You're supposed to close your eyes during this part," he says, kissing my temple.

"Shh," is all I say.

And yeah, it's kind of weird watching my boyfriend kiss someone else, but I try to just understand the fact that this is his job. He doesn't even like her, anyway. I get teary eyed at the end of the movie and Logan nuzzles into me, resting his head against mine.

"That was really good," I say when the movie's over.

"Yeah?"

I turn to look at him. "I'm really proud of you."

"Really?"

"Yes!"

"Thanks." He beams at me and it's adorable. For some reason I never thought of acting in movies as something that would be particularly hard, or something someone would be really proud of. I'm not sure why I thought that. Probably just because I never actually knew the people in them before so I never realized that doing it was actual work. And that you have to expose yourself and be vulnerable in front of people. And I'm so proud of him for being a part of this movie. I'm proud of him for doing the scene where his character cried, and when his character was so clearly in love with someone who he actually hates in real life, and when his character was making silly jokes the way Logan does. He was Logan in the movie but he also wasn't. Sometimes I didn't recognize him in the movie at all, and when I look at him on the way home, I can't stop thinking about that.

"You were actually a different person on that screen," I say.

"Of course I was. That's what acting is."

"I know, but I never thought about it too much before. And in *Neighbourly* you're pretty Logan-y, but I also saw *Neighbourly* before I knew you, so it's different. Different than seeing you in a movie after I got to know you really well."

"Fell in love with me, you mean," he says with a grin.

"Sure." I smile and kiss him. I was going to let it be a quick peck but he pulls me in, letting me drown in him.

I get into my PJs when we get back to Logan's place, and he gets into bed with me, turning on a random movie. I nuzzle under his arm and let out a big sigh.

"Is that so?" he asks.

"Yes," I say. "It's so."

"What does that mean?"

I shrug. "Nothing. I just like being here with you."

"I'm really glad the owner of Chives' aunt died so you could bring us fancy pizza and make me fall in love with you."

"It would have been nice if someone didn't have to die for that to happen," I say with a bit of a whine.

"It's okay, apparently she was really old."

"That's still sad!"

"Yeah. Okay, I feel bad saying that. I would also like it if we could have met without someone's aunt having to die."

"Maybe Chives could close for two days because they were taking their employees on a team building retreat."

"In the middle of a job they got catering a movie set? I don't think so."

"Okay then, what reasonable excuse can you come up with?"

"Well like if they had a funeral they all had to—Oooh no."

I laugh a bit. "Yeah. You're a terrible person."

"I am not!"

"Sure, whatever you say. What are we watching anyway?"

"*Ratatouille.*"

"I should have known. If I looked at the screen once I guess I would have known." I turn my attention to the TV mounted on the wall and smile. "You know I always thought this movie would make a good musical."

"Too bad I can't sing; I could have starred in it."

"Too bad," I say, shaking my head.

"You should make little *Ratatouille* guys with your clay."

"Little *Ratatouille* guys? Like all the characters?" I ask.

"No, the rat guy. Ratatouille."

"Excuse me, do you think the rat's name is Ratatouille?"

"Is it… not… Ratatouille?" He sounds so unsure of himself, and also a little afraid.

"It's Remy!"

"Then who the hell is Ratatouille?"

"No one, it's a dish!"

"A dish? What do you mean?"

"Food! Ratatouille is food."

"But it's about a rat!"

I laugh and pull back from him a bit. "Yeah! Named Remy! He *makes* Ratatouille at the end!"

"Spoilers!" he jokes.

"You've seen it and you know it." I shake my head. "Who the hell is Ratatouille," I say, mocking him. "First you think Half Moons are called Lune Moons, and now I find out you think the rat's name is Ratatouille."

"You said the Lune Moon thing was understandable!"

"Because I didn't want you to hate me!" I giggle.

"Oh I see how it is."

"You should! I mean come on, you're Logan Fu-"

"Fucking Jackson, yeah, I know, but you know who you are?" he asks.

"No."

"You're Isla Fucking Reid. And I wanted to impress you too."

Hi everyone! We're really sorry that we broke your trust by telling you all we were dating when we really weren't. We would like to tell you a story about it, so we hope you can stick around for a little bit to read it. It would really mean a lot to us. We had our reasons for doing what we did, and to be honest, they're all personal, and we don't think we need to tell you what they were in order for you to understand. Our lives are displayed for everyone to see, and for everyone to judge, and we would like at least a little bit of privacy. We hope that's okay. But what we do want you to know, is that during our time pretending to date, we were friends. We were friends before we even decided to trick you all into thinking we were the most adorablest couple there ever was. And as we continued to play this game, we grew closer, and our friendship got stronger. And we fell in love with each other. We were both afraid to tell the other person about our feelings because we were such good friends and we didn't want to ruin it. But we couldn't take it anymore, and after the secret of our relationship being fake got out, it kind of rocked our friendship

anyway. So we took the leap and told each other how we felt and then kissed on a bridge (as you can see in the pictures), and now we're real boyfriend and girlfriend. We promise. All the cute stuff that we did before, yeah, it was for show, but it was also still us. We had fun doing it. It made us realize that we wanted to do that stuff on our own, instead of just for other people to see. We care deeply about each other and that probably wouldn't have happened if we didn't pretend to date. We wouldn't have visited each other the way we did, we wouldn't have gone out on adventures, or kissed under a waterfall in a pool. We're really sorry that we made you upset when you found out it was all a hoax, but to be honest, it wasn't a hoax. It wasn't fake. It wasn't pretend. We just didn't know that yet. Thanks for all your love and support; as always, you mean the world to us. Almost as much as we mean to each other.

<3 Logan and Isla

Acknowledgments

Hello there. I haven't done this in a while. I would like to first take a minute to acknowledge how proud I am of myself, because I don't think people do that enough. And they should. You should be proud of your accomplishments, and you should tell people about them.

I spent almost an entire year not being able to write anything. For a while, I didn't want to, and then when I wanted to, I couldn't. My brain and my heart were not cooperating and any time that I tried, I felt defeated in so many ways. It was like writing turned into a reminder of my life instead of the opposite. I had friends who made me feel a little better about the fact that I could no longer use my escape to escape, and assured me that I would get it back. That needing to take a break from it wasn't a bad thing, and I wouldn't lose it forever.
And then one day an idea hit me, and instead of using my writing as an escape, I used it as more of a field trip. You know, a nice treat away from the every day, but the two are still connected; you're still learning.
And sometimes it felt like I was writing from a part of me that had never written before. It woke up the other part of me, the part that had been craving to do this again for so long.
And I wrote this book.
And I'm so proud of it.
I'm proud of me.

Now it's time to acknowledge other people, the people who were instrumental in making this book be what it is today. First, I need to acknowledge and thank Lyndsay Beech, for letting me read out loud to her basically this entire book as I wrote it. She listened and excitedly responded about every part that I read to her immediately after I typed them. Let's also acknowledge

Marco Polo for making this possible. Otherwise I wouldn't have been able to send her video messages of me reading at two in the morning, and have her listen to them whenever she had time. I read a lot of it as I wrote it to Lisa Belyk too!
Lisa Belyk, Laura Kulson, and Sandy Dunsford read the first draft for me, which is always helpful in figuring out which parts work and which ones don't. It was Laura's idea to add in the Instagram hate, which was an idea I obviously loved, and I'm also really proud of how I worked it into the story. So take that! Stefanie Ferguson and Lia Martel read a later draft, which I really appreciate, and Laura Kulson even read my final draft for me to find typos and read all the changes I made! She read it twice, you guys! She also made the adorable cover for me! Laura is just the master at everything, it seems *insert silly face emoji*

Also thanks to Sarah Chadwick for editing my final draft for typos and mistakes!

And of course, thank you to all my Kickstarter backers, including:
Emily, Nicholas Hartman, Stefanie Ferguson, Heather Engebretson, Yannick Noah Schlossmacher, Emily Pazuk, Gary Hampton, Lady.Dragron, Lisa Belyk, Laura Kulson, Amber Force, Normal (HA! I'm assuming you mean Lyndsay Beech?), Nicole Graf, Kayla Joy, Andrew & Holly, Alexis W, Adrienne Montgomery, Colin Schulte, Anthony, Brent Bowman, Rhonda Chartrand, Jamie The Beerman, Lauren Loader, Stephanie Austin, Sara Orton, Sherry Mock, Keisi, Angela Turner, Katie Vlanich, Kathryn, Jamie (SkiaSymphonia), Shervyn, Holly Dallaire, Liz, and Uncle Richard!

www.ingramcontent.com/pod-product-compliance
Lightning Source LLC
Chambersburg PA
CBHW021814110726
47902CB00006B/1772